FOLK HAVEN TALES

FOLK HAVEN TALES

A COLLECTION OF FOLK HAVEN NOVELLAS

LAUREN CONNOLLY

For anyone who wants to live in a small town full of magical beings rather than the real world.

CONTENTS

DEVOTED TO A DRAGON

FLIRTING WITH A FIREBIRD

WINNING OVER A WOOD WITCH

A SELKIE'S SECRET

She's here to claim her mate. So, why is she looking at his best friend?

Isla Brown saw the will of the Gods when they revealed her fated partner at the age of sixteen. Isla has returned to her childhood home on Lake Galen, ready to build a life with her selkie mate. But a certain human is tempting her to stray from her fated path.

The night he almost killed her, he discovered her secret.

Finn Hammond knows Isla is a selkie. He also knows that he doesn't deserve her. Not after an almost fatal mistake he made years ago. But when she offers him the opportunity to dive deep into a single night of passion, he can't find the will to walk away.

. . .

A new day brings honesty, and when secrets are revealed, both Isla and Finn must choose a different future.

CONTENT WARNING

This book includes scenes involving a near-death accident, a DUI incident, and cutting in relation to controlling magic.

1

ISLA

As a responsible thirty-year-old woman, I have accepted that I finally need to collect my fated mate.

Hopefully, he will make the task easy.

I approach the front door of the MacNamara homestead. The collection of houses this selkie clan has on this expanse of lakefront property might be enough to earn the label of *compound*. But that word is too clinical for this family. And *estate* is too grand.

The moment I push through the door, a familiar face greets me.

"Isla! You came." Sorcha MacNamara, matriarch of the family and host of today's backyard barbecue, bustles down the front hall to stop in front of me, a sunburn flush on her normally pale white cheeks.

She reaches out to give my shoulder a squeeze, and I appreciate her remembering my preference. The woman is a hugger. She pulls people in tight to her breast, wrapping them in strong, loving arms, and even goes so far as to wiggle them around while the embrace happens, as if needing to shake her love into them.

The first time I watched the spectacle, all I could do was stare in horror.

Then, she turned to me.

But even at the age of four, I knew what I wanted—as well as what I did not.

When she leaned in, I held up staying hands and expressed a firm, "No, thank you."

Unlike many adults, Mrs. MacNamara listened. When she asked how she could greet me, I provided the shoulder option, and she has kept to it ever since. Even when it's been years since I last saw her.

"I thought it was time I came," I offer.

The woman's smile stays soft on her pretty, round face. "Well, come on in, girl. Everyone is in the kitchen or out back. The kids are about to take pictures in their fancy clothes."

Tonight is Folk Haven High School's prom, and since the MacNamara parents love to host a gathering, they've decided to throw the town's biggest pre-prom party. Which will no doubt bleed into a during-prom celebration. As well as a post-prom shindig.

All the MacNamara children graduated high school a decade or more ago, but that has never stopped their parents from celebrating. Everyone knows the school event is an excuse to invite half the lake over.

The thought of so many people crammed into this place has my skin tightening.

"Is Owen here?"

Sorcha throws me a curious look over her shoulder as we traverse her large yet comfortable house, dodging chatting partygoers along the way. "He is. Seems like most of the town is. And some guests"—she lowers her voice—"are humans. So, keep that in mind when conversing."

"Of course." Keeping the fact that I'm a mythical creature a secret is normal for me.

I spent years living in Portland, Oregon and no one in that city had reason to believe a selkie was walking among them. Even in Folk Haven, a town with a larger mythic population percentage than anywhere else in the world, a good portion of people I interact with on a daily basis are humans.

I know how to be circumspect.

Unfortunately, this means I'll have a harder time managing a candid conversation about matehood. Surely, I can convince Owen to join me in a quiet room somewhere.

We arrive in a kitchen filled with warmth and laughter and people. Lots of people. I clutch my bag closer to my side to avoid inadvertent touching.

"Look who I found at the front door," Mrs. MacNamara announces to the group, like I'm an exciting addition to the party.

I'm not.

My appeal is in my unlikeliness to spill or break something in another person's home. Not to provide entertainment in any way—unless this group would like to start a debate team–like discussion centering around electrical engineering, I'm not on the top of anyone's social list.

Still, I do my best to smile at the assembly and acknowledge the waves in my direction. I know many of these people from my early years spent in Folk Haven. They know exactly how much to expect from me.

"Hi, Isla," a husky voice calls my attention, and I find Moira MacNamara—the eldest of the MacNamara siblings—approaching. "Are you here for fun or to warn us that the dam is about to break and flood our party?"

I cross my arms over my chest, clasping my elbows to make myself more compact as teenagers in formalwear scoot past me in the crowded area. "You would receive notice of that through emergency alerts. And if the dam were to fail, Lake Galen's water level would slowly lower. Only those downstream would need to worry about flooding hazards."

Moira stares at me, her smile staying in place. Waiting.

"You were joking." *I should have realized.*

"And I always enjoy your practical response more than half-hearted laughter." She leans in to mime an air kiss an inch away from my skin. Another agreed-upon greeting. "Glad to see you out of your office." She turns toward the other side of the room. "Calder," Moira yells her brother's name. "Get Isla a ginger beer, one shot of vodka, and three lime wedges."

The youngest MacNamara grins over at me from his spot at the bar and gives a wave of acknowledgment. I nod back, a content hum filling my body that this family knows me so well. Growing up, I always felt more comfortable in their household than my own, where the rules were looser and love flowed without the undercurrent of anxiety. Hopefully, this familiarity will help me meld into the MacNamara clan once I officially mate their brother Owen.

If only I could find him in the crowd.

Moira gets caught up in another conversation while I move to collect my drink from Calder.

"Hey, Isla. Done earning your PhD?" he asks while staring over my shoulder.

I nod. "Six months ago." Which is why I returned to Lake Galen. My educational and professional goals have been reached—for now. Time to pursue personal matters.

"That's impressive." He lowers his voice. "I'm actually working on my master's in business. Tougher than I thought, going back to school."

"It's a good choice. You'll likely earn a high GPA and find the degree beneficial."

Calder's cheeks color—a habit I remember him having whenever people discuss him in a positive manner.

"That's nice of you to say."

I shrug. "It's the truth."

Most people who return to earn a degree later in life take their studies more seriously and earn higher grades. They also tend to choose degrees that more closely align with their careers, meaning the education will be more useful.

But I'm sure he knows that.

"Hey, uh, did you happen to see anyone else out front when you first got here?"

"Please be more specific." I sip my drink and mentally list off the people I observed when walking from my car to the house.

"She ... well ... she's this beautiful woman. Dark hair like yours but a lot longer." He eyes my inch-long tresses before glancing back at the door. "Sometimes, she wears glasses. Her name is Delta. New to town."

"I didn't see anyone like that."

The man stares at the cups he's been stacking in an impractical pyramid formation. "Oh."

"If I meet a dark-haired woman named Delta, I'll inform her that you're looking for her."

Calder gives me a full-faced smile. "Thanks for looking out."

After a nod, I ease away, noticing how a larger crowd has formed around the bar, which means around me. A greater population of people does increase the likelihood of locating Owen, but the presence of so many bodies presses against my skin in an uncomfortable way. I head for the back door, discovering another MacNamara sibling sitting by himself on the porch. But it's the wrong one—again.

"Hello, Seamus."

The man turns to me, brushing curly brown hair out of his eyes. Moira and Calder have the same unruly mass as their brother, but Owen shaved all his off at the start of our senior year in high school and never stopped, last I checked. A practical choice.

"Isla. Good to see you." Seamus's smile is reserved in the same way I imagine mine often is.

However, I've watched this man become boisterous and outspoken when among his family. I'm never boisterous and only occasionally outspoken. Normally, the anomaly occurs at work when a man attempts to tell me how to do a job I was hired for.

"You're not enjoying the party," I point out.

His smile widens, and I wonder why the fates did not pair the two of us together. Our personalities are a much closer match.

But maybe the gods prefer variety in their pairings.

"Are you?" Seamus watches me as I sip the drink his younger brother made me.

"This tastes good, and I have a task to complete. I enjoy striving for and reaching goals."

"And drinking vodka while doing it?"

"That helps." We share a smile. "Where is Owen?"

Seamus raises his eyebrows until they disappear behind the curls that still linger over his forehead. "Down at the dock. You need him?"

"Possibly." I stroll away, heading for the stone path that leads down to the large dock, which juts proudly out into the greenish-blue waters of Lake Galen.

Do I need a mate?

Not particularly.

Do I want one?

I'm here, so it would seem that, on some level, I do.

In that case, yes, I do need Owen.

After skillfully maneuvering through another crowd by the water that must surpass triple digits, I finally spot him. Owen MacNamara stands on the far edge of the dock. As I watch, he tilts his head back, downing a beer in a few deep swallows, his strong neck muscles working with each pull. Everything about Owen is strong. The man has a broad chest and defined arms, all on display, as he's currently shirtless. In the years I've spent away, he's gained more mass to his figure. Not that I'm complaining. There are many ways that ample muscle is useful, both inside and outside of intimate relations.

He is a view to be admired, and I appreciate his form as I approach.

"Hello, Owen."

At the sound of his name, the man faces me, a smile lighting up his broad features.

Promising.

"Isla! It's been forever."

An exaggeration, but I'll allow it as he reaches forward to squeeze my shoulder in much the same way his mother did. Soon, we'll have to elevate our forms of intimacy, but for now, I am content with the affectionate greeting.

That contentment evaporates when Owen steps back and hooks an arm around the waist of a tall woman. Her hair holds a curl much tighter than his, and her skin is darker than his pale Celtic ancestry could ever hope to achieve.

I would know, having descended from the same area of the world as him.

"Ramona, this is Isla. An old friend. Isla, this is Ramona. She's a professor in the Environmental Studies Department at Ramla University."

My conclusions deviate. One part of my brain informs me I should feel some sort of jealousy. My future mate has partnered with an attractive, intelligent woman who is prime competition for his affections.

Yet another section of my brain points out how perfectly her professional interests align with Owen's, as he runs his own recycling company that serves all of Lake Galen and the nearby town of Folk Haven. Perfect pairings always bring a sense of ease to my nerves when they are on edge. And nothing puts me more on edge than a crowded party.

My attention longs to focus on the lake surrounding the dock. Not many people are swimming. Despite the warmth of the day, Lake Galen holds onto a chill through the spring. But the cold temperature would never bother a selkie. Approximately thirty feet out, the water is empty. Under the surface, just there, I could find a section of peace. Quiet solitude.

But I can't leave. Not when I have a mate to procure.

"I enjoy meeting people in the field of academia. They tend to speak of their area of study with great passion and in-depth knowledge." I hold out my hand for her to shake.

Ramona smiles wide at me. "Most times, people can't get me to shut up about it. Luckily, Owen is a fan."

"Because of his company." I nod in understanding and try not to sigh.

Owen watches his date with the fascination of the newly infatuated. The sight doesn't spark the mixture of anger and doubt I associate with jealousy.

Instead, I feel as if I ran a long race, only to come upon another hill. One more grueling leg before I can rest. One last obstacle to overcome before I can settle in with the man the fates have chosen for me.

Best I push on. Try to establish my claim. We've never had a frank conversation about our fated-mate status. I am aware there are certain selkies who, while they still pray to The Finned One along with the other gods, don't believe the lore we followed in the past still applies. If the MacNamara family falls in this group, then I will need to convince Owen that I am his perfect match by other means. If only I were charming, I could attempt to dazzle him with my wit. Or if I were funny, I might try a joke.

Why can't I woo a selkie mate by presenting him a well-

formatted résumé? My academic and professional accolades are numerous and impressive when typed in a bulleted list.

As I consider my mate-catching avenues, I notice movement over Owen's shoulder.

Then, *he* steps forward, and I grind my teeth against a groan.

Finn Hammond.

The man is dark-haired and beautiful, like the woman Calder searches for.

And he's staring at me. A bad habit Finn formed in high school.

The problem with his attention has never been that the pressure of his gaze is unwelcome. It's more that I find myself making unconscious adjustments for it.

When his gray-blue eyes rest on me, I turn, so the side of my face with more pleasing angles faces him.

My voice increases volume, as if intent on including him in the conversation.

My fingers flex with the need to set his messy black hair to rights.

My teeth bite into my lower lip to keep my mouth from ...

Doing something.

"Hi, Isla." The way he says my name is entirely inappropriate.

Only I've yet to identify the reason why that is.

"Finn Hammond. It's been three years since I last saw you."

And I remember the day, the hour, the minute exactly, but I realize just in time that those are not details people tend to share with one another.

He steps closer, tilting his chin down to hold my gaze, encouraging me to stare back at him. "It's been two years since I saw you."

"I—no. What?" Only Finn does this. Makes me trip across my words as if his statements were sticks on a normally smooth-paved path. "How is it you've seen me more recently than I saw you?"

The man has the gall to shrug. "Maybe you weren't paying attention."

"Incorrect. I always pay attention."

One of his thick, dark brows rises. "Do you?" he asks, as if I'd lie about this.

"Of course. When I last saw you was at Coffee & Claws. It was raining, but you had forgotten your rain jacket, so your red shirt was wet." The material clung to his chest in a distracting way. I almost suggested he remove it. "You ordered a hot chocolate. And that was three years ago. See? I pay attention."

As Finn continues to study me, I wait for him to admit that he was wrong.

"Where's Owen?"

"*Where's Owen?*" I repeat the odd question once and then twice in my head before I comprehend the arrangement of the words. When the meaning clarifies, I jerk my head around and realize that in the short moments of speaking to Finn, Owen and his date wandered off.

And I didn't realize it because I wasn't paying attention.

Damn it.

I turn back to Finn to find him still intently watching me, absentmindedly tracing his thumb over a thin scar on his forearm. There was a time when we were teenagers, I considered if Finn's staring might have been caused by romantic interest.

What a disaster that would have been.

If attempting to establish a relationship with Owen—a man of my own kind—is a jog up a steep hill, then dating Finn would be akin to scaling a mountain.

The man is human after all.

That fact alone would cause my parents to expire on the spot. Another selkie or nothing. No doubt they'd rather I live a life of spinsterhood, wrapped in bubble wrap and stored in a bulletproof box in their attic.

A romantic relationship with Finn is impossible.

Why am I even pondering the impossibility? Owen is my mate.

Or he will be soon enough.

"You don't need to stare at me so hard," I inform him. "You'll give yourself a headache."

Finn blinks, his head giving a slight jerk, as if he didn't realize what he was doing.

Maybe he didn't. Sometimes, when I'm pondering a particularly challenging problem at work, I will retreat fully into my brain, only to come back to myself and realize I've been gazing at a wall. Or a lamp. Or a trash can.

I hope my colleagues don't assume I am fascinated by trash receptacles.

Am I a trash can to Finn?

The thought encourages me to retreat into myself even more than Owen's quick abandonment did. Which is unacceptable because I am required to care much more about Owen's opinion than any others.

Starting today.

Long ago, the gods made it clear that Owen MacNamara was my fated mate. Not Finn Hammond.

The human is not mine and never will be.

2

——————

FINN

She's back.

Thank God. Or thank the gods, as her kind like to say.

The sight of Isla Brown still has me entranced even though I've had all my life to get over my infatuation. I've known since I was sixteen that nothing can ever happen between Isla and me.

Not after one shitshow of a night.

"I can't be expected to pay attention when someone is actively distracting me." Isla turns warm brown eyes on me after realizing Owen disappeared.

People might scoff, hearing me describe anything about Isla as warm. With her blunt way of speaking, most everyone considers her to be robotic. Cold.

But she's just honest.

And that honesty heats me up. Like everything else about her.

"Is that what I was doing?"

Vague questions always catch her attention. She wants to

16

sand off their uneven corners. Organize them with clear-cut answers.

"Yes. Although I doubt it was intentional."

But it was. Isla's focus often lands on Owen, and I have an idea why. He saved her life. Perfectly normal for Isla to develop hero worship for the guy. Maybe I should stop trying to distract her when Owen is around. But I can't help the painful tug of jealousy in my chest whenever Isla stares at my friend, her focus trained solely on him.

"Your hair is shorter than the last time I saw you. Two years ago," I repeat the time frame. Giving her another rough edge to catch on.

Isla bites into her plump lower lip as her eyes spark, every ounce of her attention adhering to me. Her hand curls in an unrelenting grip around the strap of the bag hanging from her shoulder. She wants to tell me I'm wrong. But both things I said are accurate. Her ebony hair sits in a pixie cut that shows off all the curves and angles of her face.

Which isn't how it looked two years ago.

"Fine," she relents. "When did you see me that I didn't see you?"

I consider teasing her more, but then I'd risk her getting frustrated and leaving. Isla doesn't stay in conversations she doesn't want to.

"I visited a friend in Portland two years ago. We were leaving a brewery, and I saw you walking on the other side of the street."

Isla's brow furrows, creating a V-shaped wrinkle above her nose that I want to trace. "Why didn't you say hello to me?"

Why?

The truth is, I was too stunned. Which I shouldn't have been.

When I'd booked my flight to Portland, I had known that Isla was in the same city, studying at a university there and writing up her dissertation. I'd thought about trying to get her phone number. Asking her to meet up.

But I'd denied myself. Something that's much easier to do when the temptress is not standing directly in front of me, wearing a sundress. She had on a dress that day too. A long green one that swirled around her legs as she walked purposefully down the sidewalk.

And by the time I recovered from the random sighting, Isla had already turned a corner.

I couldn't let her go. I chased after her, sprinting across the street, dodging cars and pedestrians as my friend shouted behind me. As I turned the same corner, I saw the skirt of her dress disappear into the backseat of a car. Before I could reach the spot, the car pulled away.

Taking her out of my life again.

"What would you have done if I had?"

Her brows dip further. "Said hello back."

Of course. So simple. Why do her candid statements wreck me? All I can think about is pulling her into my arms and kissing her neck while she tries answering my questions with the same neutral tone. Until she can't keep steady because of her gasping.

"Next time, say hello," Isla instructs me before turning her back. Leaving me.

I should let her go. That's what I tell myself every time.

And every time, I fail to heed the warning.

"How does the dam work?"

Isla pauses mid-step and then slowly rotates to face me, eyes wide. "What do you want to know?"

I've got her back. "Everything. I didn't pay attention on that field trip we took sophomore year."

Isla steps fully into my space now, bafflement parting her lips. "How could you not? That was the most informative day of the entire year!"

Of course she would get passionate about the Folk Haven Dam. One more thing I love about her.

I shrug. "I was distracted."

Some of the shock clears from her face as she nods in understanding. "By the beauty of it? I missed the first five minutes of the tour because I was staring at the structure in its entirety. But I found the guide before we got on the bus and asked her to repeat what I'd missed. You should have done that."

The guide would've needed to repeat the entire speech because Isla was wearing a white button-up shirt and a plaid skirt that day. My horny teenage mind couldn't stop playing out schoolgirl fantasies. Didn't help that she raised her hand every five minutes, asking some intelligent question that got my blood up.

"You could tell me about it now." *Please stay and talk to me.* "Start from the beginning. How did they even make the dam?"

Her mouth pops open, cheeks flushed, gaze sparking with excitement, her entire form thrumming as she readies to give me a lecture on dams.

But then she pauses.

Don't stop. Focus on me.

Isla shakes her head, as if hearing my thoughts. "I want to, but I can't."

So close. "Why not?"

"I need to enact a plan."

"And that plan is?"

"Secret." She smiles with an air of triumph. Proud of her ability to keep a piece of knowledge to herself.

Which only makes me want to tease it out of her more.

"Can I help with your secret plan?"

Isla examines me, as if I'm a potentially handy tool, and I can imagine her working through scenarios in her head. Ways to use me. Does she have any idea how badly I want to be used?

Leave her alone. You've done enough to mess up her life.

As the guilt begins to bite at my gut, her words distract me. "You can remark on how attractive I look in my bathing suit."

Damn this woman. How can she be so honest yet always surprising?

"You want me to objectify you?"

Isla frowns, and even that expression has me mesmerized. "Only when you have my permission. Which you currently do."

She's serious. Of course she's serious. Isla almost always is.

"You have permission to objectify me too." I make the offer just to see if I can get her to blush.

I should've known better.

"Is there someone in attendance you'd like me to speak to about the attractiveness of your body in a bathing suit?" Isla scans the party, somehow thinking there's anyone here I'm more interested in than her.

"Before I can admit that, I need to know what you'll say." The light teasing in my tone hides how much I want to hear what she has to say.

Isla turns back to me, and I shiver as her gaze travels the length of my body.

There's that blush. A small reddening along her cheekbones. "I would say that the blue of your suit pairs with the blue of your eyes."

I glance down at my swim trunks, not able to hide my grin. "You think so? What else?"

Isla steps back, intently studying me, and I try to flex my muscles without noticeably putting effort in.

"I would point out your farmer's tan."

"You—my what?" I glance at my arms and realize there is a line across each bicep, denoting where my T-shirt normally sits. My chest is also a few shades paler than my forearms. "How is that attractive?" Unless it isn't and Isla's just being baldly honest about my good and bad characteristics.

"It means you are outside a lot but wearing a shirt, which means you are likely working. Probably something that involves manual labor, which is a fact supported by the muscles in your arms, chest, and"—Isla strolls around behind me—"back." She returns to face me. "And because you have less sun exposure here"—her hands indicate my middle—"you are less likely to develop skin cancer in close proximity to your vital organs. Which reminds me." She digs through a floppy bag hanging off her shoulder, coming out with a colorful tube. "Have you properly applied sunscreen? This one is reef safe. I'm aware we don't have reefs in Lake Galen, but the aquatic life could be affected by chemicals."

My mind struggles to keep up while also permanently recording everything she said about my body to memory.

"Finn?" Isla says my name, and all I want is for her to do it again.

"Hmm?"

"Do you need sunscreen?"

"Sure."

She nods. "I do too." Then, with no fanfare at all, Isla sets her drink on the dock, drops her bag beside it, and strips off her sundress, leaving her in a polka-dot two-piece fit for a pinup model.

"That suit is perfect on you," I blurt before realizing my mouth is moving.

"Good. Just like that. Maybe louder next time."

At Isla's comments, I remember that she asked for compliments.

Then, she starts to apply sunscreen to herself, and the precise movements should not turn me on as much as they do. But that's what this woman does to me.

"I am not flexible enough to evenly apply it on my back. Will you help me?" Isla extends the sunscreen, and she might as well be offering me a gold bar with the way my hands reach to eagerly snatch the thing.

When Isla turns around, I almost swallow my tongue. But, God, the way the suit cups her ass should be illegal.

You've seen her in a swimsuit before. Get yourself together.

Growing up, I spent plenty of time swimming at this house with the MacNamaras. Isla often joined, with her being a close neighbor. I drooled over her then too. But now, she has a woman's body. Fuller and softer.

And the normally standoffish woman is asking me to touch her.

I won't mess it up.

Affecting as much detachment as I can muster, I coat my palms with the white lotion and start on her shoulders. Warm under my touch, Isla's muscles relax with each pass of my hands.

I'm doing her a favor as a friend, I remind myself as I work to cover lower. *Keeping her safe in the hot sun.*

That's the thought that helps me finish the task with determination rather than lust. Keeping Isla safe. I never want her hurt again.

When I get the lowest exposed point, just above the high waist of her suit, my fingers feel the way her smooth skin turns rough in one area. The edge of a scar.

A stark reminder of why I am the last person who deserves to touch Isla.

"Do you need help?" Her voice makes me want to close my eyes, so I can listen to only her.

"Yes." *In so many ways.*

Isla turns abruptly, grabbing the sunscreen and circling around to my back. There's the unattractive squirting sound the bottle makes and the slick noise of her rubbing her hands together.

Then, she's touching me.

If only I had a railing or table to grip and brace myself. I'm worried my knees might give out.

Isla covers every inch from my shoulders to my hips, rubbing vigorously, pressing the protection into my skin. And of course, she's thorough, sneaking her fingers under the edge of my waistband to coat the parts of me that might be exposed if the material shifts around.

Go further, I silently beg.

Instead, I cup my hands over my groin to hide my body's reaction to her touch.

"That should last for the next few hours, but it is always smart to reapply multiple times a day," Isla announces, as if reading off the bottle. "I'm going to swim."

Before I can turn to thank her, she's already tossed the bottle onto her bag and executed a perfect dive off the dock. When her head pops out of the water, she's a good fifty feet away. The distance seems impossible with how quickly she reappeared.

But the woman is a selkie, so I'm not surprised.

3

____

ISLA

I FLOAT FAR ENOUGH beneath the surface of the murky water that no one above can see me.

But I can see them. Selkies have superior eyesight in the water, even in our human forms, and I use it now to watch one man.

Unfortunately for my plans, that man isn't Owen.

My future mate disappeared about an hour ago, taking Ramona out on a set of Jet Skis. When I realized he had gone, I decided to stay in the water. Let the cool embrace calm the unfamiliar tension that tightened my chest when Finn put his hands on me.

When I handed him my SPF 70, I braced for the discomfort of his touch. Coming into contact with people has always grated against the delicate edges of my nerves. But Finn's steady movements didn't irritate me the way I'd expected. Instead, a heady flush rose throughout my body.

Unsettling but not necessarily unpleasant.

Now, with the cool water all around me, I'm balanced again,

even as I stare up at a butt in a blue suit sticking through the hole of an inner tube.

Why do I want to bite that butt?

The thought has me remembering an old game us selkies used to play, inspired by the movie *Jaws*. Finn played, too, but the human was never very good at it. The human was always fascinated by how long Owen and I could hold our breath underwater. Of course, the two of us never stayed under so long to offer real suspicion.

I should probably surface soon. I've been down here for at least five minutes. If any of the human guests think I've drowned, the whole party will search for me. The idea of that attention tenses my muscles.

Still, I'm not ready to give up my observation of Finn's posterior.

Why do I always focus on him?

Maybe the gods believe he can help me woo my mate.

I ponder the idea of spending more time around Finn. Showing him the areas of myself that a partner might find appealing, so he can pass that knowledge on. Finn has been Owen's best friend since high school, and now, they co-own a recycling company. He is in the perfect position to talk about my positive traits to my future mate.

This is a good plan.

Stealthily, I approach the surface, and when I am just underneath the man, I give a strong kick, popping up beside him and grabbing hold of his inner tube.

"Shark attack!" I yell and then tip Finn and his shocked face straight into the lake. As he flounders for a moment, I claim the tube, heaving myself onto the slick surface and reclining on the floaty. Lying there, I let the late afternoon sun dry the droplets from my skin.

"You got me." Finn grins, treading water at my side.

"I'm much sneakier than you."

I could always tell when he was trying to creep up on me when we were younger. Sometimes, I'd let him catch me, just to hear his triumphant, booming laugh.

Finn shifts to float on his back, giving his limbs a rest. Humans don't have the same stamina in the water as we selkies do. When I spy goosebumps forming on his skin, I use the small power I have over water to coax warmer currents to surround him. No reason for Finn to be cold just because I'm better at the shark attack game than he is.

Recalling his question from earlier, I let a wave of hope rise in my chest. "Do you still want to hear about dams?"

Finn perks up. "Yes. But only if I can hang on to the tube while you talk."

"Acceptable."

He crosses his arms on top of the rubbery surface and rests his chin on their pillow as his body relaxes.

"The first thing that needs to happen when building a dam is temporarily redirecting the river. This means creating a diverting tunnel ..."

As I detail the step-by-step process of how the Folk Haven Dam was constructed, Finn keeps his eyes on my face the entire time. I'm about to start on recent updates when a shout grabs our attention.

"Hey! Finn! Isla! Burgers are ready."

Glancing over, I realize that Owen was the one yelling.

When did he get back? And when did the sun start to set?

"How long have I been talking?" I turn to look at Finn, who's still staring at me.

"Not sure. Lost track of time. You hungry?"

At the hollowness in my stomach, I realize I am. "Yes."

With a quick move, I fold my body and slip through the inner hole of the tube, sinking into the water, only to surface next to Finn.

"You distracted me," I inform him.

The man grins before swimming toward the dock, towing the water toy behind him with one arm.

When we rejoin the party, I accept another drink from Moira—this one, a hard seltzer. The bubbles zing in a pleasant way against my throat, easing a soreness I didn't realize was there. I must have talked for a long time. With so much noise going on now in this larger group, I don't get the urge to speak. I gather my food and settle on a bench roughly built from a tree trunk. Ready to observe, telling myself to focus on Owen and figure out the best way to earn his lifelong devotion.

Normally, I would not approve of the idea of pursuing a man who hasn't shown much, if any, interest. But there is a key component that makes our situation different.

Fate.

Well-known lore among selkies states that we will identify our mate when they save us from great danger. When I was sixteen, I almost died. Owen rescued me that terrifying night, and once I recovered from the experience, I realized the weight of his actions. The gods had spoken, and I listened as intently as anyone with true respect for their divine power would.

Owen would be my mate.

Of course, I was a child then, with plenty of life goals I wanted to achieve without the burden of matehood. So, I put it off. For a few years.

For fourteen years. I might have gone for fifteen if it wasn't for the way my last relationship ended. The man had cried. A lot. Because he thought we were going to spend the rest of our lives together and I only wanted the occasional sexual partner. After escaping that emotional display, I admitted the day had come to date the man fate had provided for me.

Today is that day. Or at least, the start of it. Because I am not the type of woman to shove someone out of the way to declare my intentions. I would rather Owen realize I am here and that we are destined to be together and then come willingly.

Eagerly would be preferred.

I'd opt for a mate to be excited about our pairing rather than resigned to it. Advice I might need to apply to myself now that I consider the idea.

I cannot say that I am particularly energetic about the idea of being with Owen.

He's a good man. A good friend. He'll make a good mate.

All of that is ... good.

I like good, I remind myself.

As the sky darkens, people gather on the shore and the dock to watch the sun set over the trees. I spot Calder walking hand in hand with a woman exactly how he described, and I'm satisfied to know he found her. Once the light fades, partygoers either start to head home or settle around a fire Moira built in the large firepit.

I stay. The shrinking size of the group helps with my comfort level, and I still have a mission to complete. Not that I expect I'll make much headway tonight as I watch Owen pull Ramona into his lap in an Adirondack chair across the way.

The size of this hill I need to climb to claim him only seems to grow, and I stifle a sigh.

A presence that is somehow warmer than the flames settles in the open space next to me on my tree bench.

Finn. The name, even as I think it, flows through me. Filling me up.

He holds out his plate. "Want one?"

Finn offers brownies. And pretzels.

"Is this a coincidence, or did you remember?" I pick up one of the gooey chocolate treats and carefully arrange pretzels on top before biting down. Soft, sweet, salty, crunchy.

The perfect dessert.

"I pay attention," he murmurs.

I nod in approval.

"Isla." Sorcha crouches by my side. "I wanted to let you know we have a free bed if you want to stay over."

"Thank you. I'll consider it."

The kind woman squeezes my shoulder before strolling off.

Staying over at the MacNamaras' was one of my favorite things when I was younger. I'd watch movies late into the night with everyone and then gorge on the delicious breakfast Mr. MacNamara made in the morning. The offer appeals to me as much as it used to because it means a break from my parents and their endless rules.

I love the two people who raised me more than I love the gods themselves. Unfortunately, Ann and Patrick Brown are rigid. They have many fears, most related to the possibility of our discovery. The human world would cause quite a commotion if everyone found out about mythical creatures, and my parents have outlined every gruesome outcome in detail to me.

I appreciate their candor, and I know I get much of my practical manner from them. But I find I am not ruled by the same worries they are. Aware of them, of course. I am cautious when not around my kind. But, while I might not enjoy large gatherings, I do like being around people different than me even if some things get lost in translation.

Moira, Folk Haven's premier—and only—real estate agent, is helping me find a piece of land to purchase. Houses tend to pass down through generations, and I don't want to wait around for my parents to pass away to have a home of my own.

If my mother lectures me about properly locking my car again, I might set up a tent on a piece of land rather than wait around for a house to be built.

Sorcha's offer of a night away from their hovering is welcome.

Unfortunately, I won't be able to accept.

"Are you staying over?" Finn asks before picking up his own brownie and taking a hearty bite.

"Likely not."

He swallows his dessert. "Why not?"

Despite my normal habit of honesty, I hesitate before sharing. The truth is, I don't enjoy people knowing how I lose control.

But Finn waits patiently as I convince myself there is no reason to be ashamed.

"I often have nightmares if I don't follow a certain routine before bed," I admit. "I'd rather not wake people up with my screaming."

"Screaming?" He leans closer, his shoulder pressing against mine. "Those must be bad."

I nod. Things often are when they're based on actual trauma.

The pressure of his body against mine is nice. Soothing. I lean into him as well.

"There's no way to re-create your routine here?" he asks.

If only I'd packed the proper supplies. I frown down at my towel bag before shaking my head. "The most important part is relieving stress. Which I do by providing myself with two to three orgasms."

There's a choking sound, and I glance over to find Finn coughing. I get up, hurrying over to a cooler with drinks, and grab him a bottle of water. When I hand it off, he downs half the thing in two swallows.

"Thank you," he rasps. Then, he drinks some more as I return to my spot beside him. After finishing the bottle, the human continues, "So"—he clears his throat—"orgasms, huh?"

"Yes." The carbonation of my seltzer diminishes with each moment, and I set it to the side. "I was relieved when I found out they worked. But I can only ever manage one with my hand. I need a vibrator to get more, and I didn't bring one with me." As honest as I am with my parents, I don't know that I want to return home to grab a self-stimulator, only to immediately head back out.

With Finn quiet beside me, I realize I must have overshared. I tend to mix up what is and what is not acceptable to discuss in relation to sex.

Maybe I should place him in the same category as my parents.

But that doesn't seem right. "I apologize if I made you uncomfortable."

"What about with a partner?" His question isn't one I expected.

"A partner?"

Finn stares into my eyes, focusing on me in the method he seems to have perfected, coaxing me to float forever in those gray-blue depths. "Has a partner ever gotten you to more than one orgasm?"

Blinking away from his hypnotizing stare, I consider my past liaisons. "One. But that was because he was a particular fan of cunnilingus."

Finn goes quiet again.

Since I don't have anything further to add to the conversation, I stretch my toes toward the fire, enjoying the way my skin tingles in the heat. A scent drifts past my nose. A cedarwood soap, mixed with the earthy smell of lake water. Must be Finn's still-damp hair.

"What if I offered to help you relax before bed?" the human asks, his voice lower than before. "Would you stay over?"

All of my nerves clench, as if I pressed as close to the fire as I could get without setting myself aflame. "Define *relax*."

"I could help you achieve your orgasms."

An image enters my head—Finn fully bare, in a bed with me.

Straining. Panting. Sweating.

I tuck my feet close to my body, suddenly overheated.

"That would not be a good idea." The words fall from my

tongue without consideration, which is not how I prefer to converse.

"Why not?"

Because I like the idea too much and you are not who the fates chose for me.

"Do you recall the plan I mentioned earlier? The secret one?"

"Yes."

"The plan is to seduce Owen. And I cannot do that while you are seducing me."

4

FINN

She wants to seduce Owen?

Owen MacNamara?

"Why would you want to do that?"

Isla rarely shows emotions on her face, but if anything, she's gone stonier. The woman crosses her arms over her chest, grasping her opposite elbows, as if she needed to protect her inner organs.

"We're meant to be together." Her lips thin, as if she were trying to suck the declaration back into her mouth. "You wouldn't understand. It's a family thing."

Family? More like selkie.

I'd bet my half of Clean Haven Recycling that this has something to do with the society of mythical creatures Isla and Owen belong to. The one that she doesn't know I know about.

Is this some arranged-marriage type of situation? The idea has me gritting my teeth.

Not that I have any aversion to arranged marriages. My

coworker Adity has one, and she's in a loving relationship with her husband. Good for them.

My problem is with Isla Brown partnering herself off with Owen.

Could I do it? Could I watch Isla walk down the aisle with my best friend? Watch them be together for the rest of my life?

Holding hands.

Kissing.

Going off to bed together each night, where he'd …

I might be sick.

But then I glance over at my business partner, where he's laughing, having a good time with Ramona. The guy has always been a flirt, never tied down for long by any relationship. But he's loyal as hell, and I find it strange that he's flaunting another woman in front of his supposed future partner.

So, maybe it's not a set-in-stone arrangement, but Isla seems to think Owen and she should be a match, and that's what I don't get.

"Does he know you're trying to seduce him?"

Isla glances over to where Owen is whispering something in Ramona's ear, which causes the woman to chuckle.

"I haven't informed him." She averts her gaze from the couple. "I thought a natural seduction might be the best approach."

"As opposed to an unnatural seduction?" I can't help poking at her clinical wording.

Isla smooths her hands over the skirt of her sundress. Water spots linger on the floral fabric, where her damp suit presses against the material.

"You caught me. I'm unsure of the proper vocabulary to use to describe my plan. Enticing maybe." Her head tilts in thought. "Encouraging."

"Foraging," I throw out.

"What?" Her brows dip as she stares at me. "No. I'm not *foraging* for Owen. He's not a blackberry bush."

When Isla's focus is on me, all common sense leaches out of my brain, leaving only my longing in place. No memory of why I'm unworthy of her. Which has me returning to our original topic.

"Obviously, I'm not grasping your secret plan. But I think it's clear, Owen is spoken for tonight. Which means you're open to accepting other offers." *You can stop thinking about him for a few hours and see me instead.* "Do you want to stay the night here?"

Isla reaches for the last pretzel on my plate, crunching on the snack before answering. "Moira makes good mimosas. And Mr. MacNamara always cooks his bacon to the exact right amount of crispiness."

I press my lips together, not sure if I should laugh or groan at the knowledge that the breakfast offerings might determine if I get to spend the night with the woman I've wanted since freshman year of high school.

Setting aside my plate, I turn to fully face Isla, letting our knees brush. She doesn't shift away, which is her normal reaction to someone moving closer to her.

"Do you want me to give you a minimum of three orgasms?" I'm glad our bench is on the opposite side of the fire from most of the gathering. Less likely to be overheard and have a random person butt in to the conversation when they realize what we're discussing.

"You are confident you can achieve three?" She eyes my hands, as if they'd provide references.

"I don't give up easily." Leaning in to catch her gaze, I stare into the mocha irises that haunt my dreams and fantasies. "And I won't just use my fingers."

Her focus drops to my mouth, and she tips forward, as if my words had a magnetic effect on her. The same way hers always draw me in.

Then, Isla sits straight, whatever spell I was briefly able to cast broken. But before I accept the rejection, the selkie reaches a hand out, carefully pinching my index finger, brushing her thumb over the pad in a gentle caress.

"I would only need your help tonight."

One night. More than I ever hoped. More than I deserve.

"Just tonight." The words are a promise to her and a warning to myself.

Do not try for more.

Whether or not Isla continues to pursue Owen doesn't matter because she's not mine.

"I'll stay the night," she says.

Exhilaration pulses through my muscles. I want to scoop her up and sprint to the house, find the closest bedroom and worship her until the sun rises. But Isla makes no move to get up, so I stay still beside her, all quivering tension and need.

"Let me know when you're ready for bed."

5

ISLA

WHEN I STEP out of the bathroom in my borrowed sleep clothes, Finn is waiting for me in the hall. He's out of his swim trunks, dressed in athletic shorts and a T-shirt. Covering up his farmer's tan.

Disappointment trickles through me at finding him so thoroughly dressed. Which is an illogical reaction. It's not as though he needs to take any of his clothes off for what we're about to do.

"I won't just use my fingers."

What that simple sentence did to me should be a crime. All my functions and thoughts were sent into a flailing mess, just like when I tipped him from his inner tube.

I need to reestablish control over the situation. This is one night. A service between friends. There can't be anything more. Proven by my parents' response when I texted to let them know they shouldn't expect me home tonight.

Mom: *Be careful. We've heard the MacNamaras invite humans to their parties. If you feel unsafe, call us, and we'll come pick you up.*

If only they knew what *I've* invited a human to do. But there's no reason to share that piece of information.

As I approach Finn now, he watches me with those blue-gray eyes. But that's not new.

I pass by him, reaching for the door to the bedroom I was assigned. Pushing it open, I turn to face a still-waiting Finn.

"Ready?"

"Are you?" he asks back, falling into his habit of answering me with questions.

And I fall into mine of answering with the truth. "Yes."

In fact, I've been ready for years.

Just because I know that being intimate with Finn could never lead to anything permanent doesn't mean I've never thought about it. When I touch myself before bed each night, he is the most common partner I picture myself with. Fantasies of slowly peeling off that damp red shirt he wore in the line to get coffee three years ago. Having him bite me instead of the bear claw he ordered. The two of us disappearing into Coffee & Claws's single-user restroom, where he would press me up against a wall and drive into me.

Outside of my head, I would never approve of a public restroom as a sexual environment, but in my dreams, every surface is as sanitary as I need it to be.

All this to say, yes, I am ready for the real thing.

The true question is, will I be ready tomorrow morning to never let this happen again?

He precedes me through the door, which I close and lock behind me. Finn halts in the middle of the room, staring at the bed.

"Who's in charge here?" he asks.

The possibilities cycle through my mind. "You, but I maintain veto rights. And we're agreed that the goal is two orgasms."

"Three," he corrects. "At a minimum."

"Three," I agree because he seems confident. "Where would you like me?"

Finn jerks his chin toward the bed. "Sit on the edge."

I make sure not to slouch as I settle on the mattress and briefly wonder if good posture assists in achieving orgasms. I'm about to pose this question out loud when I meet Finn's stare.

There's some intense emotion on his face, but I always have trouble reading feelings from faces.

This one is starvation, maybe?

"Are you hungry?" I ask. "There were still plenty of brownies. I could get you one."

Finn closes his eyes, and I become fascinated with the long sweep of his lashes. What an impressive sweep. I'd like to measure the curvature. Can protractors be used on lashes?

"That's not what I'm hungry for." His voice rumbles between us.

"There was pie too."

Finn laughs, a small puff of breath, before stepping toward me. When we're both standing, Finn is only a handful of inches taller than I am. But now, he looms, towering, his dark hair flopping over his brow as he gazes down at me.

"Where can I touch you?"

Interesting. I assumed he would focus entirely on my vulva, but Finn's eyes trail over more than the space between my legs.

"Neck down." I decide, suddenly worried he might try to kiss me. That would do things to my brain I can't even contemplate.

He nods. "I plan to use my hands and my mouth and tongue."

"Yes. Fine. Good." I shake my head, realizing how my rapid-fire words paired with his statement. "I didn't mean those to match up, as in your mouth is only fine. I'm sure your mouth is exceptional. I amend my response to amazing, exceptional, fantastic."

Finn kneels in front of me, pressing his fists to the bed on either side of my hips. The muscles in his forearms strain, making his scar stand out against his pale skin. I catch sight of his wide smile before he leans in to trace his lips along my collarbone. The highest spot I've allowed him.

There's less air in the room. I'm unsure how that's scientifically possible, but a moment ago, I was breathing fine, and now, I can't seem to locate the oxygen.

"Let's take this off." Finn grips the bottom of my shirt, easing the material up and over my head. "Isla," he groans my name.

"What?" I stare between the T-shirt Moira lent me and my bare chest. "I'm going to bed after this. I don't wear a bra to bed."

Finn sits back on his heels, staring. Again. Always staring.

"Are you formulating a strategy?" Maybe I should have provided notes on my pleasure areas prior to this starting.

The human reaches forward, warm hands clasping my sides while his thumbs press just under the curves of my chest. Finn holds my body in his determined grasp, as if he plans to lift me or pull my torso toward his. And all the while, he stares, nostrils flaring, breaths unsteady.

Oh good. I'm not the only one experiencing oxygen issues.

Without warning, Finn dives forward, latching on to my nipple and sucking the bud into his mouth. A storm forms in my body, originating from the single tip of my breast. Pleasure and wildness crash through me.

"Where can I touch you?" I gasp the question, berating myself for not asking sooner.

He lets go with a pop. "Anywhere. Everywhere." The two words brush hot against my nipple, and then he returns to his suction, and I dig my fingers into his messy, damp hair.

Finn spends a stretch of time with my breasts, plumping them with his hands, licking and teasing my nipples. The hurricane of ecstasy he creates rolls downward to between my legs. He's stimulating me without even removing my bottoms. When his lips offer another strong tug, I can't help whimpering and rubbing my thighs together, craving friction.

"Spread your knees," Finn commands, even as his grip digs into my thighs, guiding my legs apart.

Losing the small bit of pressure drags an insensible note of protest from my throat. Then, the man settles his body in the newly made space, and with a hand on my behind, Finn drags me to the very edge of the bed. Suddenly, my aching middle is pressed flush against his abdomen.

"Oh. I like that." Eagerly, I wrap my legs around his torso, grinding against him.

"Can you come like this?" Finn's lips brush the hard tip of my nipple with each word, sending small splashes of pleasure through my body. But I want the massive crashing waves from a moment ago.

"I've never tried. If you suck on me hard like before, I think I can."

Finn groans deep and then locks his lips around my areola, pulling, tugging, and meanwhile, I rock my hips against him. Then, he bites gently yet still hard enough for a sting. The shift in sensations surprises me. Suddenly, an orgasm rolls through my muscles.

With a hiccup, I collapse back on the bed, limbs both loose and pulsing. My legs fall open, releasing their hold on his trim waist.

"One." Finn grins down at me.

I meet his eyes over the length of my heaving chest.

Gods, he might get me to three.

The talented human leans in to press a kiss against my breastbone and then again an inch lower, and he continues tracing a trail down my belly until he reaches my waistband.

"Can I?"

"Yes."

He hooks his thumbs in my shorts and underwear, sliding the fabric down my legs. There's a pause, and I realize Finn stopped touching me. Propping myself up onto my elbows, I realize he's staring again.

"You have a tattoo," he murmurs.

"I do." Reaching to my hip, I finger the neatly drawn lines permanently imprinted on my skin. "It's the Tower Bridge in London. Did you know I went to London?"

Finn shakes his head.

"I visited on my own a few years ago." An adventure I never told my parents about. They likely would have had mutual panic attacks if they'd discovered I was on a different continent than my selkie skin for two weeks. But I don't tell them everything in my life, which the tattoo is a constant reminder of.

"Must have been a good trip if you got a tattoo." Finn continues to examine the detailed image the artist spent four hours sketching into my flesh with her needle.

The picture is beautiful, but it's not going to contribute to my orgasm. I sit all the way up.

"Do you find tattoos unattractive?" My fingers spread, obscuring the image. "I might be able to achieve another orgasm on my own, if you'd prefer to stop."

I didn't think to warn him beforehand. The possibility that Finn might be turned off by the piece of art I love so much has me wanting to crawl under the covers. But as I move to shift away, he clutches my hips.

"Beautiful," he rasps. "The tattoo. You. I want—" The sentence doesn't finish with a word but instead an action. Finn dives between my thighs, pressing a hot, openmouthed kiss to my core.

Sensitive from the first orgasm, I can't help a yelp of surprise, but then I have my hands buried in the silky strands of his hair, squirming as he licks up and down my vulva lips.

"Gods!" my voice squeaks when he brushes my clitoris.

After the treatment my nipples received, I'm almost scared for him to keep going.

But I'm more terrified he'll stop.

The first suck has my thighs shaking.

The second overwhelms my toes, curling them painfully tight.

I brace for a third, but he pauses.

"Can I penetrate you with my finger?"

"Yes!" The word comes out as a sob. "Please," I beg.

"How many?"

"As many as you have!"

He chuckles against my clit. But I can't explain to him that I've become so lost in his touches that I can't remember how many fingers a human has.

Is it the same as me? How many do I have?

I don't care.

Then, a pressure enters me. In wonder, I gaze down, watching Finn ease his touch in and out of my vagina, his skin growing slick with my pleasure. His chin tilts up until our stares meet.

"For me?" he whispers.

My shaking hands cradle his head. "Finn." His name is my breath. I survive off him.

Gray-blue eyes grow dark as a storm, but they don't leave mine as he bends forward to take my clit between his lips. This time, when he sucks, his fingers curl inside me.

And I let him watch as the second, larger wave rushes through me.

Two.

6

———————

FINN

ISLA WILL ORGASM a third time if I die trying. And who knows? Maybe I am dead and was a decent enough guy in life that I'm in heaven. Because I can't imagine a better paradise than the space between this woman's legs.

But that can't be right. I was never good enough for her.

The only thing that would make this better is if I could ease the ache in my cock. Which definitively shows I'm not in heaven because I'm obviously a selfish bastard.

Still, I take a chance.

"Isla?"

Her head lolls to the side, eyes hazy as she gazes down at me. My heart hurts with how gorgeous she is, lying here, lax from the pleasure I've given her.

"Finn," she says my name like it's the answer. Just like she did a moment ago when I thought I'd break in half from wanting her.

"Do you mind if I touch myself while I take care of your number three?"

Slowly, she sits up. "You're aroused?"

Pretty much since the moment I saw her in that high-waisted swimsuit. "Yes."

"Let me see."

Curious what she'll do, I stand up. The tent in my shorts is impossible to ignore.

"I would prefer your clothes off." The selkie stares intently at my erection, which only gets me harder.

"Whatever you want." And I mean it. If she asked me to dig my still-beating heart out from under my rib cage, I'd do it for her. I tug my shirt off, then drop my shorts, and kick them away.

"I want to be in charge now." Isla digs her teeth into her lower lip, and my dick pulses at the move.

"Go for it."

My breaths come in short bursts as she rises off the bed. When Isla steps in close, my tip brushes her belly, leaving a drop of pre-cum on her skin. The sight and sensation drag a needy sound from deep in my chest.

Isla scoops up my hand and steps around me, giving enough of a tug that I realize she wants me to pivot. I rotate with her, ready for more direction.

"I'm in charge," she murmurs, as if I need reminding.

"I'll do anything you want."

The woman shoves my chest hard, so I topple backward on the bed. Before I can move, Isla brings her hands down on my thighs. That touch has me groaning. But then the temptress crawls over me, centering herself where my hard dick lies against my stomach.

"Don't worry, Finn." She pats my pec, and my muscles twitch in frantic anticipation. "I'll get number three."

"But I—holy fuck." The curse spills out in response to Isla lowering herself onto my hips, sandwiching my aching cock between my stomach and her hot pussy.

She draws more expletives from me as she begins to rock, rubbing her slick core along my length.

Using me the way I always wished she would.

The ecstasy forms a hazy fog over my mind, demanding I simply experience the sensations. That I allow myself to sink into nerve endings and become a beast of only physical touch.

But I battle that urge. As much as I crave this pleasure, more than anything, I want to remember. To sear every moment of this time with Isla into my brain, so I'll never forget, even when years have passed since this night.

My eyelids grow heavy, but I force them open, cataloging the rhythm of her hips and the angles she sways them. Noting the exact pitch of each of her gasps, cherishing the few guttural grunts when a certain spot presses into me. I cup her swaying tits, measuring the curve with my hands. Isla's nipples taunt me, the peaks still hard and flushed from my earlier attention. I rear up, capturing one point in my lips, desperate to savor the flavor of her skin.

Mistake. At my first lick, she cries out, body curling around mine, riding through her orgasm.

Her third bout of pleasure.

I never want this to end, but Isla bears down hard as her fingers tangle in my hair. With her pressed against me, the heat of our bodies mixing until we're one, I can't stop my rolling wave, and the crest crashes through me. Out of me.

My groan is half-pleasure, half-pain, and I jerk as I spill in the space between us, my orgasm throwing up a barrier.

"Three," Isla murmurs against my neck, her voice sleepy. Already, she's fading, just as she promised.

I've fulfilled my role, but I can't let her go. Can't admit that this brief, perfect moment is finished. That I got all I can ever have from her.

"You should sleep here," the selkie mumbles, resting her head on my shoulder.

"You don't mind?" Good thing she's so out of it because I struggle to mask the desperate hope in my voice.

Isla slowly shakes her head. "Thank you for helping with the nightmares." Her voice is barely audible as she nestles closer to me. "Hate to dream of drowning."

Guilt tears through me, ripping apart the joy and glow of this night.

Isla has nightmares about drowning.

And it's my fault.

As I try to focus on the memory of her pleasured sounds, another recollection shoves to the front of my mind. The hard thunk of a boat propeller hitting an object just before a scream of pain.

Carefully, I lay Isla down on the covers. She barely stirs, already asleep. I retreat to the bathroom, where I wash my cum off my torso and then wet a hand towel before returning to the bedroom. With gentle strokes, I wipe Isla's stomach, taking special care around her tattooed hip even though she's long healed.

Beneath the ink, I can still see the twist and pucker of skin she tried to cover with her beautiful image. The scar that I caused.

I should leave. The slightly decent part of my brain reasons. *I don't deserve to be near her.*

But then a louder, more selfish part roars an opinion. *She told me to stay!*

Grabbing a quilt off the foot of the bed, I spread the patterned blanket over Isla and then slip under the cover. Without encouragement, she turns into my body. This woman, averse to most physical touch when awake, seeks to plaster every inch of her naked body against mine while she sleeps.

I hold her close, wishing that what we just shared could eradicate my dark memories.

But as Isla sleeps, content, my mind drags me back to that night.

I dived into chill waters, searching for the owner of the pained sound. In the darkness, I felt a large, slippery form and dragged the mass to shore. In the muted light cast from a nearby house, I stared down in horror at a twisted creature that resembled a clumsy attempt at melding the human body with an animal's. The mouth that gasped in pain belonged to Isla, the girl I could never take my eyes off during classes.

How could she have been that thing?

Then, I saw the blood. A jagged gash on the part of her body that was other. Despite the odd form, I desperately pressed my hands to the torn flesh and tried to get my brain to work.

Next thing I knew, another water creature crawled onto the shore. As I watched in horrified fascination, the seal-like being dug its clawed flippers into its chest, and a moment later, my best friend shucked off the skin, as if the animal form were a costume.

"Owen?" I choked on his name.

"I'll explain later." All his focus was on the creature under my hands. "What happened to Isla?"

"It is her?"

Then, she shuddered and moaned, and I set aside my questions.

Owen did something, peeling away the strange parts of her body until she was simply an injured, naked girl under my hands. The sight was somehow worse.

"What do we do?" I looked to my friend, hoping he'd have the answers I didn't.

Owen's face, normally relaxed and teasing, was stone. He clutched two shimmering cloaks, which I later learned were Isla's and his selkie skins.

"You have your keys?" he asked.

Daring to remove one bloody hand from Isla's wound, I fished the keys out of my back pocket. Owen snatched them and took off at a sprint, the two glimmering pelts slung over his shoulder.

"Meet me at the road!" he yelled.

I managed to wrap my shirt around Isla's waist as a poor attempt at a bandage before lifting her in my arms and carrying her to the road. Owen tore toward us in my rusty car. I slid into the backseat, Isla cradled against my chest. She began to shake, letting out pained whimpers.

"Hospital?" I asked, mentally cursing the forty-minute drive to the nearest one.

Owen shook his head, speeding down the twisty back roads. "There's someone closer."

I thought he meant a local doctor.

But Owen took us to someone else. My knowledge of the world expanded in a lot of ways that night.

Isla was unconscious the entire time though. Once she was fixed up as could be, Owen sat me down. Told me about selkies. Then, he made it clear how hard my life would become—and Isla's too—if I repeated anything about the night.

I easily agreed to keep my mouth shut. Gladly.

Selfishly.

Because a naive me believed Isla's injury was all that needed to heal.

Turns out, I scarred more than her body that night.

7

ISLA

I NEVER IMAGINED myself as a snuggler. But then I wake up, tucked in Finn's arms, and have to recalibrate the view I have of myself. With this man so close, my body responding to every rise and fall of his chest, there's an insistent push for me to alter multiple ways I approach my life.

For example, my idea of partnering with any person besides this perfect human.

This is what I've always imagined it would feel like to lie next to my mate.

But Finn *isn't* my mate.

I need to find Owen and transfer this longing to him.

There's a sudden pressure behind my eyes, and a moment later, tears start to flow down my cheeks.

Wrong, a voice shouts inside of me, but I can't solve the puzzle. I don't know where the piece fits. Where I fit.

Finn sleeps heavy enough that I successfully slide out of his hold without him waking.

But the minute I'm free, I want his arms to capture me again. My body still hums from what we did last night.

All I want is to wake him up and see if we can surpass three.

Instead, I remind myself of the dictate the gods gave me all those years ago. But their divine voices have never been quieter. I pull on the borrowed sleep clothes I didn't end up wearing to bed and leave the room. Downstairs, wonderful sweet and savory smells waft from the kitchen, and I find most of the MacNamara clan up and eating along with a few more guests.

"Morning, honey." Sorcha offers me a relaxed smile while she waits by the French press. "Fill your plate. There's plenty to go around."

"Thank you. Am I the last one up?" I already know the answer is no, seeing as how I just left Finn in my bed. But in my initial scan of the room, I didn't spot Owen.

She glances around. "Still a few stragglers behind you. I told everyone they should sleep in. Didn't stop Owen and Ramona from getting on the road before the sun was up."

My hand freezes over a stack of waffles. "On the road?"

Sorcha nods, covering a yawn with her hand. "They're driving down to Key West for the week. Wanted to avoid traffic best they could."

He's gone.

The man I am fated to mate is gone. Drove off with another woman. Probably going to have a week full of unending orgasms together.

I should sigh.

I should be frustrated.

I should be jealous.

Instead, I'm relieved. As I work my way around the counter, gathering more food, I poke at the emotion, wondering why my heart can't follow the gods' simple dictate.

Fall in love with the person who saves you.

Aka Owen MacNamara. The man who pulled me from the

water after I was clipped by a boat propeller and almost drowned. Or bled to death. There were lots of life risks he saved me from that night.

I crunch on a salty strip of bacon as I gaze out of the house's panoramic windows, overlooking the sprawling waters of Lake Galen. The gentle, glittering waves bring clarity.

Maybe Owen has the right of it.

What's the rush? We could wait another year. Another ten. Absence makes the heart grow fonder, right?

And in the meantime, I can pursue other things.

My mind continues churning as I head toward the stairs, balancing my breakfast plate in one hand.

When I play with the idea of partnering myself to Owen ten years from now, the deadline still looms too close.

How about never?

I pause with my hand on the knob of the bedroom door, experiencing another rush of relief at that thought.

I don't need a mate.

What's the point, really? A partner for life might sound good on paper, but I've done fine on my own.

So, no, I don't need a mate.

I don't need Owen MacNamara.

What I need is …

I need …

"Gods." I'm not sure if I'm speaking to them or cursing them. "I need Finn."

For however long he agrees, we'll have … something.

This lack of a plan is disconcerting, but the one piece I do have—Finn—is absolutely right. I also have determination as I push through the door and stride up to the bed, where the human in question still sleeps, snoring softly. His lips are parted, emitting the cute noise.

I settle on the bed at his side, waiting for him to realize I'm here.

He doesn't.

Tired of waiting on him, I take charge.

"I want to kiss you," I announce.

Finn jerks awake, eyes wild as he stares around the room, his attention finally landing on where I sit, cross-legged beside him.

"Isla?"

"After you brush your teeth, I want to kiss you." I extend a piece of bacon. "If it wasn't clear, I'm doing away with the *neck down only* rule I established last night."

Finn blinks at me, his long, fascinating lashes brushing his cheeks with every downward stroke. He doesn't answer.

"Are you still waking up, or are you trying to find a nice way to tell me you don't want to kiss me?" Maybe if I maintain my normal detached demeanor, the second response won't hurt as much.

"I want to kiss you." His quick reply eases a tension in my chest I didn't want to admit to.

"You can eat first." I hold out my plate of assorted food offerings. "There's more downstairs. Best get your strength up. I want a vigorous make-out session. Possibly more orgasms. We can discuss it."

With a slow-moving hand, as if he expects me to yell *shark attack* and dump the breakfast in his lap, Finn reaches out and retrieves a slice of avocado, swallowing the piece in one bite. He shifts to mirror my seated position, keeping the sheets bunched around his waist.

"You've changed your mind since last night." His fingers carefully retrieve a raspberry.

"Yes." I watch as the juicy little fruit passes through lips I want to explore.

"Are you still planning to seduce Owen?"

"Unlikely. If I do, it won't happen for another decade."

Finn's lips thin, but I still find them very kissable. "Why? You're not interested in him, are you?"

"No. I should be, but I'm not."

"Why should you be?"

"I said before, it's not something you'd understand. A family thing."

Finn gives me his hard stare, and the weight of his focus strokes along my nerve endings. "You mean, a magic thing?"

The man's question triggers an instinctual warning, the blaring bell in my head only made stronger by my parents.

He knows something.

If he knows anything, it's too much.

What did I do? What mistake did I make?

My heart rate speeds and my breath with it.

"Isla?"

My eyes flick to the door.

Should I run? The MacNamaras are just downstairs. I could tell them ...

Realization crashes over me.

Finn is Owen's best friend. Coworker. Has spent countless hours in this house.

He might have learned about my kind. Many humans in Folk Haven know. But not all.

"How well do you know the MacNamaras?" I use my most neutral tone to ask the question, attempting to ease away from a panic that won't serve me.

"Very well."

"How well?"

Finn sighs, dragging a hand through his hair, which messes up the dark mass more than usual. "Well enough to know what happens the night of the dark moon."

The night of the dark moon.

His phrasing reveals the truth. That is how most selkies speak of the one night a month we decree it safe enough to bring out our second skins and take on our other form. On the pitch-black nights, with no moonlight to reveal us, we can reconnect with our animalistic selves, become one with the water, and replenish our souls.

"Owen told you."

Finn grimaces. "Yes. But only because he had to."

"You forced him?"

"No!" Finn leans toward me and then immediately back again.

Then, he stands from the bed, and I catch a glimpse of his bare ass before he pulls on his discarded shorts. Now partially clothed, he paces the floor, and I watch his movements, trying to figure out the proper reaction to this situation. Or at least come up with a question to ask that'll help me understand.

Suddenly, Finn crouches beside me, and when he speaks, the pain in his voice reverberates off my bones. "Owen told me to help me understand the extent of the harm I'd caused. Because I was there the night you were injured, Isla." He bows his head. "I'm the reason you have nightmares."

8

―――――――――

FINN

I DON'T KNOW if I'm doing the right thing.

But I hope I am. Hope that knowing more details about the event might in some way help Isla sleep through the night without fear.

"I was with my dad," I start, lowering myself to the floor. Placing myself beneath her.

Isla shifts until she's sitting on the edge of the bed, her feet flat on the floor. The same position she was in last night when I tasted her. It would've been so easy to kiss her this morning, but this lie has lingered between us too long.

"Your father is in prison," she points out.

"Now, he is."

A few years ago, he got wasted at a bar and punched a guy. The man pressed charges, and now, my dad is serving time for assault.

About time he got in trouble for something.

"We went out on the lake, and he brought a cooler of beers. Which was normal for him." I rub the back of my neck, not

56

liking how that sounds like an excuse. "I just mean, it wasn't the first time he did this, and I let him get away with it. He was wasted when we headed home. After dark. The only light on the boat was out, and we couldn't see anything. I tried to get him to let me drive, but he wouldn't. I tried to get him to slow down, but he only gunned it faster. And then ..." The dull thud and scream echo in my ears now.

"Your father was the one who hit me." Isla's hand presses to her hip, where the proof lies in the jagged lines of her scar.

"*We* hit you. I never should have let him drive."

The selkie eyes me, her brown gaze piercing into me, as if I were the one with a second skin she was peeling back.

Her nails dig into the covers. "You shouldn't have left me there."

"Never," I rasp. "I didn't know it was you until I pulled you out of the water. Even then, I didn't know what I was seeing. You were half and half and bleeding. But I knew your face."

Isla stares at me. "Owen pulled me from the water." Her voice wavers.

Shame tugs at my gut as I reveal the lies we offered her.

"He found us after I got you out. He took off your selkie skin and then got my car while I stayed with you. Owen drove while I tried to stop the bleeding. He took us to ..." Out of everything I witnessed that night, the next bit is still the strangest.

"Madeline. A witch," she finishes.

I nod. "I thought Owen went to her house because she was the school nurse. Then, she pulled out that old book and started lighting candles and burning herbs and things. Talking in this foreign language. She healed you."

Isla slides off the bed, kneeling in front of me. I barely hold up under her focus.

"If you're going to tell me the truth, then tell me all of it." Her voice strikes me hard in the chest. "Witches don't just wave their hands and fix things."

I hang my head, chastised. "Madeline said she needed a sacrifice of the body to heal yours. I told her to take whatever she needed."

I run my thumb along the scar on my forearm, remembering the cold slice of her knife into my skin. She held my bleeding cut above Isla's wound, and where my blood touched the selkie's injury, skin slowly started knitting together.

For a time, I wondered if my blood in Isla's veins was what drew me to her. But that was a desperate man looking for a scapegoat.

Because I'd loved Isla Brown well before the accident.

"Witch's spells aren't free," the selkie insists.

I dare to meet her eyes, a rueful smile twisting my mouth. "Mowed her lawn for the rest of the summer."

Soft, piercing eyes hold mine. "You exchanged yard work to halt my death?"

All I can offer is a shrug. "It's what she asked for." I would have emptied my meager bank account. Given her my car. Hell, if the witch had demanded I be her errand boy for all eternity, I would have signed my soul over.

But she just wanted her weeds whacked.

"You were out of it the entire time and then fell asleep after the spell. I wanted to take you to your house, but Owen insisted we go to his. Because of your parents." I thought he was being ridiculous until my friend laid everything out. "How they're more worried than most about getting discovered by humans. How they'd probably pull you out of school. Maybe even move away from Folk Haven. That was when Owen told me what you all are. Not everything about you, I'm sure. But how your skins allow you to take on another form. How you only swim on the dark-moon night to keep yourselves safe. We thought you would worry less if you didn't know I was there. If only another selkie had discovered you. I promised to keep your secret." I hold out my hands, palms up, as if that'll somehow show my honesty. "We never spoke about it again after that night."

Isla's not looking at me anymore. She stares over my shoulder, but when I turn my head, all I see is a blank wall at my back. Nothing for her to be so entirely focused on.

But if she needs to zone out, then I'm not going to stop her.

I sit still, waiting. And while I wait, I catalog every inch of her, wondering if this is the last time she'll willingly be in a room with me. My gaze travels over the slope of her cheek to the bow of her lips. Lips she wanted to kiss me with. Her short hair is a bedhead mess I want to drag my fingers through. Massage her scalp until that deep V wrinkle between her brows smooths.

The large T-shirt hangs off her shoulders, hiding all her curves under its blockish cut. I'll have to rely on the shapes my hands and mouth traced last night for those memories.

Surprisingly, Isla's hands are what call to me most strongly. They sit limp in her lap, fingers relaxed. As if waiting. Waiting for my hands to slip into them, tangling our fingers, pressing palms together. Holding on to each other to stay steady through this life.

Isla's hands reanimate along with the rest of her body. She detaches her stare from the wall and stands, moving with jerky motions around the room, collecting her few items and dropping them in her bag.

All the while, I sit still.

She steps toward me and then around me, heading to the door.

"This changes things."

Then, she's gone.

ISLA

Finn saved me.

That fact plays on a loop in my mind as I sit at the outdated desk in my childhood bedroom.

"I'm making you tea." My mother's voice sounds through my doorway.

"Thank you, Mama."

Since she grew up in England, tea is her reaction to most problems. Not a solution. Merely a response.

Not that she knows what the problem is. I simply walked into the house and announced I'd be in my room, reevaluating my life. Both of my parents opened their mouths, no doubt ready to interrogate me about what, exactly, I meant by *reevaluate*. However, I'd exited the kitchen and jogged upstairs before they could. I'd have rather not made the announcement, but living with my parents requires some basic communication.

I need my own house.

But that's not the most important factor in my life to address at the moment.

Finn saved me.

With Owen's assistance, but it was Finn who dived into the dark water and pulled me out. Finn who tried to stop my wound from bleeding. Finn who cut himself open for the spell to heal me.

By all rights, he is my fated mate.

After the decision I made this morning to stop pursuing Owen, one might say this is a positive discovery. Instead, my mind twists, as if caught up in a whirlpool, as I struggle to understand the sudden shift.

Why did he tell me now? Does he know what saving a selkie means in our lore?

Finn's words come back to me.

"We never spoke about it again after that night."

Owen would have had no reason to tell his friend about our mating myths if the two agreed to keep Finn's involvement secret.

A small sting burns in my chest, and I realize I'm angry. Angry with Owen.

Since I was sixteen years old, the morning after that accident, Owen MacNamara has been in my future. The gods' will was clear. A traditional selkie mating was inevitable. Every long-term plan I made, Owen's shadow loomed as a required component.

But that's all he was. A shadow I let follow me around. Not concrete. Not something I longed for.

Not like Finn.

Now, when I switch out the selkie for the human, every part of my brain lights up, wanting to make plans with Finn as a necessary part of the structure. Something I should have been doing from the start.

Finn saved me.

As I imagine what the man saw, what he went through, I am in awe. That boy found an injured creature—something I have to admit must have looked nightmarish to a human. But he stayed with me. Held on to my life with his firm, unwavering grip. Then, he offered the witch whatever she demanded.

And after, more than a decade later, Finn still keeps our secret.

"Here's your tea." My mother appears before me, and I wonder if she moved quietly into my room or if I was so lost in my head that I just didn't hear her.

She pushes the hot mug into my hand. "Come tell us what changes you want to make. We'll discuss them." Then, she walks out of my room, leaving the door open, expecting me to follow.

My parents are very different than Finn's father, but I think we react to them in a similar way.

When Ann and Patrick Brown were younger, they lived in England, near the coast, swimming in the ocean on the night of the dark moon. One unfortunate time, my mother got caught in a fishing net. The experience almost killed her and left the pair with a fear of the ocean they'd once loved. So, pregnant with me and worried over the safety of their child, they moved here, to a lake in the United States mythics had started to whisper was safe for our kind.

But even in this new home, where they've lived for decades, their anxiety remains. And I have always done my best to appease them.

When Mr. Hammond shoved his son's hands away from the wheel and demanded to drive, I can easily see how Finn gave in. Just as I allowed my parents to grab hold of parts of my life I'd rather keep control of. Like the idea of who I could love.

Their fear made the idea of mating with a human seem a mountain to climb.

Maybe the difficulty of that trek is real. But if so, Finn is worth reaching the pinnacle.

Ignoring the open door, I step into my closet, choosing my

favorite dress. The one that cups my boobs almost as well as Finn's hands did last night. Only after making sure I'm as physically pleasing as I can get, I follow my mother down the stairs, finding her and my father on the back porch, each drinking their own tea.

"I need you both to get in the car and come with me," I announce, not willing to allow them an opportunity for an argument.

They stare at me. Then at each other. Then move to rise from their chairs.

One thing is certain. The Browns are unwaveringly honest about what we need.

On our way out, I grab my keys and a box from underneath the coffee table, gathering the necessary supplies required for my climb.

10

———————

FINN

"You're over-mixing the batter. Give it here." My grandmother comes to relieve me of the bowl. "What's going on behind that frown, boy? You've been a storm cloud ever since you got here. And I know it's not my baking that's made you so grumpy."

She's right. I was a swirling mess of depression long before I got home from the MacNamaras' house.

I did the right thing.

I know I did because Isla was still suffering. If she hasn't moved on from the accident, then I hope knowing more about what happened might help. Knowing the driver of the boat is off the lake, behind bars.

Of course, I'm still here. Free to torment her.

"I blew a shot with the woman of my dreams."

"The Brown girl?"

My head pops up at that, and I watch my grandmother's smug smile curl.

64

"Don't think I haven't seen the way you stare at her whenever she's nearby. Come on. I'm old, but I can still see."

"I didn't think I was *that* obvious." My response is all grumble.

Grandma snorts, and I'm about to smile until I'm hit with another bout of reality.

"Well, doesn't matter if the whole town knows. I messed everything up."

"Last night?"

Hell, last night. The best night of my life. Isla was in my arms, and everything was perfect.

"More like this morning. And also, years ago."

"You enjoy talking in riddles? Want me to do a puzzle to figure out what you're saying?" she scolds me while rummaging through the fridge before coming out with a stick of butter. Her long gray braid swings with each movement.

I huff out a breath. "Isla got hurt when we were younger, and I could've stopped it from happening but didn't."

Grandma barks out a laugh. "That's a lie. Biggest one I've ever heard from your mouth."

"I'm not lying!"

How does she always make me feel like I'm thirteen rather than thirty?

"Don't you raise your voice in this house."

"Sorry." I keep my voice low and steady this time, though I want to argue.

My grandmother gives me a hard look. "You're saying, you *knew* she would get hurt, and you didn't do anything?"

"No," I admit. "But I knew someone could get hurt."

"And you did nothing?"

Not after my dad shoved me away from the wheel. He would get rough sometimes after drinking too much.

"I could've done more."

My grandmother rubs the stick of butter around the inside of a metal pan. "This have anything to do with your daddy?"

"Don't see why that's relevant," I mutter.

She reaches for a wooden spoon and tries to jab my side with it as I shimmy out of her reach. "If your daddy was involved, then he was probably the one doing the hurting. And Lord knows, I was never able to control that man. So, don't go thinking you could either."

Maybe not when I was little. But by the time I was sixteen, I was just as tall and weighed almost as much. I could've wrestled the control of the boat from him. It would've been a fight, but I should've done it.

"Everything bad in the world could've been stopped if only we'd known about it first." My grandmother keeps going. "But you *don't* know beforehand. So, you can't be taking on that shame. Especially when it's your daddy doing the bad thing."

Wouldn't that be great if I didn't have to carry the guilt of that night around with me? But even if I find a way to forgive myself, that doesn't mean that Isla will suddenly appear in my life.

A loud knock sounds on the screen door.

"Got it," my grandpa announces, strolling through the kitchen with a half-empty container of seeds he was no doubt using to refill the bird feeders.

The timer goes off, and since my grandmother's hands are busy, I pull on a set of oven mitts and go to pull out the first two layers of cake. Tomorrow is my grandpa's birthday, and she prefers to get a head start on the celebration. I still need to wrap the bat box I built for their backyard. The man loves to sit on his porch every evening and listen to the squeak of the little flying creatures as they hunt for bugs in the dying light.

"Looks like we got some guests." Grandpa returns to the kitchen with a small group behind him.

When I see who the new arrivals are, I almost drop the cake tin I'm holding. I barely manage to make it to the cooling rack.

"Isla." Her name chokes from my throat.

"Finn." She steps forward, looking gorgeous in a dress that sways around her legs and hugs her chest as tightly as I want to. "These are my parents, Ann and Patrick Brown."

The two people have the same short stature, pale complexion, and dark hair color as their daughter, but only her mother has the same shade of mahogany eyes. Her dad's gaze is darker, and both of the Brown parents stare at my family as if we were a pack of wolves about to devour them.

Owen wasn't kidding when he described Isla's parents as the cautious sort.

"Nice to meet you." I move forward with slow, obvious steps, and then I hold out my hand, shaking both of their reluctant ones in turn. "These are my grandparents, Ethel and Barty Hammond." I face my family. "And you've met Isla before."

Grandma nods with a broad smile, wiping her hands on her apron. "Sure have. Why don't you all come in? Take a load off. I'll get you a cup of tea."

"Tea?" Mrs. Brown perks up at this.

"Finest sweet tea in Folk Haven," my grandpa assures them, pulling out chairs at the kitchen table.

"Of course. Sweet tea." The brief flash of hope in Mrs. Brown's face folds in on itself.

"My mother drinks hot tea," Isla announces to the room. Just as I'm struggling for a way to smooth over the misstep in Southern hospitality, Isla keeps going. "She's from England. So is my dad." Isla points at the unobtrusive man. "Hot tea is a staple for them. Did you know teatime is a huge strain on the power grids over in England? There's a surge in demand for electricity because everyone is using their electric kettle at once. I prefer sweet tea because of the high sugar content. I had yours at the town's spring picnic fifteen years ago. Finn brought me a glass. I enjoyed it but didn't understand why he was bringing me beverages. Now, I think it's because he had a crush on me."

Another silence descends over the room as Isla pauses to dig something out of her big, floppy shoulder bag, providing a respite for everyone gathered to absorb her twisting road of a speech.

I do remember that day. Isla volunteered to help build the stage for the evening musical acts, and she looked parched after hammering in all those nails. So, I brought her some tea and silently wished she'd confess how much she liked me, so I wouldn't have to shore up my pathetic teenage boy courage and ask her out myself.

Instead, she thanked me and asked that I hold her hammer while she drank.

"That's kind of you to remember my tea," my grandmother finally says, a slow smile deepening the laugh lines around her eyes. "And I have a nice selection of tea bags. A warm cup before bed always helps me sleep better."

The Brown parents offer their own hesitant smiles at that news.

"That's good. Here." Isla finally surfaces from her bag, pulling out a box. "I brought you all a puzzle." She tilts the box, so we can see the picture—*Hoover Dam, 1000 Pieces*.

"That was nice of you. Love a good puzzle." My grandfather grins, hands out to accept.

Isla passes the gift over. "I thought you four could work on that. My parents need to get out of their comfort zone and meet new people."

The Browns share a look before turning skeptical glances back on their daughter.

Isla points at them both, a warning in her eyes, as if she expects them to misbehave. "This is good for you." Then, the mythical woman turns all her piercing focus on me. "I need to speak to you."

She extends a hand, palm open, fingers spread.

Waiting for me.

As if there were any doubt that I'd take it.

I slide my hand in hers, and she pulls me through the house, out the back door. Twigs and leaves crunch under our feet as we enter the woods that separate my grandparents' house from the lake. I've stopped thinking of it as my house ever since I moved into the studio apartment above their garage, which is a separate building. There are apartments and the occasional house available for rent in town, and I can afford to buy a place of my own. But not on the lake.

And the lake always reminds me of the woman I love, so I don't want to go too far from it.

"Tell me everything you know about selkies," Isla orders after pulling me along for a stretch.

I glance back but realize she's taken us deep enough into the woods that I can't see the house anymore. Our conversation won't be overheard even if my grandparents decide to sit out on the porch.

"I know you have a second skin." Facing Isla, I meet her eyes and draw up the information Owen shared with me all those years ago. "And that you use that skin to transform into another shape. You can do that whenever you want, but the group that lives on Lake Galen mainly agreed only to turn on nights when there's no moon. Figuring the darker it is, the safer you are."

She nods, so I keep going. "I know that you are a selkie, and so are your parents. I know that Owen, Moira, Calder, Seamus, and Mrs. MacNamara are selkies, but Mr. MacNamara isn't."

When Owen first told me that, my heart tried to give me hope that I had a chance with Isla.

But that would only work if I ignored what I had done.

What your dad did, a voice in my head that sounds an awful lot like my grandmother insists.

"Owen said your parents had a bad experience and were extremely cautious. That if they found out what had happened to you and that I—a human—knew, they'd probably move you all away." That was the worst threat my friend could've thrown at me to keep my mouth shut. "I know there are others like you, but Owen didn't name names. Oh, and that the school nurse is a witch. At least, she was fourteen years ago. Ms. Madeline might have retired by now."

"What else?" Isla presses when I fall quiet.

I shake my head. "That's all I know. I mean, I can guess there's probably a textbook amount of info he didn't give me. But Owen made sure to tell me just enough to understand. And to keep quiet."

"Nothing about mates?"

Mates. The way she says the word, I can almost feel the heavy meaning behind it. And I'm suddenly ravenous for her to tell me more.

"No. I don't know anything about mates."

Isla steps forward, holding me with the power of her eyes. "Legend says a selkie will know their mate when they are saved by them."

My mind stutters over the new information. "Owen." The name pops out of my mouth, and Isla's quest to seduce the man makes more sense now. "Owen is your mate."

The guy's quick thinking is all that got us through that night. The only reason Isla is alive.

But she shakes her head. "I thought so too. Tried very hard to make my heart want him. I thought maybe if he wanted *me,* then my body would listen to what the fates had told me all those years ago."

Again, the image of my best friend holding the woman I

love invades my mind, and I squeeze my eyes shut, desperate to get rid of the sight.

"Then, I woke up this morning, next to the man I'd always wanted, and I decided that fated mates were overrated."

I blink my eyes open, staring down into her lovely, upturned face. "What are you saying?"

Isla's hands settle on my shoulders and then drag down to my chest. "I asked you to kiss me because I'd decided to stop chasing a future I thought I should want and instead pursue the one I actually craved. I was fully prepared to tell the gods they were wrong. But then you told me the truth, and I realized they weren't."

"So, you do want Owen?"

Her brows scrunch together as she stares up at me. "No. I want *you*. I've always wanted you. And it happens to be convenient that you're the one who saved my life. That you're my mate."

"Whoa. No." I move to step back, but Isla fists her hands in my shirt, holding me in place. "I'm the one who endangered you. You can't say I'm your savior when I'm the one who hurt you."

"Your father hurt me."

"I let him drive."

"Parents command a large amount of influence over their children." She sounds so reasonable, and I want to believe her.

"Looks like you can handle yours pretty well." I jerk my chin toward the house.

The selkie continues to hold me in place. "Now, I can. Because I'm a grown woman." Isla traces my face with her gaze. "Would you let your father drive intoxicated now?"

"No way. Never again."

"And I won't let my parents' fear of humans keep me from the person I need in my life."

"Isla—"

"You, Finn. I need you."

A groan cracks out of my throat, and suddenly, I'm gathering her up in my arms, holding her close to me as I bury my face in her neck. "I need you too," I whisper against her neck.

"Tell me who hurt me," she demands.

"My father did." And the truth is a stone weight removed from my shoulders.

"And who saved me?"

I can still feel the jab of the knife and my warm blood dripping down my arm onto her wound.

"I did."

"Tell me who my mate is." Her arms are tight around my neck, and I revel in the way she clutches me.

"I am."

There's electricity in the air, raising goose bumps on my arms.

"Will you kiss me now?" She loosens her hold enough that our gazes clash.

"I don't think I can stop with a kiss."

The woman I love told me I'm hers. My whole body is hot with need to show her that she'll never have a reason to regret her choice. That I don't need a drop of magic in my body to be the best mate a selkie has ever had.

"Then, don't stop." Isla leans in, flicking her tongue against my bottom lip.

Next thing I know, my ass is on the ground, and my woman is straddling me. Our mouths are so close that we share a breath, just before I tilt my chin up and claim a taste of my selkie mate.

11

ISLA

Finn kisses me like he'll never get the chance to again.

Easing in and then taking, never breaking away.

I can hold my breath underwater for hours, yet somehow, this man gets me to start panting.

But a sudden realization has me pressing him away.

"No," he growls, dark eyes tracking my mouth.

"That was a convincing animalistic noise. I'm impressed."

"Isla." His voice comes out with a deeper rasp the second time as his fingers dig into my waist.

"I needed my mouth free to talk to you about something important."

When my pause stretches, he snaps forward, trying to capture me in another kiss. But I'm faster and a touch stronger than he is, holding him at bay.

"Eyes up, human. Focus on my face."

Finn's hungry gaze flits to my eyes and stays there, his dilated pupils showing just how aroused he is. Of course, I'm also sitting on a very prominent erection, so I'm not surprised.

"I'm focused," he claims. "*Extremely* focused."

"Good. I fell in love with you senior year, when you picked me first for your kickball team in gym class."

For a full count of five, my human just stares at me. "But that was after you thought Owen was your mate."

"I know. Which I told the gods was extremely inconvenient and cruel and that they should take the emotion away."

"Did they?"

"I thought so." Suddenly, I realize that I have permission to touch Finn, so I reach up and comb my fingers through his unruly mop of black hair. "Then, right before graduation, you ran back to my car to get my flip-flops after one of my heels broke. And I fell in love with you all over again."

With each word I speak, a smile creeps wider over Finn's face. "You've been in love with me since graduation?"

"Of course not!" I scoff. "I reminded the gods that they'd chosen Owen as my fated mate, so they *really* needed to get rid of the love I felt for you. And I'm positive they did."

"Is that so?" From the lowering of Finn's eyelids, I can tell he doesn't believe me.

"Yes. But then it was raining. That time at the coffee shop three years ago. And you came inside, all wet, with your shirt clinging to your chest." Now, I hook my fingers under his black T-shirt and tug the material off over his head to see the offending chest.

"You fell in love with me because I was wet?" His chuckle brushes against my neck as he leans in to press kisses to the sensitive area.

"That's ridiculous." I tilt my head to give him better access. "I fell in love with you again when you said you wished Folk Haven had a bookstore."

Finn straightens. "And that made you love me because ..."

I still remember him stepping up to me in line, his eyes

wide and searching as he said hello. Finn asked how long I was in town for, and I told him I was heading out again that afternoon. In fact, I had to leave right after getting my coffee if I wanted time to go to the bookstore in Atlanta before catching my flight.

And he said, with so much regret that it infused every inch of his body, that he wished Folk Haven had a bookstore.

"Because I think we were envisioning the same thing. The two of us getting coffee and then walking over to the imaginary bookstore, talking as we went, rediscovering each other. Then maybe making out between the shelves. And the fact that you wanted exactly what I wanted did it for me."

"Did you ask the gods to take the feeling away again?"

"Yes."

"Did they?"

"I pretended they had."

"Until when?"

"Until I saw your delicious butt sticking through that inner tube."

Finn barks out a laugh as his arms tighten around me. But I don't let him close off too much space, my hands intent on sliding down his torso until I reach his fly. He stills under the caress.

"If it's not clear, I'm trying to tell you that I love you." I undo the button on his shorts and slowly pull down the zipper. "I have for years even if I tried to ignore the feelings." I slip my hands into his pants and find the flap of his briefs. "And I never plan on asking the gods for it to go away again." I free his dick, the hard length standing warm and straight in my grip. "Because I need to love you."

Finn's forehead falls forward to rest against mine, heavy breaths bellowing as I stroke him.

"I love you too. Think I have from the day I met you."

Shifting forward on my knees, I position Finn's cockhead right at my entrance. In preparation for something like this outcome, I decided to come over here in a dress without any panties. No point in overdressing for the occasion.

"Finn."

At the sound of his name, he lifts his gaze to mine.

"I take my birth control pill promptly at eleven a.m. every day and have done so for the past three years. And it is widely speculated among our kind that mythics cannot contract venereal disease. Also, my gynecologist gave me a clean bill of health two months ago. What's your status?"

"I—oh hell—you mean, you want to ..." He's some kind of flustered, hands fisting in my skirt, eyes tracing over my face and then fixating on our laps.

"Finn. Status. Now. Or I'm climbing off you to find a condom."

"No STDs!" the man practically shouts. "I'm good. So good. Sit down. *Please.*"

I do appreciate being asked nicely. With a measure of control, I lower myself, focusing on the press, the push, the widening of myself to fit around the hard length of my human. When I've gone so far that my thighs rest on his, I realize a sheen of sweat covers my chest. My heart races. I feel everything.

"You're inside me," I tell Finn, untangling his hand from my dress so I can draw his palm up and press it flat against my chest. Directly over my heart.

"Hell, Isla. I never want to leave." He stares at our hands on my body the same way he used to stare at me from across the room. Like there's only one thing in the world he can see.

All he sees is me.

All I need is him.

Searching for more—the pinnacle I promised myself I'd reach to claim my mate—I begin to rock my hips. Slow at first, but then he groans, and the power of that sound infuses me, driving me on faster, harder, with unending love and absolutely no mercy.

"I wanted to take my time with you," he gasps out before both his teeth and eyes snap shut.

"I plan to take my whole life with you," I inform him while guiding his hand under the fabric pooling around my waist.

Realizing what I want, Finn takes over, his strong fingers finding and stroking my clit as I clench down on him with my inner muscles.

Curses and praises spill from his mouth, but his touch doesn't let up, and soon, I'm curling into him, my body shivering with a release even better than the ones he helped me with last night. Because this time, the word *love* floats in the air around us.

"Isla," he moans my name, his voice torn with it.

I plan to hear myself referred to in this manner many more times over the course of my life.

We have years to make up for, the ones when I naively believed I knew the will of the gods.

My mate and I sit, curled around each other, bodies heaving with gulping breaths that soon turn into giddy laughs.

"Your knees are going to give us away." Finn points out as he glances down to where I brace them in the dead leaves, no doubt smashing dirt into my skin even now.

"My skirt is long enough to hide them. But you'll have to hide your butt. Your shorts are a mess. I rode you hard."

He skips a breath at that and then smashes his mouth into mine, plundering a deep kiss I'm happy to have stolen.

Eventually, we convince each other that this is not the last, but instead a continuation of many intimate times together. Only then do we rise off the ground, doing our best to wipe away debris before walking hand in hand back to the house.

Where we discover an interesting scene.

"I need one that is mostly gray with just a small bit of blue in the corner," my mother announces.

"Here. Try this one." Mr. Hammond passes a puzzle piece across the table, where a partly finished picture of the Hoover Dam is spread.

"Mimosas are ready!" Finn's grandmother strolls in from the kitchen, a pitcher in her hands.

"Fantastic." My father stands from his chair, accepting a glass from her and holding it steady as she pours. "I've never had a morning cocktail, come to think of it. But I do like orange juice. And champagne." He takes a deep sip and then catches sight of us. "Isla and Finn are back. Did you two have a productive talk?"

Words remain just out of my reach as I attempt to understand the sight before me, where my parents are easily mingling with humans. This is what I wanted, but I half-expected to return and find they'd retreated to my car and locked the doors to maintain a safe barrier.

"We did." Finn raises my hand to his mouth to press a kiss to my knuckles.

"Oh good. It seems I was right." My mother nods to herself, attention still on the Hoover Dam.

That truly throws me off-balance. "What do you mean by *you were right*? It's not as if you knew I'd been in love with Finn for years. I barely ever admitted it to myself." In fact, I'm perturbed at her tone after tying myself in knots about how to convey this to them.

"You drew a heart around his picture in your yearbook. All four years." My mother could not sound less surprised with this situation as she examines pieces of the puzzle.

"You did?" Finn gives me a smirky grin I will likely have to kiss off his face.

"That's not proof of anything. I also circled Owen's picture."

"Only in the last two yearbooks," my father offers after another sip of his drink. "And you drew a square around him. In black marker."

"We thought you might be intending to harm him in some way. A blacklist maybe," Mama adds.

I find myself extremely miffed with this turn of events. "I did that because I thought Owen and I were meant to be together," I growl, knowing this is not a battle I have any reason to be fighting. "And because our *families* are similar," I say carefully, aware that Finn's grandparents are still in the dark about the magical creatures that live in Folk Haven.

Both my parents glance at me then, matching scowls on their faces.

"You and Owen MacNamara? Oh no. That would never do," my mother chides.

"He's too wild. Only follows the rules he likes. No. We prefer Finn." My dad raises his glass to my human, who seems to be fighting off a terrible coughing fit.

But then I see the grin grow wider and realize Finn is struggling not to laugh.

"Since when?" I press, unable to move past my parents' sudden acceptance of humans.

My father hums a happy note as he sips more of the drink. A noise he usually saves for only the most perfectly brewed cup of tea.

Mama takes up the explanation. "A few years ago, some men came to fish on the lake. They used *nets*." She grits out the word as if it were a curse, and to my family, it is. "The police were called, and they were escorted from town." Her fingers shake as she sorts through puzzle pieces. "But they left the nets in the water."

Anger rises in a slow tide through my body. *How dare they!*

"Finn dived for an entire week, searching every last one

out." My mother grants her attention to the human at my side, fixing her eyes on him. "We never properly thanked you for that."

"They were dangerous," my mate mutters, his fingers fisting in the back of my dress.

Both my parents nod, almost in unison.

Mama takes that moment to remember there's a pair of not-in-the-know humans in the room. She offers Finn's grandparents a tight smile. "I used to swim every day when I was a young woman. In the ocean near my home. When I was pregnant with Isla, I would still swim. One evening, I was caught up in a discarded fishing net. I almost drowned."

Mrs. Hammond gasps, and her husband wraps a comforting arm around her shoulders.

My mother nods. "I might have died if Patrick had not cut me free."

"You are a good man," my father says to Finn. "A protector of the lake and everyone living here. We would be happy to have you as part of our family."

The proclamation shoves through me, as if The Finned One speaks in my father's voice.

"Fine!" I announce loudly to the room, breaking the emotionally heavy moment I'm not sure how to handle. "You approve of the man I love. Fantastic. I will just shred all my well-planned arguments I had for convincing you that we're perfect together."

"You had written arguments?" Finn asks as he relaxes his grip to slip an arm around my waist.

His easy touching elicits only positive responses from my body, as if my skin recognized him merely as an extension of myself.

"Not yet. I was drafting them in my head. I planned to type them up tonight after this went badly. But now, everything is going perfectly smoothly, and I didn't plan for that. What do I do now?"

Finn cups my cheek with his hand, guiding my eyes to his. "Start typing up plans for our future."

EPILOGUE

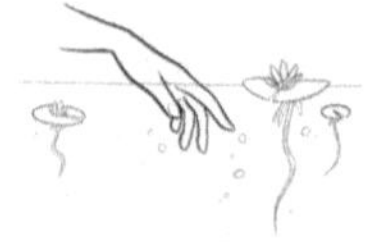

ISLA

"D*ID YOU GET ENOUGH TO EAT*?" My love's voice pulls my attention away from the window.

My mind takes a moment to focus on the words he said. "Yes. Plenty. The water is distracting me."

Finn sets the plate full of foodstuff down and adjust the bag on his shoulder before wrapping me in his arms. Any other night, his embrace would be all I needed. But it's been a month since I wore my second skin, and my body longs to sink into my other form.

"Of course," he murmurs, pressing a kiss to my neck. "Let's walk down. Looks like Moira and Calder are already on their way."

He's right. I spy the two siblings stepping off the back porch of the MacNamara house, making a straight shot for the lake.

"You coming?" Owen sidles up to the two of us, his arms clutching his selkie pelt.

He grins easily, like he always does, but I get the sense he's more relaxed now that the truth is out about the night of my accident. The man actually apologized to *me*, not realizing I'd interpreted the event as a fated mates' catalyst. Turned out, Owen had known about Finn's crush, and he'd figured if I was interested in the human, I'd want to reveal my true nature on my own terms.

Because Owen is a good man who cares deeply, I found it easy to forgive the misunderstanding.

"So, you're sticking with the whole *dick out for the world to see*, huh?" Finn deadpans at his best friend, indicating Owen's naked form.

"You're mated into a clan of selkies. Better get used to some nudity." Owen claps Finn on the shoulder before strolling into the dark night, the pale globes of his ass cheeks the only moon on display.

Finn hooks an arm around my waist. "Are you wearing that robe for me?" he asks.

I glance down at the thick terry-cloth covering. "Yes." He frowns, so I explain further, "You have to spend the rest of the night without me. I thought you would appreciate my attempt to desexualize myself, so you don't suffer too much lustful longing while I'm gone."

"Lustful longing?" Finn snorts. Then, he shows how right I was when he pulls me to a spot on the back deck in shadow and presses me against the side of the house. "Okay. You're right. I'll miss you." Then, he fuses our mouths together, kissing me with enough heat that I almost forget the call of Lake Galen.

Almost.

He breaks off, panting. "That's not helping."

I pat his cheek. "We'll get better over the years. Besides, you'll like how I am tomorrow morning."

In the darkness, I make out the bright flash of his grin.

Selkies always get light-headed, almost drunk, after taking on our finned forms for the first time after a long stretch. When

I return to my human shape tomorrow, I'll be overly enthusiastic and handsy, which Finn said he can't wait to experience.

"Come on then. Let's get you wet."

I let him take my hand and guide me toward the shore. Soon, I overtake him, pulling ahead. When the water brushes my toes, a needy shiver rocks my body.

"Here. You give me the robe, and I'll hand you your skin."

Glancing behind me, I watch Finn carefully remove a shimmering mass from a bag slung over his shoulder. I shuck off my robe, so we can exchange. Though my selkie pelt begs to wrap around my limbs, I hold off long enough to steal another kiss.

"I love you." Wet clay slides along my soles as I step farther into the water.

"Be safe. I love you too." Finn remains rooted to the shore, waiting for me to finish the change and slide beneath the surface.

My human skin is suddenly sensitive, overexposed. I wrap my selkie skin around me, sighing in pleasure with the way the hide melds to my body. My limbs flex into their new shapes, and I allow the water to claim me.

Everything is right again, the inside of my body calming from a clamor built up over days. My mind eases, and I let the current take me.

For a time, I drift, blowing bubbles of acknowledgment to others of my kind who swim by. Some selkies experience a rush of energy, taking on this form, and they spear through the water, coaxing others to play and celebrate the freedom. I tend to drift toward meditative. Which might be why I seem to be the only one who notices when one of ours swims with purpose toward the mouth of the cove.

There is no law stating we must stay in this branch of Lake Galen during our change. But it is understood this is the safest place for us. I experienced firsthand what can happen when we stray. When I gave in to a desire to explore all those years ago, I ended up in the wrong part of the lake just as Mr. Hammond was speeding by. Lucky that Finn dived in and Owen followed me.

That acceptance of both their important roles in saving my life has me making a decision now. I won't let this member of my clan travel into the lake alone.

I follow.

The figure ahead of me doesn't meander. They have a destination. I flick my tail harder to keep up while spreading my awareness darting all around me. Finn was right that knowing about the perpetrator and how he's off the lake have helped ease some of my worries. But I still get the occasional nightmare.

The selkie disappears up ahead, and I realize they rose to the surface. Following suit, I carefully peek only my eyes above the water.

We're at a dock, one in a section of the lake not home to any selkie families. As the mythic removes his skin, I realize I've been following Calder, the youngest of the MacNamaras. He hauls himself onto the floating platform, approaching a woman. The dark-haired beauty from the party.

A human? Maybe a potential mate he wishes to pursue?

She must be someone special if he would reveal himself in such a way to her.

They embrace, and their actions slide into passionate territory. Just as I've accepted Calder is safe enough that I can head back, the woman tilts her head toward the lake. Purple irises glow bright in the dark night.

Not human.

Not selkie.

Another mythic of some kind.

I sink below the water and carefully retrace my path. Calder is not in any danger. Not at the moment anyway.

When it comes to selecting a mate, mythics pair either with

one of their own kind or a human. The first is easiest. The second is harder because they need to be introduced to our world, but it's still widely done with our kind.

But a partnership between two different mythical creatures carries a stigma in our community.

Silently, I wish Calder luck with his pursuit of love. He'll need it.

Because when mythics mix, that's how the world gets monsters.

~

MOONING OVER A MONSTER

Satine expects to spend a lonely life on the shores of Lake Galen. She does *not* expect a charming bear shifter with a monster crush.

Satine lives in the small town of Folk Haven, a place full of mythical creatures. But even among shifters and sirens and dragons, she's still seen as odd. Because Satine is a monster. With no human face to wear out in the world, she has to live hidden in her house on a remote corner of Lake Galen, alone most days other than the friends she has online.

Alone until a bear shifter delivery man takes interest in her...

Can Mahon convince Satine to come out from the shadows? Can she break down her walls to accept the passion he offers? Or will Satine also hide from love?

CONTENT WARNING

This story contains discussions of parental death, self-harm, body image issues, feelings of exclusion and abandonment, and bigotry.

FRANKENSTEIN'S MONSTER fucking The Creature from the Black Lagoon doggy style is inspired. I never thought of myself as an artistic genius until this moment.

But will my audience be impressed?

A long time ago, I convinced myself not to care what other people thought. At least, not enough to affect me emotionally. But I still can't go out in public. Not when most humans' opinions when they see me are …

Ah! Monster!

Terrifying beast that's come to devour my soul!

Run!

Call the authorities!

Shoot it!

Much worse than leaving the house on a bad hair day. So, I avoid everyone, even as I refuse to care about their opinions.

But I do care about *him*. My delivery guy. The single audience member for my front yard setup.

Through the glass of my upstairs window, I hear the buzz of his engine approaching. I know it's him because I live at the farthest corner of Lake Galen. The road to my house is a ten-minute dirt lane from the closest paved surface.

Through the trees, a bright blue moped appears. He must have some durable tires to make the trek on that silly machine. But he does make it once a week, as he's been doing for the past few months on the days I treat myself to lunch and caffeine from Coffee & Claws—Folk Haven's best and only coffee shop. Bonus for me: seeing the burliest, handsomest deliveryman I've ever spied on from my bedroom window.

Yes, I'm a creep. Might as well lean into it.

The guy shuts off his engine and kicks down the stand that keeps his scooter upright. With a turtle-shell helmet clipped under his chin, the only hair I see is the vibrant red beard covering the lower half of his milk-pale face. But the bushy mass can't cover up the wide grin or muffle his booming laugh.

He likes it.

Over the years, I've collected life-sized figurines of my favorite classic movie monsters. Actual monsters that go around, murdering terrified fictional humans. Not monsters like me, who just happened to be born more different than most.

A few weeks ago, on a whimsical urge, I arranged the figures outside for a monster picnic. Only I forgot to bring them back inside before ordering myself lunch.

The delivery guy came upon my creepy garden scene.

When I heard him laugh, the delicious deep bellow rising from his belly, I immediately developed an addiction for the noise.

The next time, I had Jason chopping wood while The Wolf Man cooked marshmallows over a cardboard fire.

The week after, Dracula and The Mummy danced the waltz under a disco ball suspended from an overhead tree branch.

Then, there was a poker game.

A bake sale.

A cheerleading pyramid. That required three hours to arrange and a lot of strategically placed wire.

Still, they were all tame scenes until now. This was a risk.

Delivery Guy takes his time observing my pornographic arrangement, fists planted on his hips, intoxicating chuckles leaking from that glorious beard. I went so far as to blow up an air mattress and fit it with sheets—rumpled from vigorous sex play, of course—and pillows and condom wrappers.

I am committed to my craft. Just like the creators of the figurines, apparently, because when I pulled down Franken-stein's monster's pants, I discovered an apple bottom, green as a Granny Smith. No dick though. Bummer.

Delivery Guy finally turns toward my house, and I step back from my window even though I know he can't see me through the wildly expensive glamour I paid a witch to equip the glass with. Even if he could spot me, according to Heath—the bear shifter who co-owns Coffee & Claws—the guy wouldn't care.

"He's my cousin. A shifter. So, don't be worried none about him seeing you," Heath said when I called a few weeks back about getting food delivered to my place.

Yeah, right.

Even among the massive number of mythical creatures who live in Folk Haven, I'm an oddity. Most mythics have a human form they can change into to easily navigate the world. I'm not so lucky. And my inability to blend in freaks other mythics out. Like being around me will somehow screw them up too.

A loud knock sounds on my front door as I settle on the top step and gaze down at the portal I let less than a handful of people through. Delivery Guy isn't one of them.

"Hey, Satine!" His voice booms through the thick oak door, undeterred by the barrier. He says my name as if he knows me when we've never conversed other than my odd artistic displays in my front yard. "Your food's here! And I gotta say"—he keeps talking to my door, assured that I'm listening, which, of course,

I am—"ten outta ten. No contest. My favorite by far. I always knew they were a bunch of horny dudes."

My cheeks ache from grinning so hard, and I bury my face in my hands even though he can't see.

"Hope you enjoy your sandwich. Better get out here soon, before the ants get to it. I snuck a bear claw in the bag 'cause Heath had a few fresh from the oven. Thought you'd like something sweet at the end of your meal."

I don't say anything. No, *Thank you,* or, *That was thoughtful,* or, *Can I touch your luxurious beard?* Just keep my silence, like always.

"All right. I'll leave you be." The sound of his heavy boot on the gravel of my drive lets me know the best part of my week is coming to an end.

I don't bother using the stairs, instead extending my wings and gliding down to the first floor. I peek out a lower window to watch as he retreats to his moped. The door will stay closed until his taillight disappears down my wooded drive.

Nibbling on the sharp point of my thumb's claw, I wait for the puny roar of his scooter's engine, fighting a smile as the compact machine dips under the weight of his broad body.

Five, four, three, two, one ... I arbitrarily count down, as if I can guess the exact moment the key will turn.

But I guessed wrong because there's no thrum of an engine coming to life.

I count again. And another time.

Then, I stumble back a step when Delivery Guy stands from his moped.

"What are you doing?" I whisper the panicked question to myself.

I want him to go. But I also *don't* want him to go. And that confusion, along with his deviation from routine, spikes my pulse.

From the safety of my home, I watch the shifter raise his

arm in the air, turning back and forth, as if searching the sky for something. That's when I see the phone clutched in his grip and let out a groan.

There's no way he's going to get reception this far out.

Delivery Guy strolls toward my door.

Oh no. Oh no, no, no. I'm not ready for this. Maybe one day, after tons of preparation and at least a week of psyching myself up mentally. But sprung out of nowhere?

"Hey, Satine?" A gentle yet decisive knock sounds on my door, as if he knows I'm standing just on the other side. "My ride won't start, and I don't have service out here. I'm sorry to ask it of you, but could you help a guy out? Just looking to use your landline to give my buddy a call."

A response. He requires a response.

I can talk to him. Talking isn't seeing. My voice is normal enough. No reason for him to cringe away at that.

Now, I only have to deal with the mortification of him knowing I've been lurking, watching him this whole time. But what's my other option? Stay quiet and make him hike miles back to town?

I'm a monster, but I'm not monstrous.

Stepping in close to the door, I finally break the silence on my end of our relationship. "I can call you the mechanic."

He doesn't need to be the one to use my phone, I reason. I can just as easily contact whoever he needs.

"Hey, Satine!" His voice vibrates with something like excitement. "You *are* there! This is so cool. I wasn't sure."

"Yeah." That comes out too breathy to be heard, so I try again. "Yeah, I'm here. I'll go call the auto shop." I step as if to move farther into my house when, really, I could use my satellite phone here if I wanted to. I don't have a landline, just a supercharged signal on my high-tech device.

"Wait!" His shout has me pausing. "Could you call my friend instead? They've got a truck I can toss my baby in the back of. No need to get Francis out here, charging me an arm and a paw."

My best guess is, Francis is a local mechanic. I wouldn't know because I barely drive my car anywhere and can change the oil myself.

"Sure." I lean my shoulder against the door. "What's their number?"

And please don't ask me why I'm not opening the door.

Delivery Guy rattles off a string of digits, and I type them out on my screen, pressing the device to one of the slits on the side of my head I use to hear.

"Hello?" a feminine voice answers the call, and my gut twists in a painful jerk, made all the worse because I didn't brace myself for the hurt.

"Hi," I croak the word, frog-like, and then clear my throat of the amphibian tone. "Hello. My name is Satine, and I live on 913 Dark Wood Road. I have a deliveryman here, experiencing vehicle troubles, and he asked I call you to come pick him up."

"I'm sorry, who?" the lovely-voiced person asks.

"Satine."

"No, I got your name. Who's the delivery guy?"

"Oh ... uh, just a second." I cover the receiver with my webbed fingers. "What's your name?" I yell through the door.

"You don't know my name?"

"No." I always refer to him as Delivery Guy. Keeps a needed distance between me and dangerous emotions. "Heath just called you his cousin."

There's a mutter that sounds like *unhelpful asshole* and then, "Well, I'd like to formally introduce myself. I'm Mahon Vernon Deepcave the third. But you can call me Mahon. Or any other complimentary name you think up for me. I'm flexible like that." He lets out a rumbling laugh. "Yeah! Make a note of that. I'm *very* flexible."

I stare at the door, slowly blinking both sets of my lids,

wondering for the first time if the creature on the other side of the entry might be stranger than me.

"Hello?" The voice from my phone recaptures my attention.

"Sorry, I'm still here. He said his name is Mahon."

There's a groan and then a muffled shout that has me thinking this person is doing the same hand-over-the-phone maneuver I just did.

"Calder! The silly bear broke his scooter again and wants to use my truck."

Calder. I know that name. Calder MacNamara is a selkie in town. And if the gossip I've heard during my stealthy excursions is right, the water mythic just found his mate. Is that who I'm talking to? For some reason, the idea eases the wave of queasiness in my stomach.

"What are they saying?" Mahon calls through the door.

"Hey, Satine. Tell him Calder will be there in a bit. This is Delta, by the way. Hopefully, Mahon's not giving you too much trouble."

"Satine?"

Every time the shifter says my name, my scales tingle.

"Delta says Calder's on his way," I call. Then, into my phone, I say, "Thanks. And he's fine. You can give Calder this number in case he gets lost and needs to call."

"Weird to think there might be a corner of Lake Galen he doesn't know, but thanks," the woman muses. "I'll do that. Try not to stab the whiny bear while you wait. He means well. Nice to talk to you, Satine."

"You too." And it was. I don't talk to many people in this town. The food places I order from. My friend, Levi. That's about it.

Everyone else I connect with is either through my remote work as a digital marketing designer or in virtual chat rooms for gamers. Delta somehow seemed more real to me. Maybe because of her connection to the all-too-real man just outside my house.

"All right. Well, I guess I'll just wait out here then," Mahon calls to me.

When I press my eye to the peephole, I see him settling his butt on the top step of my front porch.

"You know, just sit here. All alone."

Was that a sniffle?

"No company." He hangs his head. "By myself."

If I had pupils, I'd roll them.

"Do you need a thesaurus?" I ask.

His head pops up. "Huh?"

"To come up with a few more ways to say *alone*?" Even as I snark at him from inside my house, I can't stop the upward tug of the corners of my mouth.

In the rounded image of him in the peephole, I pick out a broad grin.

"No, no. I think you get the message."

Then, the shifter starts whistling "Nobody Knows the Trouble I've Seen."

The put-upon act should annoy me, but I find myself fighting a laugh. And contemplating a bad idea. With a flick, I extend my wings, and then I jump into the air and flap my way back to the second floor. The maneuver comes naturally to me. Living on my own in this open–floor plan, high-ceilinged house, I fly as much as I walk.

I also don't bother with clothes most of the time. As I pad into my bedroom, I glance down at my bare body. Indigo skin melds seamlessly with scales of the same color, covering my body in beautiful patterns I've learned to love over the years. The harder surface still leaves some soft parts of me exposed. Like my nipples and my vulva. Both a lighter blue than the rest of me. Same with my lips.

I press the pads of my fingers to the plush skin surrounding my mouth, and despite the thinness of them, I'm glad the gods let me have a set. I'd rather have lips than ears. Who needs those fleshy satellites sticking out from the sides of their head anyway?

My walk-in closet is sorely underused. I don't bother with clothes most days of the week. Today is a rare occurrence. Snatching a loose set of black sweatpants and an extra-large hoodie, I slip the fabric pieces over my body. With my wings tucked tight against my back, they hide under the material, and everything fits fine. In fact, the outfit engulfs me, but that's what I'm going for.

Less on display for him to judge.

This time, I use my feet to get down the stairs, walking barefoot until I reach the front door, where I slide on a set of slippers. The getup is cozy, and I might be more amenable to clothes on a daily basis if the seams didn't snag on my scales.

I can still hear the delivery guy's mournful whistling through the door. The tune lures me to him, as if the man were part siren.

But he's not. If Mahon had any blood in him other than shifter, he would lose access to that term. Just like I can't call myself a dragon even though that's what my father is. And I can't call myself an undine even though that's what my mother was. The mixture of the two makes me other.

Makes me a monster.

With my fingers wrapped around the doorknob, I pause and reconsider.

Will Mahon cringe away from me like so many others have? Can I handle it if he does?

I glare at the dark wood of *my* front door, on *my* property.

Of course I can handle it. I am a work of art, and if he doesn't see that, then fuck him and the scooter he rode in on.

Besides, I think as I unlock the dead bolt, *I'm hungry.*

2

THE INSTANT I STEP OUTSIDE, the whistling stops. I focus on picking up my bag of food and still-warm café au lait. July in northern Georgia is normally stifling, but today, a breeze inter-twines with the ever-present humidity. Something in my phys-ical makeup has always allowed me to regulate my body temperature to fit the environment, so wearing sweats on the hot day doesn't bother me.

Focusing on the weather is my vain attempt to think of anything other than the mythical creature lounging on my front porch. My eyes stay on the wooden planks beneath my feet as I settle beside him on the step, plenty of space between us. Then, I pretend to be fully absorbed in my first sip of coffee.

All a ploy to give Mahon time. Time to school his shocked features. Time to come up with an excuse to make a hasty departure.

But after a seemingly endless stretch, I can't keep my eyes to myself any longer. Not when I finally have an unobstructed view of him. Not when I have his freshly mowed grass and tangy tree-sap scent teasing the slitted nostrils on my tiny bump of a nose.

Bracing myself, I turn my head.

He's staring. That's not new. But the delighted, wide-mouthed grin is. The shifter almost appears joyous.

Did I turn into a giant bar of chocolate and not notice?

Finally, he snaps his mouth shut. Only to open it a moment later and set me further off-balance.

"I *love* blue." Mahon points to his T-shirt, which happens to be a vibrant shade of royal blue that matches my scales. The material stretches over a beefy chest and a set of biceps I'm not sure I could wrap my fingers around even if I used both hands. "It goes great with my hair," he continues, unclipping the helmet. When he takes the covering off, a mess of red waves spills out, the color darkened by sweat. Mahon messes the strands further with his broad palm.

Our roles have reversed because now, I'm the one speechlessly staring. Never have I had such an easy acceptance of my appearance. Even Levi, a monster himself, did a triple take when we first met.

"Don't hold off eating on my account." Mahon waves at the bag he drove all the way out here to deliver. "You gotta be starved."

Still lost for words, I silently take out and unwrap my turkey and avocado sandwich, robotically biting into my lunch as my mind tries to make sense of this odd man.

When I swallow, his joyful grin returns. "Good, huh? Heath makes a mean loaf of sourdough. Tried to teach me a few times but got all grumpy, saying I was killing his starters." The redhead shrugs. "I wasn't *trying* to murder them. Sometimes, things die of natural causes, you know?" He glances my way.

With my mouth full, I just raise my brow ridges.

"Exactly! He didn't agree. Put me on delivery duty instead. Much better job. I wish you'd order more though. Yours is my favorite house to come to. Get to fly down that last stretch of road before your drive. And no one else bothers putting on a show for me." He waves toward my monster fucking display. "Like I said before, *genius*."

His chortles have me smiling as I take another bite of my sandwich.

"Thank you," I mumble through the food. The tone of my voice surprises me, as does my posture. *When did I start talking shyly and slouching as if I'm ashamed?*

With a jerk, I straighten my spine and meet Mahon's eyes. At least, I try to. But his focus is on my relatively flat chest.

"Did you go to Ramla?" He points, and I realize he's not attempting to find my mosquito-bite boobs, but instead reading the logo on the sweatshirt.

Ramla University. The academic institution just south of Folk Haven, secretly serving a populace of mythics, just like our town provides a home for a good portion of mythical creatures.

I nod while swallowing. "I was their first fully online student." Now, they're looking into improving virtual offerings. But for me, the professors jumped through a lot of hoops. "Got a degree in marketing. That's my job now. Digital marketing. Can do it all from home." I wave at my house, trying to forget how my boss has been pushing for face-to-face meetings lately. If he makes them mandatory, I'll have to quit and go on the job hunt again.

"Consider me impressed. You're looking at a guy who barely made it to high school graduation." The shifter offers a sheepish smile that crinkles his beard in a delightful way. "Still don't know what I want to do with my life. Just work a bunch of odd jobs around town for now."

Mahon describes his situation as if there were something wrong with it. But, gods, the freedom in that way of living starts up a subtle longing in my chest. I like my job. I'm great at it. But I can't just show up someplace and ask about their Help Wanted sign. I have to do a whole digital song and dance to keep from exposing my unusual face to the world.

"Do you need any help around here?" Mahon's question brings my focus back to our conversation. "Maybe a gardener? I can do it shirtless." The shifter wiggles his eyebrows, crimson hairs dancing like caterpillars above a set of friendly hazel eyes. It's almost as if he's flirting with me.

But that can't be right.

Still, I fight the traitorous curl of my lips as I answer, "Sorry, not in need of any half-dressed employees. Despite the setup in my yard, I promise you I am not filming pornos here."

Mahon barks out a laugh as he reclines on his elbows. Suddenly, I'm regretting not requiring he take his shirt off. Right now, the cotton strains against his meaty body.

The opposite of mine, which is just a collection of sharp angles.

"You have a big ole cast of characters already—that's for sure."

I follow his stare to the bawdy scene, swearing Mahon's eyes run over the generous globes of Frankenstein's monster's ass.

"Which one is your favorite?"

The shifter glances back at me, and I drop my gaze to his arm, attention caught by the abundant amount of ginger hair on his pale skin.

"The Wolf Man," I blurt out, fur on the brain. When I flick my eyes back to Mahon's face, I find the bearded man pouting.

"You gotta be kidding me, Satine. You're breaking my heart over here. Wolf shifters always think they're hot shit." He waves a dismissive hand in the air. "Bears are *so* much better. Trust me."

"Well, you are the expert." Digging my teeth into my lower lip, I keep my snicker to myself. Reaching into my to-go bag, I pull out the bear claw Mahon was kind enough to bring me. I split the pastry in half and offer him a piece.

He leans toward me, his scent increasing with the proximity. "You honor me," he says, tone serious.

Then, the bear shifter plucks the treat from my fingers and takes a substantial bite. I'm so focused on the flex of his jaw that I almost don't hear the crunch of tires on my gravel drive.

But my sense of self-preservation kicks in, and I whip my head to the side in time to watch a truck amble toward my house. Without considering the move, I pull the hood of my sweatshirt up over my hairless head, leaving only my face and hands uncovered.

Even though I know of Calder, it doesn't mean he knows of me. This casual chat with my delivery guy has shone on my day like an unexpected ray of sunlight, and I don't want the joy marred by a selkie flinching at the sight of my differences.

Mahon levers himself up from the stairs with a groan that my mind translates into a sexual noise for some unexplained reason. Or maybe I can blame my yard art for putting my brain in the bedroom.

Shit. Calder's going to see my monsters fucking.

I only meant for my nameless delivery guy to see it. I was going to break the setup down after he was gone. As Calder steps out of the cab of the truck, his focus goes straight to the green booty. I wonder if he'll keep the sight to himself or if all of Folk Haven will learn about the backwoods monster's twisted sense of humor.

At least while the selkie is distracted, I can retreat to the nonjudgmental emptiness of my house. While I gather up my trash and my coffee cup, Mahon strides across my front yard, reaching his moped in seconds and barely pausing before he squats down and heaves the entire thing over his head.

All plans to retreat are delayed, as I'm mesmerized by the strain of the shifter's biceps against the blue cotton shirt. His crimson hair really does pair nicely with the sapphire color.

The truck sinks under the weight of the scooter, and I tear my gaze away.

"Satine!" My name booms through the trees and freezes my feet once again, just steps away from my door.

With a slow turn, I watch Mahon bound toward me, wide grin parting his beard. He vaults the steps to my porch and skids to a stop in front of me, extending his hand.

Guess the guy has good manners. I set the leavings of my lunch down before straightening and accepting his handshake. At least, that's what I think he's offering.

Instead, Mahon tugs me into his warm body and slings a strong arm across my shoulders. My wings gather even closer to my back under my loose sweatshirt, but the bear doesn't seem to notice as he guides me toward the new arrival.

"Calder! Come here. Have you met Satine?"

The selkie finally looks away from my yard art, his eyes finding mine. To his credit, he merely blinks a few too many times before smiling at me. He holds out his hand, which I shake in a firm grasp, all the while staying tucked in close to Mahon's side.

As if our relationship were more intimate than having met face-to-face a short while ago.

"Nice to meet you, Satine. Hope Mahon didn't talk your ears off."

Suddenly, feeling comfortable enough to joke with these two mythics, I let the first response I think of come out of my mouth. "Actually, he did." I tug down my hood, revealing my ear-less head.

Calder's eyes widen, Mahon's laugh roars, and I bite my lip, fighting a smile. This is the goofy rapport I have with people online but rarely in person. The interaction is heady in a way.

After a second of shock, Calder grins wide and exhales in relief.

"Wish I could stick around." Mahon lets his arm slide away, and I try not to think about how I miss the warmth. "But Heath is already going to chew *my* ears off for taking so long." The bear shifter affects a dramatic pout. "He's going to make me mop. And it's not fun anymore since he said I can't use the handle as a microphone and serenade the kitchen."

The image he describes is easy to conjure in my mind. This wild redhead could do all manner of things at this point and not surprise me.

"I'll let you go." With a step toward my house, I can't help feeling like I'm returning to a cage. Maybe today is a good day to go for a swim.

"Nice to meet you." Calder waves as he climbs into the driver's seat.

I return the gesture before facing Mahon.

The delivery guy stares into my eyes. I wonder if he's searching for pupils among the purplish clouds shifting over the surface of the orbs that allow me to see. He won't find any.

"Can I see you again?" he asks.

You want to? I barely keep the vulnerable question to myself with a reminder that I don't care if people want to see me or not.

"Sure."

The shifter beams, leaning forward to snatch one of my hands. He brings my palm to his mouth and presses a surprisingly intimate kiss to the webbing between my thumb and forefinger. Left speechless, I hold my hand against my chest when he releases it.

"See you soon, my blue beauty."

3

———————

THE SKY SPREADS in a black mass above my perch, a void illuminated only by stars. Some call this the night of the new moon.

Among mythics, we call it the dark moon.

This is a night of shadows. Without light, we can easily hide yet also be free in that secrecy.

I stand easily on a thick branch, gazing over the treetops that spread for miles. Folk Haven sits in the foothills of the Appalachian Mountains, among the Chattahoochee National Forest. The wilderness pushes in on all sides. I love it, and tonight, I'm going to explore as much as I can from above.

I'm not the only one venturing out. Selkies have pulled on their magical pelts to swim in animal form, diving deep under the surface of Lake Galen. Sirens have freed their wings and play games in the air above their cove of the lake. Many other mythics let loose in the darkness.

But I'll spend the night on my own, as I've always done.

Sometimes, I pretend the bats are my companions. Their little squeaking voices fill the cool night air, and I watch their fluttering bodies glide back and forth. Once I take to the sky, they'll find somewhere else to hunt, scared my size makes me their predator. I don't blame them. I'm used to being feared.

Just as I ready myself to launch into the air, a loud rustling sounds beneath my tree. Glancing down, I spy a large mass lumbering among the trunks.

A bear.

Folk Haven has had the occasional black bear stray into town limits. But this creature is massive, and if my night vision isn't failing me, he's a reddish color. As the scent of freshly cut grass drifts up to me, I know exactly who has wandered into my territory this dark moon night.

When Mahon made his promise to see me again soon, I was left without a timeline. Of course, his delivery was yesterday, so I shouldn't have continued to glance out my window and at my phone every hour. The bear shifter doesn't even have my number.

And one day? How needy am I?

Apparently, very because I immediately swoop down from my perch to land a short distance in front of him.

Shit. Until I'm on the ground, I don't realize the result of my impulsive move.

This night, I left my baggy sweats at home. Despite expecting to be alone, I maintained a sense of modesty by pulling on a tight set of black bike shorts along with a matching sports bra. The straps of the top are all Velcro because that's the only thing I'm able to manage with my wings.

Wings that are now on full display. If Mahon has night vision anywhere near as good as mine, he'll see my extra limbs along with the scales that cover me from toe to hip, climbing up my back and then spilling over my shoulders and down my arms.

A living, breathing lizard person. Exactly what one could expect from mashing together a human and a dragon. Not that

I'm ashamed of my appearance. It's the way that others react that cuts.

Why can't they see the beauty of me?

Already in front of Mahon, I have no other choice than to stand tall and give him the best view possible.

The bear plops back on his gargantuan ass, beady black eyes tracing over my form as his wet nose sniffs the air.

Shifters are an interesting breed. In their other forms, they appear almost like the real animal. But something is always different. My bet is, no true bear has a ginger coat. Unless we're talking about red pandas. If Mahon could transform into one of *those* cuddly creatures, I'd have to kidnap him and keep him forever just because the adorableness factor would be too much to handle.

The man is pretty cute too.

Bear Mahon heaves to his feet and trundles forward. When the furry creature is almost in my personal space, he reaches out a paw the size of a Frisbee.

And he pushes me.

The gesture doesn't feel aggressive, and even though I stumble back a few steps, the push wasn't hard. Not compared to what an animal his size could manage if he wanted to attack me. Mahon lets out a huff that sounds a lot like a laugh. Then, with surprising agility for such a chunky body, he pivots around and sprints into the dark woods.

Did he just ... start a game of tag?

"Oh, it's on," I mutter, a grin stealing over my face.

With a powerful flap, I thrust myself into the air, leveling out over the treetops. I don't even need to search between the cluster of branches to try and locate him. The pines quiver wherever his heavy body runs, and I follow the shaking. When I'm above his location, I pick up speed and then dive down to land right in his path.

The bear lets out a surprised bark, tumbling as he tries to

stop and recalibrate his too-fast momentum. While he struggles, I lunge forward and slap his meaty shoulder.

"You're it!" Then, I wing myself to a branch at least fifty feet above him.

Bear Mahon lets out a series of protesting grumbles and whines as he stares up at me. Then, the massive beast digs his claws into the trunk and starts to climb.

Teasing him, I allow the guy to get halfway to my perch before I glide over his head, landing in a crouch on the forest floor. Then, I tuck my wings in close to my back and sprint into the woods, keeping to the ground to allow him an actual chance at catching me.

Because I find I want to be caught.

The ground shakes, and I hear the crashing sound of his big bear body charging through the woods after me. My underutilized legs pump as hard as they can, but I know he'll reach me soon enough.

A laugh bursts breathlessly from my chest when I hear his panting and sense his looming presence, and then I squeal in surprise at the cold press of his wet nose against my lower back. Whirling around, I tumble to the side as he charges past and disappears into the shadows.

"I'll get your furry ass!" I shout after him and receive a roar in response.

We go back and forth like that for so long that I lose track of time. All I know is, my legs burn, my wings tire, and I've never had more fun in my life.

Eventually, the two of us collapse side by side at the top of a cliff. Lake Galen rests below us, down the sheer rock face. The high vantage point emphasizes the freedom I've felt this night. As if the world grew vast as we tore through the woods.

As I lie on my back, cushioned by my wings, sucking in deep breaths to calm my racing heart, I notice a shift in the color of the sky above us. A lightening that lets everyone know that dawn is approaching.

Time for me to return to the safety of my home, no matter how much I'd like to linger here, on this cold rock, beside a panting bear. But when I stand and glance to my left, the bear is gone. A man lies in his place.

A naked man.

"Mahon!" I yelp and then cover my eyes with my webbed fingers. And yet, somehow, I'm still left with a sliver of a gap between the digits. Enough to watch as his muscular body tenses when he moves to stand.

Gods, he has that vibrant red hair everywhere. Arms, legs, chest. There's an especially dense cluster at the apex of his thighs ...

Before I can take in the newly revealed part of him between his legs, Mahon steps in close to me, warm, grassy scent embracing me, even as he keeps his touch to himself.

"Thanks for a fun night, Satine." He rumbles the words through a playful smirk. "Can I get a proper good-bye?"

I drop my hands, so I can meet his eyes. "What's a proper—"

Mahon cuts me off with a kiss. His mouth teases against mine so quick, there and gone, that I lose the chance to memorize the sensation.

Next thing I know, he's sprinting the few steps to the cliff's edge, the globes of his ass bouncing with each powerful step. Mahon launches himself into the empty air, briefly flying before he plummets into gravity's embrace. I reach the edge in time to watch his perfect dive, and a moment later, a bear bursts from the water's surface.

"That was extremely rude!" Even as I try to chastise the wild man, I laugh through my scolding.

A mishmash of bear noises is my only response as he

reclines on his back, floating away toward what I assume is his home.

Spurred on by the rising sun, I leap into the air and glide in the opposite direction, wondering exactly when I'll see that troublemaking bear again.

4

"I wouldn't do that if I were you."

Levi pauses, his fingers pinching the nipple-like top of his bishop piece. I bite my bottom lip to keep from smiling as I watch the consternation envelop his handsome features.

"Are you going to explain?" he asks.

I shrug. "Where's the fun in that?"

My friend scowls at the chessboard between us, trying to discern if my advice was honest or a trick to throw him off his game. The chances are fifty-fifty.

As Levi takes more time deciding, I ponder over how, even put out, he's a sight worthy of an audience. Inky locks frame a well-carved face with a prominent nose that somehow fits perfectly with the rest of his features. Classically handsome, which is a good thing, as he dislikes taking on his other shape.

Nice for him to get that choice.

Levi's random roll of genetics allowed him a human form and a monster form. He can move freely through the world in a way I cannot. But I don't resent him that option. Especially because he seems to be having a harder time accepting the label our society has given us.

"You're trying to trick me," he mutters, still fingering the chess piece while his other hand fiddles with his full lower lip as his brows dip with doubt.

"Guess you'll find out," I sing back to him, all innocent tone.

Yes, the monster is gorgeous. And yet he doesn't stir anything romantic in my chest.

We tried once. Not long ago, Levi and I decided to give dating a chance. The sex was good—not that I had a lot to compare it to—but outside of the bedroom, there was only ever friendship. The passion, when it arose, felt forced. Like blowing on smoldering kindling underneath a pile of wet wood.

Luckily, Levi felt the same, and we ended things on a mutual note and have successfully maintained our friendship. Thank the gods because I already have a limited number of offline acquaintances. No need to chip away at the miniscule group.

Although the number might have recently increased by one.

"Not falling for it." Levi scoots his bishop diagonally across the board, and I smother a grin of triumph.

Three moves later, and he's muttering curses as I checkmate his king.

"Told you so."

"No one likes a cocky winner." His long fingers work to meticulously place the pieces back in their wooden case.

"If I remember correctly, you twerked last week when you won in Scrabble."

"I did no such thing." He affects an affronted tone, even as the corner of his mouth curls. "And I would've won this time if I wasn't distracted."

"Hmm. Distracted by me? Or by some council issue?"

Last year, all the monsters living within Folk Haven's town limits voted on who would represent us on the town's Mythic Council. Levi won with more than eighty percent of the votes.

"Oh, wait. Maybe you were distracted by a council *member*."

When my friend glowers at me, I can't fight a grin anymore. He's too easy to rile. Besides, I'm positive I know what's had him off his game. Moira MacNamara. Fellow council member and Calder's older sister. My guess is, Levi is half in love with the selkie woman even if he won't admit it.

One more reason I'm glad we're not an item.

"My mind is on my *business*," he retorts, standing from the straight-backed chair he always sits in at my house. The least comfortable chair I own, as if he thinks he's not allowed to relax. "Nothing else. Or have you forgotten that I'm opening my own spa in less than a month?"

Sure. And hopefully, that place has some comfortable chairs to sit in.

"Ah, yes. How silly of me." I stroll with him to the door, tucking my hands in the pockets of the linen shorts I wore because I knew he was coming over. Same with the loose black halter top that covers my itty-bitty titties while leaving a gaping opening for my wings.

"Let me know when you want to come by the spa." Levi's grumpiness from my teasing fades as he opens my front door and smiles down at me. "I'll set up a private room for you. And all the employees are monsters, so it'll be no problem."

Yeah, no problem. Not like usual, where simply my existence is an issue.

I keep those sharp words to myself.

"I'll think about it."

Levi's enthusiasm dims. "Satine—"

"Hi!" The booming greeting has me jumping backward, ready to lunge inside and separate myself from the new arrival before they can comprehend the oddity of my appearance.

Then, I spy the red beard, and my panic evaporates.

"Mahon." I step to the edge of my porch. "Hey."

The bear shifter lingers in my driveway, looking rugged

when compared to Levi's business casual appearance. The big man has on heavy working boots, faded jeans, and a gray T-shirt that's worn on the edges. He clutches a scuffed-up cooler in one hand and a blanket in the other.

But his expression is what catches my attention. The normally jovial man glances between Levi and me, brows raised, eyes ... sad.

"Sorry. I should've called. Only I don't have your number. So, I showed up." Mahon raises his shoulders but doesn't let them fall in a full shrug. Like he's trying to brace himself for a blow.

My heart aches, and I stroll forward without thought.

"Don't worry about it," I say.

The shifter blinks, as if surprised to find me at his side. I wrap my hand around his wrist and tug him forward, strangely worried that he'll barrel off into the woods and I'll never see him again.

"Have you met my friend, Levi Abadi? We play chess sometimes, and I just beat him mercilessly."

Mahon glances at my hold and then into my face, his lighting up with a grin. "Of course you did. No one compares to you."

Warmth flushes through my body, and when I look at Levi, I can tell my friend is doing his best to suppress a smirk. Suddenly, I'm regretting my shortsighted teasing from earlier.

"Levi ..." I put a warning in my voice. *You'd better not embarrass me in front of the adorable bear.* "This is Mahon Vernon Deepcave the third."

When I release my hold on Mahon, he drops the blanket on the ground and reaches out to shake the monster's hand.

"Nice to meet you, Mahon the third." Levi keeps a cordial tone that tells me I'm in for it during our next hangout session.

"You too, buddy. Are you guys dating?"

My friend covers a laugh with a cough while I wonder if Mahon is this up front all the time.

"We tried that a while back," Levi answers. "Didn't work out. We're friends now."

The bear gives his hand a vigorous shake. "Good for me!" Then, Mahon turns his beaming face my way. "Want to go on a picnic?"

5

WE END up in my backyard because going any distance from my house when the sun is up is not a risk I'm willing to take. Maybe if all the inhabitants of Folk Haven were either mythics or humans who knew about mythics. But this lake attracts tourists, and some unaware humans move into town because they like the quaint feel of the place.

There's no witch strong enough to work a protective spell that would cover an entire lake and town. That would take hundreds of witches, all with a protective focus. I'm not sure that many exist in the world, much less in Georgia.

"I brought sandwiches," Mahon announces as he unfurls the blanket, the fabric settling on the shaded grass under my favorite laurel oak. Long branches stretch outward, glossy leaves providing relief from the glare of the sun.

On this hot day, we would have been cooler, sitting by the water, but I have an urge to protect my small dock. One of the few places in the world that's mine. Though I like Mahon, I'm not ready to take him there even if it's only a short distance away.

"I can't believe you brought me lunch." I settle cross-legged on the blanket.

When Levi and I were dating, he never surprised me with a meal. Sure, he'd bring me food. But eating together was always a preplanned event.

Before today, I would have said I didn't like surprises. Maybe I'll have to reevaluate.

"I bring you lunch all the time." He chortles at his own joke, and I toss a twig at him. Mahon merely grins as the projectile bounces off his broad chest. "You're a violent woman. I like that. We should wrestle."

At the outrageous wiggle of his eyebrows, I find myself sinking into laughter. This shifter is impossibly easy to be around. Helps that he brought food. Popping the top off the cooler, Mahon pulls out sandwiches, like he promised, and a pitcher of brown liquid that I'm hoping is sweet tea.

And a full watermelon.

"Do you want me to go grab a knife?" I ask. "To cut that up?"

"That'll ruin my whole plan!" Mahon scoops up the melon, holding the gourd away from me, as if I want to steal it.

"What plan?" I get the sense I should approach all of Mahon's ideas with caution.

"To impress you with my brute strength." Then, the bear stands up, clutching the watermelon with both hands, and brings it down in a swift move across his knee. The rind cracks, and Mahon digs his fingers into the fissure, tearing the melon in two with a mighty roar.

Juice goes everywhere.

Droplets fall like cool rain on my face, and I'm glad my clothes are dark colors. When I seek out Mahon's gaze, I watch his triumph dim at the sight of the red splatter, including the stain forming on his shirt.

"Oh shit."

Burying my face in my hands doesn't do much to smother my snorts, and from the small puffs of air, I know my wings are quivering along with my hilarity.

"I pictured this going a different way." Mahon's face holds a ruddy blush when I glance over my webbing at him.

"H-how"—I sputter on my words as more giggles spill out —"did y-you see it going?"

"Well, I thought you might compliment my muscles. Maybe gasp. Clutch your pearls." He offers a sheepish grin when I choke on a laugh. "I do this all the time as a bear. But I guess I don't worry about getting dirty. I just jump in the lake to wash my fur." With careful movements, Mahon sets the two watermelon halves on the top of the cooler before grimacing down at his shirt.

"You can take it off." The words pop out of my mouth without warning. Or maybe my vulva learned how to speak because the horny parts of me are suddenly rabid to see the shifter shirtless.

Or naked.

The image of his muscular, pale ass is burned into my memory.

If I thought Mahon would be weirded out by my offer, I obviously need to stop expecting him to act like everyone else. The bear doesn't hesitate, shucking off his T-shirt and tossing the material to the side like the covering offends him. I try not to stare, instead picking up one of the sandwiches and putting all my concentration into peeling off the brown paper wrapper. A smile tugs at my mouth when I realize he brought turkey and avocado—my usual.

"So, Satine, tell me about yourself." Mahon affects an almost-formal tone while simultaneously pouring me a cup of the brown liquid. "How do you fill your days in that big ole house of yours?"

Accepting the cup, I do a quick sniff check and immediately relax. Tea, like I thought. "Work takes up a lot of time." I sip and try not to pucker my lips at the wild amount of sugar. Almost like drinking straight from a bottle of honey. "I try sticking to an eight-to-five schedule, but then the end of the day rolls around, and I'm still working on projects. Or putting out digital fires. Sometimes, I'm going ten-plus hours a day. Still, I like it. A little bit of art, a little bit of management, and a whole lot of problem solving."

Mahon keeps his eyes on me as I talk, and then he drops his focus to my mouth when I bite into my sandwich. If I had hair follicles, no doubt his attention would cover me in goose bumps. As it is, my nipples pebble against my flimsy top.

"Who are you working your marketing magic for? Any places I might know?" The shifter snaps off a smaller corner of the mutilated watermelon and offers the dripping fruit to me.

"Our biggest client owns a string of gyms on the West Coast. Not sure you'd know them. But I've done a few smaller projects for businesses in Folk Haven. Just helping with setting up their social media pages and working out some style guides. That kind of thing. That's how I got to know Heath. Of course, Sonya was the one to hire me." I refer to the siren who co-owns Coffee & Claws. "But Heath is the one I work with mainly. Your cousin has gotten pretty skilled at photographing his pastries. That's prime digital marketing content."

A new blush rises on the tops of Mahon's cheeks, the red easy to see on his alabaster skin. His eyes shift to the side. "Guess he wasn't lying," the bear mutters almost too low for me to hear.

"Lying about what?"

I watch the big man fidget, and my heart melts at his adorable evasiveness.

Mahon scratches the back of his neck and then sighs out his

explanation, apparently unable to be even the slightest bit deceptive. "It's only ... well, a couple weeks ago, I went in the café's kitchen. Heath had his phone waist height." The shifter gestures toward the crotch of his pants, and I struggle against the urge to stare in that direction. "I saw the flash go off, and I figured he was ... taking a picture of his branch and berries."

Oh gods. I weld my jaw shut, worried that any noise might interrupt what promises to be an amazing story.

"So, I told him, 'I'm all for admiring the abundance The Clawed One gave you, but I suspect a place of business might not be the best environment for the photo shoot.' You know?" He scratches his beard, appearing almost thoughtful. "My guess is, most people would prefer a few layers of fabric between their pastries and a dong."

A high-pitched giggle sneaks out before I can stop it. Then, a rolling wave of them follows.

And Mahon keeps going, face flaming and mouth grinning, sharing his embarrassment with no further hesitation. "So, Heath said 'I was just taking a picture of my croissant.' And I said, 'I don't know why you'd call it a croissant unless there's a curve in it.' But then I thought that might make him feel bad, so I told him 'It's fine if your dick is a little curvy; I'm sure your future mate will love it, no matter what.'"

I can't—oh gods—I can't breathe. The laugh that forces its way out of my throat is almost a scream.

"He got real mad," Mahon admits. "Threw a croissant at my head."

Unable to even sit upright any longer, I lie out flat, face-down on the blanket, wondering if I'll die of this laughter and realizing I'm so happy in this moment that I'd be okay if this was the way I went. Giggling myself to death, next to a charmingly oblivious bear.

Eventually, I calm down enough to turn my head and meet Mahon's warm gaze.

His mouth curves at the corners when our eyes catch. "I used to think the buzz of a honeybee was the most beautiful sound in the world. But your laugh kicks that sound in the nuts."

"That's sweet. I think." I push myself upright, wondering if I'll ever be able to predict the next thing out of his mouth.

"I'd like this to be considered a date."

Guess not.

I only hesitate for a second, and that's so I can catch up with the change in conversation.

"Okay." *Why not?*

The guy is handsome and funny and brought me food and said my laugh is beautiful. What would this be if it wasn't a date?

"Awesome. We're on a date. How am I doing?" Mahon leans forward, his bare chest with its heavy muscles and blanket of ginger curls threatening to distract me.

"Do you want to be ranked on a scale?" I've never given a man feedback on a date before.

"The only scale I care about is if I'm doing good enough for a kiss or not."

At his words, I'm drawn back to the night of the dark moon. More accurately, the morning after, when his lips briefly touched mine. That gentle pressure set off a turbulent storm in my body, one that hasn't fully abated.

What would happen if we really kissed? Deeply? For a prolonged amount of time?

For one, I'd probably feel more connected to a person than I have in a while. In years.

The temptation drives my answer. "Yes. You are doing that well."

Mahon's face lights up, this time not with a blush, but with shining joy. As if getting the chance to kiss me is a magnificent gift. As if he sees me the way I've always hoped someone would.

Suddenly, the world shifts, and I realize the bear has scooped me up in his arms, drawing me into his lap. With an assured palm on my ass, Mahon lifts and tilts me until I'm able to settle my knees on either side of his hips, pressing into the soft blanket. The heat from his thighs soaks into the scales on my legs, and I allow him to arrange my arms around his neck.

"Is this good for you?" he asks once we're still, facing each other.

On top of him like this, I'm simultaneously in control and surrounded. My normally thin lips now feel plump, eager for his mouth. My wings quiver in anticipation.

"Yes. I'm good." To prove it, I cross the scant distance between us, taking what he offers.

Mahon is hot as sunshine and just as soothing. Just as dangerous. Because as I move my mouth over his plush one, I sense the cells in my body begging to connect with his. Threatening to wither if ever removed from his presence, like a plant pulled from daylight and shut up in a basement.

Will I be the same after this?

Mahon parts his lips on a deep breath, allowing me to delve into him. I flick my tongue along his, tasting watermelon and sugar and the darker flavor of man. The combination is so good that I suck, reveling in the moan I draw from him.

Weight on my back. Hands pressing against my hard scales, drawing upward until the searching touch meets the joints of my wings. I gasp into the kiss, unfamiliar with contact on that part of my body. Even I have a hard time reaching the place on my shoulder blades where my wings extend.

"Good?" Mahon asks with his lips moving against mine.

"Amazing," I respond before dragging my tongue along his.

My reward comes as fingers massage into the neglected area. As if he found a hidden button, my wings snap wide, and I'm glad we're outside. No accidental destruction from them knocking knickknacks off shelves.

As he continues to knead my muscles, the press and release encourage a similar pattern in my hips. I rock, pushing my pelvis against his. When I comprehend exactly what's happening, I force myself to stop and break away from the bear's intoxicating mouth.

"Sorry," I mutter.

"Use me," Mahon growls, eyes half-lidded.

One of his hands drops to my butt, encouraging the rocking. A new hardness greets me, and I glance down to find the outline of his arousal pressing against his jeans.

"Are you sure?" My question lacks conviction as my hips sway forward again, and I watch where our bodies meet.

"I would be honored if you humped me." His words are so solemn that it takes a moment for them to register.

Giggles bubble up just before I reclaim his mouth, plastering my chest against his. The whiskers of his beard tickle my more sensitive face scales, and I kiss my way across his cheek to explore the mass, nipping his jaw when I find the hard angle.

"Yes," he grunts. "Bite me. Use me. I'm your bear."

Why is that so hot?

His panted words crash through my body, exciting all my pleasure points. Through my shorts, I grind my clit against his pelvis and thank the gods this part of me chose skin instead of scales.

"Say it," he growls the command. "Say that I'm your bear." Both his hands are on my ass now, holding me against his erection.

The need in his voice feeds the erotic storm within me. Mahon wants me. Begging me to claim him. I have all the power.

Sliding my legs around his hips, I lock my ankles behind his lower back, pulling us even closer together. My fingers work into his messy red locks, and I have enough control to make sure my claws don't slice his scalp. I make fists and draw his head back, putting the column of his neck on display, licking the strong pump of his pulse.

"You're my bear," I whisper against his skin.

"Satine. My Satine," he moans, thrusting himself against me. "I want to lap at your pussy lips until your wings flap so hard that you threaten to fly away." One of his arms circles my back, locking me against him, while the other massive palm grips my thigh, soft cream against hard sapphire. "By the gods, I'll hold you to the ground and drive my tongue deep into your slick depths until you scream my name and the whole lake knows I'm your bear. Fuck yes. I'm *your* bear."

"Oh—oh I—" The storm hits, and I discover that dirty talk does everything I need to bring on the most intense orgasm of my life. My wings flap, just as he predicted, and I wrap my pulsing, quivering limbs around Mahon, terrified of accidentally separating us and losing this intense pleasure.

"Your bear," he groans into my neck. "Satine's bear." Then, his body jerks, and a strangled noise cuts off any more naughty words as he comes against me.

When our breathing levels out and I regain the ability to think over the demands of my vulva, something like panic tightens my muscles. I force myself to relax enough that I can unwrap myself and slide my butt out of Mahon's lap. He lets me go, even as his rough fingers drag along my retreating scales.

When there's a buffer of air between us, I risk meeting his eyes and come up against a sleepy, satisfied gaze. The shifter reaches over to the cooler, setting the mangled watermelon aside so he can open the lid.

"What just happened?" I ask. Is the question for me? For him? For the gods? I have no idea.

One moment, I was agreeing to a kiss. The next, I was claiming a shifter as mine and orgasming in his arms.

Didn't I just officially meet this man a few days ago?

Mahon finds what he was looking for, coming up with a ziplock bag full of pastries—no doubt from his cousin's café. He cracks the seal and plucks out a croissant and offers the flaky bread to me.

"You just rode a bear. Fun, huh?"

6

AFTER OUR HOT and heavy picnic, I hurried the too-enticing bear off my property. Mahon took my retreat good-naturedly, only asking for my phone number before he left, which I gave.

I haven't seen him in five days.

And I miss him.

I could have convinced myself the bear lost interest after messing his jeans with me, but even though I haven't seen him doesn't mean I haven't heard from him.

Mahon texts me. A lot. Like whole paragraphs of the things he's doing or funny incidents that have happened to him at the café or around town.

Reading them has me feeling like I'm living the day with him, and I find myself snatching up my phone whenever I take a break from work to get another dose.

After the first five or so that I didn't respond to, Mahon even did the gentlemanly thing.

Mahon: Hey ya. I know I'm texting a lot. Am I bothering you? I'll stop now unless you say otherwise.

I only held out five minutes before responding.

Satine: You can keep texting.

Mahon: *Great! Here's a picture of the squirrel that stole my potato chips. Cute as hell, but don't trust him!*

Maybe I should've applied that advice to the man, too, but less than a week has gone by, and I can't stand going to bed another night without seeing his face.

So, I invite the bear back over.

This time though, I'm going to make sure I have control of the situation. That I'm the one throwing *him* off-balance.

I stare at the innocent white square in my palm. The object both excites and terrifies me. And when I hear the distant thrum of Mahon's scooter engine approaching my house, I peel off the back of the adhesive and stick the patch on my wrist.

Sharp pain splits through my body, as if a hornet stung my wrist and decided to have a go at a few more spots. My weight alters, my sight loses an edge of clarity, and gravity dials up a handful of notches.

After I take a series of deep breaths, the pain fades to a manageable level. To get used to the change, I go through a few quick yoga poses, my feet feeling sticky against the hardwood floor.

Sweat glands, I remind myself. *Those little fuckers are everywhere.*

When I've gotten as comfortable as I can hope for, I peer out the window next to my door, spying like I used to whenever Mahon came to my house. And like all those times, he's currently chuckling at my latest monster display.

The Wolf Man and The Creature from the Black Lagoon are in the middle of a game of badminton. I kitted them out with sweatbands and rackets on their respective sides of the net, and I even flew up to a high branch to suspend the shuttlecock from a strand of fishing wire, so it appears to be in play.

Not as shocking as my last creation, but I figure Mahon and I heated up my property plenty without needing more fictional monster bed play.

While the shifter is distracted, I carefully slip out my front door and move to stand on the top step of my porch, arms akimbo, every inch of me on display, except for the small bits covered by my shorts and sports bra. Finally, he finishes taking in the sporting event and faces my house. Hazel eyes land on me, and he stumbles. We stare at each other across the distance, him no doubt admiring my new, supple form while I moon over every ruggedly handsome inch of him.

Somehow, Mahon became even hotter in the last few days, and I'm not sure how he managed it. Maybe he got a witch's help, like I did.

Unfreezing, Mahon raises his nose in the air, nostrils flaring, before refocusing a curious look on me. "Satine?"

I smile, my face feeling softer than wet clay without my scales. A panicked thought has me pressing my fingers into my cheeks, worried I'm so soft that all my parts might start slipping off. But no, they're still in place. Even the protruding nose in the middle of my face. I keep catching glimpses of the fleshy add-on in the corner of my eye. How do people focus with the constant distraction?

"Is that you?" Mahon steps toward me, hesitant puzzlement in the tilt of his head.

"You guessed it." I perform a three-sixty turn, so he can admire every inch of my transformation.

"I'm confused." He stops at the foot of the porch steps, staring up at me. "I thought you didn't have a human form."

"I don't." Raising my arm, I display the patch stuck to my wrist, successfully stifling a wince from the pain caused by the movement. "Bought a few of these off a transformation witch. I thought they might be helpful if I needed to be among humans. But I don't use them much."

"Is your skin supposed to be red like that?" He tilts his chin, brows dipping.

Following his gaze, I realize the pale flesh around the patch has flared an irritated color.

"Well, a human's skin shouldn't be. But yeah. The witch warned this was a side effect. One of the reasons I don't use them often." The other is that they cost a fat stack of cash.

Mahon steps closer, bringing his summer scent and heavy presence with him. I gasp when he settles his palms on my shoulders, his hands rough against my abnormally soft skin. Carefully, he drags his touch down my arms, as if examining the changes.

"Do you like looking like this?" When the question comes, the words hold none of his regular boisterous enthusiasm.

The muted reaction has my thoughts stumbling over one another.

"I—" I stare down at the delicate, pale hands, so different from my normal pebbled flesh. "The world likes me like this."

You'll like me like this, I can't help adding silently.

"But this is hurting you. You're in pain." Mahon's massive palm cradles my wrist, where the skin around the paper has darkened in anger at the offending object.

"Not bad."

The witch compared the initial discomfort to a sunburn. Having never had a sunburn before, I had to take her word for it, but now, I wonder why humans don't constantly coat their entire bodies in SPF 150.

"She said the pain would get worse after an hour." Skin bubbling. Acid in my veins. All that fun stuff.

"Please, Satine. I don't understand." A growl rumbles from his chest. "Do you need to go somewhere in town? Interact with humans?"

"No," I admit. "Not today."

"Then, why? Why do this?"

Mahon's eyes haven't left my wrist, all his focus on that tiny patch of discomfort. He's not admiring my smooth skin or my soft curves. He's not commenting on my silky, long burgundy hair. He hasn't gazed into my eyes with their green irises and normal pupils.

All he cares about is the pain.

My pain.

And that itself is a balm.

"Do you care?"

Mahon dips his head to blow on my wrist, as if he could soothe the flushed skin like one would cool off a too-hot slice of pizza.

"Care about what?" He mutters the words in a distracted manner. "Can we put ice on this?"

"Do you care what I look like?" I ask, ignoring his second question.

That finally has him glancing up to meet my searching stare. "I only care that I get to see you."

My insides, the most human part of me, fracture and reform at his simple statement.

Over the years, I've found small ways to love myself on my own. But I've never admitted how fragile those discoveries were. That I fear the rest of the world could pulverize my hard-won self-assurance.

And here is this man. And he is everything good I never let myself hope existed in the world.

"I shouldn't have put the patch on," I say. "I have them for emergencies. If someone I don't know comes to my house or if I need to go somewhere that humans will see me." Shoring up my courage, I stand taller. "I thought you might like to see me like this."

Mahon's brows dip low. "But I can't see you. All I see is the witch's glamour."

His grip might appear to be about my wrist, but I'm certain the shifter has found a way to plunge past my rib cage and cradle my heart.

"You're right. I want to take it off."

"Do you need help?" There's a trembling in his big hand, as if he's holding himself back from tearing the magic off himself.

"No. But there are some more side effects when I remove it. We should go inside." Stepping away from his comforting presence, I push the front door open and try not to think too much about what's coming next. "There's food in my fridge and cabinets. Help yourself. I'm going to need fifteen, maybe twenty, minutes."

"What are the rest of the side effects?"

Of course the pushy bear would ask that, following me toward the bathroom rather than staying in the kitchen, like I directed.

"Some indigestion. Nothing to worry about."

"You're a bad liar," he announces. "Now, I'm more worried. Unless you tell me you're gonna shit your drawers, I'm not leaving you alone when you take that thing off."

Whirling fast, I slap his chest. "I'm not going to shit my pants!"

By all the gods, this man knows how to ruin a romantic gesture.

I shake out my hand, the delicate human skin covering my bones smarting after the impact.

Mahon grins down at me, even as worry continues to cloud his eyes. "Noted. I won't dive for the wet wipes. But I won't abandon my Satine. Not when you're hurting. Not ever."

My heart throbs hard, and I long to not be distracted by the growing burn of my wrist. Having reached the bathroom, I lean back against the sink and meet his understanding stare.

"Fine. But I warned you."

Bracing myself for the effects, I tear the spell from my skin. With a snap in the air, like a thunderclap, my true form reclaims me. For one breath, I feel right again, every part of me as it should be.

Then, I dive for the toilet and puke my guts up.

Mahon's chest is comfier than any pillow I've ever owned. My torso is propped over his as he lies, sprawled on his back across the cushioned platform I use in place of a couch. If I need to, I can fold my wings in tight enough to use seating with a back, but I'd rather give all my limbs room to stretch.

"More popcorn?" the bear asks.

In response, I open my mouth, which has him chuckling. The vibrations press directly against my scales, and I love the sensation. Sometimes, I forget how good it is to simply touch another living being.

Mahon reaches into the massive bowl at his side and hand-feeds me a few butter-covered kernels. Normally, I'd handle the job myself, but my fingers are busy on my gaming controller.

After I puked for almost ten minutes straight, my stomach finally stopped heaving, and I collapsed in a quivering mess on the bathroom floor. Instead of retreating with a grossed-out expression, Mahon wiped my face clean with a washcloth, and then he picked me up and carried me to my living room, where he sat down and cradled me against his chest until the after-shocks of the spell eased.

"What would make you feel better?" he asked.

"Ginger ale and video games," I mumbled back.

His deep chuckle also helped my recovery.

An hour later, here we are, acting like a couple in my home, and I feel better than I did before I adhered that patch to my scales. Even though I'm the only one playing the game, the bear shifter doesn't seem interested in switching up the activity. His eyes stay locked on the screen, watching as I direct a CGI cat to explore a postapocalyptic city. He occasionally asks questions about the game while feeding me popcorn and holding the straw in my ginger ale up to my lips.

This is a certain kind of heaven.

"Have you ever gone to an all-mythics gathering in town? Like when the MacNamaras hold an only-in-the-know party at their house? Not using the human-looking spell, I mean."

Since this question veers off from the video game, I press pause and meet his gaze. "No, I haven't." Not even with the patch.

"Do you just not wanna? Or is there something else?" There's no judgment in the dip of his ginger brows. Just curiosity.

Levi has brought up this topic before too, trying to get me out of my house. As if I don't want that myself. But having only mythics in the room doesn't solve all my problems.

Still, I don't get the urge to snap a response at Mahon like I have with Levi.

"When I was younger, my mother took me to a few mythics-only playdates. She wanted me to be able to interact with other kids my age."

His kind face twists in a grimace. "Did those cubs bully you?"

Letting my chin rest on his belly, I shrug. "Not exactly. They just acted like kids. I was a strange-looking thing to them, so they poked me. Laughed. Ran away. It wasn't fun, but that's not what stuck with me." When I have to force out the last few words, I realize I'm clenching my jaw. Taking a moment to relax, I keep going. "It was the parents. They were the ones who looked at me like I was scum. Like I was a toxic waste that could pollute the air and water around me. And"—I choke, clearing the angry blockage from my throat—"they insulted my mama. She was the sweetest woman. A gorgeous undine. Every move she made could have been a dance. And they said she was dirty. Told her giving birth to me was a mistake. Who says that to a person?" I'm not actually asking, just accusing the universe for putting that hatred near my family.

A soothing caress smooths over my skull, and I realize Mahon is petting along the scales that cover my head. Comforting me with his stroking.

"I'm so sorry, my Satine. So sorry." His beard quivers in a rare frown. "Give me their names, and I will steal their tires."

The absurd threat entices a giggle from my lips, and I bury my face in the warm cotton of his shirt, breathing in the grassy scent of him.

"Where are your parents?" The question is all hesitation, as if he already knows the answer will be sad.

"Mama died the year after I graduated college. Car crash when she was driving to Atlanta for a shopping trip. She loved nice shoes." I wiggle my clawed toes. We'd have endless playful bickering about my insistence on only ever going barefoot or wearing slippers. "Dad ... he was always a keep-to-himself kind of guy. Mom would get him to open up. When he lost her ..." Even the memory of the vacant stare has me shuddering. "He couldn't come back from it. One day, he decided to go beast. Live as a dragon." Once a dragon shifts into their other form, they must stay that way for a few decades. "He's in the Antarctic colony. Last I saw him was seven years ago."

"You've been alone for a while." Mahon's heavy hand slides down to my neck, thick fingers pressing into the tense muscles.

"Yes." No use denying it.

I try, in small ways, to keep a connection to the world. Talking to people online. Inviting Levi over. Spying on the Folk Haven townsfolk when they aren't aware I'm around.

But still, every night, I remember that I'm on my own.

As Mahon continues to stroke me, every cell in my body relaxes until I'm on the edge of sleep. Which is why I'm not sure if I dream the words he speaks.

"You're not alone anymore."

8

THE SUN just starts to sink below the tree line as I lead Mahon down toward my dock. When I woke up from my nap, still sprawled over him, I worried I'd kept the man too long.

"I'm off work today. Keep me as long as you want," he assured me with a cheeky grin that had my nipples tightening under my Velcro sports bra.

At some point in the last few hours, maybe when he cared for me while I hugged the toilet or when he offered to commit a crime against the people who'd hurt my mama, I lost the hesitation about bringing him to my small inlet of Lake Galen. Now, I cannot wait to dip the shifter into my water.

My house sits at the northwest part of the lake, closer to the Appalachian Mountains, which means the shore is steep enough to require switchback stairs to descend to the waterline. Normally, I'd just glide down. But with my webbed fingers wrapped around Mahon's wrist, I keep my feet on the ground.

The rush and trickle of a waterfall greets us. The cascade is less of a massive curtain off a ledge and more a leapfrog down a series of large rocks. But I love living next to one of the tributaries to the lake. The falls ensure my inlet has freshwater year-round unless there's a drought.

"You have a paradise, right in your backyard." Mahon stares wide-eyed around my cove as we break through the last stand of trees.

I have to agree. The steep banks block most of the sun, even when the glowing mass sits high in the sky, but that only means this space is greener, lush from shade and water, the falls cooling the humid air until I shiver.

Of course, that might be anticipation.

"This is my favorite spot." I face the bear and reveal a vulnerable piece of my heart. "You're the only person I've brought here."

If I thought his eyes were wide before, they're planetary now.

"Levi?" he asks.

I shake my head. "He has his own lakefront property. And we rarely swim together." One more indication he wasn't the man for me. Because more than almost anything in the world, I love to swim.

"I am honored." He places a fist over his heart, as if pledging fealty to me. If only I could inspire that type of deep loyalty.

"Even more honored than when I humped you?" I tease, needing to lighten the weight of this moment.

Mahon beams, stepping in close to settle his grip on my hips. "Equally. And doubly if you honor me with a humping here."

My laughter bounces off the large stones that litter the bank, and I know for certain that inviting him into this space was the right choice. But I'm not done with the acts of vulnerability.

"Did you know that I have a second form?" As I ask, I slide away from his grip, stepping carefully to reach the short gangplank that stretches to my floating dock.

The wooden platform is small, only big enough for a couple of chairs or to lounge on. One of my fondest memories is swimming in this inlet as my parents shared an evening cocktail in their folding chairs. I'd bring them the smoothest rocks I could find and then set the stones back in the exact spots I'd found them, not wanting to steal anything from Lake Galen.

"A true second form or another spell?" The humor has left Mahon's voice, and I turn to find him watching me with concern.

"A true form," I assure him. "But I'm not going to show you until you get in the water."

The tense wrinkles ease from his forehead, replaced with crinkling crow's-feet as his beard curves with a smile. "I'll do anything you want, but fair warning: I didn't bring a swimsuit."

Pushing against the air with my wings, I descend on the dock before facing him again. "That didn't stop you last time."

A beautiful blush tints his cheeks, clashing with his beard in the best way. "You naughty woman! You've been looking for a way to strip me down since the dark moon, haven't you? Saw something you like?" He gives me his back, glancing over his shoulder. "Was my ass, right? You could bounce a quarter off the thing. At least, I think you can. I've never been able to get the angle right."

I press my knuckles against my lips but can't help the snorts that escape out the slits of my nose.

Mahon's hazel eyes twinkle with humor as he tugs off his shirt. My breath speeds as his hands drop to his waist, and a second later, I find out the bear goes commando.

Good to know.

Feeling playful myself, I stick my fingers in my mouth and let out a perfectly executed wolf whistle. Or bear whistle, in this case. And despite his bawdy humor, I swear the blush spreads to that coin-ricocheting butt of his.

Mahon gives a loud whoop as he cannonballs into the

water. The ground is so steep here that I have no concerns about him hitting the bottom. Just a few feet from shore, the depth drops to double digits. When his ginger head breaches the surface, Mahon executes a perfect mermaid hair flip, immediately ruined by his mouth.

"Damn The Cold One! How's it so chilly here? I've got an icicle where my dick used to be." Mahon treads water expertly as he complains.

"It's the waterfall. That's pure mountain water. And don't go around, insulting the gods, or else you will lose your parts. And I happen to want them to stay exactly where they are." As I scold the blasphemous bear, I settle myself on the edge of the dock, slipping my bare feet into the water, loving how clear everything is in my cove.

The shifter guffaws, and then proving he was just grumbling for grumble's sake, he paddles to the mouth of the falls, where the clean water spills through a V created by two boulders.

"There's fish here!"

His delight has me smiling, and I get the sense the more time I spend with Mahon, the more beauty I'll see in the world. The man seems to find joy whenever and wherever he can.

"Hey, curious bear, want to see something cool?"

Mahon faces me, having found a shallow enough part to stand. The water laps around his waist, but through the clear liquid, I catch a distorted glimpse of his cock. Suddenly, I want a much closer view.

"What's this cool thing you're bragging about?" he challenges with a smirk.

I respond by melting. My clothes fall to the surface of the dock as every part of my body transforms into H_2O. I flow into Lake Galen, immediately one with all the water around me.

My other form.

This version of me is exactly right, according to the lore of mythics. In this watery body, I am like every other undine. It's as if I had two slots and three options, and the universe decided to carefully place undine into one and forcefully shove dragon and human into the other.

Both feel right to me. It's the rest of the world that cannot handle one.

Sinking into the gentle current, I flow through the inlet, reintroducing myself to every rock and root and stretch of clay. This lake bottom is home. I've traversed almost all of Lake Galen this way, but no part inspires such loyalty as this cove.

"Satine?"

Even deep under the surface, I hear his voice. With a shift, I flow to the space in front of Mahon, and I pull on my power to rise from the surface, presenting a watery form to reassure him.

"Gods, you freaked me out there. My fault." He offers a rueful grin. "Forgot you're part undine." He steps forward and tries to wrap his thick arms around my waist. But the muscular limbs pass straight through. Mahon frowns, brows dipping low.

"Pouty bear," I tease. "Let me make you feel better."

"Wha—"

Before he can finish asking, I sink back into the lake. I might not be able to create a fully solid figure from water, but that doesn't mean I can't exert pressure.

Mahon's bare legs stand firm, like thick tree trunks plunging into the water. And there's his branch, bobbing in the gentle current. Almost as if he were waving to me.

Can't let that greeting go unacknowledged.

Leisurely, I weave my body through and around his legs. Then, giving in to desire, I form my mouth and ease my liquid lips down his length until he juts straight and proud.

"Holy gods. I-is that you, Satine?"

With a flick of my form, I gently splash his chest, all the while continuing to taste him.

"It is. It is you." His hands dive through the water, seeking some solid part of me to hold on to as I pleasure him. But there's nothing, and he growls out curses, digging his fingers into his hair instead.

I suck and lave him, coaxing warmer water from a sunnier section of the lake to wrap around him. With teasing currents, I press against his testicles, watching the balls bob and loving the needy grunts I earn in response.

Then, acting on a particularly naughty urge, I direct a strong stream straight at his anus. The bear roars, cum spurting from the tip of his cock. I ease back, and with a flick of power, I send the milky liquid out into the lake.

"Satine," Mahon pants. "Come back to me. Please. I need to hold you."

Again, his longing for my form, the one even my parents agreed needed to be hidden from the world, fills me with joy.

Mahon wants me.

I allow my corporeal form to manifest, rising from the water with droplets flowing off my scaled skin. Before I can speak, Mahon has his arms about my waist, nose buried in my neck, as if he can breathe me in.

"I felt you here, but I couldn't scent you," he groans the words, as if the loss pained him.

"What do I smell like?" Carefully, I comb my claws through his hair, enjoying the soft tease of the strands against my webbing.

"Mmm." Mahon presses a series of kisses up my neck. "Warm rocks."

"What?" I bark, not sure if I should laugh or be offended.

The shifter has his cock pinned between us, and with subtle rocks of his hips, he presses his length against my belly.

Is he getting hard again? Already?

"You know when you find a big rock that's been baking in the sun all day? You just want to lie on it and soak in that warmth, and the scent in the air is hot stone?" Mahon meets my eyes now, his almost glazed over as he keeps up his subtle thrusting. "That's what you smell like."

He claims my thin lips in an eager kiss.

I'm so drugged by his lustful response; I barely notice him dragging me through the water, toward the dock. Somehow, the bear kisses me and swims at the same time. It's only when he breaks away from my mouth and lifts me to sit on the old wood that I realize we've relocated.

"Wha—"

This time, I'm the one cut off by erotic attention. Mahon presses my knees open, putting my vulva on display. That part of me is similar to human females from what I've seen in porn and pictures online. Everything, except—

"Blue." The shifter beams up at me. "My favorite color."

Then, he dives in and consumes me as if I were his favorite food. And just as he described during our naughty picnic, Mahon laps at me until my wings flap and I shout his name.

Letting all of Lake Galen know he's my bear.

9

BEFORE LEAVING MY HOUSE, I memorize the directions to the address Mahon gave me. Electronic navigation around Lake Galen is always spotty, leading people to the wrong place or shorting out completely. From what I've heard, the disruption occurs naturally rather than because of some witch's spell.

The suspension in my SUV keeps the ride on back roads smooth, and as the sky slides to the darker side of twilight, I flip on my headlights. That's the only illumination coming from my car, as I've made sure to dim my dashboard display until the information is barely legible. All to keep the interior of my car as dark as possible. But even if the world was noontime bright, no one would be able to see through my windows, all of which have been tinted far darker than the legal limit.

Not that I'll get pulled over for breaking the rule. The whole of Folk Haven's small police department has my license number on file and knows not to stop me for the violation. One of many reasons I'm glad Levi is on The Council. Within a month of his election, my friend implemented measures to help me and other mythics without human forms to move more easily around town.

Of course, the cops can still pull me over for speeding. But if they do, I won't have to use one of my emergency human-illusion patches because all officers have been briefed on my appearance. Still, I keep two in my glove box, just in case.

When the sign for my turnoff appears, I ease on the accelerator, immediately missing the rush of the high velocity. Despite the discomfort of cramming my wings behind me in this bucket seat, I consider driving more often in the future, just for the joy of rushing down empty back roads, surrounded by dense greenery that threatens to overtake all the land lost to civilization.

The last stretch of the drive has me on a dirt lane, but the way is almost as smooth as pavement. When I round a bend, I find a traditionally styled farmhouse with white siding and blue shutters. To the right of the house sits a large barn, and that's where I spy movement. Pulling up next to a familiar truck, I try to figure out what I'm seeing.

Are they hanging a sheet on the side of that barn?

The approach of a large form distracts me. The figure is shadowy in the dusk, but I know that body just from the outline.

Mahon.

He steps into my headlight beams, and I catch my breath at the sight of him. Tonight, he's dressed himself up in a pair of dark pants, a crisp white button-up, and a set of suspenders that stretch over his broad chest. The change in his normal casual appearance eases my nerves about my own outfit choice. I smooth a hand over the silky skirt of my black dress. The material falls far above my knees and plunges in the back, leaving plenty of room for my wings.

Then, there are the boots. This morning, I crawled into the attic and pulled out all the boxes labeled *Momma's Shoes*. When she passed, I knew I should donate them, but I couldn't find the will to let go of her little treasures. Tonight, I'm glad I held on to them.

Collecting the gift bag from the passenger seat, I turn off the headlights and climb from the car, taking a moment to straighten my clothes. Then, I hear a wheeze and glance up to find Mahon staring at me, his mouth as wide as his eyes.

I guess the thigh-high heels are doing their job.

Thanks, Momma.

"Since you gave me zero direction, I hope this outfit works," I tease as I approach the stunned man.

In answer, Mahon stumbles forward and hooks me around the waist, fusing our mouths together. His heavy hands explore the many exposed parts of my body until my scales tingle with needy pleasure. When his thumb brushes under the short hem of my skirt, I wonder if he'll skip all the preamble and just fuck me on the hood of my car. The shifter wouldn't hear any complaints from me.

Instead, Mahon rears his head back with a gasp. "Gods, you are fucking perfect. I'm jealous of your dress. The thing looks better on you than I ever could, but damn, I want to be on you all the time. And your shoes. I never want you to take them off. But also, I need to peel them off slowly. Kiss all your scales as I go."

My nipples harden, pointing through the thin fabric, and he groans when he notices. But before the bear can get any more dirty talk out, I shove my gift bag in his face.

"Happy birthday!" My words come out breathy.

Mahon loosens his hold, putting enough space between us to hold the gift in front of his chest. "You didn't have to get me anything. Anything other than a night with my face between your thighs, of course."

When I let out a scandalized gasp, the bear chuckles. Despite protesting the need, he digs past the tissue paper, and I suddenly find myself self-conscious. In a short amount of time,

I've let down most of my walls for this mythic, but we still know so little about each other. I wasn't sure what kind of gift he'd like, so I had to guess.

"It's not much. Since I only had a few days. I can get you something better with more time."

He pauses in his digging to swoop forward, stealing a quick kiss. "I love it."

"You don't know what it is."

His broad shoulders shrug under the dress shirt. "It's a gift from my Satine. So, I love it."

When he pulls the first item out, I'm busy, rubbing my chest, just over my heart because the organ is about to bust out of my rib cage and tuck itself in his pocket.

"Honey?" He holds up the mason jar, a delighted curl to his lips.

"Well, you're a bear." *Good job. Way to sound super caring and smooth.*

Mahon's expression freezes, and his nostrils flare. I brace myself to discover I've made a misstep. That gifting honey to a bear shifter is offensive in some way.

With jerky movements, Mahon unscrews the lid and practically shoves his nose in the golden goo, sucking in a deep breath.

"Is something wrong?" I hold out my hands, ready to take the gift back and hide it in the SUV in shame.

"Is this honey from Violetta's hives?" He names the witch who is also Levi's mother.

"Yes. Can you tell that just by scent? Is her honey okay?"

"Is it okay?" The question gasps out of his throat. "H-how did you get this? She *never* shares."

Really?

"She gives me a jar sometimes. Violetta and my mama were friends." Two women with monsters for children. "She looks out for me."

Mahon moves in close again and plies me with a series of rapid-fire kisses that have me giggling by the time he backs off. "This is the most delicious honey I've ever had in my life. And I've only had it once because I took some from a hive when I was a teenager. When Violetta found out, she cursed me to lose my coat for an entire *month*. I was a butt-ass naked bear! Then, she hired a protection witch to set a spell around her bees. I never got another taste. Until now."

And with that, he scoops up my hand and dips one of my fingers in the nectar, and then he sucks my digits into his mouth, tonguing the sugary coating off so thoroughly that I'm worried I might orgasm just from the hot slide of his licking.

As I try to recover, Mahon screws the lid on and reaches back into the bag. Realizing the other small gift can't compare to the honey, I move to tug it away.

"Don't worry about the other thing. It's a joke."

He grins, hand already coming up with the bundle of blue material. "I love jokes."

"You don't have to wear it," I persist.

Mahon lets the fabric unroll, and I watch his eyes track over the letters I ironed onto the material. Suddenly, he's setting aside the honey, as if forgetting the golden treasure he just proclaimed it to be. The shifter shrugs off his suspenders, unbuttons his dress shirt so fast that I'm worried he'll pop off a few buttons, and then tosses the top aside, replacing it with the simple T-shirt, displaying the two words on the front—*Satine's Bear.*

"I want six more," he declares, voice serious. "One for each day of the week."

"You're ridiculous." And I can't help pressing myself into him and kissing the hell out of my bear.

A throat clearing breaks up our make-out session. I'm glad I can't blush when I realize Calder and a stranger hover just a few feet away. Then, it registers—a person I don't know can see me in all my wide-winged, blue-scaled glory. My body stiffens, and I'm about to launch into the sky to escape when Mahon wraps a staying arm around my waist and grins at the pair.

"Delta! Calder! Check out my badass shirt." The bear points to my craft project like I gave him a designer suit.

Calder reads the words and then turns to his partner. "I want one."

The dark-haired woman rolls her eyes, even as she smiles. Delta steps forward, extending a hand in a kinder greeting than I expect from strangers.

"Nice to meet you. You'll have to tell me where you got that."

"I made it. But I can show you how," I offer as I carefully shake her delicate hand.

Everything about her appears human, and I wonder if she is or if this face hides another form. Despite my lack of time among Folk Haven's population, I do know it's rude to interrogate a mythic about what they are, and I don't want to alienate Mahon's friends.

But maybe Delta, who hasn't even tilted a brow at my appearance, would be willing to get to know me well enough that I could ask if those are acrylics or claws on her pale hands.

"We'll leave you two to it." Calder steps forward to give Mahon an affectionate slap on the shoulder. "Happy birthday."

As his friends climb into the truck, Mahon uses his arm around my waist to guide me toward the barn.

"This is your day, but I feel like I'm the one getting the surprise." My eyes take in the suspended sheet and what appears to be a giant pile of pillows.

"You can surprise me next year," Mahon offers, as if us being together a year from now is a guarantee.

My heart thunders with happiness that his mind has reached the same conclusion that I want. That we aren't a quick fling. That this is more.

"But since it's my birthday, we're watching my favorite monster movie."

The bear directs me to sit on the cushions as he fiddles with a projector. When the sheet lights up like a movie screen, I can't stifle a delighted squeak at the title.

Hellboy.

"I like this one," Mahon explains as he reclines on the pillows next to me and encourages me to sprawl on his chest, "because the monsters save the world."

Which is the exact reason I love this movie too.

Could I also have fallen in love with this sexy, silly, sentimental bear?

Did I ever have a chance?

As the film plays, we cuddle and share snacks and drinks pulled from a cooler. Strategically placed citronella torches keep most of the bugs away, not that they'd bother me with my impenetrable scales, but I'm glad for the protection of my shifter's vulnerable skin.

When the credits roll, I wonder if we could start from the beginning. Just keep playing the movie all night and never leave this perfect moment. But I'm guessing the owner of this property will eventually want us to stop squatting.

"Is this Delta's land?" My claws idly trace over the proclamation on the shirt I gifted him. I assume it's hers because we're not in water mythic territory, which is where Calder would own a home.

Mahon's stomach bounces with a chuckle. "Nah. This is all mine. Twenty acres."

That has me sitting up, meeting his hazel eyes in the dim glow of the half moon. "This is your house? And you're working as a delivery guy? Is your mortgage super expensive or something?"

Mahon slowly shakes his head, his focus on my mouth, as if he's more interested in kissing than conversation, but I keep a staying hand on his chest, wanting to know everything about him.

"My parents owned this place. Used to be a horse ranch. They missed the cold, so they moved up to Canada a few years back and left this all to me outright when I said I didn't want to go." His warm palm covers the back of my hands, thumb idly tracing the design of my scales. "I do odd jobs because I'm not sure what work I want."

"Why'd you stay?"

Don't ask that! I silently shout at myself, not wanting to give him any reason to leave.

The curve of his lips threatens to distract me. "Folk Haven felt like home. Like there was something important here for me. Or someone."

Could he mean what I think he does? I find I'm too much of a coward to ask outright.

"Have you come up with any ideas? Deciding what you want to do?"

Now, the curl of his mouth is pure naughtiness. "I have in fact. Got a good idea that just popped into my head right now. And I think I need some help with it."

The shifter leaps to his feet and pulls me up with him. Next I know, the bear tugs us toward the shadowy forest.

10

Mahon halts in a random spot. Not even a clearing really, though the moon's light does pierce through the treetops. He drops his hold, fingers going to the suspenders, which he drags off his shoulders as his hungry gaze meets mine.

"Since it's still my birthday, I'm asking for one more gift from you."

"What's that?" I try to keep my voice teasing, even as he pulls off the T-shirt I gave him, revealing his broad chest, covered in ginger curls.

Mahon carefully folds the material, as if the gift is precious to him, and hangs the fabric over a low tree branch. Then, his fingers find his fly.

"I'd like you to ride me on the forest floor. I want to feel the earth beneath me. Feel your body on top of me, driving me into the ground." With a shove, the shifter's pants fall to his ankles, revealing an already-hard cock, pointing straight at me. As if every part of him is drawn to me.

The scales on my upper thighs slide slickly against each other, damp from my core at his fantasy. With eager fingers, I unzip my boots and place them to the side, and then I shrug off the straps of my dress and let the silk pool at my feet. The outfit was sexy, but I want to be as bare as Mahon is.

When he drapes his pants over the same branch, the shifter dips fingers into a pocket and pulls out a whole sleeve of condoms, holding up the foils with a cheeky grin. "Guess I was optimistic."

A smirk tugs at my mouth in response, and I hold up my hands, claws glinting in the moonlight. "You'll have to handle those. Don't want any accidental breakage."

His chuckle is deep and erotic, dragging over my body the way I want his hands to.

Mahon tears open a package, rolls the latex down his deliciously impressive length, and then sinks to the ground. The birthday boy reclines back and palms his sack as he rakes his stare over my naked body.

"I'm ready for you to ravish me."

"Oh, are you?" I taunt, launching into the air, letting my wings hold me just above the aroused shifter. "Maybe I'll just stay up here. Take in the view while I stroke myself." As my wings gently flap, I sneak two fingers down and spread my intimate lips, giving him an unobstructed view of what he wants.

"Satine!" he growls, the sound grumpy and needy and begging, which only makes me wetter. "Please. Gods, I want you more than anything. Just the sight of you has me hard as oak. And your scent drives my bear wild. I would tear down concrete walls just to be close to you." He reaches a hand toward me. "I don't want doors between us. I don't want space. I don't even want a breath of air. Please, come to me."

How can a monster say no to that?

Relaxing my wings, I descend, my thighs settling on either side of his torso. Mahon moans as my core presses against his lower belly.

"You're very good at begging." I attempt to keep my voice

conversational as I gently scratch my claws against the skin under his fiery beard.

Mahon's hips jerk up at the contact. The demanding movement elicits a responding clench of my inner muscles, and I find I can't tantalize him anymore. Not when I want him as much as he wants me. Maybe more.

Lifting my hips, I stare into his lust-hazed gaze. "Hold yourself straight for me."

The shifter lets out a strangled noise in the back of his throat as I find his cock with my core and press down slow, taking him inch by inch, fully appreciating how many of those inches there are. When I'm settled, his balls cradled against the cleft of my ass, everything in the world is perfection. And yet I suspect this will only get better.

I draw Mahon's warm, rough palms to my breasts, wanting the heat of him to drag against my sensitive nipples. He cups and strokes. Pinches the peaks and licks his lips as his eyes track the action. When I begin to move, the rise and fall are slow. Still, his legs twitch and then thrash, as if I'm torturing him with pleasure.

The same brain-melting ecstasy that threatens me at the stretch of him inside my body.

My knees dig into the dead leaves and dirt beside his hips. My wings unfurl to their full expanse, pulling the muscles of my shoulders in a glorious stretch. Moonlight filters through the membrane, casting a sapphire glow onto Mahon's pale skin.

This experience seems to have broken his ability to weave his deliciously crude sex talk.

Which means I'll have to take over.

I lean forward, shifting where his cock caresses in the best way. My palms hit his shoulders with a smack, and then I'm digging my claws in just to the point before they might pierce skin. Capturing his attention with my cloudy stare, I make sure Mahon is paying attention.

"You're my bear." I slam down hard, driving him into the ground like he wanted.

Mahon moans, low and lovely, so I repeat the motion. This earns me an animalistic grunt. More follow as I fuck him hard.

Then, I tear my heart open for him.

"I'm your monster."

Mahon's expression slackens in surprise, morphing quickly into ecstasy as I don't let up with my thrusts. And something must have revitalized his vocal cords because the shifter's groans bring dirty, seductive words with them.

"You're my gorgeous, incomparable monster," he rasps. "The most amazing being I've ever known. You are everything that is beautiful in this world. I always want you. Cannot stop thinking about you. Not that I've tried. Gods, I need you, Satine. Be mine." He pants as his thighs give a telling clench beneath me. A thick finger leaves off teasing my nipple and descends to my clit, stroking in steady, unrelenting circles. "Be my monster." Mahon heaves his hips off the ground, driving into me, even as I sink as deep as I can onto him. "Be my mate."

I don't know if the skill of his touch or the emotion in his words claims my orgasm. All I'm aware of is my muscles tightening and releasing in tandem, drawing me to a height of pleasure that should only be available to the divine.

From the roar Mahon releases, I expect he's going through something similar.

After a time, I can finally focus my thoughts enough to realize I'm draped across my bear's chest, listening to the easing pound of his heart.

"Be my mate."

At first, I think I'm remembering the statement, but then I realize Mahon repeated himself. Hope and fear battle in my heart.

Pressing myself upright, I meet Mahon's searching gaze.

"How can you already know you want to mate me? We've only known each other for a few weeks."

His hands cup my shoulders and then stroke down my scaled arms to my elbows before repeating the motion, as if to soothe a skittish creature. Which is maybe necessary.

"I fell in love with you when I saw Frankenstein's monster getting his rocks off in your front yard."

I push myself higher, looming over him. But I don't separate myself enough for his soft cock to slide out of me. Not yet. "You hadn't even met me at that point."

"You can learn a lot about a person from their art. Like how they're odd." He chuckles at my frown. "And how they're clever. And creative. And funny. And have a wonderfully dirty mind." Mahon reaches up, placing his finger on the barely existent ridge between my nose slits, and traces a track up and over my scaled skull. Mapping the profile of my face. "How could I not fall in love with you?"

While I struggle to accept his claims, Mahon sits up abruptly, keeping me pressed to his torso by bending his knees. His massive hands cradle my face, thumbs brushing over sharp cheekbones.

"I know I'm a lot of talk and fur and not much else. But I promise you, Satine, I will work hard to become the best shifter I can be. Someone you'll be proud to call your bear. Officially. One day."

The desperation in his normally easy, kind eyes erases all my own doubts, and I become the unyielding, unquestioning force in our pair.

Careful of my claws, I stroke my fingers through his sweat-dampened ginger strands, shivering in delight at the silky touch against my webbing.

"Silly bear," I murmur. "Didn't you read the shirt? You're already mine. And I want all of Folk Haven to know it."

11

MAHON

A Week Later

I JOG—OKAY, I sprint—down the public dock when my inner animal senses Satine. Without her hot, steamy rock scent in the air, I know to search the water instead of the sky for signs of her. My knees hit the damp wood with a thud, and I scan the calm surface for any sign of my lady.

"How'd it go?" the most beautiful voice I've ever heard whispers just as Satine's familiar face forms in the waters of Lake Galen.

Even the impression of her smooth head and adorable not-really-a-nose have me wanting to plunge my face below the waves to kiss her.

But she scolded me last time I did that because I accidentally breathed in water.

"Hello, my sexy little mate!" Even though I want to boom my greeting, I manage to keep my voice to a low grumble, aware that anyone could show up on this dock that serves as a popular space for launching fishing boats. Luckily, the water around us is empty for the moment. "How's your day going? Did you miss me?"

"Mahon!" Satine flicks water at me and then giggles when I bite at the droplets in the air. "Stop stalling. Tell me how the interview went."

I'm about to give her a silly response, but I stop myself. Satine loves my jokes, and I'd always rather be funny than serious. But this morning's meeting had me anxiously pacing when we were together last night, and I discovered another benefit to finding my perfect mate. She let me be the mess I felt like at the moment, comforting and encouraging me as I fretted. I'd never thought I'd need that kind of support, and now that I have it, I love her even more.

"Good. Really, really good. I mean, Owen and I are buddies, but this is his business, you know?"

Owen MacNamara, Calder's older brother, started a recycling company in Folk Haven. I always knew about Clean Haven, but it wasn't until I was in Satine's pristine inlet that I realized how important a clean lake was. Watching my mate become her liquid form before sinking into the water drove home that any pollution might harm her. I want to do my part to keep Lake Galen a safe place for her and every other mythic who finds refuge here.

"When I told him I was up for anything, he said he'd be happy to have me on the team. And that I can try a few different positions until we figure out where I fit."

"That's fantastic!" Satine sends up a few more flicks of water, like tiny wet fireworks. "I knew you'd be great."

If anyone's watching me, they probably see me grinning with a loving gaze at what they'd assume is an overactive fish.

"And what are you up to, oh monster of my wet dreams?"

Her laughter sounds like soft bubbles popping. "Wow.

Applying for a job really made you horny, huh?" She tosses a few more droplets my way. "Don't answer that. And I've just been drifting around. Listening to the town gossip."

I grin, thinking of how clever my mate is to learn about the townsfolk by spying in her undine form. She knows lots more about Folk Haven than people would expect of a recluse.

"I found Levi moping on a rock," she adds.

"Ah, lady troubles," I say with all the wisdom I can muster. But I'd take a hefty bet I'm right.

That monster pretends he only wants to fight with Moira MacNamara when, in reality, the guy wants to make sweet, sweaty love to that selkie.

Unfortunately, she hates his guts.

Poor guy.

"That was my thought too," my intelligent, perceptive mate agrees.

"I wish we could help out."

Levi is Satine's best friend. I want him to be as happy as we are.

Her watery mouth curves into a sneaky smirk. "Don't worry. I've got it covered."

That triumphant tone has me half-hard. Most things about my mate turn me on, but when she wins, all I can think is how I'd like to be her prize.

"I want to make your wings flap." Lust adds gravel to my words.

Another flick of water, this one chiding. "You have a shift at Coffee & Claws in twenty minutes."

"You should order a sandwich. So, I can come *deliver* for you."

Satine giggles, and then her face disappears. Sensing her lingering, I dip my hand into the water, as if checking the temperature.

At first, the caress is gentle, barely noticeable. Then, my

fingers experience a warm, firm suck along with the dragging pressure of a tongue.

"Naughty mate," I growl under my breath.

There is a gurgle of water that sounds like a laugh. Then, her presence fades from my awareness, and I know she's drifted into the mass of Lake Galen.

Leaving me fully hard.

Standing, I adjust myself and hope my dick calms down before I get to the café. I wish Satine could come to the coffee shop like everyone else. Then, I'd pull her into the storage closet and make her wings flap there.

She'd probably knock everything off the shelves. Heath would be pissed.

The thought has me grinning, but the spike of happy anticipation tumbles away when I acknowledge that she can't.

Yet.

I settle on the cushy seat of my scooter and clip the helmet strap under my chin, giving my skull some relief from the relentless summer sun. As I accelerate through town, wind in my beard, clear path of the future ahead of me, I command myself to hope. In the past few months, I've heard of more inter-mythic couples hooking up.

Can't believe the traditional mythics thought they could stick a whole bunch of us in one place and not expect some cross-species hanky-panky. Maybe the monster stigma is dying as a new, open-minded generation grows into adulthood. Maybe townsfolk will realize that monsters are an important part of the future.

Maybe these are wild hopes, born from my longing to see the woman I love happy.

But I know one fact for sure.

Things are changing in Folk Haven.

~

DEVOTED TO A DRAGON

All Lee longs for is to return home, find his mate, and not disrupt her life. He does *not* long for a front-row seat to her happily ever after with someone else.

Lee fell in love with Esme when they were both teenagers, but he was unceremoniously ripped from her life and dropped in the middle of an Antarctic dragon colony. Now, years later, he has found his way back to the small magical town of Folk Haven and the harpy he never stopped loving. But he's a different man than he used to be, inside and out. Will Esme recognize him? Will she still want him?

Or will his sudden reappearance ruin her life?

CONTENT WARNINGS

This story contains scenes with violence, emotional abuse, physical abuse, a near-death experience, and prejudice. This story contains scenes describing killing someone in self-defense and suicidal thoughts.

1

Fresh Feathers Dry Cleaners used to be owned by an old male griffin who enjoyed roaring at kids who skateboarded on the sidewalk outside his shop. Now, the store belongs to a beautiful harpy I've thought about every day since I left this town.

I'll be lucky if she remembers who I am.

"You sure you want to do this fake-name shit?" Xavier asks as he walks around the front of his truck to meet me on the curb.

The dragon has designated himself as my Folk Haven liaison. Up until this moment, I've been grateful. But I can't have him letting people know who I am. Not yet.

There's still a chance I'll leave.

"Not fake," I rasp. The damage to my vocal cords makes speaking difficult, but I don't much notice the pain anymore. At least I'm still alive. There were a lot of days I had to remind myself that was a good thing.

"Fine, *Lee*." Xavier puts more emphasis on the nickname than he needs to.

"You swore," I remind him, and the towering Black man grimaces.

171

"Yeah, fine. Just sayin'." He doesn't push again, letting the disapproval ease off his face, replaced by curiosity. "You ready for this?"

Glancing at the storefront's large glass window, I catch a hint of my reflection in the surface.

I don't recognize the ragged stranger staring back at me. Brown hair, roughly shorn at the shoulders; beard, grown scruffy enough to obscure the bottom half of my face; and thick glasses, distorting the top. My body is strong and lean from living too long on the edge of survival, fighting claw and fang to find my way back to Folk Haven—this small town in northern Georgia. I've traversed continents with nothing more than stolen clothes and a killer instinct.

All to get back to her.

"No." I smooth a hand down the flannel shirt Xavier gave me to replace the threadbare T-shirt I'd shown up in. The material is too hot for September in the South, but I'd asked for something with more coverage, and this is what he gave me. "Let's go," I mutter.

Coward that I am, I let him lead the way into the shop. A tinkling bell alerts anyone inside to a new arrival. The first thing I smell is cleaning supplies. Lots of cleaning supplies. Makes my nose itch until I'm forcefully holding back a sneeze. But after another breath, the industrial scents fade away.

All I smell is *her*.

Flowers, baked in the sun and caressed by a breeze. Gentle, comforting, and a memory I held on to as long as I could. It took years for the harsh bite of frost to obliterate the fragrance from my mind.

I breathe deeper, then choke on air when Xavier strolls farther into the shop, his large shoulders shifting enough to reveal *her*.

Esmerelda Sharpwing.

Esme.

"Hey, big man. What's up? You got your nice suit smelling like smoke again?" Esme stands behind a counter, barely glancing up from where she's bent over a notebook, pencil scratching away.

She's changed.

Of course she has. It's been a long time, and neither of us is a teenager anymore.

The girl I once knew is now a woman. She used to be soft with rounded cheeks, but years have honed the angles of her face, somehow crafting her into a more beautiful creature than the image of perfection I held in my mind. The same shade of dark blonde hair falls in curls over her naturally tan shoulders, but I spy a handful of white strands.

Bleached by the sun or age?

I couldn't have cared less if I'd returned to find her stooped and wrinkled with a head full of white. Only that her changed appearance would mean she had lived a lifetime without me.

They took half a life with her from me. If I think on it too long, rage will cloud my mind, and I won't be able to soak in this moment.

Every muscle in my body tenses, quivering, demanding I stride across the room and gather the harpy into my arms. To hold her close and breathe her in and promise never to let anyone or anything take me from her again.

But I wait. Esme hasn't glanced up again from her drawing. Hasn't reacted to my presence on an instinctual level, like I have with her. As much as I long to, there's no way we can simply start where we left off. Too much time has passed.

"I'm calling in my favor," Xavier announces.

That gets her attention. Esme straightens with a snap, her amber eyes wide and focused on the man.

"Of course. Anything. Tell me what you need," she says.

At that word—*anything*—my hackles rise. I don't like the idea of her leaving herself so open to someone else's whim.

Protect yourself, I want to warn her. *You are too precious for this world and the cruel beings living in it.*

But I keep quiet.

"Favor is for my friend actually." The big man turns and looks ready to drop his hand on my shoulder but thinks better of it. He tilts his chin my way. "A new dragon in town. He needs a place to stay. I figured he could crash in your upstairs apartment since those witches left."

Her eyes flick to me, running over my face and my body in a quick sweep.

There's no flash of recognition. No gasp or shout or angry glare.

Esme's expression only holds mild curiosity.

"Really?" The corner of her mouth ticks up. "I thought you were gonna ask for something hard." Esme sets down her pencil before strolling around the counter, coming closer.

A pulse of needy energy picks up in my body, the thrumming increasing as she approaches. Starved for any detail of her I can claim, my eyes eat up this mature version of the harpy.

The softness of her youth is also gone from her body, replaced by toned muscle. She looks strong. Like she could take down someone twice her size. Like she could wrestle me to the ground.

I would give anything for her to do exactly that.

"Hi." She smiles wide, staring up into my face, so open and sweet and welcoming and ...

Fuck. I want to *devour* her. And then I want to worship her.

"Hi," I mutter.

"Nice to meet you, newbie. I'm Esme." The woman I've loved since I was seventeen years old holds out her hand to shake.

Because I'm a stranger.

With both eagerness and reluctance, I slide my palm into

hers, noting the new calluses that rub against mine. When she curls her fingers around my hand, gripping tight, I bite down hard on the inside of my cheek to keep from blurting out the truth. To hold back the confession of who I am and what she is to me.

Because I couldn't stand it if the lack of recognition in her golden eyes remained. If, armed with my name, Esme still struggled to recall who I was.

Her hand releases mine, and I want to snarl at the loss. But she doesn't back away, continuing to gaze into my face.

When I realize she's waiting on a response, I force one out.

"Lee," I grunt.

Her grin, already enchanting enough to stop my heart, manages to stretch wider.

"Man of few words?"

My fingers twitch with the urge to rub the scar on my neck. Nasty thing, but my beard and buttoned-up shirt cover it.

I give her a silent nod.

"That's all right. I have plenty enough for the both of us." She whirls on Xavier. "This is *barely* a favor. I wanted a new renter anyway." Esme crosses her arms and contemplates the dragon, who leans against her counter, totally at ease in her space.

"He'll need some time to find work," Xavier explains. "Won't be able to cover rent to start off."

Shame coats my insides. There was a time in my life when money meant nothing to me because I had an abundance. Now, my pockets are empty, and I'm a burden.

Esme shrugs with a glance my way. "No problem. You pay when you can." She tilts her head, eyes to the ceiling, as if in thought.

"A quarter," her sweet voice declares. "This only covers a quarter of the favor. I still owe you three-fourths."

The dragon snorts, his mouth curling in amusement.

"You're shit at bargaining. But fine. If you want to still owe me, that's on you."

Curiosity twists in my gut. Why does Esme owe him anything? Did she get into trouble and need his help out of it?

Why wasn't I here to keep her safe?

That last question is pointless. I know why, and I couldn't have stopped it. But now, I'm back, and while I'm in Folk Haven, I will make sure nothing harms Esmerelda Sharpwing.

"Let's go check out your new digs." Esme slips behind the counter again, coming up with a set of keys. "Entrance is around the side."

She strolls to the front door, and I follow in her wake. When she reaches to flip a sign to *Closed*, Xavier stops her.

"You two go. I'll watch the shop. Let people know you're coming back soon."

Esme offers a grin over her shoulder that has my heart stuttering. "Thanks, bud."

We walk around the side of the brick building to find a set of exposed metal stairs. They're sturdy, barely making a sound when both of us climb them. As hard as I try to be a gentleman, my baser urges have me studying the way her round ass shifts under her tight black pants. Leggings, Xavier told me they're called. He's been giving me a crash course in the changes in the world since I've been gone. Just the advancements in phone technology are hard to grasp.

But this style choice? I can get on board.

"The lock sticks sometimes. You need to press down on the key as you turn it." Esme pushes the door inward and ushers me into an open space.

The room has furnishings—a table, an overstuffed couch—and through an open doorway, I spot a bare mattress on a bed frame.

"There're two bedrooms, one bathroom, a full kitchen, a view of Main Street ..." She strolls past the couch to tug open a set of curtains. "Pretty nice place, if I do say so myself. Feel free to make it yours. Just try not to damage anything." She tosses her honey curls over a shoulder as her eyes trace down my body again. "Are you in an *I've only got the clothes on my back to my name* kinda situation?"

I can't stifle a grimace. Even the clothes on my back aren't mine.

"Xavier"—his name is gravel in my throat, but so are most words—"gave me some ... things." Never thought I'd be so grateful for a toothbrush. The man offered plenty more, but *this* is all I really wanted. An introduction to the woman I used to know so well.

"Okey dokey. Well, I've got plenty of extra things too. When I get a Bed, Bath, and Bargains coupon, I *have* to use it. And they send me one, like, every week. It's a problem, but today, it's a solution!"

I think I remember what that store is, though I never used to have to buy those items for myself. My parents had staff for that.

"I'll drop off some bed linens and towels. I don't know if you use loofahs, but I've got at least six, so you're getting one. And I'll see what else I've got around my place."

"You don't—"

"Don't tell me I don't have to because I'm already doing it in my brain, which means the action is unstoppable." Esme reaches out and gives my chest a gentle pat.

Every part of me tenses, wanting to lean into the affectionate caress. Esme misinterprets my reaction, backing up a step and folding her hands behind her back.

"Sorry. I'm a touchy person. Half the time, I don't realize I'm doing it."

"You ... can touch me." *Please do. Run your fingers over my body, like you used to.*

"Noted." Esme's smile is softer this time as she gazes at me. "Any questions about the place?"

"Why don't"—I have to clear my throat to keep my voice working—"you live here?" This seems like the perfect spot for her. Above her business and near the heart of town.

Did she need more space because she doesn't live alone? Did Esme find a partner while I was gone?

I couldn't—wouldn't—blame her even if I have the overwhelming need to find the shadowy figure and tear their throat out with my claws.

"I used to, but people don't respect closing hours when you live above your business." She fiddles with her key chain as she talks. "There're only so many times a girl can get a knock on her door at eight p.m., asking about a clothes pickup, before she snaps and moves. So, I did. Got myself a little place on the other side of town."

"Just you?" Despite my sore throat, the question sneaks out without help.

The harpy smirks, so adorable with her playful expression that I almost kneel at her feet and beg her to let me be hers. "Wouldn't you like to know?"

Yes. I want to know everything I missed.

She hands me the key and leads me downstairs, telling me to stop by the shop if I have any questions or problems.

Though I'm terrified to leave her sight, sure she'll disappear when I turn away, I force myself to go with Xavier.

"Changed your mind yet?" he asks once we're in his truck, heading to his house to pick up the few belongings he gifted to me.

I shake my head as I watch the vibrant greenery speed by the window, still thrown off by so much color after years of white and gray.

Xavier grumbles low in the back of his throat, "Guess I

learned my lesson. Never make a blood oath without all the facts."

The dragon rubs a small mark on his wrist, a pale white scar from where a knife drew blood. I have a similar one on mine, but it's not as obvious among my many other healed wounds.

When Yuito helped me escape, he gave me the name of a dragon in Folk Haven—Xavier. But when I made it here and found the man, I refused to tell him who I was until he swore not to share the information with anyone without my permission. I made him swear not to interfere with my purpose in Folk Haven. Dragons talk to each other, and even with Yuito's good word, I wasn't sure of the stranger's loyalties. In turn, Xavier only agreed to enter the blood bargain if I swore I'd hurt no one in town unless first attacked. An easy enough agreement to make. I'm done fighting.

We cut our wrists and spoke our oaths as the blood mixed.

Then, I told him my name and reason for returning, and he growled a whole string of curses at me.

"Just ..." I watch him grind his teeth, no doubt struggling with words that come too close to interfering. "Thank you," I say, getting the sense this dragon *does* want to help me. But I cannot allow him my full trust. Not with the betrayals that lurk in my past.

He's done what I asked, and now, I can complete this task on my own.

Without disrupting Esme's life or causing her pain, I will discover if my mate remembers me.

2

———————

Eighteen Years Old

I CAN STILL TASTE Esme on my tongue as I hike through the dark woods back to my house. Still hear the way she squealed and laughed and moaned when I snuck my head between her legs and licked her delicious nectar. Just the memory has me half hard. How I can manage that after going through three condoms is a mystery for the gods.

When I catch the hint of lights between the branches, I pause.

They're awake. They're waiting for me.

Knowing that the magic of this night is about to be broken by my parents, I hesitate. Not because I'm scared to face them. But because I want to partition off the joy so their scolding can't taint the gift Esme gave me.

Her first, just as she was mine.

I tried to be gentle, but my eager harpy dug talons into my back and demanded I be rough. She is a force and a light and my everything.

You're young, they'll say.

This isn't love, they'll claim.

As if there's a specific timetable to follow before I'm capable of realizing that Esmerelda Sharpwing is a woman worth giving my heart to.

Pressing my shoulders into the rough bark of a tree, I close my eyes and remember. Play through the way her hands stroked and teased and drew phantom scales on my flesh while she called me her dragon. In my memory, I hear her gasp at my first clumsy attempt to sheathe myself in her tight, wet heat. Then her groans as I got better, found my rhythm, and stroked her clit.

With my eyes closed, I bring up the uncertainty, then determination in her eyes when I asked her to shift. To show me all of her. Esme's body stayed the same shape, but golden wings stretched from her back, and her flesh transformed. My fists clench on empty air as I recall the brush of feathers on skin as I spilled inside my beautiful harpy.

I won't let anyone ruin this night for me.

And so I imagine the night is over. That this is a new night, the next one, and all that happens now is separated by a buffer of hours from when I held Esme as she whispered and laughed and panted my name.

Soon, I won't have to make buffers. Soon, I'll leave and make a home for myself and for Esme when she's ready to join me.

I press off the tree and stalk toward the grand house my parents constructed on the shore of Lake Galen. Their palace in the small town of Folk Haven. The soundtrack of gentle waves slapping against the protective riprap on the shore accompanies me as I enter the back door into the kitchen.

If I thought the rear entrance would save me from discovery, I was wrong.

My parents wait by the large wooden island, where staff prepare our meals throughout the day before carrying them into the main dining area. My mother sits on a stool with her shoulders bowed inward as my father paces, halting with flared nostrils when I enter the room.

"What have you done?"

I flinch back at the menace in his voice. Since my last growth spurt, he no longer towers over me, but the older dragon exudes the power of decades as he stalks toward me.

"N-nothing." I hate the way I stammer. The way I feel the need to describe what just happened between Esme and me as nothing.

This night was everything. The start to my future with the woman I love.

In my soul, I know she is more than my first infatuation or even my first love, though she is certainly both those things.

Esme is my mate.

The reminder has me standing steady in the face of my father's rage.

"You were with that girl. The harpy." He sneers the name of her mythic designation as if she were beneath him. "I can smell her on you."

"I love her." Crossing my arms, I stare him down. "She is my mate."

My mother lets out a sound that mixes a gasp, screech, and sob, as if partnering myself with a smart, kind, beautiful woman were some horrendous crime.

"She is not," my father bellows in my face, the heat of his internal forge scalding footprints on the kitchen tiles. "You're a foolish child. Even a human would be better. You will not sully yourself with anything so crude. You will not blight the Blaythorn line with monsters."

Of course that's all he cares about. Our legacy. Not my happiness.

Mythics must only breed with their own kind or humans to maintain the purity of the gods' creations.

But how can that be what the gods want when I felt the approval of The Winged One when I held Esme in my arms tonight? When I slid inside her body, I felt phantom wings on my back, lifted with a wind of purpose.

She is joy and love and meaning.

Esme is my mate. And even if the gods did disapprove, it would not matter.

And neither do my parents' prejudices.

"If you can't accept us, then that's your problem. I'll leave." At eighteen, I'm an adult by human standards, and I can work and live on my own.

"No, dearest, please." My mother appears then, standing between my father and me, facing him, as if in my defense.

Hope takes flight in my chest. I am not alone.

"Please, do not leave. Sleep here tonight. Let us speak again in the morning. When tempers are not as hot."

As I mull over her words, my father's eyes drop to her face, and they share a silent communication. A skill I've begun to develop with Esme. Not true mind talk, like some of the strongest dragons can manage in their beast forms, but the simple ability to interpret the meaning of the minuscule muscle twitches on the face of the one you love.

Whatever my mother conveys calms him enough to step back, turn abruptly, and stalk out of the kitchen.

"Everything will be better in the morning." She pats my chest.

I trust her.

I shouldn't have.

3

Present Day

A JOB in construction fits my skill set perfectly after I spent the last two decades in a land of snow and ice, living as a mythical beast. Mainly, the foreman has me lifting heavy things.

Today, we're finishing up the kitchen in a lakefront house, and I maneuver through the front door, carrying a five-hundred-pound granite countertop. On my own.

"Look at you go! Fucking glad we added you to the team." Adrian, a white guy with shoulder-length red hair, damp with sweat, pats me on the back, and I manage not to flinch.

I'm still braced for an attack, expecting a heavy body of claws and scales to slam into me and try to wrestle power from my grasp. That was the way of the colony. The constant brutality was something most of the dragons living there respected and prided themselves on.

I just wanted to survive long enough to escape.

But it seems leaving the place didn't automatically free me from the violent lessons I'd learned while there. It's going to take time for me to reacclimatize to this mostly civilized world.

After working with me for two weeks, the crew is used to the fact that I don't talk much, so the redhead accepts my nod as I settle the load onto the lower cabinets. He strolls away, toward the foreman. Both are mermen. Most of this crew is merfolk.

When I asked Xavier about work in town, saying I'd take anything with a paycheck, he came up with a list. The top two were this construction team and a recycling company—one owned by a merman, the other by a selkie.

The same as when I grew up here, there are more Of the Fin—aka water—mythics than any other in town. But I couldn't care less if I worked with my kind, other mythics, or even humans, as long as it was a job. I figured with my supernatural strength, might as well try out a building team. Fortunately, Bardo, the owner of Lake Castles Construction, found space for me on his crew despite me being Of the Wing, like all dragons.

"Love when I finish a task right when it's time to clock out." Callisto, a mermaid and the plumber for this build, rolls out from under the sink and grins my way.

I give her the same silent nod I gave Adrian. She wipes her hands on a rag, then waves before strolling out the door. I fiddle with the counter for a minute, creating a buffer.

The first day here, I learned Callisto's sister is the police chief in town. Even though I haven't committed a bigger crime than snatching some clothes and food, I still have the urge to avoid the law. To stay away from anyone who might find my true identity interesting.

"Hey, you want a ride into town?" Adrian throws his thumb over his shoulder, and even though I enjoy walking in the lush Georgia forests, I nod.

Anything to get back faster. Hopefully in time to catch sight of Esme before she closes the shop for the day.

I have no plan. Not anymore. Nothing other than figuring out if Esme would be happier with or without me.

But I've spent all my time surviving among dragons in a colony in Antarctica and zero time learning how to discern the inner workings of a woman's mind.

For now, all I can do is observe. Count her smiles. Look for hints of discontent.

Find out if she sits by her window at night, staring up at the moon, praying to The Winged One that, one day, a dragon mate will come fulfill her life.

I roll my eyes at my own immature hopes.

Esme was never a pine-and-wait type of girl. Once, when she was sixteen and with me and our friends on a boat—my parents' new speedboat that I was using to show off—the engine crapped out on us, leaving our group stranded in the middle of Lake Galen. Back then, we didn't have convenient cell phones to call for help. Without a moment of hesitation, she dived into the water and swam to shore, calling out she'd get us a tow. An hour later, the fancy speedboat was hooked to an aging pontoon, and I was crushing hard on a girl who never needed to be saved.

"You're above Fresh Feathers, right?" Adrian asks as he turns his truck onto Main Street.

"Yeah," I grunt. "Thanks."

"No problem. Feel like you've halved the heavy lifting since you started. Figure I owe you." The guy flicks the rim of his baseball cap as he pulls up to the curb. "See you tomorrow. We're going to happy hour after work at Local Brew if you want to join."

"Maybe."

My twenty-first birthday came and went while I was in Antarctica. I've never had a sip of legal alcohol. Still wouldn't be able to if they carded me. Got no card to give. And under this shaggy beard, I don't look much older than when I left even if I feel ancient.

Adrian's truck spurts out a plume of black exhaust as he drives off, and I fixate on the sign on Fresh Feathers' front door.

Closed.

Disappointment bows my shoulders, but as I turn toward the steps leading to the apartment, the ringing of a bell stops me. Esme emerges from the shop, carrying a backpack, keys, and my bloody, aching heart.

She doesn't know about that last one though.

"Lee!" The harpy grins wide, gold eyes sparkling as if I'm some kind of beautiful view. Gods, this whole town must be in love with her by now if this is how she approaches strangers. "Done working for the day?"

"Yeah." I glance down and realize I have a light layer of sawdust coating my skin.

Not that I mind. Just a sign that I have a job, that I'm contributing to a community I *want* to be a part of. I don't have to deal with the shame of squatting in her apartment anymore. Since I don't have an identity as far as anyone is concerned, Bardo is paying me under the table, and I was able to start right away. He made it clear he's giving me the amount the other workers get after their taxes are subtracted, and the taxes he'd normally pay, he's donating to the town's Mythic Council.

Even if I don't trust him enough to tell him my real name, I've got to admit, he's a stand-up guy.

"How's the apartment working out? Hopefully better than crashing on Xavier's couch at least."

I nod. "He has pinball machines." Talking gets easier every day—especially around her—but I still keep my words as minimal as possible. "Loud ones."

"Oh goddess, I almost forgot." Esme chuckles, and I lean forward at the sound. "His hoard must be huge by now. Such an oddly specific thing for a dragon to grow attached to, but whatever works for the guy." The harpy tilts her head, the gesture quick and birdlike. "And are you creating a hoard of your own odd objects upstairs?"

I shake my head, wishing I could give a different answer. Name something that would make her smile, make her laugh, make her fall in love with the shell of a man I've become.

But nothing draws me, except for her. Not all dragons hoard, but a lot of our kind do. My father hoarded something more traditional—money.

Despite the comfortable life it gave me for my first eighteen years, I'm glad I don't have the same compulsion. Especially after the expectations he had for how I would pay him back for the support from his hoard.

"Sorry, that was probably a personal question. Ignore my nosiness." Esme hooks her thumbs in the straps of her backpack, looking more like a college student in that moment than a woman in her late thirties. "Any plans for the evening?"

Only if attempting to make edible food from a recipe in the *Cooking for Beginners* book I picked up off Never Judge a Cover's bargain shelf counts. The siren who owns the local bookshop has been helping me find how-to books for the skills I forgot or never had.

If only there was a *Wooing a Harpy for Beginners*.

I shrug. "Shower. Eat." *Think about you.*

No doubt that pity for the strange, boring dragon with no life prompts her next question.

"Do you want to come with me to my favorite place in the world?"

4

Eighteen Years Old

Cold.

It's the first sensation I register when I wake up. The chill makes no sense to my sleep-muddled mind and even less as hazy half dreams fade.

Did the AC go into hyperdrive? Early fall in Georgia still means heavy, humid air, which causes the sheets to cling to my skin, so I normally wake up with an urge to take a shower. This dry, frigid sensation isn't exactly uncomfortable. The mystical fire that always burns in my chest and hands keeps my body toasty, even in winter.

The discomfort comes from the strangeness.

Why am I cold when I should be hot?

When I force my heavy eyelids open, my surroundings answer none of my questions. This isn't my bedroom with its high ceilings, broad windows, and walls plastered with band posters. These walls are bare, metal, and close enough that I can reach out and touch one.

I sit up, immediately regretting the move when my brain rocks and tilts, as if I were drunk.

No, wait. I'm not the one rocking. The room is.

Just then, a door swings open, one with rounded corners and a circular window.

"Good. You're awake." My dad strolls in, taking up too much space. "We'll be docking in a half hour."

If anything, I'm more confused, both by his words and his outfit.

Maximus Blaythorn spends most of his days in a suit. Dressing down means slacks and a polo shirt. Even his pajamas have buttons. If he puts on a coat, best believe that tailored garment is a peacoat, made of the finest wool.

So, why is he wearing a bright orange puffy coat, unzipped to show a set of army-green overalls?

"Where are we?" I croak the words and realize I'm fucking thirsty.

"Antarctica." He glares down at me, his blue irises glowing the way all dragons' do when experiencing strong emotions.

"What?" The blaze of my own reflects off his pale face. "How? When?"

Damn The Winged One's tricks. When I fell asleep, I was in Georgia, exhausted from a night of loving Esme for the first time.

This is impossible.

"Your mother gave you a sleeping draft. We knew you would cause problems, and frankly, I have no patience for your disrespect. After that, it was simply a flight to Ushuaia in Argentina and a passage on the colony's transportation ship."

By flight, he means on his private plane, of course. I bet no commercial airline would be cool with him hauling my unconscious body into a first-class seat.

"Why?" But that's naive. I know why. I stepped out of line for love. "Why here?"

My parents discussed spending a stint in the dragons' Antarctic colony when they got older and I was out of the house. This was never supposed to be a family trip. There's no point to me being here when I have no intention of taking my dragon form.

"Because you obviously do not comprehend how much you lowered yourself. We never should have moved to that town. Anywhere else, the distinction would have been clear. We are Blaythorn dragons, distinguished, even among our kind. Our internal forges burn like no other. Here, you will see the respect we deserve. Here, you will understand how much more you can demand from the world." His expression is feverish by the end of his preaching of his self-aggrandizing worldview.

I've heard it all before.

"So, what? You want me to interact with colony dragons? They're all in beast form." And stuck that way for roughly forty years from the time they released their beast.

That's the difference between our kind and other shifters. We can't blink and go between forms.

When dragons transform, we must hold that shape for decades.

Hence the need for a colony far from prying human eyes. Seems like a failing rather than a bragging point to me.

"Plenty of our kind live near the colony in our two-legged form." His jaw tightens as he stares toward the door, as if he can already see our destination. "And there are other ways to communicate. In just the first day, you will see the difference. You will understand what my words haven't been able to teach you."

I hate this, but I'm trapped. My father holds the power now, having cut me off from the rest of the world. No money. No connections. No way to leave a fucking frozen wasteland, inhabited only by mythical beasts. The only way I can get back to Folk Haven, return to Esme, is if I play along. Ooh and aah over these great dragon traditions and impressive family lineages he always waxes on about.

And when he's convinced himself I'm properly brain-washed, he'll take us back to civilization. Maybe not directly to Folk Haven if he's written off the place, but somewhere that I can get away. Leave his house forever. After this, I'll never trust my parents again.

Get through this. Get back to her.

"Fine," I agree with resentment in my tone. Can't fully flip my switch and become the devoted model son or else he'll get suspicious. "I'll communicate with whatever dragons you want me to." I glance around the stark cabin. "Is there a phone on this boat I can use?"

What is Esme thinking? We sleep together, and I disappear the next day. She's the smartest woman I know, so she'll figure out this isn't just me blowing her off. But I can't imagine what I would do if the roles were reversed. If I didn't know where she'd gone.

I'd tear the town apart.

"So you can contact that harpy?" He shakes his head, disgust in his sneer. "You will forget her."

Never.

"Get dressed." He strolls toward the door. "We're leaving as soon as we dock."

When I'm bundled in the best quality winter gear money can buy, I meet my father on the deck of the vessel. Icy wind tries to cut at my face, but doesn't bother me much. The extra layers mean I don't have to call on too much of my internal fires to stay warm.

Still, I miss the balmy heat of Georgia.

Navigating through icebergs, we come upon a settlement that looks more like a space station. There's nothing meant to be aesthetically pleasing. These structures were built for survival.

I expect my father to lead me into one of the buildings, sit me down in a chair, and have some other pompous assholes lecture me on what a glorious thing it is to be a dragon with a well-known family name. Instead, with a firm hand on my shoulder, he directs me to a vehicle.

"Where's Mom?" I ask, looking around for her slender form.

"She'll be here in a few days."

Fuck. So, this isn't going to be just a day or two visit.

A man with a bushy beard and rosy cheeks gets behind the wheel, and my father sits in the passenger seat, leaving me on my own in the back. As the man drives us through the intimidating landscape, I silently wish Esme were here. Not only because I miss her and want to be wherever she is. But also because the curious harpy would find this place fascinating. She would make this trip fun rather than my personal hell.

After an hour of driving, a note of foreboding sounds in my head. "How much farther?"

"Ten minutes to the boundary," our driver responds.

The boundary of the town? At least, I hope there's something like a town, where our kind live in human form near the colony. But what structures or businesses could last in this harsh climate?

When the vehicle stops, I don't see anything but a long stretch of snow outside the window.

"On foot from here." The bearded man pushes open his door, and my father follows suit.

Could I steal this truck? Drive back and sail away?

But there's no road, and I doubt the boat captain would leave without my father. So, I climb out and trudge behind the two men. Not long until the bearded guy reaches up a hand in a clear signal to stop. Despite the below-freezing temperature, he removes a glove, does something with his hand, and presses his palm against what I thought was empty air.

A red light erupts from his hand, patterns spiraling out

until we stand in front of a glowing arch of light-infused symbols.

"Through. Now."

Too confused at the display to protest, I allow my dad to shove me forward, under the arch. The air is just as cold on the other side yet calmer.

And that's when I hear the roars.

"Welcome to the colony," the bearded man grunts, his expression stony.

The archway collapses behind us, and in that moment, I know I've made a mistake.

"Fuck!"

I try to charge back the way we came, but I crash into a force that flings me spinning backward through the air. I hit the ground hard, wheezing with the impact. Lying facedown in the snow, air knocked out of me, I can't fight when my father takes the opportunity to grasp my arms and twist them behind my back. Painfully cold metal surrounds my wrists.

"Wha—" I gasp, still choking on my breath.

"Magicked cuffs. You want out of them? Then shift. They can't contain a dragon." His harsh words make no sense.

Shift? Get stuck in a form I can't leave for forty years? No way in hell.

The true purpose of this pilgrimage slams into me harder than the magic of that barrier.

He means for me to live here. To give over to the dragon and separate myself from the human world for decades.

Fifty-eight. If I shift today, Esme will be fifty-eight next time I see her. A life lived without me.

My mate stolen from me by time.

"No!" I roar, fighting against the bonds. "You can't make me!"

"We'll see." He hauls me to my feet and drags me forward.

I don't know how long we walk for. Or how long he walks and I fight. But soon, great, scaly forms come into view, soaring overhead. Any other time, I might find the sight glorious. Now, all I care about is escape.

My father hasn't gotten weak with age, and he keeps hold of me until we reach the edge of a massive, icy pit. Dragons lounge around the exterior and on ledges that jut out from the steep sides. The bottom is relatively flat with only a few jagged rocks piercing the icy white surface.

The place looks like a stadium. An arena. Like something a gladiator would fight in. A red dragon the size of a fire truck waits in the pit, sharpening his claws on stone, the way a cat might on a scraping post.

"Transform now," my father growls. "Or face him on two legs."

"What?" I try to back away from the ledge, but he holds me in place. "You're trying to kill me?"

"You're a Blaythorn. He's a nobody. A human father. His inner forge is dimmer than the winter sun. In your beast form, he'll stand no match. Transform, begin your climb to dominance, and these years in the colony will be the best of your life. When it comes time to change back, you likely won't want to leave." My father's voice turns ragged with anticipation, as if he were sprinting while speaking.

"You're fucking crazy. I'm not fighting him or anyone!"

"Yes," he snarls, "you are."

Maximus Blaythorn shoves me over the edge, and I tumble down the steeply sloping side toward the middle of the pit. Ice shards nip at my skin, and every time I roll, it feels like the same stone bruises my ribs. I land in a groaning heap at the bottom of the incline, lying on my back as I try to orient myself. Silhouetted above me against the bright sky is my father. Dazed, I watch him strip, see his shoulders bow, track how a glowing red fire seems to grow hot and pulse under his skin. He spreads his arms wide and screeches at the sky as his skin splits open, and a massive sapphire creature of myth takes over his body.

He did it. He changed. There's no going back for him.

But I still have a chance.

Scrambling to my feet, I'm upright only for a moment before a sledgehammer hits my side. At least, that's what the dragon's swipe feels like. I fly through the air farther than the barrier flung me. Big Red slinks after me, letting out a huff that sounds like a laugh. He swats at me again, and I go tumbling.

No matter how much I roll and duck and dodge, he always gets me, sapping even my supernatural strength. With my hands cuffed behind my back, I'm hampered. He's too big. Too fast.

And after the fifth strike, it's clear he's just playing with me.

Because on the sixth, he lets out his claws.

The diamond-hard, razor-sharp tips rake down the front of my body, shredding my winter gear, leaving me exposed but unharmed, other than the shallow cuts on my chest. If he'd wanted to sever my head from my neck, he could have.

But it's still a game. I'm a mouse under a lion's paw.

I could be a lion too.

The mouse must be boring him because the next swipe is not so gentle.

He tears open my throat.

At first, I don't feel a thing, as the cut was so quickly made. But then every nerve in my body screams in agony, and I'm sure that death must be pure fire. As my blood spills onto the snow, crimson on ivory, too much for any mortal to survive, I make a choice.

Survive. You'll never see her again if you die.

With a roar of rage and despair, I do the one thing I've been warned never to do.

I release the dragon.

Esme. Her face is the last thing I see before a black rage clouds my vision and my mind.

Cuffs fall to the ground, and I attack.

5

Present Day

THE ANSWER IS YES. There is nothing in the world I want to do more than go with Esme to her favorite place in the world.

Wherever that is.

She directs me to take a shower and meet her outside of Wolf Trust Bank, which—surprise—is owned and run by the local werewolf pack.

After speeding through my wash and barely bothering with a towel, I'm clean, out the door, and jogging down Main Street. There's a constant fear festering in my chest that Esme will disappear if she's out of my sight for too long.

But there she is, standing on the sidewalk as she piles her sunlight curls in a messy bun on the top of her head. Luckily, I'm in good shape, so I'm not panting when I arrive at her side. Reaching up, I make sure my glasses are in place, sitting securely on my nose and camouflaging the glow of longing in my eyes.

"That was fast. I bet you didn't take the time to properly

condition your hair. That is going to puff up in the humidity, just you watch." She playfully tugs on one of the damp strands hanging low, leaving wet spots on my shirt.

I wish she'd fist her hand in the mass and use the hold to drag me to her. But Esme lets go and waves for me to follow.

When we were younger, she teased me about my hair all the time. How I drove an hour and a half to Athens to get it trimmed at an expensive barber. How I used more products than she did to arrange the brown strands in a sleek style. I remember staring at myself in the mirror every morning, going through my hair routine, grinning at the thought of how she'd try to mess the whole thing up the first moment she saw me.

How I'd pretend to be exasperated but secretly always liked the style better once her hands dug into it.

The care I put into my appearance is distant to me now. All the money and effort. If that's what Esme wants from a mate, I'll do it again, but after so many years in the wild, the ability to brush my teeth and shower seems like a luxury.

Besides, this lack of grooming keeps me unrecognizable for now. Or at least, I can tell myself that instead of admitting Esme has probably forgotten me.

"Okay, so this is *not* my favorite place. Not to say it's not good, but it's just a stop on the way," she says before pulling open a door and ushering me inside a shop with a warm atmosphere and the scent of coffee beans. "Coffee & Claws is pretty cool. Also, I'm one of those horribly unhealthy evening espresso drinkers, and I'm jonesing for my fix."

Then, something amazing happens. Esme hooks her arm through mine, guiding me toward the counter.

Every part of my body lights up, fueled by an internal sun that blazes bright for her. My muscles want to curl around Esme until I encase her with my body. The hot-flower scent gets me drunk, and I never want to sober up.

"Lee?" Her voice drags me from my happiness haze.

"Sorry. What?" My question sounds harsh, but there's no changing that. Not after that red dragon tore out half my throat when I was still in my mortal shape.

I don't think I was supposed to kill him once I released my beast, but no one had taken the time to explain anything to me before shoving me into that battle pit.

So, I took his head. And I'll never forget the life that faded from his glowing eyes. The scar on my throat will always act as the reminder that I'm not innocent.

"I asked if you wanted anything. Doesn't have to be coffee. They've got lots of good stuff here. Oh, and this is Sonya." Esme waves toward the tall Latina behind the counter. "She's one of the co-owners. And"—she lowers her voice in the event there are any humans around—"she's a siren."

"What can I get you?" Sonya asks, friendly smile in place with a set of shrewd eyes taking me in.

Xavier claims I look intimidating with my wild hair and *I've seen shit* aura. "Nothing." I try to gentle my voice, but it still comes out as a rasp.

"Uh, yeah, nonsense. I'm getting you something." Esme squeezes my arm, unaware that she's all I need in the world. "Any bear claws left?"

When we exit the shop, Esme has me hold her drink and the pastry as she fishes out her car keys.

"Sorry, I forgot to say we need to drive to get to my favorite place. Is that okay?"

She doesn't know I stowed away in the dank hulls of multiple ships for days just to get back to her. A short car ride with her at my side is pure pleasure in comparison.

"Yeah."

Esme likes to sing as she drives. I don't recognize the songs on the top hits radio station, but she makes every one beautiful with her joyful harmonies. Her old car doesn't have cupholders, so she asks me to hang on to her latte, accepting it for quick sips at stoplights. I stir up my internal forge enough to heat my palms and keep her cup warm.

I could stay here, riding beside her, for days. But eventually, we pull into a parking lot.

"Welcome to Bed, Bath, and Bargains!" Esme parks and wiggles her fingers toward the front of the store. The place she claims sends her endless coupons.

"Your favorite?"

"Yes. I spend way too much money here. Well, other people probably think it's too much. I think it's the exact right amount. Come on. Let's find some things for your apartment. My bet is, you're still functioning with the bare bones."

She's right that I haven't added much, but anything after the crude dwellings of the colony is the high life.

"Here. Snack first. Get a good sugar high going." Esme reaches into the bag I forgot about and pulls out the pastry, drizzled with frosting and sprinkled with sliced almonds. She splits it down the middle. "Half for me. Half for you." After passing the larger piece to me, Esme takes an impressive bite of hers. "You know"—she speaks with a full mouth, as if she were running out of time—"dis wast—"

The harpy did the same thing in high school, and I'd always cover her mouth and say, "Bite, chew, swallow, speak."

"After that?" she'd mumble against my hand, her eyes sparkling with mischief.

"Make out with me," I'd growl.

Then, she'd smile and chew *really* slow just to drive me wild.

The memory has my chest clenching with longing, and I have to do something.

I set my hand on hers, stopping the harpy mid-sentence. "Chew. Don't choke," I chide her.

Her nose wrinkles with a puffed-cheek smile, but she

listens, swallowing before going on. "I was saying, this was made by a bear shifter. The other owner of Coffee & Claws. He's kind of a grump, but a nice grump, you know? Anyway, I think you're going to like it in Folk Haven. At least, I hope you do." Then, her eyes drop pointedly to the untouched pastry in my hand.

I eat the bear claw in more respectable-sized bites, enjoying the treat. "Good," I tell her, and Esme beams.

Beautiful.

As we enter the store, she bounces on the balls of her feet, pushing a cart in front of her. Within the first aisle, she flits off, and I'm able to claim cart duty, following behind as the harpy adds random items to her haul.

A table lamp.

An orange omelet pan.

A fluffy bath mat.

My attention catches on a wall full of pillows. They're all stuffed to bursting and look so soft. I pick up one with a purple checkered pattern and cautiously press the cushion against my chest, not sure why I'm so wary of the object.

Maybe I just don't trust soft things anymore.

"Those are on sale! Let's get four." Esme tosses the matching pillows into the cart, and I like seeing them there. Knowing they're coming home with me.

"Towels next. I always leave them for last because they're my *favorite*." She strolls into a section with towels in every color a person could hope for. "I just really love terry cloth. There's something about it, especially the plush stuff." Her fingers stroke the stacks, coming to land on a royal-blue set. "I want to drape myself in terry cloth. And, yes"—she grins over her shoulder at me—"I know I have a problem."

My fingers automatically check that my glasses are still on my face, blocking the telltale glow of strong emotion. All I can think about is her stepping out of a shower, dripping wet, slowly blotting away the droplets with one of her precious towels.

I wish I were made of terry cloth.

6

———————

In the Past

I NEED two things to escape. Two seemingly impossible things.

But with decades in the colony stretching before me, I have nothing else to fill my time than trying to achieve the impossible.

My first taste of hope comes from Hotaru Watanabe, one of the elders in the colony. She finds me when I am living feral on the outskirts, attacking any who approach. She, more powerful than any dragon I've ever met, presses her thoughts into my mind and shows me there is a way to regain my human form earlier than the normal time span.

"Trust me," her voice hisses in my skull. *"Trust me enough to teach you."*

I can have what I want if only I put in the time. If I train. If I want it bad enough.

And, gods, I do.

I'm not sure why she chooses to share her knowledge with me. Why I'm worth this secret other dragons would kill for.

Whenever I ask, she simply says that the world needs less violence and more love.

Hotaru shows me the magical meditation practice passed down her family line. Guides me through all the subtleties. Drills into me the thought patterns I need to follow to overcome the power of my dragon soul.

I practice every day.

In a decade, I finally master the skill. When I sit still, listening to the power and magic flow through my veins, I can feel my two-legged shape locked within me, waiting to come out.

My heart begs for me to change now and run back to my mate. But I am not only trapped in my beast. I am also trapped in these magical walls.

The second impossible task is to rise so high in the hierarchy of the colony that I receive the gate spell to breach the boundaries. Only a few are allowed access for the safety of the group.

So, I return to the pit, and I fight. The easiest way to rise in the ranks is to dominate in the pit. I never kill another dragon, not after that first one. But I gain a reputation I doubt Hotaru—with her preference for love over violence—is proud of. But she must understand because she does not shun or betray me.

Every morning, even in the winter when the sun never rises, we meet on the same high peak to meditate. Our thick, scaly hides and internal forges keep us warm in the frigid temperatures. Icy wind plucks at the wings on my back, and I find, knowing I can leave this form now, I don't hate the shape so much. I even discover a small amount of contentment when I take wing.

But never enough to justify remaining.

"Why do you stay?" I ask her the morning after a particularly savage battle. My leg still aches from the break that healed overnight. At least I came out on top, although bloody when I got there.

For a long time, she doesn't answer. I don't begrudge her the silence after she's given me so much.

"My mate was human," her voice whispers softly against my mind. *"They are gone now. And I worry, when I go, we will not meet. That I will simply fade."* In her two-legged form, she would age like a human, as we all would, moving closer to death. Our dragon form stretches our life span. *"So, I will live a little longer. And their memory with me."*

While I appreciate the honesty, her sadness spurns a wildness in me. A desperation.

Time is running out for Esme.

The world is full of dangers; what if she's already met her end?

The next day, in the pits, I leave rivers of blood in the snow.

Finally, after years of battling and falsely proclaiming myself as a lover of the dragon way of life, I'm ruled as the best warrior and therefore master of colony protection. The elders, Hotaru among them, feed my blood into the boundary, giving me the key to leave.

Twenty years of dedication, deception, and destruction.

In the dark of the night, I flee. After breaching the barrier, I fly only a short way before testing Hotaru's gift to me.

At the sight of my naked human body, I weep in relief, the tears freezing on my cheeks. Terrified I'll never be able to make the change again, I hike miles in the deadly cold, hoping my inner forge doesn't run out before I make it to the camp. Somehow, I manage the trek, but my problems aren't over.

"Breath of The Winged One, you're in rough shape." The captain of the ship off this icy hell dimension stares down at me, his pale forehead wrinkling as he furrows his gray brow.

"Come on, Veritas. You're acting like you've never seen a

return before." A man with hooded eyes approaches me cautiously. "A fighter? In the pits?" he asks.

The scars littering my body tell my tale. Seems he knows of the brutality that exists in the colony if you want to earn an honored space. Or if you're a teenager who stepped out of line.

Despite living in the same area as my parents, I haven't spoken to them in years.

I give a jerky nod.

"I've seen a return before, but he's not on the schedule. The records list three females in the next month. No males."

Records. Of course they keep documents of arrivals and departures—one of the many safeguards for the colony. I should have known it wouldn't be as easy as showing up and requesting a ride home.

"What's your name? The name of your family?" The captain scowls down at me, distrust clear in his eyes.

This, at least, I can give an excuse for not answering. Raising my chin, I display the sloppily healed wound on my neck. The one that would have been fatal if I'd stayed in my mortal form. The one my magic barely managed to knit back together.

At the sight of my mangled throat, the captain's eyes widen in shock, then narrow.

"So, you can't speak? Fine. You'll write your answers. I'll be back." Veritas zips his coat and pushes into the frigid day.

Dread scrapes my insides with the clanging shut door.

The moment he disappears, the young man turns back to me with urgency. "You're running, yes? You need to get away from here?"

Over the past twenty years, I've only allowed myself to trust one other. Everything in me rebels against allowing this stranger to know the truth.

"Please, I want to help. But we need to act fast."

That's when I see the onyx glow of his eyes. The same color as Hotaru.

"Watanabe."

Despite the shock in his expression, he doesn't freeze. "My grandmother."

If I can put my faith in anyone, let it be one of her line. I nod, staring into his eyes.

"You'll need to knock me out, then run southeast until you spot a rock formation that resembles a turtle. Under the largest stone is a cave. Shelter there, and I'll find you. We'll have to smuggle you onto the ship when the scheduled dragons come. If he finds out the secret my grandmother taught you, he will take you back. Or worse. Do you understand?"

Another nod. Of course, the trials continue.

"We'll make a plan as we wait for the others to arrive. For now, you need to run. Hit me and go."

When I hesitate, tired of bloodshed, the young man shoves my chest. "Now!"

I do. His eyes roll back in his head as he falls to the floor. I snatch a coat and run and hide.

For three weeks, I live beneath a rock, venturing out to catch fish in icy waters, sometimes cooking them with the heat of my hands and sometimes devouring them raw. Antarctic sushi.

Yuito, Hotaru's grandson, comes when he can, bringing supplies that won't be missed and teaching me the many ways the world has changed in my absence.

"Do you have someplace to go?" he asks one night.

Not in the way he means. There's no shelter waiting for me in the world. But I have a destination.

I simply nod. After another week of pushing and a blood oath not to share my location, I relent and tell him.

"Folk Haven? I've never been, but I've heard of it. A town in Georgia. A safe place for mythical creatures looking to coexist."

I grunt in confirmation. Good to know it hasn't disappeared. Would have made the job of finding Esme that much harder.

What if she left?

I push the thought away. If she has, I'll search until I find her.

"I know a dragon who planned to move there. Xavier. Nice guy. Think he's a firefighter. If you need help, you might want to find him," Yuito offers.

With a nod of thanks, I store the information away. Hold on to his name when I hide in the hull of the ship as it sails to the southern point of South America. Silently chant the name when Yuito presses a wad of cash into my hand and wishes me luck before I blend in with the city crowd. Whisper his name after Esme's each night when I fall asleep in a grimy alley or a hidey-hole on another boat, the one that brings me to the States.

During the long, painful journey is the only time I miss my dragon form. The body with powerful wings that could carry me across a great distance, straight to her. But I will never again risk getting stuck in that form, even knowing the secret of early transformation.

After weeks of scraping my way through the modern world, I find myself in Georgia, hitchhiking north.

A trucker lets me off in Toccoa with a granola bar and a gruff, "Good luck."

I walk the rest of the way, sleeping in the woods when I'm too exhausted to take another step.

At the sight of the Folk Haven town sign, my throat tightens, the longing a more painful ache than any injury I sustained from the pits.

Almost there.

7

Present

Two months in this town, and I realize with a sense of trepidation that I've begun to settle in.

I stare at the bags from Bed, Bath, and Bargains, full from another trip to the store. My fourth since Esme showed me the place. Something keeps drawing me back.

I unpack every item but one, keeping it in the small plastic bag and clutching it tight in my hand as I descend the stairs from my apartment and circle around to the entrance of Fresh Feathers.

This isn't what I came here to do, I remind myself.

I'm supposed to determine if Esme is happy with the life she has. If the sudden reappearance of a dragon mate would be a bad thing.

If I'm honest, I think I know the answer.

She has a thriving business. Friends all over town. Smiles for everyone.

What about love? Does she have that?

It's the final question. The one I'm too much of a coward to dig into.

When I push open the shop door, I find she has customers. Not wanting to interrupt, I lean back against the far wall, waiting for my harpy to be free. When I pick up the thread of their conversation, my body stiffens.

"When are you going to make an honest man of me, Esme? You're doing this town a disservice by letting me stay on the market." A stocky white guy with a flirtatious smile leans on the counter.

I'm about to step forward, make the asshole back the hell off. But then I spy Esme's affectionate smile, and my heart and feet freeze.

"A disservice? That sounds terrible. You're saying I'm putting the entire town in danger by *not* dating you?" From her playful tone, I can tell Esme is enjoying the exchange.

I want to set the man on fire.

"That's exactly it. I'm a hot commodity. People are fighting in the streets, dueling for the chance to lock down this rockin' bod."

"Gods, Owen." The man's companion groans. "Can you stop talking about yourself for a single minute so I can pick up my pants?"

The flirter throws his arms in the air. "Help a guy out! You already have a winged woman of your own. Now, it's time for you to be a *literal* wingman and help me get mine." Owen turns back to a grinning Esme, shaking his head in mock disappointment. "Seamus is so selfish sometimes."

"This is why I don't take you on errands with me," the taller man grouses.

Owen and Seamus MacNamara. With their names, I remember the two selkies from my childhood, both a few years younger than me. We never hung in the same circles. But their parents own Float 'N Dive, the water sports shop, and they're a certain kind of royalty in Folk Haven. One of the founding families.

I think my parents always resented the families that had that claim. The Blaythorns are rich, but they didn't build Folk Haven. As a teenager, I didn't pay much attention to the politics, so I have no idea if they were spurned in any way, but I do know they showed up at the Antarctic colony with all the pride they knew our name garnered.

Blaythorns were one of the founding families there.

Nothing to be proud of, as far as I could tell. What did they truly build? Witches established the protective barriers. The buildings are crude caves for the most part.

It is basically preserved land. Good fucking job if all you wanted was to protect animals.

But that's not what dragons are. At least, it's something I refuse to be anymore.

"Well, despite the very real and serious danger it might put the population in, I can't help you. My answer remains the same." Esme reaches out and taps Owen's nose with a single finger. "Someone already has dibs on my heart. You're too late."

Too late.

The words fling through the space, poisonous, deadly daggers.

The final answer to my question.

My cue to leave.

Not yet. Just a little longer, then I'll go.

As I deal with the agony of my fracturing heart, I don't hear the rest of their conversation. With my chin tucked to my chest, I don't even see them leave.

Suddenly, there's a set of golden eyes glaring into mine.

"Traitor!" Esme jabs me in the chest with a finger, and I wish she'd keep going, digging past my rib cage and tearing out the ravaged organ.

Then, her accusation registers, and I feel my brow furrowing.

"You went to Bed, Bath, and Bargains without me," she clarifies, eyes dropping to the bag in my hands. "How did you even get there? Bought yourself a car?"

"Xavier took me." I force the words out, trying to be whatever version of normal I can manage. "Errands."

"But *I'm* your B, B, and B buddy."

That first time we went, she tricked me. I bought my pillows, and she bought everything else in the cart. Then, she carried all the items up to my apartment. Took me that long to realize she'd been shopping for me.

I tried to pay her back, but she ran away before I could get my cash out.

Need to be smarter to get one over on Esme Sharpwing.

We've gone to the store together twice since then, and she keeps pulling the same shit, claiming she enjoys shopping for someone else, but she keeps dodging my cash.

To pacify her, I extend the bag. "Got you this."

They were just setting up their fall display when I arrived at the store, so I'm pretty sure she doesn't already own it.

Esme's attempt at a scowl drops away with an excited gasp. She plunges her hand into the bag and comes out with a set of pumpkin-patterned hand towels.

In an unusual shift of personality, Esme doesn't say anything. She just stares at the silly item, and then her eyes slowly move to my face.

"Terry cloth," I say by way of explanation.

Something changes in her stare, almost as if she's in pain, and I panic at the sight. I don't know what I did wrong, but I have to fix it.

"Sorry." I reach to take the towels back.

Esme steps away, moving faster than me. "Mine. They're

mine." She clutches the gift against her chest, the way I wish she'd hold me.

But she never will.

Too late.

My hand falls to my side.

The harpy shakes her head, eyes on the floor, and when she looks my way again, her normal smile is in place. "I love them. These are so cute and soft." She rubs the towels against her face, and I'm jealous of the material. "They're perfect. You get an A-plus for gift giving."

Strolling behind the counter, she tucks them away and comes up with one of her sketchbooks. "How's your day going? I was working on some designs before the MacNamaras stopped by. Want to see?"

I nod, joining her at the counter. As she flips through the pages and talks about her sketched ideas, I push away the knowledge that I need to leave and try to enjoy this simple moment of just being with her. The scent of hot flowers fills my lungs, Esme's sweet voice caresses my ears, and I'm the happiest I've been since I was eighteen years old.

"The sirens in particular love this style because the racer-back shows off their wing marks. And allows them to fly at a moment's notice."

She tilts her sketch pad my way. We stand side by side now, elbows on the counter.

Esme has evolved from the teen with a garage-sale sewing machine to a full-scale designer. Turns out, the dry cleaning is just the storefront and a small part of the business.

"Harpies too?" I ask.

"I mean, it technically works for us." She fiddles with the corner of the page as she contemplates the drawing. "But wearing a top when we shift is uncomfortable. Because of the feathers. Best to be topless. Or completely naked."

I must make a noise because her head whips up and a delicious blush infuses her cheeks.

"Sorry! Too much info." Esme straightens, running an agitated hand through her hair. "If you saw me in my other form, you'd get it."

I have, and I do. Thinking back on the time when she changed for me, I have to bite my lip to stifle a grunt. Her heather-colored feathers created a soft coat over her skin, covering her nipples but provocative in the way they shaped perfectly to her body.

"Oh goddess, that sounded suggestive." Esme's voice is tight. "I-I swear I didn't mean to, like, proposition you just now."

Her words have my eyes narrowing, studying her closer. I note again how oddly Esme is acting. Normally, she's bubbly confidence. But there's an air of anxiety in her words and jerky movements as she shuffles farther behind the counter and adjusts small items that don't need to be rearranged.

"Something wrong?" I ask.

She freezes in the act of arranging pencils in a cup on the counter.

"Wrong?" she repeats, then covers her face with her hands and groans. "Yes. Something is wrong."

"What?" Whatever it is, I'll fix it. Maybe that can be my role. I'll solve all the problems Esme faces. Then, I'll go when she has no more problems and her life is entirely perfect. "Tell me."

She drops her hands and stares hard, studying me and no doubt seeing a husk of a man. With a quick step, she's next to me, her palms settling overtop one of mine. It's all I can do not to drop my head and press my forehead against the back of her hand. Try to imprint the shape of her bones on my skin.

"The problem is," she sighs, "I like you, Lee. A lot."

Her words are lightning, infusing my body with a painful explosion of energy.

"But," she continues, "I've devoted my life to someone else.

And I don't want to betray them. Not that I'm sure I would be. Not by *liking* you. But I also might ... as time goes by ... well, anyway, I'm sorry. Just know you're not doing anything wrong."

Who are they? I long to growl. *Can I kill them?*

With the hand that's not under hers, I rub the bridge of my nose—hard—trying to dispel the fury and lethal rage that someone else has her heart.

"Lee?"

The sudden press of her palm on my chest makes me flinch, causing my thumb to bump my glasses. They slip off my face.

"Oh shoot," Esme says as the thick spectacles clatter to the floor. "Let me grab those."

"No. Wait." I lunge forward the same time Esme bends over, but she's too fast for me, her strong fingers plucking the lenses up from where they fell.

When she straightens, her body is too close, brushing against mine. Through my flannel, I feel the soft curves of her breasts, the gentle press of her hip, and the steadying pressure of her hand. Rage bleeds to desperate wanting. She smells like warmth on the wind, and my throat aches, holding back the groan of longing.

Curse The Winged One's tricks. I've missed you, Esme.

She offers a rueful smile as her eyes meet mine, but the expression falters, as if disconcerted by our proximity.

"Your eyes," she murmurs, her gaze fixed on mine. "That blue ..."

And that's when I notice the glow on her skin. A reflection from my gaze, shining bright with passion for her. With want and need and love. No spelled lenses to mute the vibrant color and block out the mystical reaction I have in her proximity.

Without the shield of magic-infused glass, I reveal more than my feelings.

With the Blaythorn blue, I've revealed myself.

"Lee?" Esme's golden brows twist with confusion. "Lee ..."

Understanding dawns in her wide sunshine eyes. "Su-*LEE*-en? *Sulien?*"

She remembers.

I knew I wanted to hear my name—my true name—on her lips at least once more. But I didn't know how much until my entire body shudders with the simple pleasure.

She remembers me.

That single gift, my name spoken in her sweet voice, is more than I let myself hope for. Now—maybe—I can leave Folk Haven. Let her live a happy life with her new love.

"You're here?" She pants the question, and my brief spike of triumph morphs into concern when I spy the wildness in her gaze.

"Essie—" The nickname slips out.

"You're *here?*" Her features sharpen in a flicker, taking on the beautiful angles of a hawk, as she digs her fingers into my beard, searching for the shape of my face. *"YOU'RE HERE!"*

A harpy's scream.

The words pierce my skull like needles shoved into my eardrums. Painful. Powerful.

The last thing I hear before the world goes black.

8

As I slowly awaken from a strange dream, I hear muffled voices speaking around me. Part of my mind wants to pay attention to them. But another part—a more demanding part—wants me to turn over and bury my face deeper into the most comfortable pillow in the world.

I'm distracted from the internal argument by the gentle brush of fingers through my hair. Someone is touching me, and it feels *good*.

If I could stay in this half-wakeful state forever, I would. But there's one problem.

My ears itch. When I reach up to rub them, my fingers come away, coated in an oily substance.

"Don't do that. It's a healing potion." The sweet voice coaxes me to open my eyes, meeting an amber set above mine. "Sorry. I ruptured your eardrums when I screamed." Esme scowls. "I mean, I want to throttle you." Her hands fist in my shirt, and I watch her glare go soft. "But I didn't mean to hurt you."

"Yes, well, he's fine now."

Glancing to the side, I spot a Black woman with iron-gray

hair in braids, washing her hands in my kitchen sink, and I realize we're in my apartment.

"Easy enough fix. Easy for me, of course. Doesn't mean it won't cost you."

"Madeline is a healing witch. One of two in town," Esme explains before leaving off staring at me to glance the stranger's way. "And of course. What payment do you want? Money or favor?"

Madeline packs up her bag, tucking away glass jars full of colorful liquids. "Favor," the witch declares. "I want you to stitch me a dress for the Halloween Ball. Something that'll make Georgiana choke on her snobby tongue."

Even from my lower angle, I can see the curve of Esme's smile.

"I can do that."

"And do I get a favor for carrying his heavy ass upstairs?" The familiar voice comes from the couch, and I know who it is without looking.

"Don't get me started on you, Xavier."

My pillow shifts with her movement, and I realize I'm not lying on fabric and stuffing. My head is in Esme's lap.

Now, even more than before, I want to bury my face into the plush surface.

But before I can roll over, her strong hand cradles the back of my skull, and her legs disappear, quickly replaced by an actual pillow. A grumble of protest sneaks out of my throat, but she doesn't seem to be paying attention to me anymore.

"You knew this whole time, didn't you?" The harpy advances on the dragon, face fierce.

"Hmm. Not my kind of drama. I'll be in touch about the dress." Madeline heaves her workbag over her shoulder and exits through the front door.

"I wanted to tell you." Xavier holds up his hands in surrender. "But he swore me to silence before I knew who he was."

"Are you kidding me?" Esme hisses, all sweetness gone.

"Blood oath." Xavier points to the healed slash on his wrist, where the skin is pink against his normal dark brown. "Swore I wouldn't interfere with his plans as long as he didn't harm anyone in Folk Haven. I couldn't say *anything*." He sits up abruptly. "But now, you know. Figured it out on your own, no thanks to his secretive, brooding ass." Xavier rises from the couch, looking mighty pleased, even in the face of Esme's wrath. "Looks like my work here is done. Send me an invite to the mating." His eyes flick my way, and he offers a sympathetic grimace. "Or the funeral. Whichever. See you both around."

The dragon strolls out of my apartment, leaving me with an angry Esme. My strength slowly returns to my limbs, and I'm able to push myself into a seated position as the harpy paces around the living space, unnervingly silent.

I expect the obvious questions.

How are you here?

Why did you come back?

Why didn't you say who you were?

Instead, Esme, like always, surprises me.

"Why do you have so many throw pillows?" She snatches two off an armchair I bought at a yard sale.

Glancing around, I realize I do have a lot. Probably twenty in this room, and there's more on my bed. Every time I went to Bed, Bath, and Bargains, I would toss a few in my cart.

"Missed soft things," I say, now realizing that's the reason.

Everything in the colony was hard and sharp and cold.

Throw pillows are the opposite.

"You're hoarding them." Esme tosses one my way, and it hits my chest like a lobbed marshmallow. "You're hoarding throw pillows because you want soft things," she mutters.

I shrug. Collecting them simply felt natural. Like being around Esme.

She continues to pace, not meeting my eyes, clutching a piece of my hoard to her chest, as if it will comfort her.

"Tell me," she commands.

So, I do. In slow, halting words, I tell her about leaving against my will, only realizing my father's intentions once he shoved me into the fighting pit. How I had to change to survive, but then I just wanted to die. How a dragon saw my torment and shared her sacred secret with me. How I trained and meditated and fought every day to get back to myself. Back to her.

"But you didn't come back to me though. Lee did," she points out.

"Would've left," I say. "If you were better off. Better without me."

Esme crouches in front of me, her eyes wild, tears on her cheeks. "I'm going to kiss your fucking face off, you fucking infuriatingly dense dragon."

My sluggish brain takes a moment to register the words. The deliciously perfect threat.

"Yes."

Esme flies forward, straddling me, plastering herself to my chest as her fingers dig into my hair. Her lips crash into mine, dragging a groan from deep in my chest when I taste her hot flavor on my tongue. She kisses like a woman starved for my mouth, and I want nothing more than to be her feast.

Until I can't fight the urge to consume her myself.

There are so many throw pillows in my place; a handful have toppled to the floor. I roll Esme over onto her back so she's cradled among the soft cushions, and then I drag my mouth from hers, licking my way down her neck to her collarbone.

"Sulien," she moans, and I grow hard at the sound.

Shoving up the thin cotton of her shirt, I continue my trail of kisses over her bare flesh, enjoying not only the salty, sweet taste of her skin, but also the way she twists and laughs and groans. Just like she did all those years ago.

The two times blend together, and for a moment, I can imagine I haven't lost decades of this magic.

I dip my tongue in her belly button as I pull down her leggings and underwear. Golden curls, pressed flat by fabric, greet me. I nuzzle them, breathing in her scent, rubbing my bearded cheek against this intimate part of her.

"Sulien!" Her voice is half scolding, half giggle, and I feel the demanding tug of her fingers in my hair, as if she's trying to pull me away from perfection.

I snarl as I palm her thighs wider and nip at the soft flesh of her lower belly.

"Fine, you evil dragon." Her voice is breathless, and I glance up to find her face flushed, chest heaving, as she tries to glare down at me. "I want an *I'm sorry I didn't tell you who I was the moment I stepped into your shop* orgasm. Got it?"

A wicked grin spreads over my face. I don't care who the bastard is she's devoted her life to, but they're forgotten with my face inches from her pussy. She'll never think of them again once I'm done with her.

Because I'll never be finished.

"One for every day," I rasp.

Her sass disappears with a hard swallow. "One orgasm for each day you've been here? No, that's, like ... more than thirty orgasms. I'll die." Despite her morbid words, there's heat in her eyes, and her lips press tight, trying to suppress a smile.

"Die happy," I say with a smirk before swiping my tongue up her vulva, collecting the wetness that's all for me.

"You're *evil*. Oh gods." Esme's head drops back to a pillow, and her legs hook over my shoulders, heels digging into my shoulder blades to urge me forward. "You'd better fucking kill me," she mutters as her hips rock against my greedy mouth. "Because I'm going to murder you."

I suck her tight clit and growl a wordless response. The

sound must create the right vibration because, the next thing I know, she's tensing and convulsing and shouting my name.

"One," I grunt before sucking on her inner thigh, just hard enough to leave a hickey.

That's how I plan to keep track.

I slip two fingers inside her and get to work.

When there are five hickeys, Esme uses her feet to press hard on my chest and shove me away. I could probably win against her shaky legs, but I decide to give my harpy a respite. A short one. Crawling up her body, I kiss a trail as I go and try to ignore my demanding hard-on. My cock wants to slide into her soaking wet channel so fucking bad.

When I'm sprawled beside her, head propped on my hand so I can gaze down at the woman I love, I watch as she raises her hand, fingers still twitching with post-orgasmic shocks, slides it under my beard, and wraps the digits around my neck. As if she wants to strangle me.

I lean hard into her hand, liking the idea of her fingers leaving impressions on my skin. But she's not trying to choke. Instead, her touch traces the thick scar. The proof that I had to change or die.

Please, forgive me.

"Does it still hurt?" she asks.

I shake my head. When compared to the pain of losing her, it was nothing.

"You can't leave again," she says, her tone allowing no argument.

"Your partner. They'll want me gone."

And they could get me to leave. Whoever they are, they wouldn't need force or might. If it came to a fight, I'm confident I would win.

No. All they would need to do is take Esme into their arms.

I would go, if only to survive the pain.

Her brow dips. "Who?"

Hmm, were my orgasms that good?

"You're devoted, you said"—*Was that just a few hours ago?*—"to another."

Esme's mouth drops open, and now, I feel the strength in her fingers, tightening enough to make me pay attention.

"I'm devoted to *you*, Sulien Blaythorn. Only you."

Does she mean what I think she means? After all this time, I'm the one who holds her devotion?

"You still want me?" I rasp.

"Want you?" She stares at me, expression bewildered. "I was coming to *get* you."

9

ESME HAS an entire room in her house devoted to research on Antarctica and dragons.

Books on shelves and open on tables. Scrolls unraveled. Pictures of great, scaly beasts scattered about. Maps pinned to the walls with notes about different areas.

The largest is a detailed image of the Antarctic continent.

There's a blue pin placed exactly where the colony is.

"Did you ever wonder why I owed Xavier that big favor?" Esme asks as I stare around in wonder.

After her cryptic confession, the harpy righted her clothes and dragged me out of the apartment, not caring that my body was obviously still in *I want to fuck you* mode. Even after the car ride to her house on the edge of town, I'm still half hard.

Silently, I nod.

My harpy strolls up to the map with the blue pin. "Because he promised to take me to the colony twenty years from now."

"What?" The question comes out hoarse—and not just because of my injury. The idea of Esme in that place is my nightmare.

"When I found out a dragon moved to town, I sought him

225

out and pestered him until he agreed. Only took a few months." She smirks, all cocky and triumphant. "He promised to guide me there, help find you, and get you out."

"Twenty years. You'd be almost sixty." An even more fragile version of herself, braving the Antarctic wild.

"So? Yuichiro Miura climbed Mount Everest when he was eighty years old, and that guy was human." She crosses her arms, glaring at me, like she still plans to go and needs to convince me to let her. "I've been training since I was eighteen. Designing some kick-ass magical winter gear, better than Gore-Tex." She jerks her chin toward a corner with a rack of clothing that looks like it belongs in a ski apparel shop.

"I knew I couldn't change you back. At least, I couldn't *find* record of any dragons changing early, other than one." Her eyes flick to a shelf of scrolls. "But they used a god artifact that was lost on a sunken ship hundreds of years ago."

She stops next to a pinned-up map of the world, tapping her finger near Japan before sliding south to the giant white ice patch at the southernmost point of the world. "But I figured if I was *there*, if I was nearby when you transformed naturally, I could save you from your parents. Prove whatever they might have told you was a lie."

She shoves her fists in the pockets of her shorts, glaring at the floor. "Your mom came to my house. The day after we slept together. She told me you and your father were already gone. That you were so ashamed of what you'd done, you wanted to live in the colony as a dragon to repent for your *sins*."

Wrath boils in my gut, and my parents are lucky there's a world between us.

My harpy straightens her spine. "I knew it was a lie. She knew you were mine, and that terrified her. So, they took you from me. Thinking I'd forget. But I never did. Not for a single day."

The magnitude of what she's telling me threatens to rupture my brain.

"All this ... time ... your loyalty."

Esme grimaces, her eyes sad. "I'm not perfect. There were times—a whole year once—when I convinced myself it was impossible. Or that I'd go through all this, find you, and you'd shift back into a young man, and I'd be an old woman, clutching too tight to the past. That you'd pity me for never letting you go."

Pity? More like worship at your feet.

I'm humbled by her.

"What changed?"

Esme shrugs and fiddles with the pages of an open book. "I realized it didn't matter. If you had moved on and were happy with some lady dragon, then I'd hurt, but I'd deal. Or if you simply didn't want me, I'd live with that too. But one thing I was absolutely sure of was, they had *forced* you to go to the colony. And when you could shift back to your human form, I wasn't going to let you face them alone if you wanted to escape. I could not live the rest of my life, knowing you were trapped."

She would've been there. Four decades apart, and she would have come for me. Done her best to save me.

No less than I'd do for her, but I've spent so much of my life among selfish, backstabbing creatures that I can't comprehend this commitment.

"I don't deserve you." I stare at Esme and wonder if I'm dreaming. If I fell asleep on the icy tundra and my internal forge finally ran out and I'm now drifting toward a death dimension. One that gives me every joy I never had in life.

"That's a ridiculous thing to say." The harpy circles the research-covered table to face me, staring me down with her golden gaze. "Do you want me? Because I want you."

Blue light flickers across her skin in response. "Yes."

"Do you love me like you used to?"

Like I used to? We were both barely more than children then. What I feel now eclipses those fledgling feelings.

"More."

She grins as tears spill down her cheeks. "And you're not mad I was this close"—she holds up her fingers in a pinching motion—"to cheating on you with you?"

"Do it," I growl, lunging forward to scoop her into my arms.

Esme laughs against my mouth as I kiss her, tasting the salt of tears and scenting hot flowers. I sink to the ground with her atop me.

"Do you ..." I groan when she reaches between us to palm my erection, fully stiff again.

"Do I what?" Her quick fingers undo my fly and pull out my cock, stroking until I almost forget my question.

But the answer is too important.

"Love me?"

Esme pauses with her fingers around my heated flesh, meeting my eyes with a look that says, *Seriously, you dense dragon?*

Then, she smirks, all sass and teasing.

"Oh, I see. An entire room devoted to you isn't clear enough. My dragon needs to hear me say it. Do I have that right?"

Her dragon.

Fuck yes, I'm hers.

I nod, a quick jerk of my chin.

"Fine, you want to hear it? I"—she stands my cock up straight, positioning me at her entrance—"love"—she sinks down an inch—"you." She slips the rest of the way.

Fully seated inside her, I've lost the few words I had.

Then, with each rock of her hips, the teasing harpy gives me a different variation.

"I love you, Sulien."

"I love you, Lee."

"I love you, my infuriating bearded dragon."

"I love you, my ... mate."

"Wait," I croak, my balls tight, on the verge of spilling. "I am?"

Mating is different for every kind of mythic. I knew the fates had chosen her for me when I first filled her with my cock and felt as though wings had sprouted from my back and my chest caught on fire and my heart reformed to the shape of her small palm.

"That first time"—she moans as I thrust into her again, then licks my neck—"you asked to see my other form. You wanted all of me. Every last feather." As she talks, I nod. "Your soul lifts my wings. Of course you're my mate. Now, stroke my clit."

Her profound words, followed by the crude demand, have me chuckling and falling further in love. I do as I was told, and soon, I'm rewarded with the fist-tight clench of her around my cock.

"Gods," I shout, slamming deep and locking an iron arm around her hips, keeping Esme close as I spill inside her. Over and over, filling her with my ecstasy and love.

Later, when we lie, spent and panting, Esme's fingers twisting my hair around her fingers, she brings up the future.

"Everyone is going to know something is up with you. My devotion to Sulien Blaythorn isn't a secret. If I suddenly abandon my mission and start making out with you in public—which, let's be honest, I'm going to do every time the urge takes me—people will ask questions. If you want to remain anonymous, we're going to have to leave Folk Haven."

Leave her business? Abandon her friends, this house she bought? Run away, like I did from the colony?

That place was hell and deserved to be abandoned.

Folk Haven is different. A place where we could be safe and happy.

"I won't hide. Not anymore." I speak the words against her hair, breathing in the warm floral scent. "I want to stay."

My parents might come for me, demanding ... retribution? Obedience? I'm not sure. But whatever they might want, they won't be able to lash out for twenty years. Plenty of time for us to prepare. They're as stuck as they tried to make me. And when I see them again, I won't be a naive teenager. I'll be a warrior dragon with allies and a fierce harpy mate at my side.

"Good." Esme pushes herself up until she sprawls over my chest, our naked bodies pressed together. She brings her mouth to mine for a series of kisses. "Welcome home."

EPILOGUE

Esme claims the research room reminds her of the decades we spent apart, so after only a week of her knowing my identity, she boxes everything up.

"The Shellys might want the dragon books. They're the witches who used to rent the apartment," my harpy explains. "Have you been by their library?"

I shake my head as I help her arrange the heavy boxes in her car.

"Then, prepare yourself for a treat." Esme flits to my side, pressing a hot kiss to my neck while my hands are full.

She enjoys doing that, I think, as a small means of torture. Giving me lusty kisses when my hands are occupied and I can't grab her.

She's a sneak, and I fucking love her for it.

She's also brazen with her affection. The memory of how she laid me out on her bed and kissed every scar on my body makes me half hard. After packing the last box, I rearrange myself and slide into the passenger seat.

Then, I wrap my hand around the back of her neck, drag her in for a scorching kiss, shove my fingers past her waistband until I find her greedy little clit, and mercilessly stroke her until she's coming while strapped into the driver's seat. Luckily, the car is in park.

"You bastard," she pants. "Now, my underwear is going to be damp for this whole errand."

I dip my fingers lower, stroking the wetness, then drag my hand free and suck her pleasure off my skin like the sweet treat it is.

She glares, even as her cheeks flush hot and needy. "You've turned evil. I've mated an evil dragon."

"Mmm," I rumble. "Yes."

As Esme backs out of the driveway, she goes on a rant. "I don't know what happened to you. You used to be this sweet, preppy boy with styled hair and a closet full of polo shirts. I used to make *you* blush." Eyes on the road, she reaches over to poke my chest, and I chuckle at the playful assault. "Remember that time you took me on your boat? You thought you were so cool and confident, up until I lost my top in the water. You were the color of a tomato! You could not form a single word."

"Not true," I argue, fighting my grin at the memory. "Think I said *one*."

"Oh yeah. How could I forget? When I climbed out, you said, 'Boobs.' Like, *really* loud."

Gods, I was dense. And obsessed with impressing Esme, who made the task impossible, which only made me try harder.

We turn down a road with lush green forest pushing in from all sides. How most of the roads around Lake Galen look.

"And now, you're this confident, swaggering seduction master. It's not fair. I'm going to have to up my game," she declares just as she pulls into the driveway of a Victorian house.

The place looks kind of spooky in the evening light.

Perfect house for a set of witches and their magical library.

Esme throws the car in park, shuts off the engine, and turns to face me.

"Get ready," she warns.

"For witches?" I ask.

"No. For me to up my game. Right now. Are you ready?"

I bite my lip to keep my laughter at bay. She's too fucking cute, wanting to out-seduce me. Not like she needs to work at it. She walks into a room, and I'm already looking for a surface to bend her over. Still, I'm not about to complain.

At my nod, her smile grows wicked.

"I love the way your beard feels against my thighs."

Damn her. I palm my dick through my pants and swallow hard. "Yeah?"

She nods slow. "Whenever you see me looking at your mountain-man facial hair, I want you to know, in that exact moment, I'm thinking about riding your face."

"Fuck, Esme."

I go to claim her mouth, only to get held up by my seat belt. As I wrestle with the strap, she giggles and escapes the car. When I get out, I have to tuck my hard cock into my waistband to hide what her words did to me.

"*You're* evil," I tell her as she pulls a box from the trunk.

"Then, we're a perfect pair."

My mate gifts me with a chaste kiss on the cheek, and I silently vow to make her come so many times on my tongue that she forgets her own name when we get back to her house.

The inside of the house looks like a library in progress. Some books are on shelves, but most are in stacks around the dim rooms.

"Thanks for these." A curvy white woman with russet hair accepts the box in Esme's arms. "I'm hoping to build out our sections on the different mythic groups." Her eyes flick to mine. "I'm Morgana Shelly."

"Sulien Blaythorn."

I've decided to use my real name, parents and past be damned. Still debating on trying to find the legal documents my parents had for me or getting a new set forged. It's not the most uncommon thing among our kind. A safety measure some use.

"Would you be willing to verify the validity of these texts?" Morgana asks me as I set down my box of books on one of the few clear surfaces in the room.

"Sure." I feel no loyalty to my kind. No reason to keep their secrets.

"Are any of those grimoires?" The question comes from the stairs, where a woman with hair as red as Morgana's and pale skin, covered in freckles, descends.

"Sorry, no." Esme moves to my side and smiles at the new arrival. "Just dragon stuff. Sulien, this is Amethyst Shelly. Ame, this is my mate, Sulien."

A bolt of pure pleasure goes through me. She's called me her mate before, but this is the first time she's used it in an introduction. I wrap an arm around her waist, pulling the lovely harpy into my side.

"Bummer. About the grimoires. Not about the mating. That's a good thing." The witch's green eyes meet and hold mine, and I feel like she sees more than I mean to reveal. Suddenly, the woman smiles wide. "You're exactly what Esme has wanted all this time."

The words are odd, but also kind of endearing. Before I can think on them more, a territorial growl sets my hackles up. But then I see the noise emanates from the throat of a small black cat lingering on the steps.

"This is Bee," Amethyst says. "Don't take the aggression personally. He doesn't like anyone."

I meet the cat's dark eyes, and for a moment, I'm held by the intense stare. There's something in the depths, more than animal.

Understanding. Intelligence.

Rage.

"He's a cat?" I have to ask, tearing my eyes away and meeting the freckled witch's.

She tilts her head, wearing a sad smile now. "I'm ninety-six percent sure he's not."

Whatever he is, I sense familiarity.

He is what I was. A beast held captive.

"Don't worry," Amethyst assures me, as if hearing my thoughts. "I'm working on it." Her attention flicks to my side, and I realize she's holding Esme's stare now. "Even if it takes forty years, I'll figure it out."

"Good luck," my mate says, her tone sympathetic.

We leave then, both of us needing distance from the somber reminder of our forced time apart. When we reach the car, I stop Esme from climbing inside, pulling her in for a kiss. Not one of passion and sex and craving.

This one is a thank-you.

When I pull back, I find her lashes glimmering with tears, though her mouth smiles.

"I love you too," Esme whispers. "For my whole life, I will always love you."

"My mate," I say in response, the words holding everything that's in me.

Then, her eyes dip, lingering on my beard, before flitting back to my face as she smirks.

The tension breaks as I rumble a chuckle.

"Evil mate," I mutter.

The next kiss is full of promises.

～

FLIRTING WITH A FIREBIRD

Broderick knows that the beautiful firebird he freed from a curse wants nothing to do with him. He does *not* know why she suddenly shows up in his office with a list of questions.

Broderick Shelly moved to the small magical town of Folk Haven to be closer to his witchy sisters. Before he even finds a place to rent, the man is shirtless on the night of a full moon casting spells to destroy some twisted magic. But when his hard work reveals a gorgeous woman with fiery powers, Broderick is immediately smitten.

Unfortunately, Ophelia the firebird flies off after he makes an ill-advised compliment. Certain that he's ruined his shot, Broderick decides to keep his pining to himself.

But Ophelia has other plans...

CONTENT WARNING

This story contains descriptions of self-harm for spell work and life-threatening stunts, as well as discussions of death, captivity, child neglect, and emotional abuse.

1

BRODERICK

"I DON'T SEE why this spell requires me to take my shirt off."

My younger sister, Ame, continues to light the necessary fires as she answers, "You wouldn't have to if you agreed to let me perform the spell." She pauses and tilts her head, as if in thought. "*I* might have to then. Take my shirt off. Jack will be grumpy about missing that."

"Nope. No. Never mind."

It is in everyone's best interest that Ame's werewolf boyfriend stays un-grumpy.

Or at least less grumpy than his normal amount.

"We need skin-to-skin contact for you to draw on our magic. Closer to your heart, the better," Mor, my older sister, explains as she reads through the steps in the grimoire. "I can't believe you performed this on your own, Ame."

The youngest of us stands up and offers a mild shrug, her long red hair sliding over her shoulder with the gesture. We all share the shade, along with our pale skin, and magical heritage. Our current group is missing the fourth sibling, but even though Anthony, my twin, is in town, none of us expected him to join. The man hates magic.

"It was uncomfortable," Ame admits.

Which probably means it was agonizing. Ame is not a complainer.

With a sigh, I reach for the buttons on my shirt and prepare for multiple discomforts. Along with whatever magical bothers I'm about to deal with, there's also the fact that it's cold. Georgia might stay warm longer than England—where I just spent the last few years—but this full moon night in December is only just above freezing.

As I slip the buttons free, my eyes seek out the reason we're all out here on this frigid night.

In the center of a chalk-drawn diagram sits a fluffy rabbit. The creature is the color of milk chocolate with ears that droop and an overall aura of fear. The tiny thing quivers.

Guilt hits me hard in the stomach and hurries my fingers.

I'm an ass, bemoaning my momentary discomfort, when there's a person trapped in the wrong body only feet from me.

A few years ago, Ame found a black cat on the side of the road. Instantly, she knew there was something other about the feline, and she spent all her time trying to figure out what. Eventually, she broke the curse placed on him, freeing Jack Lim. A werewolf. A man who now is thoroughly in love with her.

Turned out, Jack had been captured and transformed by a sorcerer—also known as a human who utilizes twisted spells to steal magic from mythical creatures. He'd been feeding off of Jack for years before the guy managed to escape.

When Ame, Jack, and a group of other powerful mythics sought out the sorcerer who had cursed him for retribution, they found the evil man had taken another captive.

Tonight, we free them.

And I volunteered as the curse breaker this time around.

"Okay. That's everything." Ame stands up, wiping her hands off on her overalls. A small fire burns with pungent herb-filled smoke, matching three more she lit around the circle. "Moon is high. Time to do this."

The aptly named Cold Moon is round in the night sky, its full glow blotting out the surrounding stars. Energy seems to spill from the orb, encouraging our casting. A shadow flits across the spotlight of the moon, and a soft hoot alerts us to the presence of an owl. Hopefully, it's not eyeing Bunny for a midnight meal.

One more reason to get this over with. The world is a dangerous place.

Despite how tiny the rabbit is, I feel like I can hear the animal's panting, terrified breaths from where I stand. Goose bumps trace over my skin, but not from the cold. There's a tug on my magic I normally only feel around distressed humans.

Calm them, the urge whispers in my mind.

Instead of staring directly at Bunny, I focus on the space around them. In the air where auras sometimes appear. When I relax my eyes, I spy the vivid orange of anxious terror.

Power pinches along my shoulders, a sensation born of my natural magical aptitude. All of us Shelly witches have abilities tied to emotions. Ame is desire, Anthony is jealousy, Mor has a more general connection to all emotions.

I sense fears and have the ability to soothe them.

I want more than anything to comfort this rabbit.

But before I can ask if that would interfere with the spell work, a black cat lopes into the circle, straight for Bunny. The feline curls its dark body around the shivering animal and starts up a soothing purr that rumbles through the quiet clearing.

"Thank you, Lucky," Ame calls out to her familiar. "She'll keep Bunny calm while we work." My sister points to a spot on the edge of the circle, sitting equally between two fires. "Here's where you go, Broderick. Probably best to kneel."

I do as she directed, and when Mor places the grimoire on the ground in front of me, I review the spell once more. An invention from sunder witches.

The curse breaker.

There's a hiss behind me, and I glance back in time to see blood well on Ame's thumb, where she nicked herself. Mor takes the knife and cuts her thumb too, then wipes the blade clean and hands it to me.

Each of them places their hand on my bare shoulder. They speak a string of words in the witch language, and I gasp as a shot of electricity races down my spine. Suddenly, my skin feels overly full of an abundance of power.

"Now," Ame, normally the softest spoken of us, commands.

As I read from the tome, I mimic her unwavering attitude. I chant the spell in an unrelenting tone I would never use in my daily life.

But tonight, I cannot waver. Cannot doubt or shy away.

"Take of my body. My blood to break," I say as I reach for the silver dagger lying innocently next to the grimoire.

The blade is warm when I drag it in a stinging slash across my palm. I hiss through my teeth at the painful bite of steel. With the flow of my blood, I feel the draw on my power. On all of our powers. Energy from Ame and Mor feeds into my body from where they clasp my shoulders.

"A curse before me," I say in the witch's tongue, "break it."

Then, I repeat myself, over and over, as the pain intensifies.

The injury on my hand burns more than a cut should, as if a hand were pressing hard on the wound. A corner of my brain is horrified at the realization my younger sister did this alone, no magical assistance. This agony would only have been amplified.

I'm determined not to bow to it.

"Break it," I growl in a voice I've never used before.

Fury rises fast in me, toward the dead sorcerer who forced this on an innocent mythic. The vile man made my sister suffer so she could free them.

Wind rustles the tree branches, the spindly limbs looking like grasping fingers in the night sky. The flames grow brighter as magic seeps from me. The scent of smoke and burning herbs is thick in the air. Lucky lets out a yowl and sprints from the middle of the circle.

But still, the rabbit doesn't change.

I will not fail in this. I will not fail them.

"Break it!" I snarl. "BREAK IT!" The words scream out of me with a rush of power, and the world goes white.

And like a switch being flicked, everything shuts off. The surge of magic, the bonfires, the ringing in my ears—it all ceases.

We're left in the forest clearing, under the light of the full moon, and the only sounds are an owl hooting and four people panting.

Four.

I push myself to my knees, having fallen forward in that last wave of power, and I cast my eyes to where the animal was once crouched. Bunny is gone.

A woman remains.

She sits on her knees, back bowed, head bent, hands held in front of her with fingers stretched wide. I watch as she flexes each one, as if testing their authenticity. Long blonde hair trails over her shoulders, only partly covering her nudity.

"Hello," I say, my voice cracking on the greeting.

Her head jerks up, gaze clashing with mine, and I swear her irises have their own golden light.

My sisters and I didn't discuss this. What to say when the curse was broken. We brought clothes because Ame had explained Jack was naked when he transformed. She also warned that there might be some attempted kissing, but that also could have been particular to Jack.

Honestly, if this woman wants to kiss someone, I volunteer.

Stop that. She is obviously terrified.

I can still see the toxic orange aura of fear around her.

Or wait ... is that her aura?

"You're safe," Ame informs her from over my shoulder.

"The sorcerer is dead," Mor adds.

The woman's eyes widen, and trembling overtakes her body. Just like when she was a rabbit. I want to say something to ease away that fear.

"I'm Broderick," I offer with what I hope is a disarming smile. I clear my throat, vocal cords ragged from screaming out spell words. "Nice to meet you."

She doesn't respond. Only shakes.

"We have clothes. And blankets."

The sound of movement behind me is probably one of my sisters grabbing those things, but I don't want to look away from our new arrival for even the moment it would take to check.

"We're here to help. Whatever you need. You've actually been living with us for the past month," I babble, not sure if my words are helping the situation. But something in me needs to keep her attention my way. "We live in a library, not far from here. There's room in the house, if you'd like to stay with us. Even with you taking up more space than you used to." I try for an easy smile, but the joke falls flat. Most of my jokes do. "I just meant, since you're a person now. Not a bunny. That's what we called you—Bunny. Only because we didn't know your name. You were a very cute bunny."

She flinches, and I immediately regret the comment. I should've left the talking to Ame and Mor.

"I'm not"—her voice crackles like the logs on a fire—"a bunny."

"No. Of course no—"

She bursts into flames.

Mor, who had stepped toward the woman with a blanket, stumbles to a stop. Meanwhile, I scramble forward, desperate for a way to put out the consuming fire.

"The flames are hers."

Ame's warning shout stops me when I'm inches away, hands stretched toward the fire, as if I could simply pat it out. Blood oozes from my open wound, dripping onto the grass between us.

The freed woman stares at me as she burns, but her skin doesn't char or melt.

"You're a phoenix?" I gasp the question, heart beating at a rapid, irregular rhythm.

As close as we are, I watch the emotions play across her face. Anger, pain, devastation, fear, fury...

"Not a phoenix." Her eyes leave mine to stare into the sky. "I am free."

She launches herself into the air, body changing as she rises. A flaming creature with wings that spread wide.

Mor walks up to my side, my shirt in her hand as her eyes watch the mythic disappear over the spindly, leafless treetops and spires of pine. "Phoenixes only catch on fire at the beginning and end of their life cycles." My librarian sister educates me in a distracted voice.

"Then, what is she?"

The farther she flies from my sight, the more my chest aches at what feels like a sudden loss.

"A firebird."

2

———————

BRODERICK

Six months later

I'VE MADE it a tradition at the end of each semester, when the final grades have been entered into the electronic system, to treat myself to a drink.

From the bottom-left drawer on my desk, the one I keep locked all semester long, I unearth my favorite brand of scotch. The amber liquid probably deserves to be poured into a beautiful crystal decanter, but all I have is my hastily cleaned *Read the Syllabus* mug. Oh well. At least, this way, if any stragglers happen by my office, I'll appear to be a responsible faculty member rather than a man getting tipsy on the job.

But I doubt anyone will see me. The students donned their graduation robes a week ago, and most of my colleagues are off enjoying their summer. Or at least finishing their grading at home. I prefer to work here, in my not-so-large office that has grown from organized to cluttered in a matter of months. I've only recently moved out of my room in the Folk Haven Public Mythic Library—aka Mor's Victorian house that she converted to hold all her magical texts. My rental is a small house on the edge of town, and with the hectic nature of starting a new job this semester, I haven't unpacked much more than my bed and my teapot.

The alcohol is heady on my tongue with a slight sting as it slips down my throat. I'm in the middle of savoring the subtle flavors with my eyes closed when there's a light knock on my door.

"Professor Shelly?"

Oh gods. Her. It's her.

I spin my chair so fast that some of my scotch sloshes over the rim of my mug and onto my hand. But who cares about booze when there's a vision in my doorway?

The firebird. The woman I haven't gone a day without thinking about since my sisters and I broke her curse.

"Ophelia." I gasp out her name, in love with the elegant sound of it ever since I learned the moniker.

She didn't fly far that night, just to an undeveloped plot of land owned by Moira MacNamara—local selkie and member of the Mythic Council. Because of Ophelia's rather spectacular display that evening, our small town's magical ruling body had to be notified in case any humans unaware that mythical creatures lived in Folk Haven saw her. But there were no calls to the local authorities about a fiery bird flying through the night sky, so the incident was contained.

Georgiana, a siren and the Of the Wing council member, took charge of Ophelia's care—all flying mythics are considered creations of The Winged One and therefore given the Of the Wing designation. One might argue a firebird is actually formed from The Bright One's hand, but there are so few fire-based mythics in Folk Haven that they don't have representation on the Mythic Council. Georgiana learned Ophelia's name, provided the mythic a place to stay, and helped her find a job.

A job that brings her by my office every Wednesday.

"Are you here for the recycling?" I ask. "I don't have any bins in my office."

The first time Ophelia showed up in the English department faculty offices, I about perished on the spot.

She wasn't a huddled, terrified woman on fire. She stood straight, her golden hair glossy and smoothed back in a ponytail and her glorious body clothed in fitted jeans and a Clean Haven Recycling polo shirt. But the firebird wouldn't meet my eyes or engage in conversation with me for more than a few words.

Ophelia is shy, and I am awkward.

Also, I'm pretty sure she'll always dislike me for that "cute bunny" comment.

I still curse myself for that horrible slip of the tongue.

"I already collected the bins." She waves over her shoulder toward the cart she trucks around Ramla University to dump the recycling in. "Can I talk to you?"

Talk to me?

There's nothing I want more in this universe. Instead of saying such a dramatically needy comment, I manage a much more respectable, "Of course."

Setting my mug of scotch on the far end of my desk—hoping she doesn't smell the booze on me—I hurry to clear student papers off the cushioned armchair in the corner of my room. I want to encourage student visits, which means having comfortable places to sit.

Ophelia silently watches my frantic movements, then settles on the edge of the chair when it's cleared. That's when I notice she's holding a notebook and a pen.

"How can I help you?" I ask as I resettle in my chair, at a loss for what she could want to discuss with me.

The longest conversation we've had was when I asked her about golden apple mythology. After a break-in at the library a few weeks ago, Ame found an apple hidden in a wall of the library that gave off intense power vibes, and according to legends, firebirds are fans of apples. But when Ophelia was done telling me one of the stories she knew, the woman scampered off, making it clear she liked to spend as little time in my presence as possible.

No need to focus on how that feels like a jagged wound to the gut.

She clicks her pen, tosses her golden ponytail over her shoulder, and flips open the cover of her journal. The academic preparation has my blood pumping hot through my veins.

"Could you please tell me some things that Jack Lim likes?"

She waits, pen poised, eyes on her paper, unaware of the spiraling despair in my brain.

She likes Jack? She's here, asking me for advice on how to get to know Jack better?

Of course she likes the guy. He's got that brooding werewolf energy that I could never re-create if I tried. I'm one hundred percent nerdy witch professor, and there's no changing that.

Still, though I have no illusions it'll raise my level of attractiveness in her eyes, I need to point out the obvious.

"I'm sorry, Ophelia. Jack's in a relationship. With my sister Ame. And he's ... well, he's kind of obsessed with her. Like bordering on unhealthy. But if you tell him I said that, I'll deny it because I want to keep my head on my shoulders." The man has used decapitation before. "All this to say, you're an amazing woman any person would be lucky to earn the affection of, but Jack's not the best candidate."

The firebird stares at me now instead of her paper, golden-brown eyes widening further as I ramble. My mouth loves to ramble around her.

"I'm not trying to seduce Jack," she says when I finally shut up, her voice soft and melodic. "I want to get him a gift. Because he helped me. By taking part in slaying the sorcerer."

"Oh. Oh. Yes. Right. Well, that makes sense." I clear my throat. "And I'm an ass."

Ophelia's plush lips twitch in the hint of a smile. "You can redeem yourself by helping me." She taps her journal.

"Of course. What does Jack like?" I lean back in my chair, twine my fingers together, and rest them on my stomach. My pondering pose, one student called it. "Well, as I mentioned, he likes Ame. A lot. Probably more than anything else."

Ophelia raises her notes, turning them to face me. *Ame* is written in a lovely slanting script, underlined multiple times with stars around the name.

"Got it."

I grin and think more on my brother-in-law. "He likes technology. He and his friend Niko watch soccer sometimes. He eats an ungodly amount of bacon every day. Hopefully, werewolves cannot develop high cholesterol."

Ophelia bites her bottom lip, as if fighting off a smile as she flips a page. "And what does Ame like?"

"Jack," I say, and my chest warms when Ophelia snorts. But it's true. My sister isn't as obvious about it, but I can tell she's gone for the man. "She loves animals, especially her familiar, Lucky." I almost add *whom you've met*, but am proud of myself for stopping and remembering that Ophelia probably wants to avoid talk of her time trapped as a rabbit. "She also enjoys tech. Oh, and action movies." I list off a few of her favorites. "Funny thing, they all star bald men. The other night, I overheard Jack asking if she wants him to shave off his hair."

Ophelia gasps out a chuckle. "Oh no. Jack has such nice hair." She waves toward my head. "Not as good as yours though."

Silence falls between us as Ophelia's sun-tanned cheeks

flush a deep red, and I make a silent vow to never cut my hair again.

Do you want to touch it? I long to ask. *Comb your fingers through it?*

I'd curl at her feet for a chance to receive that kind of affection from her.

She drops her eyes and flips to a new page. "Do you know Niko?" She names Jack's best friend and the kappa who rents one of the free rooms in the library.

I've said hi to the guy plenty of times when we lived in the same space, but he worked late hours at a restaurant in town, so we didn't cross paths much.

"Not well. Best you ask Jack."

Ophelia nods and makes a note. "Mor. What does she like?"

"Books, coffee ..." I rattle off a few more things as Ophelia writes each down. "I can tell you about Anthony too. But he was still avoiding magic back then, so he didn't do much to help." I keep my voice light and joking.

My twin has changed his tune, working through his hang-ups after he fell in love with Zara Ironfeather—the town vet and a proud harpy.

Ophelia gives a slight headshake, then leans forward in her seat. In the small office, the change in position almost feels like she's crowding me. Or it would if I didn't have the overwhelming urge to pull her into my lap.

"Next, I want to know what *you* like."

"Me?" I croak, struggling with words and thoughts and breathing when her eyes hold mine.

She ignores my discomfort, never releasing me from her stare.

Which is why I only manage one word.

"You."

3

—————

OPHELIA

"You."

I watch as the witch's pale skin turns as red as his fiery hair. Even flustered, the man is handsomer than any other I've ever encountered. Even his twin cannot compare. There's something about Broderick Shelly that puts me at ease. I think it has to do with his genuine nature.

Or that he's bad at lying.

Maybe those two are the same thing in a way.

All I know is that I don't feel unsure of any of the words that he speaks to me. Every time Broderick opens his mouth, there is a resounding ring of undeniable truth. And not even a harsh truth.

He seems kind.

I have not experienced much kindness in my life.

And so, hearing him, with his genuine nature, answer my question with the simple *you* fills me with comfort.

And also guilt.

The man, seeming to have realized how much his one-

256

worded statement might reveal, continues to babble in a way that he does often.

"You ... know ... *you know*, I like things that most people like. I like ... pens. And paper. And mugs." As Broderick lists off these objects, I watch his green eyes flit around his desk.

I do my best to fight a smile, but feel the expression curving my lips nonetheless.

"You seem to have many of the things that you like in your office already." My voice is as matter-of-fact as I can manage.

It feels good to make a joke. A subtle one though it may be.

I want to be able to laugh. I want to be able to see the humor in the world.

I don't want my days to be long stretches of twisted anxiety anymore.

Broderick clears his throat and fiddles with one of the buttons on his dress shirt. He is always dressed well. Not necessarily strikingly or sporting high-fashion designs, the way that his twin brother does. But the witch is usually wearing an ironed shirt and a nice set of pants and only slightly scuffed loafers. It's a professor look I see many of the faculty at Ramla University opt for. But the style looks best on him.

"Yes, well, I prefer to surround myself with things I like." As Broderick finishes making the statement, his eyes land on me, and it suddenly becomes impossible to ignore how close we are in this cramped office of his.

I want to ask if he would consider surrounding himself with me.

You don't deserve to think of him like that, I remind myself.

Now, I feel heat rising underneath my own skin, but my mortification comes from a harsher place. Broderick should not feel shame about saying kind things about me. I deserve his derision after how horribly I reacted when he freed me from that terrible curse. The man had cut himself open to help me.

Even now, I can see the scar of his sacrifice puckered on his palm. The witch cast painful magic for a stranger.

And I snarled at him. I fled from him.

And to this day, six months later, I still have not said *thank you*.

Every time I come to the university for my job, I tell myself that I will walk into his office and I will say it. It's so simple. It *should* be so simple. And yet there is a part of me, deep in a damaged corner of my soul, that is terrified of saying those words aloud. Even after all these years, with a great distance from my past, I'm scared of what will be demanded of me once I speak them.

The sorcerer might have kept me captive, but someone else broke parts of me before I ever met that evil man.

Emotional scars from my childhood remain.

And so, if I cannot speak my thanks, then I will find another way to show my gratitude to the group of mythics who ended my most recent torment.

Gifts.

I enjoy the idea of handing something special to each person to show them, even if it's through a small act, that I understand what they did for me.

"Happy hour."

I blink myself away from haunted memories and refocus on the witch in front of me. He blurted the two words, and I adore how the redness, having nowhere left on his face to stain, creeps up to his ears. A daring part of me wants to lean further forward and press my lips to the heated skin to feel if it scorches like my internal fire.

But I keep my mouth to myself and only ask, "Happy hour?"

Broderick picks up a pen from his desk, tapping it in an anxious rhythm. And because I am currently working against a bout of anxiety too—a state I am never far from—I somehow find the repetitive noise soothing.

"This Friday, if you're free, you could join my family for happy hour. We have it on the dock behind the library now that the weather is nice. If you have any gifts that you want to give to people, that might be a good time to find them in an easy mood. And I'll be there." Broderick, seeming to realize his pen tapping has grown a touch frantic, tosses the writing utensil on his desk. "Not that that's a selling point. But I thought I might mention it."

Happy hour.

Spending time with peers.

Making friends.

All things I have never gotten a chance to do. And I want to so badly.

But will my mind let me relax enough to engage?

After six months of being free, I still feel like life is on the thinnest knife edge, cutting me when I wobble. But I'm used to pain. And pain in pursuit of happiness seems worth it.

"I'll think about it."

He smiles, and my heart rate quickens. I stand from my chair abruptly, feeling the shaking in my fingers that lets me know I need time to myself. Time to breathe. Time to remind my soul that I won't be trapped again.

But before I leave, I want to give the babbling witch something that I believe he might consider to be a gift.

"Just so you know, for me, you *are* a selling point."

BRODERICK

I wait until Ophelia is gone before I collapse back in my chair and let out a groan of embarrassment. The sound arises from deep in my chest, carrying with it every mortifying thing I said back up to my brain to replay on a loop. A self-torture I don't know how to escape from.

"Broderick?"

I snap upright, trying to fling my body into a not-embarrassing position as I realize that Ophelia is at my office door. Again. Staring at me.

The firebird definitely heard my self-pity groan.

"Are you okay?" she asks, both of her golden brows raised in concern.

"Ah, yes. Good. Very good."

Oh gods. Now, she's going to think it was a good groan instead of an embarrassed one. Her imagination will start filling in all the *very good* things I could have been doing right after she left to make me feel like that.

So, I panic.

"I mean, bad. Just a moment ago, I was bad. Because I hurt myself."

She frowns and steps forward. "On purpose?"

"No. Just stubbed my knee. I mean, knocked my toe." If a portal opened and sucked me into a hell dimension right now, I would welcome it. "Both those things. At once. Which is why I made that noise. But I have a fast recovery time."

Seriously, gods, if you would like to smite me, I would be eternally grateful.

"Oh. Okay." Ophelia tilts her head as she studies me, and the gesture appears almost birdlike. But something an adorable, beautiful bird would do. "Sorry to bother you again, but I wondered if you would mind giving me your phone number?"

"Mind? No. Never. I would never mind that."

If someone overheard the way I spoke when Ophelia was nearby, they would never believe that I worked as a professor who regularly gave class lectures. Especially not lectures about how to use the English language effectively.

"That's good to know." She reaches into her back pocket and pulls out her phone, swipes it open, and hands it over to me.

"It's an owl," I say, once again showing my superior level of intelligence. But I'm surprised by the image she has set as her background.

Ophelia sidles closer, and I bite back a moan when I realize the firebird smells like cinnamon. She leans over my shoulder, and her ponytail swings forward, brushing my cheek. I think I might die right here, in my chair.

"He's cute, right?" She pinches her fingers on the screen to zoom in on the round-faced barn owl. "I like to take walks at twilight, and he joins me sometimes. I wish we could fly together."

"Why can't you?"

Her lips twist. "Georgiana says my fire is too bright. Even for dark moon nights."

Georgiana can go fuck herself. Ophelia spent however long being trapped in the wrong body, and now, someone is telling her she isn't allowed to be her full self in a town of mythical creatures?

Not happening.

"We can find ways around that." I don't know how yet, but I'm determined to figure it out. "A cloaking spell maybe. Or we'll go to a more remote part of Lake Galen, where humans aren't allowed. You're not the only fire being in town. The Mythic Council might already have a solution."

Ophelia straightens while I talk, and her fingers tangle in the ends of her ponytail. "Georgiana is on The Council."

Much to Mor's consternation. Last year, there was an election for the Of the Wing seat on the Mythic Council. My sister thought for sure someone would unseat the siren with her antiquated notions of how Folk Haven should be managed. But the siren is a charming woman with deep ties to the Of the Wing community. She ran unopposed.

"Which means she should help you find a solution. Not shut you down."

Ophelia makes a noise in the back of her throat that's not quite agreement. But I'm not about to back off this issue unless she tells me to. For the moment, I'll leave it alone, but I have all summer to work on whatever project I want before classes start again in the fall.

Discovering a way to make Ophelia happy seems like a good use of my time.

I navigate to her Contacts list so I can add my name. There, I get another shock.

Finn Hammond

Georgiana Stormwind

Owen MacNamara

Her boss, her landlord and Council representative, and her other boss.

And that's it. Those three.

Ophelia has three people listed in her phone.

"You just click that thingy, I think." Ophelia points at the plus symbol, sounding only partially sure.

Is Ophelia new to using cell phones?

As I add my contact information, I do some mental math.

Jack escaped from the sorcerer three years ago and said he was almost certain he was the only captive the man had at the time. Which means even if Ophelia was taken the day after Jack broke free, she should have lived in the world when cell phones existed.

Unless Jack was wrong. Unless Ophelia was a captive for much longer than we assumed.

I want to ask so many questions, about her captivity and age and knowledge of the world. But I want to know even more than that. Like how she's coping. Does she like her job? Does she want to keep living with Georgiana?

Are those spikes of orange in her aura normal anxiety or a constant wear at her psyche?

Maybe this exchange of numbers means the firebird might open up to me. Eventually. Now is not the time to pry.

But there is one question that's reasonable to ask.

I send myself a quick text.

"Now, I have your number too." I hand her back her phone. "I'm sorry. I just realized I've only ever called you Ophelia. I don't know your last name."

Until that moment, I didn't realize the firebird had started to relax around me. I know now because her entire body goes stiff and a flood of orange that isn't mystical fire burns in the air around her.

"No last name. Just Ophelia."

She disappears from my office, taking every ounce of warmth with her.

4

OPHELIA

THE NEATLY WRAPPED boxes fit easily in my cloth tote bag. Though my thanks are big, I'm glad I went small for size. This way, I won't overwhelm happy hour by stumbling onto the dock with an armful of gifts. They can be unobtrusive.

Like me.

I know my voice is soft, and my body has a tendency to curl in on itself. Most times, I can't help it.

Years of conditioning are hard to circumvent.

When I check over my appearance in the mirror once more and see nothing else to be fixed or altered, I know I'm wasting time as I work up my nerve.

You can do this. You can make friends.

I meet my eyes in my reflection and let my power out enough for a flicker of gold to show in the irises. The small rebellion I allowed myself all through my childhood.

"I'm in control of my own life," I remind myself out loud.

And with that declaration, I pick up my bag and head downstairs.

"There you are, Ophelia! I thought you'd hide in your room all night, silly girl." Georgiana strolls up to me with a wide smile that matches her perfectly tailored attire.

The siren is a beautiful Southern belle, blonde hair arranged in perfect waves around her meticulously made-up face. She has on a yellow day dress that makes me think of butter.

"You can help set the table for dinner. Richard has some friends coming over, and I can't wait for you to meet them."

"Oh." I wrap both of my hands around the straps of my bag. "I'm sorry. I have plans. If I had known, I wouldn't have made them."

Apologizing and lying come easy. I spent years doing both.

If I actually wanted to attend whatever dinner party Georgiana is hosting, I easily could. I only told Broderick that I would *think* about attending happy hour.

The corners of her eyes tighten, but her smile remains. "That is unfortunate. I told them all you would be here. Everyone was looking forward to meeting you."

That makes the event even less appealing. I don't want to be stared at by strangers who find me intriguing for whatever details Georgiana shared about me.

The siren continues, "With you living in our house—rent-free—for so long, I would have thought you'd also want to take part in our household." The unspoken message: *You should want to do what I say because of what I have done for you.*

I've always found it strange how the people who loudly claim to be charitable always expect a return on their supposed good works.

"I can pay rent," I offer, not for the first time.

My job pays well. Enough that I've begun keeping an eye out for *For Rent* signs. Next week, I am hoping to go to Folk Haven Realty on my lunch break to start an official search.

I want out of this house.

"No, dear. There's no need." Georgiana expertly folds her face into disappointment. I know this tactic well. "What are these plans you have that are more important than saying hello to our friends?"

Despite being aware of the manipulation Georgiana is using, I still feel a familiar twist in my gut. The insistent urge to do whatever pleases her. To tuck away my own wants and needs to make sure she is happy. The siren has been supportive since I returned to my true form. Giving me a place to live. Explaining how things work in this small, mythic-filled town. She even tried to get me a job at her husband's doctor's office, but my lack of tech knowledge would've required much more training than collecting recycling for Clean Haven did.

Those were kind gestures, but I don't owe her my life.

"I'm going to the Mythic Public Library," I say, forcing my spine straight when I realize I started to slouch forward in a form of defense. "The Shellys invited me to happy hour."

Georgiana's face sours before she smooths the wrinkled expression away. "Really, Ophelia? If you're going to abandon us, at least spend your time with other Of the Wing mythics. Not those strange witches."

My hackles rise, but in the same way I can't manage to say *thank you*, I also can't seem to force *it's rude to talk about decent people like that* past my lips.

"They saved me," is as much of a defense as I can muster.

Georgiana scoffs and waves her hand in a dismissive gesture. "I'm sure that horrid spell would've worn off on its own with that sorcerer being dead. If you ask me, those Shellys put you at risk, working more magic on you."

The siren lets a tempting smile take over her lovely face. "If happy hour is what you want, then I have some specialty cocktails that'll have you singing and dancing by the end of the night. So strong that you'll forget all your worries."

That does *not* sound appealing. At least not among a group of strangers who apparently find the idea of me fascinating.

Instead of turning her down flat, I reach into my bag and pull out a little box. "I'm sorry. I can't. But I made this for you." I press the box into her manicured hands.

She blinks in surprise. "You made something for me?"

I nod as I shuffle toward the front door. "I hope you like it. Good night."

Then, I turn and hurry out of the siren's beautiful house before she can tempt me to stay with more guilt. Too much of my life has been dictated by manipulation.

I need to practice making my own choices.

And tonight, I choose Broderick Shelly.

5

BRODERICK

"Do you have something wrong with your neck?" Anthony's voice pulls my attention back to our happy hour gathering.

My brother and the rest of the group have their eyes on me.

Heat pools in my cheeks. "No."

"Then, why do you keep jerking around?" Anthony lounges in the chair across from mine, absentmindedly petting Sin, his black rat snake familiar. The creature has its long body coiled in his lap and flicks a forked tongue out every so often, as if tasting the air.

"No reason." I try to affect nonchalance as I brush nonexistent lint off my shirt. "Just thought I heard something."

My brother narrows his eyes at me. "You are a terrible liar."

I ignore his comment and probing stare, pretending as though the lake has my full attention. The view is gorgeous. Lake Galen sprawls before us, and gentle waves rock the floating dock our group has gathered on. A hawk dives to pluck a fish from the water. On the opposite tree-lined shore, a group of deer weaves through the forest. An oddly familiar barn owl perches on a branch above the herd and lets out the occasional hoot.

Could that be Ophelia's owl friend?

Out on the water, I spy a pontoon boat slowly cruising, the setting sun reflecting off the frothing wake it leaves as it passes. At the growing rumble of an engine, I assume another boat is approaching. But then there's the crunch of gravel, and once again, I'm flinging my attention back toward the house.

"I thought Zara was working late," Moira says, the comment directed at Anthony as she references his mate.

"She is. Paperwork," Ame answers from where she sits in Jack's lap.

Zara is my sister's boss at the town's veterinarian practice.

"I tried to seduce her away from work," Anthony adds. "But apparently, my skills are fading. I blame small-town living."

"Who else is invited?" Niko asks the question everyone is wondering.

Everyone but me.

She came.

"I'll go check!" I launch out of my chair and jog away from the group before anyone can offer to accompany me.

When I reach the driveway, I discover Ophelia climbing out of a truck that looks like it's older than she is. The paint job is chipped and rusted, the body of the vehicle is boxy, and the bumper was clearly replaced at some point yet still has a handful of dents. But when she slams the door closed, I watch her turn and pat the hood, as if the vehicle were a loyal hound. Ophelia seems almost proud of the old truck.

While I turn the idea over in my mind, I study the woman in front of me and remind myself that the firebird has made no mention of her time before the sorcerer. As if she wants to forget more than just her time in captivity.

And I wonder what it must be like to start life over from scratch. To have everything you own given to you.

How that might make you want to earn something on your own.

I'd lay money down that Ophelia bought the truck soon after getting her first few paychecks from Clean Haven. Which makes it hers more than anything the town or Georgiana has given her.

"You made it!" I call out when I get closer.

Ophelia jumps, as if spooked, and I feel an immediate wash of guilt. Especially when she turns to face me and her cheeks are flushed red and there are flashes of orange in her aura.

"I did. I'm here." Her voice is tight, and so is the grip she has on her bag.

I want to focus on how I can avoid upsetting her, but I'm having trouble forcing my brain to think past the simple way she looks.

Ophelia has on a sundress. A deep red color with little white flowers. The material hugs her chest and gently flares at her waist, giving only a hint at the curve of her hips. Her hair is down. A golden screen falling over her shoulders that she pushes back to reveal two slim straps holding her outfit up.

Gods, this firebird will incinerate me.

"Hello," I croak.

Ophelia tilts her head, and her lips purse. "Are you okay? You sound sick."

"Good. I'm good." I clear my throat and tuck my hands in my pockets to keep from reaching for her. "We're all down at the dock."

She nods and steps to my side. We walk quietly together toward the group. As we approach, they aren't even trying to pretend like they aren't watching us.

"Will they mind that I'm here?" Ophelia whispers the question to me.

"No. Not at all. We like when new people show up. Gives us

someone new to interrogate." I try for the suave, teasing tone that my twin is so good at.

Ophelia stops abruptly, her knuckles white on the straps of her bag. "I-I don't want to talk about me." She takes a step backward. "I should—"

"Wait. I'm sorry. That was a joke. A bad one." I hold out my hands, palms up in supplication. "I'm bad at jokes. Anthony is the funny, charming one. I'm the awkward one."

Ophelia stares at me, her eyes wide as I babble. When I cut myself off, silence lingers between us for the stretch of one heartbeat. Then two. At three, I'm sure I've ruined things.

"I don't have to talk about myself?" she finally asks.

I try not to be obvious about my sigh of relief.

"Not if you don't want to." I nod toward the two empty chairs on the dock, one of which I was just occupying. "You can just sit and relax and listen to us chatter. And you can leave whenever you want." I lean toward her, lowering my voice. "Jack doesn't talk either unless Ame asks him a question."

Ophelia nods, and I thank the gods when she starts walking toward the dock again. This time, I let her get a step ahead of me, and when we reach the gangplank, I give everyone a warning glare that I hope they properly interpret.

Do not scare the firebird, I demand with my eyes.

"Everybody," I call out even though their attention is already on us, "this is Ophelia. Ophelia, some of these might be a reminder, but this is Mor, Anthony, Niko, Ame, and Jack."

There's a chorus of greetings, and Ophelia detaches a hand from her bag strap long enough to offer a wave.

Ame slips out of Jack's lap—ignoring his grumble of protest—and opens a cooler.

"What would you like to drink? We have water, beer, seltzers, and cider."

Ophelia focuses all her attention on Ame. "Cider, please."

Ame pulls out a bottle, pops the cap, then places it on the small table between the two chairs left open.

Then, my younger sister turns to Mor. "Have you decided if you're helping with Galen's Gauntlet again this year?"

And with that, talk turns toward the magical competition held in Folk Haven every other summer and away from Ophelia. The firebird settles into her seat and sips her cider, the tension in her shoulders easing as time goes by and no one asks her any probing questions. Slowly, the anxious orange in her aura fades from neon to pastel.

I wonder what had her retreating. Did she think we would ask questions about her traumatic time as the sorcerer's captive?

Or was it more than that?

This week, I've played multiple facts over and over in my head. First, the small number of names in Ophelia's phone. The firebird has been in Folk Haven for six months, and she hasn't made any connections, it seems, outside of work and her living situation.

Then, there's her lack of a last name and past life.

Jack mentioned his memory of the time spent as a cat had plenty of holes in it, but not of his life before his capture. He could recall growing up in California with his mother and best friend, Niko. He told us about the werewolf pack he attempted to join, but who ended up selling him to a sorcerer to fuel the man's twisted magic.

Turned out, it was only one member of the pack that betrayed him, and the rest have done their best to earn his forgiveness. The wolves even relocated to Folk Haven, much to the consternation of the established pack. But that's a can of worms I plan to stay far away from.

All this shows that Ophelia should have memories of her years before she was turned into a rabbit and used by that evil man.

Could it be that her time prior to captivity was bad in a different way? Was she betrayed, like Jack was?

Or is there simply nothing left from before?

As much as I want to know, I keep my curiosity to myself. Ophelia doesn't owe me anything, especially not explanations of her past trauma.

"I just can't commit to it," Mor sighs, and I refocus on the conversation. "The Gauntlet planning takes up so much time. And depending on the spells, a lot of energy too. I have a library to run, my magical object studies, and I still need to figure out our statue problem."

"Statue problem?" This soft question comes from Ophelia, and I try not to vibrate with happiness that she's engaging in the conversation.

Mor gestures toward a thick stand of trees to the left of the library. "There's a statue garden there. Metal sculptures created by the dragon who used to live in this house." The library was previously a residence only, and from the outside, it still appears to be a regal Victorian house. "There is one statue though that I think might be alive in some way. But frozen. I want to make sure it isn't someone who's trapped."

Ophelia goes tense once more, and Mor grimaces, no doubt realizing she brought up the very worst topic.

"Oh, look! Lucky is here!" Ame proclaims much louder than she normally would as her black cat familiar strolls onto the dock. My sister gets up again, earning another unhappy grunt from Jack, which she ignores. Ame scoops up her feline and strolls over to Ophelia. "Do you remember Lucky? She loves to cuddle."

"Oh, yes. I remember." The firebird seems perfectly content to allow my sister to set the animal in her lap before Ame strolls back to Jack.

The werewolf wraps a set of strong arms around his mate's

waist and holds her tight against him—a clear command to stay put.

I wish I could hold Ophelia like that.

I gaze at the firebird, who now strokes a purring Lucky under the chin. Ophelia has on a soft smile and leans close to the cat to whisper something only the animal can hear. The familiar purrs louder and butts her head against Ophelia's hand.

Once again, the woman is at ease.

The topic of discussion turns away from trapped beings and toward Niko's plan to open a new restaurant in town, then the happenings at Ramla during the summer months, and next what Halloween Ball dress designs Anthony is working on with Esme—a local harpy who runs a tailoring business—even though the celebration is still months away.

The more we chat, the more I notice Ophelia relaxes out of the corner of my eye. It's a struggle not to stare at her constantly, but I don't want to unnerve her. She only drinks the one cider, savoring it, and when her bottle is done, she switches to water. Lucky stays in her lap the entire time, eventually curling up and falling asleep.

I try not to be jealous of the cat.

When the sun is just about to sink below the horizon, Ophelia finally removes Lucky from her lap. She brushes cat hair from her dress and offers a soft smile to the group.

"I should go. I don't like to drive in the dark."

"Of course." I hurry to stand beside her, but she doesn't move to leave yet.

"I have something. Tokens. I made them."

In the twilight, I can still see the way a blush creeps over her cheeks.

Ophelia reaches into her bag and pulls out a small box, which she hands to Mor. "For contributing your power to break the curse. And for gathering the grimoires."

Ophelia offers a tiny, wrapped gift to Niko, which he accepts with cradled hands. "For assisting the attack. The rescue."

She pulls out another box for Ame. "For your power. And for finding the spell in the first place."

The firebird digs out one more gift and extends her offering to Jack, who holds out a large palm to accept. "For coming back," she whispers. "And for ending him."

Before anyone can respond, Ophelia turns on her heel and hurries off the dock.

I follow her, jogging to keep up. But I don't call out because I have no idea what to say. The words she spoke were simple and profound. Full of pain and graciousness.

When we reach her truck, she doesn't immediately climb in. Instead, Ophelia whirls to face me, her white-knuckled fingers clutching another small container with a tiny bow.

"For you." She presses it into my chest. "I was horrible to you that night. I regret it. You bled for me. You saved me."

"It was nothing," I mutter.

"It was *everything*." Ophelia steps in close, her chin lifting, her golden eyes taking mine hostage. "Can I ... can I hug you?"

She wants to touch me?

"Yes," I rasp. "Anytime. Anywhere. For as long as you want."

Ophelia leans fully into me, wrapping her arms tight around my torso. Her arms are strong and warm. She smells like cinnamon and ginger and fireplaces on cold winter nights.

"Can I hug you back?" My entire being aches with the need to gather her close to me.

"Please," she whispers.

Thank The Dark One.

I enfold the firebird in an eager embrace, one hand splayed on her lower back, the other grasping a shoulder. And for too short of a time, she allows me to hold her close.

When Ophelia finally pulls away, I'm horrified to see tears streaming down her face.

"You're crying," I point out, as if she doesn't know.

Her smile is sad as she brushes her fingers across her cheeks, collecting droplets of moisture. "You make me feel like I can. Like I don't have to hide it."

"You don't." *Gods, what has this woman gone through?*

But I refuse to press her. Instead, I hold up the box. "Can I open this?"

"When I'm gone." Ophelia pulls out her keys. "It's just sand and heat. Something I learned when I was younger."

I wait until her taillights disappear before turning back toward the dock, walking slowly as I savor the sensation of her hug and her trust. There's a soft, steady sound above my head, and I realize the owl has appeared again, settling on a branch that's only slightly higher than my head.

When the bird coos, I experience a surprising wave of contentment flow through my body. As if the animal has the same soothing magic that I do.

But that can't be right. I must be imagining things.

Still, I give the bird a nod, then continue walking toward the lake.

"Where did she get these?" Mor asks the moment I step onto the sun-bleached wood.

I glance over to see my older sister cradling a small glass book. The thing looks so fragile with its flipping pages. Niko examines a wolf in mid-howl, his own mouth slack with wonder. My eyes trace to Ame, who holds a glass cat out for Lucky to explore. Jack still has one arm wrapped around my sister's waist, but in his other hand, he holds a glass replica of her.

"She made them." I understand now.

Heat and sand.

Together, they make glass.

I slip the lid off my box and find a glass firebird nestled inside.

6

OPHELIA

THE WEDNESDAY after the happy hour at the Shellys' house, I approach Broderick's office with a sense of optimistic anticipation. Though I try not to get my hopes too high. For one thing, the witch might not even be here. It's the summer semester, and many professors abandon their offices entirely. Of course, if he's *not* here, then I could theoretically send him a message with my phone.

I still feel strange, using the device. I always knew they existed when I was growing up, but my father never let me have one.

My father didn't let me have a lot of things.

I push away those sharp memories and focus on the future. Focus on something new and exciting. Something to prove that I am not that girl who was given to a sorcerer.

I spy a light on in Broderick's office and smile. My body remembers the feel of his arms wrapped around me. How his hold was comforting.

More than that, Broderick's embrace was hot. His body was

the perfect kind of heat that called to my inner firebird and enticed me to sink into him.

But I'm not sure I can be with someone that way. I don't have any practice. I don't have any experience. Not with romance.

Not with affection in general really.

Not since my mother and my aunt. But those memories are from so long ago that I'm not sure how accurate they even are. Maybe my mind made up a version of those two women that I could use to comfort myself in the harder moments.

Realizing I've begun to tug on the end of my ponytail in an agitated gesture, I let my hand drop and take a calming breath. Then, I knock on the door of the witch's office and watch his crimson head pop up at the sound. An entrancing grin spreads across his honest face.

I could get addicted to this man. I might already be.

"Ophelia! You're here!"

His cheeks flush a dark red, as if he's embarrassed, but there's no need for him to be rueful about such an enthusiastic greeting. It warms me to know that Broderick likes seeing me. That the eagerness I feel whenever I know he's near is shared.

"I'm here," I agree. "Do you mind if I come in?"

"Not at all. Take a seat." The professor turns in his desk chair as he makes the offer, facing me fully.

I know that Broderick means the soft chair in the corner, but I wish he were offering his thighs as a spot to perch. The memory of Ame cuddled up in Jack's lap on the dock comes back to me. The ease with which they shared that innocently intimate embrace. I crave that closeness with another.

I crave that closeness with Broderick.

But I also know what it's like to have power taken from you. To have people act without asking. So, I won't settle on his lap just because the impulse takes me. Just like I did not hug him after that happy hour just because I wanted it more than anything in the world. I asked him first and was honored when he said yes.

I settle in the chair, deeper this time, more comfortable in this cozy office. Broderick leans toward me with his elbows braced on his knees, eyes alight with curiosity. As if he finds me fascinating.

I don't like the idea of others being fascinated with me. If people find me interesting, they'll ask questions about me. They'll want to dig into my past. They'll want to know about what happened with the sorcerer. They'll want to know what happened *before* the sorcerer.

Both of those times in my life should stay buried until I can convince myself they are forgotten.

But Broderick hasn't pried into my past. Maybe he could be fascinated by the person that I *am*. Even if that person is relatively new.

"I was hoping you could explain something to me," I say. "Something that your siblings were discussing on Friday."

"Of course. What are you interested in?"

"Galen's Gauntlet."

The event they brought up, asking if Mor might contribute to it, seemed like a competition of some kind. A challenge. And it wasn't the first time I'd heard of the Gauntlet. Georgiana was talking on the phone to someone about the event. The woman seemed to be one of the organizers. But when I asked her about it, she said it was only for sirens and witches to plan. And that I shouldn't worry about anything related to such a dangerous pastime.

The dismissiveness of her response irked me. The reminder that I am still anxious and skittish.

Like a rabbit.

As much as I hate my ever-present fear, I can't deny that I'm easily startled. That I constantly risk getting overwhelmed.

I'm weak and quivering from my time with the sorcerer, an

insidious voice whispers in my head. *So, how could I ever be considered strong enough to participate in even a recreational activity that might have a touch of danger to it?*

I don't want to be thought of that way anymore. I don't want to *be* that way anymore.

My fear infuriates me.

What if this new beginning means more than just escaping a bad situation? What if this chance to start over means finally claiming control of my life?

If I'm going to stake a claim as the new Ophelia, then what better way than to prove I will not be cowed in a simple competition?

"Oh, yes. Galen's Gauntlet." Broderick leans back in his chair and takes on a tone I suspect he uses when lecturing his students. "Admittedly, I have never seen one. I moved here after the last one took place. They happen every two years in July, and I believe they are related to the founding of the town. I'm sure I could find out more information on the history if that interests you. But as to what the Gauntlet is now, it is a competition. From what Mor and Ame described to me about the last one, it is a race of sorts, but filled with magical obstacles that competitors need to maneuver through. The victor is the one who reaches the finish line first, and they hold a position of honor in town for the following two years. They win some money. But it also takes money in order to enter the competition."

That last comment—about costing money to enter—gives me pause. I shouldn't be surprised. Most human competitions require money to enter them. Why should a magical one be any different?

Every dollar I earn from my job is precious to me. This is the first time I'm making money of my own. And the more I save, the closer I am to creating a home of my own. To becoming a self-reliant woman.

But a part of that self-reliance is also emotional. Mental. How can I truly feel at home without first proving to myself that I am not the weak girl that I once was? That control of my life is mine?

"Anyone can compete?" I ask, envisioning my bank account and estimating how much I can spare without making an uncomfortably large dent.

"Sirens can't compete because they organize the whole thing. My understanding is that any witch who contributes to the obstacle course cannot participate—so that would have included Mor last time. Also, if you are mated to someone who takes part in the organization of the competition, you are ineligible. That is a new rule after the last competition, where the selkie who won was mated to one of the sirens. Not that anyone believes Seamus got a leg up on the competition. No one other than ..." Broderick trails off, and from the expression on his face, I can see he's hesitant about sharing who exactly has an issue with the previous winner.

"Who was it?" I press, curious about any drama occurring in the town. I spent all of my life in some form of isolation, so I find I'm wildly curious about the details of Folk Haven residents. "Who thinks he cheated?"

Broderick grimaces, but he still answers, "Georgiana. And a few other sirens she is close to. They were furious when they found out in the middle of the competition that a siren song didn't affect him in the same way that it did the rest of the competitors. To be fair, I heard Seamus didn't seem to realize it either. Word is, his mate—Neri, who owns the local bookshop —was pissed at him and wasn't speaking to him at all, and he entered the Gauntlet to win her over. That's not a guy who's about to cheat. Anyway, turned out, she was in love with him, and if a siren loves you, then their song doesn't discombobulate you the way it does with everyone else."

Interesting. I'm not particularly surprised about that infuriating Georgiana. After living with the siren for so many months, I can easily see her being judgmental of a change in the norm.

But enough gossip. Back to planning.

"Other than not being affected by siren song, what do you think are the skills competitors need in order to make it through the Gauntlet?"

Broderick relaxes further in his chair, settling his hands over his torso, long fingers twining together. Their length fascinates me, and I sometimes wonder what it would be like to have those fingers trace over my skin. To be touched by him in a way that I haven't been touched before.

Unaware of my thoughts, Broderick answers my question. "Well, one of the rules is that competitors cannot overtly use their magical abilities. That means no shifting from shifters. No spells from witches and such. However, lots of mythics still have natural advantages. Superior strength and stamina. Those competitors tend to have an advantage in some challenges because of their speed and ability to potentially fight off things they might come up against. But there is a mental element. Puzzles to solve. Oh, and of course, everyone needs the ability to swim."

My stomach sinks.

As quickly as *I* would if thrown into a body of water.

"Why is swimming such an important part of the Gauntlet?" I ask, trying to keep the hopelessness from my voice.

Broderick doesn't seem to notice, and I wonder if the witch realizes that I'm more than just curious. That I'm interested in competing.

Or at least, I was when I thought I might have a chance.

"My understanding is that the trials are always set up in one of the coves on Lake Galen. While competitors don't have to swim the entire time, there is usually a good portion of the race that requires swimming."

My last feeble hope burns up in a puff of smoke. I duck my head to hide the disappointment that I'm sure is overwhelming my face.

"Were you planning on entering?" Broderick asks the question so easily, answering my silent query from a moment ago. He asks as if the idea of me in Galen's Gauntlet makes complete sense to him.

I don't sense wariness in his voice. I don't hear judgment or fear on my behalf.

And maybe that could be enough. His easy belief in me.

But it's not.

It helps, but it's not enough.

"I was considering it," I admit. "But I don't think that I would be able to. Based off your description."

Now, his voice tightens with apparent concern. "What did I say?"

I try to wipe all the vulnerability from my face as I raise my head. "Swimming. I can't swim."

Broderick looks genuinely confused by this confession. As if he cannot fathom an adult who can't keep themself afloat.

I'm sure there is a vast number of people in the world who don't know how. But this hurts. The acknowledgment that I am less than he thought I was. There are so many ways that is already true. I didn't need another.

I stand abruptly, ready to walk away from the pity in his face.

"Wait, Ophelia." He extends a hand, but doesn't grab me. "There's time."

I pause my escape, but I don't turn to face him. Not when I'm worried the pressure behind my eyes might be tears. "What?"

"We live near a lake," the witch says, his voice gentle. Cajoling. "Plenty of water. I can teach you."

He can teach me?

Behind me, I hear Broderick stand from his chair, and I can feel his presence at my back. Tall, warm, but not intimidating. I don't mind when this witch looms over me. Someone else would have my hackles raised and my adrenaline spiking. They'd set off alarms in my head and turn my breaths into anxious gasps.

But I trust Broderick Shelly. The man who bled for me.

There are times when he gestures and I catch a sight of the scar on his hand, and I know without a doubt he's a good man.

"I'm sorry if I sounded surprised," he says, unaware of my admiration for him. "I grew up in a seaside town. And then I moved here, where there are water mythics everywhere. Where the lake is an integral part of the town. It's been a little while since I've encountered someone who doesn't know how to swim, but that's completely normal. But ..." He hesitates, clears his throat, and presses on, "I can teach you. If you want to learn. If you give me a chance, I would be honored to help you, Ophelia. So you can compete in the Gauntlet. So you can *win* the Gauntlet."

That last sentence has me choking out a laugh, even as my eyes feel wet.

I have no intention of winning. But even stepping over the starting line into whatever wildness the sirens and witches cook up would be a braver move than I've ever made in my life.

Would be proof that my fear does not rule me.

Slowly, I turn to face Broderick, and in that rotation, my eyes notice a sparkle on his desk. There, next to the professor's keyboard, sits the glass firebird I crafted for him from sand and the heat of my hands.

"Can I hug you again?" I rasp, knowing deep in my heart, in the intuitive part of my soul that survived all the harshness of my past, that this witch is important to me. That he's someone to keep close. To cherish.

If only I can open myself to him.

"Like I said before," Broderick murmurs with a lovely blush on his sharp cheekbones, "anytime. Anywhere. For as long as you want."

I'm in his arms again. And the sensation is as glorious as flying.

"Yes," I say, breathing in the herb and soap scent lingering on his shirt. "Please teach me to swim."

BRODERICK

"I THOUGHT you were going to teach me in the lake."

Ophelia stands next to me outside Haven's Relaxation, a spa owned and run by monsters. Not that it means the place isn't relaxing.

"I figured this would be a safer place to start. They have saltwater pools that are shallow enough to touch the bottom. And no wake from wind or boats."

"That makes sense." Ophelia stands taller, and I watch the start of a smile tug at her mouth. "And if I panic, I can calm down with a massage."

I chuckle to cover my nerves. Only after Ophelia left my office yesterday did I consider how big of a deal this was. I'm in charge of teaching the firebird an important skill she'll use during Galen's Gauntlet.

A dangerous competition that not everyone walks away from without injury. When I checked in with Mor, she said Seamus won, but not without multiple broken bones.

Maybe I was hasty claiming Ophelia could participate. I still have no idea what she went through before landing in Folk Haven. And there's always a touch of orange anxiety creeping through her aura.

Is she ready for this?

The blue-haired desk worker with a name tag that reads *Titan (they/them)* greets us warmly, and I lay down my credit card before Ophelia can even think of pulling out a payment.

"I can cover the cost," she argues.

Like with her truck, I get the sense this means something to her, being the one to pay. But I also know Haven's Relaxation falls on the more luxurious side—aka pricey.

"I was planning on buying a membership," I explain to her and the desk worker. "Does that come with guest passes?"

"It does," Titan says with a kind smile as they type in my info on their computer. "You can have a guest accompany you twice a year."

"Great. I'll use one today." I turn to Ophelia. "You can treat me to dinner afterward to pay me back."

Like a date. That's a thought I keep to myself. As well as my preferred method of repayment—more lingering hugs.

Ophelia, appearing mollified, nods.

Another worker appears, this one tall and lean with a dark complexion and the scent of the forest clinging to their uniform. They show us around the facilities and eventually leave us at the locker rooms. There's no gender divide, just communal lockers and individual rooms for changing and showering.

I change fast, eager to start training. Wanting to assure myself Ophelia won't get hurt.

When I step out of my little room, she's still in hers, so I wait. My nerves jump and twitch, and not for the first time, I wish I could use my fear-soothing magic on myself. A relaxation enchantment would hit the spot right now.

If I had ingredients and a grimoire on hand, I probably

could work a spell for myself. But my natural magic—the kind that comes to me with only a slight amount of effort—is the ability to soothe those around me. I can sense when fear and worry spike, a person's aura filling with sickly orange.

If I want, I can twine my magic through their anxieties, dulling the sharp edges until they are calm again.

More than once, I've wanted to use the power on Ophelia. She always seems to have a tinge of orange around her.

But the woman has had magic forced on her before. I won't be another person who spells her without permission.

But if I explain what I can do and she agrees to let me help ... that is a different story.

"Are you ready?" Ophelia appears before me, seemingly out of nowhere since I was so lost in thought. Her ability to move stealthily will work in her favor during the Gauntlet.

I open my mouth to respond, but then I take her in, and I struggle for words. The sight of her undoes me.

The firebird doesn't even have on a skimpy bikini, though that would also likely short-circuit my brain. Ophelia's current outfit is entirely modest. A fluffy white robe, provided by the spa, engulfs her.

And she looks entirely too adorable, bundled up in the garment.

I can't help thinking this is how Ophelia would look while wrapped up in a blanket. Snuggled on a couch.

I need to buy a couch for my place. And a fluffy blanket.

"You look very huggable," I blurt.

Ophelia's eyebrows pop up.

Then, a smile curves her luscious lips, and I don't regret the blundering words.

"You said I could hug you anytime. Anywhere. For as long as I want?" Her voice ticks up on the last note in a question.

"Correct," I croak, throat gone dry with hope.

"Just checking."

Then, the temptress steps into my chest and wraps her arms around me. I hold her back, and she's as soft as I imagined.

Even as I revel in the sensation, a part of me feels bad that I haven't shared how much these embraces mean to me. Ophelia probably thinks I'm some sort of selfless being, offering her comfort. She might even have an idea that I'm attracted to her and that I derive pleasure from holding her because of that fact.

But there's more. As I press my arms into the softness of her robe and feel the steady heat of her body beneath, I give in to the sudden urge to share.

"I never got hugs, growing up."

Ophelia flinches. Then, she holds me tighter. "Not from your siblings?"

I let my fingers stroke the silky tresses of her cinnamon-scented hair that spills down her back. "No. I think it has to do with their magic. Getting close to people can be overwhelming for them."

"Your parents?" Her question is hesitant.

"My parents ..." I try to sound nonchalant. Aloof. But bitterness creeps in. "They weren't the loving kind."

Fingertips dig into the tense muscles of my back, and I realize Ophelia is gripping me.

The possession is intoxicating.

"My father wasn't the loving kind either." The firebird reveals a piece of her past. A hint to the life she had before her captivity.

I take the knowledge for what it is. A gift and an honor.

Ophelia doesn't let go, only shifts her head so her chin rests on my chest, gazing straight up so I can meet her eyes.

"I cannot promise you anytime, anywhere, as long as you want," she admits. "Sometimes, I don't want to be touched." Ophelia strokes up and down my back, the soothing gesture threatening to melt me into a puddle. "But I promise to hug you whenever the urge takes me. Because I ... I want to be the loving kind."

The sweet words rush through me like a wildfire, and I know that I will do anything I can to earn and keep this firebird's trust.

To be worthy of her.

8

OPHELIA

THE WATER IS WARM, and Broderick's hands are hot.

After that emotionally heavy hug, we found our way to one of the rooms with a saltwater pool. Apparently, there are multiple, each one with a wall of windows, showing the beautiful expanse of Lake Galen. We have the place to ourselves, which is nice because no one can witness me ogling the hot professor's body in his fitted green swim trunks. He's tall and lithe, not rippling with muscle, but still has an air of athleticism.

Since I haven't shared any of my past—other than that small detail about my father—Broderick has no way of knowing that this is the closest I've ever been to a man that I like.

All through the lesson, I keep bumping into the witch's tantalizing body as he helps me float in the pool. Despite the oddity of water lapping against my ears, I fight to keep my head tilted back and my body straight, lying flat on the surface as Broderick's hands support me under my lower back and behind my thighs.

I trust him to keep me afloat.

I don't trust *me* to keep me afloat.

"I'm going to step back now. Stay just like this." Broderick uses a soothing voice, and I wonder if he perfected it on panicking students.

"Okay," I squeak.

We've tried this twice before, and each of the other times, the moment he released me, I floundered.

But this round, chest tight with gasping breaths and hands making little flutter motions, I stay up. For a whole count of five.

Then, Broderick is back at my side, grinning down at me with his handsome face aglow, green eyes shining with approval. "You did it!"

Now that he's close, I relax my body and make an awkward transition to standing. "I did!"

Pride fills me, knowing that I've made a step—even if it was a small one—toward a future where I have one less thing to be frightened of.

As joy flows through my veins in a heady rush, I give in to the urge to throw my arms around Broderick's shoulders, claiming another hug that, apparently, he craves as much as I do.

He *did* say anytime, anywhere, for as long as I want.

I'm surprised that my small admission about my past—the kind of man my father was—has me feeling closer to this man rather than erecting a barrier, like I believed sharing painful memories might.

But all thoughts of my past seep away as I realize exactly what position I've put us in.

Soaking wet, me dressed in a single-piece swimsuit that leaves nothing to the imagination, pressed tight against the first person I've felt safe with in my entire life.

A man who also happens to have a very rigid part of himself sandwiched between us.

"Ophelia." He croaks my name, and I find I love the vulnerability revealed in that creaky way his voice gets. "I'm sorry. My body is … a little too excited."

When Broderick places his hands on my hips, I shiver. But then he pushes my body away enough so that I can't feel his hardness anymore.

Disentangling my arms, I'm hit with a hot flare of embarrassment, the fire burning in my cheeks. "Sorry. That was my fault. For rubbing myself on you."

I might lack practical experience with intimacy, but the internet has taught me plenty in the past few months.

Broderick shuts his eyes tight, as if in pain, and the fingers he still has resting on my hips flex. "Maybe we don't talk about you rubbing me."

I nod, but with his eyes closed, he can't see the gesture.

"Can you show me how to hold my breath?" I offer, refocusing on my swimming lessons and the Gauntlet. "Do I just go down? I don't think I'll have a fast stroke, even with practice. But maybe if I can outlast others, that would help."

Broderick grunts, releasing his hold on me to aggressively rub his hands over his face, and I get the sense I said something wrong.

"Are you okay?" I venture carefully.

Broderick drops his hands and gives me a strained smile. "Good. Yes. I'm good." He clears his throat and takes a step back in the pool. "You want to learn to hold your breath underwater. Go down underwater. Last underwater."

"You're saying underwater a lot."

Broderick nods. "I did. Let's focus on that."

For the next half hour, the professor affects an instructional air, showing me the basic way to hold my breath—by pinching my nose—but then also more helpful methods, like blowing a stream of bubbles. I only snort water twice, which I count as a success. Broderick also demonstrates some basic strokes, which he looks powerful and graceful doing. Meanwhile, I flop through them like a half-dead fish.

By the end of our lesson, I'm exhausted, my airway is raw from partially inhaled saltwater, and overall, I'm exuberant.

I kind of know how to swim!

As I wrap myself in a large towel, I gaze out the windows at the sprawling lake. The stretch of water glimmers in the evening light, and I find the gentle waves enticing.

"Do you think I'm ready to swim off the dock?" I ask, eager to try my skills in a wilder setting.

Broderick rubs his own towel over his head, leaving his red tresses in a charming disarray.

"You were treading water at the end there, so, yeah, I think we can step it up."

His confidence in my ability warms my blood in a delicious way. Broderick was supportive and careful with me all through the lesson, but I never felt coddled or stifled.

Never felt like he was trying to hold me back.

Memories of a time when that was my life threaten to rise. I almost push them away—like I've been doing for the past six months—but then I decide that I don't want to hide them. I want to expel them from me like venom from a snake bite.

"My father was a human," I blurt.

Broderick pauses in the act of toweling off his torso, his emerald eyes finding mine. In his open gaze, I see the willingness to listen.

So, I keep going. "He knew what I was. Knew what my mother was. Apparently, he called her an angel." I shake my head with a frown. "That seems so impossible to me. That he would have said something like that. Because he hated what *I* was."

Broderick straightens and steps closer. But I'm too busy seeping the poison of my past to hug him.

"My mother passed away when I was six. She was giving birth to my brother. Something went wrong, and neither of them made it. My father said if being a mythic was good, then she would have lived."

There was no logic to the hatred that grew in him, and I just wanted my mother back.

"My aunt visited when I was younger. I remember that. But she didn't come back after my mom passed. Maybe because losing her sister was so sad. Or ..." I swallow and tug on my damp hair. "Or maybe my father didn't *let* her see me again. All I know is, he demanded I hide that part of myself. Suppress it. And he mostly kept me away from people."

So much loneliness. I used to wander around the acres of land we lived on and pretend the forest animals were my friends.

"I was homeschooled, and I couldn't leave our property, except to go to church." Those Sunday mornings where I felt the preacher's judging eyes on me. Apparently, my father had told him I had a demon in me. Gone was his talk of angels.

"And there were times I couldn't contain the fire. Trying to stifle it only made things worse. At night, I would sneak off and change in the woods. Just for a short time. I never flew anywhere." Even standing in a clearing, allowing my other half to breathe, was euphoric.

"But I was a grown woman, and my father's tight reins had been chafing for years. So, I told him I was leaving." Even though I had no idea how to exist anywhere other than our homestead and had no money of my own. All I knew was that staying there felt like dying. "He refused. Swore that he would stop me. And my temper *exploded* out of me. That heat ..." I stare down at my fingers, flexing them, feeling the phantom of flaming feathers. Finally allowing my firebird side out in front of him was glorious at the start. But when I realized the damage I'd done, I was terrified. "If we'd been arguing inside, I might've burned our house down."

As it was, I melted his old truck until it was a puddle in the gravel driveway.

I thought maybe my father was right about me having a demon in me. His words were starting to blot out the firebird fairy tales my mother and aunt had told me.

"Soon after, he brought a man to our house. The stranger was kind, and I was *excited* to meet someone new. To talk to someone who wasn't my father." How naive I was, thinking my life was at its lowest point. "He said he could help me get rid of the fire." At this, a sob sneaks out of my throat. Shame overwhelms me at the memory. "I *begged* him to. Because I thought if I wasn't a firebird, then I could finally live in the world."

Broderick stands in front of me now, his face stark. He's moved as close as possible without taking me into his arms. Waiting for my permission. I make the final move, gathering him close, pressing my cheek against his bare chest, hard enough to hear his heartbeat. The scent of salt and warm herbs fills my nose. Broderick strokes my wet hair, and I feel the pressure of his lips on the top of my head.

"The man said if I went with him, he could take all the magic from me," I whisper.

The stranger wasn't lying.

"Your father agreed? To let him take you?" Broderick's words are a rasp.

"If my father ever loved me, it was gone by then." I see that now. "He saw me as a duty. A danger he had to protect the world from. Not his daughter." I swallow hard. "So, I left. Happily. And the first night, the man who was supposed to be my savior had me stand in the middle of a spell circle. And I did. As meek as the rabbit as he turned me into."

The witch continues to pet my hair, which helps ease the edge of anxiety that squeezes my lungs.

"How long ago?" he asks.

I tighten my hold. "Three years. I was twenty-three when he came for me. A grown woman still living under the thumb of her father who hated her."

I wasn't brave. I was timid. Submissive. Letting his words and teachings become my truth.

Forgetting the stories the women of my family had taught me. The love I'd experienced in the first few years of my life became a hazy fiction.

And then I was an animal, only partly aware of the world around me, but sure I was more trapped than I had ever been. Weaker than I'd ever realized I could be.

When I came back to myself in that forest clearing under the full moon, my body naked and overheated from the suppressed magic within me, the first emotion I felt was fury.

And I knew I never wanted to feel so vulnerable again.

"I've been trying to figure out how to live these past few months," I confess. "Live as a firebird, but also as a human in the world. Even Folk Haven seems big to me, though I know it's small compared to cities."

"You're doing amazing. Much better than I would have." Broderick twines a strand of my hair around his finger. "I hate that you've been hurt so many times by people you trusted."

When he puts it like that, maybe I should consider not trusting people anymore.

But with Broderick, it's not even a conscious decision.

His hands cup my cheeks, tilting my face up so my eyes meet his concerned gaze. "I didn't live a dream childhood either. With loving, supportive parents. Mine were self-centered. Sometimes cruel, but they mostly forgot about us."

His confession, painful though it must be, comforts me in a

way. I don't like that Broderick suffered, but I feel closer to him, knowing my experience isn't unfathomable.

"Still, I had my brother and sisters." His thumbs stroke the shape of my cheeks, the movement soothing. "You were alone. I wish I could have found you then."

"You're with me now." I close my eyes and inhale salt and herbs.

"That's all I want." He murmurs the words so low that I almost don't hear them. "For you to keep me close."

9

———————

OPHELIA

"I AM SO glad you decided to join us for dinner," Georgiana gushes. "You're always retreating into your room. I thought I'd have to grab a crowbar and pry you out of there." The siren smiles at me over her shoulder from the front passenger seat of her husband's car.

I don't bristle at her words because I've started to realize that they're true.

Despite coming out of my cursed form with a determination not to live under the control of someone else, I still fell into old habits. All through my childhood, my father had taught me that I needed to separate myself from society. Once Georgiana set me up with my own suite-style arrangement in her house and I got settled in with my job at Clean Haven, just leaving for work seemed like a grand adventure for me. An adventure that I felt I needed to earn by staying at home whenever I wasn't on the clock.

But after going to happy hour and swim practice with Broderick, I understand now that any limits and restrictions in my

299

life are ones I've made up for myself. Either born from habit or fear.

That's not how I plan to live anymore.

And in the same way that I started to repeat my past behavior, I might have projected some of my resentment for my father onto Georgiana. That I made her into a jailer she wasn't.

True, there are aspects of her personality that rub my feathers the wrong way some days. But not every person is perfect. And she's trying. Which means I should try too.

Which is why I accepted the invite she'd extended to join her husband, Richard, and her for dinner.

I'm going to eat out. At a restaurant!

This won't be the first time I've eaten out in my life. Sometimes, my father would take me to a diner in the small town near our house. But we'd go late at night when the place was a ghost town.

I've also bought myself lunch at Coffee & Claws and Mary Jo's bagels a few times. Sat at their tables. Surreptitiously observed the other diners. Reveled in the simple freedom.

Longed to have another at my table to share the experience with.

Tonight, that tiny dream is coming true.

Maybe this will be the time that Georgiana, Richard, and I make a connection. That we maneuver past polite, stilted conversations and become true friends. I have so few of those. I want to find more.

But I doubt anyone will match the natural closeness I feel with Broderick.

Just the thought of the witch has me smiling.

With joy warming my body, I continue the conversation. "This restaurant is one of the stops on my route, and every time I go into the building to collect the recycling, the food they're cooking smells delicious. I'm looking forward to trying some."

"I'm sure you are." Georgiana turns even more, her seat belt pressing hard into her magenta shift dress. "And you know, I was just thinking. Now would be a perfect time for you to look into classes at Ramla University. There's plenty of time for you to sign up for the fall semester. Soon enough, you could level up your career aspirations." She wrinkles her pert nose. "You don't want to be collecting garbage for your whole life, I'm sure."

My warm happiness cools, and I forcefully relax my jaw, which wants to clench at her dismissive tone. For one, garbage and recycling are two totally different things. And two, even if I *were* a garbage collector, that's still an important profession for people to have. I doubt Georgiana wants her trash piling up in her perfectly paved driveway.

But the siren makes a good point about the potential of going to the university. I like the idea of being able to attend the classes. Ones about topics that I choose. Getting the chance to educate myself on subjects that my father's homeschooling never touched on.

To explore this wide world that is now open to me.

And maybe see a little more of a certain professor in the process.

"That's a good idea. I'll look into that this week."

"Oh, good!" Georgiana claps her hands. "And I'll be on the lookout for job openings." She raises an eyebrow and tilts her head toward her husband, who seems content to drive the car and listen to a quietly playing podcast about fishing. "Accounting is always a great profession choice, you know. You can help out many businesses."

And once again, I have to fight a grimace. Math was something that I got plenty of during my childhood. I was in charge of the finances for my father's farm. Not that I was allowed to keep any of the money for myself. One more way that I felt trapped in my old life. I'm glad that I know how to deal with money now. But numbers don't excite me the way classes on history, public relations, or creative writing do.

Still, I force a smile and a nod and try to think of subjects that we could discuss over dinner that won't have me fighting off disagreeable words. Luckily, Richard asks Georgiana to sit back so he can look behind us while he parallel parks the car on Main Street.

We've arrived at Knives & Fangs.

The fine-dining restaurant is busy for Thursday night, but I assume that's often the case when living in a small town and there's only a certain number of places to eat. I hope there's enough business to support another restaurant, recalling how Niko mentioned wanting to open his own soon. The proprietors of Knives & Fangs might not appreciate the competition.

The hostess smiles at Georgiana and Richard first, and then her gaze lands on me. Once again, I'm wearing my red dress with its little white flowers—the only dress I own—and I smooth my hands over the skirt, hoping I'm properly dressed for this place.

The woman gives me a little wink and smile before saying, "The rest of your party is already here."

The rest of our party?

Confused, I follow the group to the table. I thought it was just going to be the three of us. Georgiana didn't mention anyone else when she invited me to dinner.

Maybe I misunderstood?

Maybe I was too nervous and missed part of what she said?

I breathe through the spike of panic that likes to jab me when plans get changed and instead remind myself that this night is one more adventure in the new, improved version of my life.

As we weave between tables, the hostess brings us to a four-top, where a man who looks to be in his late twenties or early thirties sits. He has a handsome face with a square jaw and dark hair that is neatly styled. His eyes are milky blue and crinkle at the corners with his welcoming smile as he stands and holds out a hand to Richard.

"Thank you so much for inviting me. I've been looking forward to this dinner ever since you told me what wonderful company we'd have."

As the man says this, his eyes land on me. My fingers twitch and tug at the skirt of my dress. I thought it was the best choice. Now, I'm wishing I had something that covered more of my arms and my legs. The man runs his eyes over me. Assessing.

What is this?

My anxiety is not so easy to soothe as it was a moment ago.

"Oh, you charmer!" Georgiana exclaims while laughing and letting the man claim her hand and kiss her knuckles. "I was so happy that you agreed to join us. Franklin, this is my house-guest, Ophelia. Ophelia, this is Franklin. He is the newest doctor at the practice where Richard works." She turns a wide smile on me, and there is an eagerness in her eyes.

"I am honored to meet you," Franklin says, moving around the table to stand in front of me. "When Georgiana told me how beautiful you were, I never expected that you could surpass her description."

I don't like this.

There's something familiar about the situation that causes a painful tug in the bottom of my gut and sweat to collect like a chilled mist on my skin. But technically, no one has said or done anything wrong, so I fall back on my previously learned coping behavior.

I go quiet.

I attempt a smile and let Franklin take my hand and put his lips on my knuckles. And I try not to be obvious when I then wipe those knuckles on the back of my dress to get the feel of him off me.

This is not a man I would ever ask to hug.

The dinner commences with Georgiana and Franklin chatting happily while Richard adds a handful of comments but stays almost as quiet as me.

I don't say anything. They don't *ask* me anything. Even though I prefer not to speak in this strange situation, a part of me knows this is weird. How they don't even try to include me in the conversation. This feels different from when I attended the Shellys' happy hour. I didn't speak much then either. But I still felt a part of the gathering. Maybe it was the fact that Ame immediately asked what drink I wanted. Or because she put her cat in my lap. Or that when I did venture a rare question, they answered it easily.

And maybe it was because I knew that Broderick knew I was there. That he was paying attention to me even if we weren't speaking.

Here, I feel as visible as the tea light in the center of the table. A decoration.

And then they start to talk about me.

"Ophelia is thinking about going to the university for accounting." Georgiana's eyes glitter as she focuses solely on Franklin. "Wouldn't that be so helpful? And I'm sure they'd get her set up with basic computer skills, so she could work reception for you all."

I go rigid in my seat.

"Accounting degrees are a good choice." Franklin smiles and nods at me as if approving of a trick I was planning to learn. "It's always refreshing when a young lady has a good head on her shoulders."

Suddenly, I realize what this reminds me of.

My father and the sorcerer.

The night he came to our house. How the two of them discussed my future. And my father gave me to him as if I were a malfunctioning object to hand off and be fixed.

That time, I went willingly.

This is a double date. I see that now. A date my host didn't bother to speak to me about. My opinion on the matter must be inconsequential. Georgiana brought me here like cattle to be viewed and considered as ... wife material?

From the way that Franklin grins, he finds me plenty acceptable. He likes the woman who has not spoken a word to him in the last hour. The woman who's getting an accounting degree and will conveniently work at the front desk in his office.

He doesn't even know my last name. I haven't told *anyone* in this town my surname because I don't want it anymore.

But maybe it's easier for him not to know. Especially if he plans to give me his.

Breath stutters in and out of my throat, my lungs tight with anger and panic. Heat flows like lava, thick in my veins, ruffling invisible feathers. Stirring the bird that I'm not supposed to let out. The other half of me that I have been told to keep hidden by the woman who is smiling across the table at me.

She is looking to sell me. Just like my father sold me.

I know that he got money. I know that a generous donation was made to the church that he attended. Everyone was paid, and then I was gone.

I don't want to disappear again.

I want to exist, and I want to be free.

And I want to burn.

The legs of my chair squeak on the hardwood floor as I push myself away from the table and stand. "I have to go."

Georgiana gapes at me, her perfectly painted lips in a shocked O. "What are you doing?" She gasps. "Sit back down."

The siren doesn't ask me *why* I want to leave. She doesn't ask me if I'm feeling all right. She doesn't have an ounce of worry for me as a living being.

She just wants me to sit down, close my mouth, and fit me into a neat plan she made without my input.

But my life is my own now.

"You gave me a place to stay when I didn't have one." I state the fact, acknowledging the gesture.

I should say *thank you*. But my father always demanded that I say *thank you* for every single thing he gave me in life. I wasn't allowed to eat without thanking him. I wasn't allowed to sleep without thanking him. I wasn't allowed to enter or exit the house without saying, "Thank you, Father, for this home." I can't say those two words anymore.

"But I'm moving out." I pull cash from my purse and lay the bills on the table to pay for the food that I didn't eat.

No need to thank anyone but myself. Ignoring the three baffled faces, I turn abruptly, walking as fast as I can toward the exit.

Only to run face-first into a warm, familiar chest.

10

───────

BRODERICK

Not to sound like a total creep, but I've been watching Ophelia since the moment she walked into Knives & Fangs. Some hidden force alerted me the second she pushed through the door. My body immediately wanted to abandon my dinner party and go to her, but the beautiful firebird was with a group. The siren Georgiana, her human doctor husband, and another man. A good-looking one, I guess. If you're into Clark Kent vibes.

What soured me on him was the way he stared at Ophelia.

His gaze was assessing.

And possessive.

She's her own fucking firebird! I wanted to shout across the restaurant. *You don't own her!*

But I don't know that Ophelia would have appreciated my defense, and my colleagues would have started asking questions about my sanity.

"I think we need to reword the rubric for the 102 midterm paper," Sherry, another professor in the English department

307

and a mermaid, says, leaning across the table to make sure everyone is listening. "That's the one I got the most emails about." She pushes her long braids away from her plate and continues eating as the table debates how to update the assignment.

There are six of us here, including Delta Novac—the previous owner of Mor's library and the newest faculty hire. The dragon shifter eagerly adds her point of view, drawn from years of teaching online college composition courses.

Normally, I would be all in on this discussion. Some professors dread teaching intro courses, but I enjoy getting the chance to encourage students at the beginning of their college careers. That first year is when they're most vulnerable. When they doubt themselves.

My need to soothe anxieties has lots of opportunity to come into play.

But my entire attention stays trained across the restaurant, where Ophelia sits. She has her back to me, blocking her expression. But the longer I watch, the surer I am she isn't saying a word.

So? She barely said anything at happy hour, I remind myself.

Just because the firebird isn't chatty doesn't mean she's having a bad time.

But there's orange in her aura. Darker than normal ... right?

It's hard to tell in the mood lighting of the restaurant.

I'm jealous. I know I am. The setup looks suspiciously like a double date, and the idea of Ophelia getting romantically involved with anyone who isn't me feels like swallowing glue.

I robotically chew the rest of my food and reassure myself I'm not missing anything super important in my distracted state. This is just an ideas meeting. We'll get together later in the summer to iron out any solid changes for the fall semester. I can continue to not-creepily watch the woman I'm obsessed with.

To make up for my distraction, I pick up the bill for every-one. It's not a big deal for me. My parents, horrible as they were —and still are—left plenty of money to their four children. Mor used her inheritance for the library. Anthony doesn't need his, having made a fortune during his years as a model and influencer. Ame ... honestly, I have no idea if my younger sister has touched the money. She lives a frugal life. I wouldn't be surprised if she donated it years ago to an animal shelter.

As my group rises, I consider if I could sit here on my own. Slowly sip the rest of my water and wait for Ophelia's party to be finished with their meal as well.

No. That would be weird.

But maybe I could hang out at the bar—

Suddenly, Ophelia shoots up from her chair, throws money on the table, and hurries for the exit.

Working on instinct, I dive after her. But, misjudging the way the table arrangements might hold her up, I end up directly in front of her.

The firebird plows into me.

Ophelia has plenty of strength in her deceptively thin body. I wobble from the collision, then steady us both with my hands on her upper arms.

"Ophelia? Are you okay?"

That didn't look like a happy, planned departure, and now that we're close, I can see the sickly orange anxiety twisting in the air around her.

She jerks her chin up, gaze meeting mine, and I spy golden flames dancing in her irises.

"I need to burn something." Her voice is soft and desperate. Shudders rack her body.

Is this the state she was in before almost lighting up her father's house?

"Okay." I wrap an arm around her, fighting my urge to magi-cally soothe her. "Let's find something to set on fire."

We hurry out of the restaurant, and Ophelia allows me to guide her to my car. Hopefully, she can hold on to her internal inferno until I get her to a safe location. Once I'm behind the wheel, I dial a number I never have before.

"What?" Jack says on the other end of the line.

He sounds grumpy. But that's his norm, so I ignore the tone.

"Hey. It's Broderick."

"I know. I have caller ID," he growls.

Jack has never been the kind of guy who feels the need to impress the brothers of the woman he loves.

"Great. Anyway, Mor mentioned something about a few dead trees that fell near the library. She said you were planning on chopping them up for firewood."

"Yeah. So?"

"So, could you drag them to the lakeshore instead?" I glance over at Ophelia, who sits hunched in the passenger seat. "Right now. Please. I'll take care of them."

There's a pause.

"Fine."

Grumpy or not, the wolf can still be helpful when he wants.

The line clicks off, and I gun it toward the library. When we arrive, I spy the werewolf disappearing around the side of the house, a massive tree gripped in his clawed hands. Jack is in his half form. Part human, part wolf. Wolfman, some might say. And apparently, it's a rare form only guardian werewolves can access.

The guy is properly terrifying. Luckily, he's in love with a Shelly, so I'm safe from him.

Probably.

"Time for a bonfire." I keep my voice light, but I'm not sure if Ophelia hears me.

She seems far away as she scrambles for the door handle and stumbles out of the car.

I meet her in front of the hood and gesture toward the lake. "This way."

Just when I'm sure she's going to race past me, the firebird sidles close, slipping her hand into mine. Her skin is fever hot. I hold tight and draw her forward.

On the rocky lakeshore, Jack is just finishing setting a tree on top of two others. Decent-sized trunks—each could have provided a year's worth of firewood. Something tells me they won't last the night.

Jack backs up on his lupine legs and uses a clawed hand to point at the pile. "Yours," he growls through a gaping maw full of fangs. Then, he lopes off, back toward the house.

"Thank you!" I call after him, determined to show gratitude whether he acknowledges it or not.

"Stand back," Ophelia commands, her voice strong now.

She detaches her hand from mine and uses it to push my chest. Then, in moves so quick that I almost miss them, she toes off her sandals and tugs her dress overhead. In only her panties, the firebird strides toward the kindling, flames sparking from her skin, feet scorching the grass with each step. The moment Ophelia stands among the wood, she emits a shriek that reminds me of a hunting hawk. And just like the night we freed her, the gorgeous shape of a majestic bird overtakes her.

But this time, she doesn't fly away.

Ophelia simply burns, the logs around her catching to build a huge bonfire on the shores of Lake Galen. Even at my distance, the heat spills off in waves, stealing the moisture from my face until my skin feels tight. But I don't retreat.

In the rising temperature, I can sense her pain. The orange of anxiety is masked by the fire, but I feel the emotion through my magic. The fear and hurt she tries to hide under soft words and ducked eyes.

Behaviors I'm beginning to believe were taught to her by that hellish father she told me about.

My parents were terrible, but at least they left us to our own devices for the most part.

Ophelia lived under the constant oppression of a man who told her this wondrous part of her was wrong. Then, he—her own flesh and blood—traded her to a monster who caged her even further.

We're lucky she hasn't set this whole town on fire with how much furious despair is pent up inside her.

I settle in the now-dry grass, ready to wait as long as Ophelia needs. There's a small log a few feet from me, and without warning, a large barn owl glides down to settle on the makeshift perch.

No, not *an* owl. *The* owl. The one that keeps appearing, as if following me around town. The one that feels oddly familiar.

Tearing my eyes from Ophelia's pyrotechnics, I take a moment to study the bird. For now, it stares straight ahead, keeping vigil over the firebird.

Is the owl here for me or for her?

Either way, I find I appreciate the company as I turn back to watch Ophelia burn. Her fire mesmerizes me, lulling me into an almost-drowsy state. Which might be why I blink and feel like I've only woken up when all there is before me is a cluster of charred wood. And a naked woman.

She crosses her arms over her chest self-consciously. I scoop up her dress and keep my eyes on my toes as I jog up to her, the sound of flapping wings at my back alerting me to the fact that the owl has taken to the air at my departure. The silky material slips over the skin of my fingers like a tease as she accepts it.

"I'm covered," she says.

When I glance up, Ophelia stares back at me, an expression of uncertainty on her face.

"Will I get in trouble?" she asks.

"For what?"

She tilts her chin toward the smoldering embers. "For letting my fire out."

"No. Of course not. Is that what Georgiana told you?"

She shrugs. "Not in those exact words. But yes."

I spread my arms wide, a silent ask. With a hesitant smile, Ophelia steps into them. Hugging me.

Gods, each one of these is better than the last.

"You didn't hurt anyone. That's all that matters." I breathe in her smoky cinnamon scent. "If you caught on fire in the middle of town, there probably would have been some PR damage control and a stern talking-to from the Mythic Council. But in Folk Haven, our kind isn't punished for what we are. I'm sorry if that's what you were led to believe."

"I don't want to live with Georgiana anymore," Ophelia confesses. "She's not near as bad as my father, but sometimes, she reminds me of him."

Fuck. One more person in the firebird's life causing her pain.

"We can find you another place to live."

I consider asking Mor about a free room in the library. There should be one since I moved out.

But as if she can read my mind, Ophelia shakes her head. "I can't live here." She tilts her chin toward the Victorian structure. "With my fire and the books, I'd be too worried all the time."

"Mor would still have you." She'd probably just start frantically researching fireproofing spells. "But there are other places to rent in town, I'm sure." Just as I say the words, an idea comes to me. "Actually, I might know of a place. A temporary one, but if they agree, you could use it while you search for another."

Ophelia stares up at me, an adorable streak of soot on her face. "What place?"

I grin. "How do you feel about selkies?"

11

OPHELIA

BRODERICK SHOULD HAVE KNOWN I was a fan of selkies. One of my bosses is one after all.

And Owen MacNamara's house is exactly the destination the witch had in mind. Well, more like the MacNamara homestead. Turns out, the family of selkies—one of Folk Haven's founding families—owns a stretch of land along one of the coves. Multiple houses litter the property.

And one Airstream trailer.

Delta Novac is mated to Calder MacNamara—Owen's brother—and she used to use the trailer as an office before she stopped working remotely as a professor and recently joined the Ramla staff. She's Broderick's colleague—also a faculty member in the English department—and mentioned to him that her trailer wouldn't get much use with her having an official office at the university.

He called her as I was busy washing ashes off of my skin in the library bathroom. The dragon shifter was happy to immediately start renting me the place for the rest of the summer, especially when her brother-in-law gave me a glowing review.

I didn't realize my work ethic had impressed my boss so much.

"Is it going to be weird, having me living here? As one of your employees?" I ask.

Owen lingers in the doorway of the Airstream as I maneuver around the compact space. He showed up with the plan to help me move in, only to discover all my belongings fit into two duffel bags.

The selkie smirks. "Nope. As long as you keep your mouth shut about my nude sunrise yoga routine."

My horror must show on my face because he bursts out laughing.

"I'm kidding!" He chortles. "It's fine. You're an outstanding employee. And now, my parents can grow enamored with you and forget about their errant son. Mark my words—less than twenty-four hours from now, you'll have a dinner invite."

I try not to grimace. After last night's horrendous dinner, I'm antsy at the thought of future social events.

Unaware of my disquiet, Owen turns to acknowledge someone over his shoulder. "And here's the professor."

I lean down to glance out the small window above the desk in time to see a red head of hair passing by. Owen steps down from the entryway, and Broderick appears.

"She found the spare." He holds up a key.

Delta greeted me when I first arrived, giving me a brief tour of the camper, then went back to the house she shares with Owen's younger brother to search for the second key. Broderick offered to go with her so I could unpack my belongings.

I find I like how small this space is. The compact camper makes it feel like the tiny number of items I own was planned.

When I returned to Georgiana's house to pack up my life, I

realized how little of a mark I'd made, even after being free for six months.

A handful of outfits.

A coat, sandals, and sturdy boots.

My cell phone. Some personal hygiene items. A few second-hand paperbacks I bought from Never Judge a Cover, the town's bookstore.

That was it.

If I incinerated along with my fire, my entire existence could easily be done away with through one trip to a trash can.

Still, Georgiana—who was up, waiting for me, when I arrived—seemed livid about my abrupt departure.

"After taking care of you all these months, this is the thanks I get?" She glared at me while I packed up my small life. "Your rudeness to Franklin, then leaving without warning?"

In a way, she was right. Georgiana *had* done a lot for me when she had no reason to, and I was making a fast exit without a thank-you.

Because those words were still so hard to say.

But I wouldn't be guilted into remaining, and I certainly didn't want to stay in a place where someone thought I needed taking care of.

There's a difference between caring *for* someone and caring *about* them.

I doubted that Georgiana could claim the latter.

"You have done a lot for me," I admitted while zipping up my bag. "But now, it's time I take care of myself. If I owe you any money, please let me know."

I'd been trying to contribute financially for months, but she always pushed the offers away. Maybe the gesture would have seemed kind to others, but for me, I only felt more beholden.

"And there is a gift. Something I made. For you."

I'd left the vase of glass flowers on her dining room table. Matching the single one I'd originally crafted for her when I made everyone else's thank-you gifts. The siren had claimed to love the fragile bloom, so I'd fashioned her an entire bouquet. Hopefully, through them, she'd understand that I did truly appreciate her generosity.

I suppose I'll find out the next time we cross paths in this small town.

"Well, it's getting late," Owen announces. "I'll bid you both good night. Ophelia, I'll see you at work on Monday. Broderick, I'll see you tomorrow. Bright and early. Ready to get your ass whooped." Owen offers a jaunty wave before heading up the hill toward the main house, whistling as he goes.

I turn to find Broderick rolling his eyes.

"What's happening bright and early tomorrow?"

He offers a sheepish smile. "We're playing cricket."

That means absolutely nothing to me. "And cricket is ..."

"Sorry." Broderick tucks his hands in his pockets, and a blush steals over his cheeks. "I keep forgetting that it's not big over here. Cricket is a sport. Kind of like baseball, but not really. It's a pretty huge thing over in England. And I think it might be the most popular sport in India. Have you met Anthony's partner, Zara?" When I shake my head, he explains, "She's a harpy and a veterinarian. You might have seen her in town. She's also Ame's boss. Sorry, that's a lot of information to throw at you without answering your question." The witch gives me a rueful grin.

"You don't need to apologize," I tell him, coming to lean against the tiny kitchen sink, where he lingers. "I like hearing you talk."

The blush he had before now looks like a full sunburn, and the heat under his skin is both endearing and enticing.

"Oh. Okay. Well, anyway, Zara's father, Sanjay, is a huge cricket fan. His parents came over from India, and he grew up on the game, then raised Zara to love it too. And Anthony wants to do anything he possibly can to get on Sanjay's good side. Not that he's on his bad side, necessarily. But when he found out Sanjay wanted to have a cricket league, but didn't have enough interest from townsfolk to get a game going, he made it his mission to conscript a decent amount of us in order to play."

"That's sweet. So, you and Owen and others are going to be playing this cricket game tomorrow morning?"

"Yep. Luckily, I played a few matches when I lived in England, so I have a good idea of how the game goes. I still have a feeling that I'm gonna get my ass handed to me." Broderick ducks his chin as he offers the self-deprecating words.

I find the witch's humble nature extremely appealing. Maybe it's from spending my life under the thumb of men who thought they knew better than me. Sometimes, you just want to be around someone who doesn't think they're God's gift to the world.

"Could I watch?" I don't really do much on the weekends. I don't do much in general. And I want to change that.

"Of course you can." Broderick glances up at me, his eyes sparkling with excitement. "But would you want to play instead?"

Do I want to play? Do I want to participate? Do I want to be part of the fun instead of an observer?

Yes.

I'm annoyed with myself that I didn't even consider asking. My entire mindset needs a shift. I need to remember that I don't have to be a simple spectator in life.

I can fully be a part of it.

"Yes. I have no idea how to play, but, yes, I would."

"I can teach you the rules." Broderick starts to grin. "And I think this will be good practice for Galen's Gauntlet."

"How so? Do they usually incorporate sports into it?"

"No." He reaches out, almost absentmindedly, claiming my hand and lacing our fingers together. "Or maybe they will. I honestly don't know what those sirens have planned. But this *should* get your competitive nature going. Because"—now, he smirks—"I don't expect any of these players to go easy on you just because you're a newbie."

A fire starts in my chest, but this time an excited one. Not an anxious, scared flame. But a beautiful, roaring, life-sustaining fire.

"Good. I think I'd like the challenge."

12

BRODERICK

EVEN THOUGH I made sure to be encouraging, I worried about Ophelia trying to play in the cricket match. After how quiet she was during happy hour and the stress of going supernova, then moving to a new home last night, I had no idea how she'd be in this competitive social situation.

But I did know that if she wanted to be here, I was not going to stop her. This was her life and her decision to make.

Still, I texted Anthony to let him know that if Ophelia wanted to leave early, I planned to go with her. In a surprising display of maturity, the guy didn't tease me.

Turns out, there was no reason for me to worry.

"That firebird has a rocket arm on her." My twin mutters the compliment as Ophelia sends another ball bowling hard toward the batter, bowling him out.

She might not have known the rules when she first arrived, but the firebird learned fast. And apparently, she is a goddess when it comes to bowling balls.

Which officially makes her Sanjay Ironfeather's favorite

person. The human is talking so much smack to the other team that I think he might adopt Ophelia as his own.

"You know this was supposed to be my chance to make him fall in love with me, right?" Anthony complains as Ophelia warms up for the next round.

"It's not her fault that you have noodle arms," I taunt back.

There's a snort from nearby, and we both glance over to see Zara chuckling at my insult.

Anthony glares at his harpy. "You're not supposed to laugh at his jokes that insult me. You're supposed to defend me. I am a damsel in distress, and he is an evil villain."

Zara saunters over and gives my brother a kiss on the cheek and a playful smack on the butt. "Stop whining. My dad approves of you for the simple fact that you got this game together. If you get pouty, you'll annoy him."

A smile cracks across Anthony's face, his eyes going hazy with adoration as he leans in to kiss the woman he loves.

"Fine," he sighs. "Cheerleader role it is." Anthony starts rooting for Ophelia, which earns him a middle finger from Owen, who's strolling up for his turn to bat.

I'm also impressed that my brother was able to arrange all this. He didn't manage to get two full teams of eleven, like an official cricket match, but he got a decent turnout. The MacNamara selkies are here, and those who have mates brought them. Then, there's my family, though Ame said that she preferred to keep score. Jack, on the other hand, is having a grand time, bowling Anthony out whenever my brother is up. The werewolf can also pelt a ball dangerously hard. However, we established the rule that mortals or mythics without extra strength could wear a set of cuffs Mor had created with a temporary strength spell.

Now that my older sister has her library up and running smoothly, she's started experimenting with some of the more interesting spells she's found over the years. The strength cuffs are her latest and most successful endeavor. She modeled them after a god object she found written about in one of the grimoires. God objects are mythical gifts, given to mythics by our deities. Mor suspects she has one—the gold apple found in a wall of the house.

But none of us knows what it does, and no one is brave enough to experiment with it.

Mor finds creating her own magical artifacts safer. The original cuffs were described to give the wearer the strength of five werewolves and last as long as the wearer had them on. Mor's version goes for about an hour and gifts the strength of a werewolf with a cold. Still, they're good enough to help a mortal compete with mythics in a backyard cricket game.

Anthony, trying to show off, decided not to use a set. Hence why he cannot handle the balls that Jack bowls him.

Zara, meanwhile, makes contact with the ball just fine. The harpy is probably the best player on the field, scoring the most runs and winning the day for her team—which also happens to be Sanjay, Anthony, and Ophelia's team.

I'm on the losing side, but I forget that fact as I watch the gorgeous firebird dance and cheer with her teammates. Everyone praises her throwing power and accuracy, and for a brief moment, there's not one hint of orange in her aura.

Happiness blots every negative emotion out.

Ophelia jogs up to me, wearing a wide smile, her cheeks flushed, her eyes sparkling with an internal fire that can only be fueled by joy.

"That was invigorating. I want to play every weekend."

Sanjay, who is passing by close enough to overhear, grins and laughs. "That's what I like to hear!"

If nothing else, I think that Anthony should thank Ophelia for being such an enthusiastic participant. She might be the reason that my brother wins total approval from Zara's father.

"Are you worn out?" I ask. "Or ... would you like to cool off in the lake?"

The offer might seem selfless, an opening for her to continue her swimming skill work. But in truth, I have another motive.

I've had to share the firebird all morning. Now, I want her all to myself.

Ophelia's eyes widen, and she blinks slowly. Her smile doesn't disappear, but her expression takes on an edge of determination.

"The lake," she says with a nod. "I want to cool off. And I want to practice. With you."

Ophelia sways toward me, and the moment I open my arms to welcome her, she presses our sweaty bodies together, wrapping her arms around my waist.

"You'll have to tell me if you ever get tired of this," she whispers into my shirt. "Because I don't think that I ever will."

Something inside my chest grows, explodes, reforms, and transforms in a thousand other ways. The simple, affectionate words, filled with vulnerable honesty, wreck me and rebuild me.

I cradle the back of her head in my hands and tilt her head until her golden eyes meet mine.

"Trust me when I say, I will always want your arms where they are in this moment."

Ophelia's smile softens. "And you said your brother was the charming one." Her fingers press into my back. "That did not sound awkward at all to me."

My gaze drops to her sweet lips that say such perfect words. I want to kiss her almost as much as I want her to keep holding me. But I won't do anything to risk this gentle affection she hands out only to me and so freely.

"Just give me a moment," I rasp, my throat scratchy with

want. "I'm sure I'll start babbling about something nonsensical soon."

Ophelia chuckles, and then her lids drift halfway shut, and I could swear that she's staring at my mouth now.

"If you start to babble, is there anything you would like me to do to help you stop?"

Could she be hinting at what I think she is?

"Feel free to shut me up in whatever way you think is appropriate. Using whatever part of you that you think is appropriate."

"Anytime, anywhere, for as long as I want?" she asks with a teasing note.

My body clenches at the idea, and I choke out a single word.

"Exactly."

13

OPHELIA

THE MACNAMARAS MADE it clear that I could use their dock whenever I wanted. That access to it was part of my rental agreement.

Still, I told Broderick that I wanted to practice at the library. Something about floundering around in a cove populated by seal shifters sapped my confidence.

Now, we sit, side by side, on the edge of the floating dock as I work up the courage to slip into the gentle waves.

"Here, let's try this." Broderick pushes himself off, disappearing slightly in the less-than-clear water. But I never fully lose sight of his fiery hair. He pops up a moment later and flicks the soaked red strands out of his eyes. "How about I stay right here?" He drifts to the ladder, then floats a short distance away. "You climb in. Don't jump. Just take it easy at first. Hold on to the ladder for as long as you want. And I'm here to help if you need me." He smiles wide. "But I bet you won't."

His confidence in me strengthens my own.

Also, I *really* want to dip my sweaty body in the cool lake.

Following his directions, I keep a tight hold on the ladder as I ease myself in. The water soothes my overly warm skin, and though it's a little terrifying to descend, the weightlessness is also exhilarating.

"That's great. Just like that," Broderick encourages. He doesn't crowd me. He doesn't tell me to hurry up—or worse, demand I get out before I hurt myself.

Broderick supports me. And I trust him.

Which gives me the confidence to let go.

"I'm doing it!" I crow as I aggressively tread water.

Waves churn around me because of my desperate movements, nothing like the effortless motions Broderick makes to keep himself afloat. The surface barely ripples by him.

But my head stays above water, and that's what counts.

I'm swimming. Really, truly swimming.

"Yeah, you are!" Broderick fist-pumps the air, and the gesture has me laughing and grabbing for the dock again because I don't know that I'm skilled enough to giggle and swim simultaneously.

Small steps, but steps nonetheless.

Broderick paddles up to me, taking hold of the ladder himself. "That was great. And you still have a few weeks until the Gauntlet. I'll come out here every day with you, if that's what you want."

The way he makes the offer, with eager hope on his face, makes one fact undeniable.

This is a good man.

A man I want.

I let go long enough to wrap my arms around Broderick's neck. Hugging him, but not like before. All those times were *only* hugs.

This time, I want to hold him close so my face has easy access to his.

"How do you feel about kissing?" I ask.

From the comment he made earlier, about shutting his babbling mouth up however I want, I think this is what he meant. I hope it is.

But I don't want to guess with Broderick. I want to know.

"Good." He chokes on the word. "Very good. Yes, very much extremely good—"

I shut his mouth up with my mouth.

These past few months, I spent most of my free time on my own in my room in Georgiana's house. But not doing nothing. With access to the internet, I watched movies and shows and searched things I'd always wondered about. Luckily, I found ethical porn websites before I got lost in the free, unrealistic porn that seems to make up a lot of sexual content online. I read romance books from Never Judge a Cover, and I binged the knowledge that my father had refused to give me access to.

So, I'm not unaware of how everything works. I merely lack practical experience.

Meaning, this is my first kiss.

I don't know if I'm lucky or if all kisses are like this. Because every moment is divine.

Broderick worships my mouth with gentle yet firm pressure against my lips. He teases and coaxes. Maybe he's awkward sometimes when speaking, but he's saved all his suave skills for kissing, and I'm glad for it, learning from him as we go.

He deviates from my mouth, kissing over my cheek and along my jaw, dragging my internal fire with him, as if the magic in me wants to chase his mouth.

"That feels so good," I gasp. "I didn't know kissing would feel this good."

Broderick pauses, and I let out an involuntary whimper of protest.

He raises his head, staring at me with wide eyes. "Is this your first kiss? You ... you ... you haven't ... of course you haven't." He closes his eyes, a pained look on his face.

And my fire rises with panic and anger and want.

"Broderick." His name comes from my throat in a hard demand. A tone I don't know I've ever used before.

His eyes snap open, and in his green gaze, I can spy a reflection of the sparks in mine.

Good. I have his attention.

"You will not coddle me," I inform him. "You will not decide what I want. When I tell you to kiss me and touch me and fuck me"—I love the simple erotic word and plan to use it again—"you will trust me. Trust that I am being honest and know what I want. Do you understand?"

If he doesn't, then this is over. No more time with the red-haired witch I crave so much.

Because even if I want him desperately, I refuse to have another person dictate my life.

"Gods be damned," Broderick mutters. "Tell me to do anything in that voice, and I will crawl on my knees to you. I trust you, Ophelia. What do you want from me?"

In this moment? Everything.

But I only say, "Kiss me again."

Broderick dives for my mouth, and this time, there's a fevered need. I respond in kind, learning quickly how to move my mouth in concert with his. I consume the groans and grunts as I wrap not only my arms, but also my legs around him. Broderick keeps us floating with two hands on the ladder, and I feel the cold metal bite into my back.

But I'm too consumed with the pleasure in front of me to care.

A hard length wedges in the space between us.

His cock.

I gasp at the knowledge that his body wants mine the way mine wants his. When I'm alone in bed, for months now, I've explored my pleasure with thoughts of this witch. Fantasies of him taking me in all the ways I learned in my research.

I think it's time to share.

Broderick frees my mouth, kissing down my neck, and I tell him my truth.

"Every Wednesday," I gasp, "when I come to the university, to your department, I want to push you into your office and lock the door behind me."

His body stiffens.

"Hells," he whispers against my neck. "Then what?"

"You'd sit in your chair." I close my eyes, playing out my favorite fantasy on the back of my eyelids. "And I'd mount your lap and rub myself against you like this." I rock my hips, angling so his shaft presses against my clit. "I think about you when I touch myself at night."

Broderick lets out a deep groan and nips at my neck. I jump from the sharp pinch, then hunger for more. Digging my heels into his lower back, I bring him against my pleasure center again and again.

"I want to come," I pant. "Right now."

Who cares if I just had my first kiss? I want what I want. No need to wait.

But will he trust that I mean it?

"Gods, yes." Broderick thrusts against me, helping drive the sensation between my legs to a new level. "Anything you want. Use me. I think about you all the time, Ophelia. Every damn second of the day, I want you." His breath is ragged against me, body straining in my arms.

"Broderick." I moan his name as we find the perfect rhythm. "I want you."

"You have me," he promises. "I'm yours."

The pleasure is a free fall on fire. I let out a scream that the witch claims with his mouth, kissing me hard through my orgasm.

When I finally return to reality, land back in my body, Broderick is still, his body hard as a rock in my hold.

"Do you mind," he rasps, "if I come too?"

I'm momentarily stunned as I gaze at him in realization. The man waits for *my* permission to seek out his pleasure. I'm in full control of this situation. Of him. Broderick has truly given himself to me.

"No," I say. "I don't mind."

His lids flutter in relief, and he rocks his hips, his erection pressing against my belly. Now that I'm relaxed in my postorgasmic bliss, I find myself bravely fascinated with my first access to a penis.

"I want to touch you," I tell him, honest, slightly demanding, but still waiting for his permission.

"Gods, yes. Anytime. Anywhere. For as long as you want."

The familiar words have me smiling eagerly as I reach between us and dip my hand past his waistband. When I grasp his member, Broderick lets out the most delicious grunt and rocks faster, stirring waves around us with his movements. Curious, I drag my thumb over the slit at the tip, where he emits a wetness of a slightly different texture than the water.

"You're going to kill me," he mutters, "and I'm going to die *so* happy."

With the hand that isn't exploring his jutting cock, I twine my fingers in the silky crimson hair at the base of his neck, tugging until green eyes meet mine.

"You can't die on me," I say, knowing he was joking. But my response is completely serious because he needs to know, "Not when I've just started living."

His emerald gaze stays locked on mine, even as his stare clouds with pleasure.

Still, I go on, confessing and claiming. "I've never had anything that was truly mine before. And I know now, if I can have anything, if I can *keep* anything, I want that to be you."

"Yes. Yours," Broderick promises as his body shudders and his cock erupts in my hand. "I'm yours."

14

BRODERICK

ANOTHER FRIDAY EVENING happy hour has me on the dock beside all my siblings as I eagerly stare toward the house, waiting for the cranky sound of Ophelia's truck engine.

"Are you expecting someone, brother dearest?" Anthony sings the question at me from his spot beside Zara. The harpy was able to get off work tonight, but her presence does nothing to dampen the bother that is my twin. "Could it perhaps be a certain bird woman with a fiery pitch?"

"If you call *me* a bird woman," Zara says, "I will shave your head."

Anthony runs his fingers through his hair while wearing a satisfied smirk. "Mmm, I love it when you threaten me."

I ignore the back-and-forth and the other side conversations everyone around me is having, not concerned about being subtle at all. They all know who I'm waiting for. Who I desperately want to appear.

Ophelia. My firebird.

Being back on this dock brings up the memory of last weekend.

What Ophelia and I did.

What she said.

"... if I can keep anything, I want that to be you."

She doesn't realize yet how easy I'll make it for her to keep me.

At the sound of a rumbling motor, I straighten further in my seat, searching for the flash of her truck through the trees. But there's nothing. Only a nudge on my arm. I glance over and realize Niko was the one to claim my attention, and he's pointing toward the water.

A pontoon boat lazily turns into the inlet, and seated at the very front is Ophelia. She faces into the wind, the breeze playing with the long golden strands of her hair. Her eyes are closed, and she's smiling.

I wonder if she's thinking of flying.

"Ahoy!" Owen calls out from behind the wheel as he slows the pontoon to a crawl and aims for our dock. "When Ophelia told me where she was headed, I thought I'd offer my services. Who wants a happy-hour boat ride?"

We have a dock, but no boat, so everyone climbs on board for the novel experience. At first, I'm worried that our whole group won't fit. But I shouldn't have been concerned. The boat is basically a floating living room, and our party of nine settles in, close, but not crowded. Especially because Ame and Jack only take up one seat.

The PDA between my sister and her wolf boyfriend was awkward at first, but I've grown used to it. Plus, it's not like they're making out in front of everyone. The werewolf simply has an incurable need to hold her.

As Ophelia settles at my side, I have a sudden, deep understanding of that urge. Despite the warmth of the summer night, I still lean closer, soaking in her hot cinnamon presence.

"Do you want something to drink? Owen stocked a cooler." She points to a large Yeti tucked into one of the few sections of the boat without seating. "He said he wants to form a selkie–witch alliance, and booze is the best friend–maker."

I already finished my first beer, but saying yes means she'll leave my side even if only for a moment.

"I'm fine. Thank you though."

Yeah, I understand Jack completely.

As Owen steers us out onto the lake, Ophelia takes hold of my wrist and guides my arm around her shoulders. Then, she snuggles deeper into my side, and I perish from happiness.

The cruise is beautiful, showing us a view of our home that can only be enjoyed from the water. Building on the lake is limited, which leaves large stretches of untouched, thickly forested shoreline. There's a wildness to Lake Galen, and the mostly opaque water holds an air of mystery.

What might be lurking beneath the surface?

As we travel past the opening to one inlet, a chill goes down my spine, and Owen makes an abrupt turn.

"What was that?" Mor calls above the drone of the engine. "Did you all feel that?"

Everyone nods, but before my worry about a malevolent force in the lake can take root, Owen laughs.

"Sorry! My fault. Forgot that's the stretch reserved for Galen's Gauntlet this year. Warding spells are already up." He grins. "No peeking allowed. Any of you competing?"

Beside me, Ophelia raises her hand, and a glow of pride lights in my chest. This past week, we've met every day after she gets off work to practice her swimming. She's treading water like a pro and even managing to swim a decent distance from the dock. She's not the most graceful, and speed isn't her strong suit. But every day, I watch her confidence grow, and that alone is a type of winning.

Glancing around, I'm surprised to see Jack and Niko also have their hands raised.

The kappa grins at Ophelia, his expression open and friendly. "Didn't know you were signing up. Want to be part of my and Jack's alliance?"

I glance down in time to watch a hesitant smile take over her lips. "I-I would. But I'm a slow swimmer. Broderick has been helping me learn."

Owen lets out a dramatic gasp, clutching his chest. "How dare you! You asked for a witch to teach you how to swim when you know a selkie? I think this might be a fireable offense."

Ophelia snorts, and I get the sense Owen has a similar personality to my brother. A tendency to tease and most of the words he speaks sounding like flirting.

"We practice in the evenings if you want to come by and offer your wisdom," Ophelia says.

Part of me wishes she hadn't because the selkie's presence will largely cut down on the end-of-lesson make-out sessions. But with Owen's help, she might learn faster, and more than anything, I want to see Ophelia's confidence in herself grow.

We can find other times and places to wrap ourselves around each other.

"Cool. It's a plan," Niko announces, holding up his beer. "You'll get some selkie training and join the Jack-o Alliance."

"I didn't agree to that name," the werewolf grumbles.

"Well, it's better than the Nack Alliance. And now, we can be the Jack-olia Alliance." Niko slips his phone out of his pocket and offers it to Ophelia. "Let me get your number. For strategy meetings."

This could be a sneaky hit-on-Ophelia tactic, but I only get friendly vibes from the kappa. Plus, when I watch her eagerly add her number to the man's phone, I remember how few contacts she has in hers.

As much as I want all of her time to myself, what's best for

Ophelia is to establish a group of friends in Folk Haven. And what better group to start with than the one we're in now?

"Why don't you get everyone's numbers," I say, "while we're all here?"

She blinks up at me, lips slightly parted in surprise.

"Come on." I squeeze her shoulder. "Where's your phone?"

After handing Niko's his back, Ophelia reaches into a pocket on her jean shorts and pulls out the device. When she swipes it open, the picture of the owl makes me smile. Then, I hand it off to Mor.

"Everyone, put your number in Ophelia's phone."

"Good idea." Ame smiles at us from her spot in Jack's lap. "That way, we don't need to go through Broderick to talk to you. We can make sneaky plans behind his back."

"I regret this immediately," I grumble, but without true heat because Ophelia is laughing.

Talking trails off as Owen navigates to a more open section of the lake and increases the speed, filling the air with the roar of the engine. The clouds take on a magenta shade against a periwinkle sky as the sun sets behind the trees. With the growing darkness, our captain points us back toward the library.

We dock smoothly, temporarily tying the boat up long enough for everyone to unload. Owen accepts our thanks with a dramatic bow.

I wish the ride could have gone on longer. That I had an excuse to hold Ophelia for endless hours.

Now, I have to say goodbye.

But when I turn for my farewell, the firebird is right behind me.

"Could you drive me home?" Ophelia asks.

"Abandoning me?" Owen shakes his head with a mock frown.

Meanwhile, I grin. "Of course."

After we untie the pontoon and watch Owen cruise off, the two of us walk hand in hand toward the house. Everyone else has already disappeared, either going inside or heading home. We're alone in the twilight.

A hoot sounds overhead, and a beautiful barn owl glides past. The bird has a watchful quality, as if it's guarding the two of us.

"That's my friend." Ophelia points to the owl. "Always joining me on walks."

I make a note to ask Ame and Anthony about their familiars. How did they know the animal was their magical partner? Because I feel a calm connection with Ophelia's feathered friend, and I wonder if maybe I've discovered mine.

When we reach my car, I try to be a gentleman by heading to the passenger side to open Ophelia's door for her.

But the firebird seems uninterested in chivalry when she presses me back against the car and claims my mouth in a searing kiss that tastes like the spices from the cider she was drinking on the boat. I groan and spread my legs to both lower myself closer to her height and to make room for her between them.

The hot press of her body against my hardening cock is a beautiful kind of torture.

Ophelia peels her mouth from mine. "Maybe we could walk for a bit." Her words are breathy and full of promise. "Before you drive me home."

"Walk." I nod repeatedly, trying to force my brain to function. "Yes. I know how to do that."

She laughs and tugs me toward the woods. And despite claiming I know how to move my legs in a normal manner, I end up a touch bowlegged until I adjust myself.

The woods swallow us, the evening growing darker with a thick canopy of leaves overhead.

"I was going to find a good tree to kiss you against," Ophelia informs me. A tight note to her voice that replaces the light-hearted tone from before.

"Sounds like a good plan to me."

And any other time, just the thought would melt me into a puddle beneath her feet.

But with Ophelia's hand in mine, I have a closer connection to her emotional state. A clearer view of her aura. Creeping orange tendrils twine through the air around her, and her fingers tighten in mine with each step we take.

Is she shaking?

"Ophelia—"

Her gasp cuts me off, and she whirls to face me with wide eyes, pupils dilated. Overhead, the owl screeches. On instinct, I gather the firebird into my arms. Her body is sweltering against mine. I send a brief prayer to The Bright One that I'm not about to be burned alive.

"You're safe," I tell her. "What's wrong? Why are you scared?"

The magical urge to soothe her terror is so strong that my skin actually stings from holding my power back.

Not without her permission.

"D-dark," she forces out through chattering teeth. "P-panic. Panic attack." Ophelia squeezes her eyes shut, but not before tears flow from them. Her breathing is erratic, short gasps and ragged exhales.

I hold her closer, not sure if my embrace is helping or hurting.

But I know something that can solve this—at least temporarily.

"Ophelia. Sweetheart. Will you let me use my magic on you?" There's a desperate rasp in my question. "I can stop the panic attack. That's all I'll do, I swear."

For a long stretch, she only shudders and sobs in my arms. But eventually, she manages a weak, "Yes."

In a secret compartment on my watch, I keep an emergency dose of the red powder us Shellys use to amplify our magic, making it easy to manipulate. I press the notch now that releases the dry potion and spread the clinging crimson dust on my palm.

Then, I cup the back of Ophelia's neck and focus on the tangled orange of fear that's suffocating her. I guide my magic over the sickly color, easing the vivid shade until it turns into the rich emerald of contentment. The power tingles along my nerves, like all my limbs fell asleep and are suddenly regaining blood flow. Not the most comfortable sensation, but worth it.

Ophelia sags in my hold, and I guide the both of us to the leaf-strewn forest floor. We settle there, the two of us breathing in time as our owl observer coos a soothing hoot overhead.

"I'm sorry," I say after a stretch. "For the magic. I know it can't be easy after ... everything." I clear my throat and try not to let my fury rise, like it does every time I think of that evil sorcerer using Ophelia as a power source for his sick spells.

"Can you explain what you did?" She asks the question against the collar of my shirt, giving nothing of her feelings away.

Now that she's not panicking, I hold off on trying to explore her aura.

"All witches have specialties. A type of magic that comes naturally to us. Shellys are emotion witches." I draw on my professor voice, pretending I'm in a lecture hall and not terrified I've screwed up everything with Ophelia. "Mor has a general kind of control over all emotions. Ame senses and can affect desires. Anthony deals in jealousy when he wants." I try not to hold her too tight to me as I explain the next bit. "I'm acquainted with fear."

"What does that mean?"

"I can sense it. See it." I clear my throat. "Not the cause though. Not unless I perform certain spell work."

"And you can get rid of it?"

"I can ease it," I agree. "Soothe the harsh edges."

Ophelia tilts her head up to stare into my eyes, her brows dipped. "How often do you soothe my fear?"

"I don't." The words rush out of me as I experience another wave of my own panic. "This was the first time and only because you told me I could, I swear."

The question is, will she believe me?

15

OPHELIA

THE RELIEF IS EUPHORIC.

Until Broderick took it away, I never realized how much fear still twined through my normal level of emotions. How close I always am to panic.

The relief is addictive. What would I do to never go back to being afraid again?

Does anyone else live like that? Keep functioning despite a constant, low-level terror?

Jack might not have had my strict father, but he did spend years trapped as an animal, used as magical fuel.

Maybe that's why everyone thinks he's angry all the time. Maybe he *is*.

As often as I feel anxiety, the werewolf seems to feel rage.

And still, he's a functioning member of society. He has a partner he loves and a full-time job in the tech department at Ramla.

But would he jump on the chance to forever rid himself of that anger?

"Ophelia?" Broderick speaks my name tentatively. "Talk to me. How are you doing?"

"I feel ... light. Weightless." And I believe him about having never worked magic on me before. Because I can't remember a time I felt this good.

Well, other than when I was mid-orgasm.

"Is that okay?" he asks, still wary.

And I appreciate Broderick's caution. That he doesn't assume I'll be grateful for his magical intervention. That he's giving me room to figure out how I feel about this development.

"It's okay. But ..." I don't want to keep talking. I want to simply enjoy this state of being. To never leave it.

And that's exactly why I need to push forward.

"But?" Broderick presses.

"But this feels too good, I think." A sigh gusts out of my chest. "I could see myself relying on it. And I don't want that. To have to rely on you."

Broderick's eyes drop from mine, but not before I spy the hurt. I pinch his chin and raise his gaze.

"I didn't mean it like that. Like I don't trust you." My thumb traces over his soft bottom lip. I love this man's mouth so much. For all the pleasure it brings me and all the soft, caring words it speaks. "What I meant is, I need to know I can rely on myself. I've never had that chance before, and I need to know I can survive on my own. Fear and all."

While his expression stays concerned in the dim light, the witch still nods in understanding.

"I won't ever use my magic on you unless you ask. I'll make a blood oath if that sets you at ease."

This man.

"I trust you. No blood oath required." Leaning in, I brush a gentle kiss against his mouth, then pull back before going too deep. "Maybe we could have a signal. I think during a panic attack, if you're nearby, it makes sense. There's no willing my way through those. They take over completely."

Broderick's expression lightens. "Yes. Good. That sounds good."

I fist a hand over my heart. A gesture my mother used to make when she told me she loved me. "If I do this, then I need your help. Okay?"

The witch nods, a solemn air to the dip, as if making a vow. "Okay." He tucks some stray, sweaty hairs behind my ear. "Do you know what brought it on? Or are they random?"

My eyes flick around us, and it truly is a display of his power that I'm calm in this moment. "The darkness. That's why I walk at twilight. Trying to get used to it." With my fear dampened, I find it easier to discuss that terrible time. "When I was trapped, the sorcerer would keep my cage in a dark room. I didn't have much light."

"Gods." Broderick rasps the word, clutching me tight against his chest. "If that bastard wasn't dead, I'd flay him alive myself."

A violent Broderick is kind of hot.

"I can't believe ... it's terrifying to think ... if I hadn't gone ..." He shakes his head, muttering to himself.

I reach up to finger-comb his red waves, not because they're in his eyes, but only because I find the gesture soothing. "Hadn't gone where?"

He gives a dry, humorless laugh. "To this random estate sale in London. Anthony was gone on a photo shoot, and I realized it had been over a year since I had seen my sisters. I was missing them, feeling lonely, and then some friends invited me to this sale. Just a lark, to see what the upper crusts owned. Not normally my thing, but I decided to join them because I had nothing else to do."

My heart thumps, slow and heavy. "What did you find there?" I ask in a whisper.

Broderick meets my eyes, though I can't see much of his green irises with night enveloping us.

"The grimoire," he says with a tone of awe. "Just sitting in this old house, on a shelf. Magic spilling off it. I knew Mor was collecting them, so I bought the book and sent it to her."

"*The* grimoire?" I rasp, remembering the old leather book open in front of him the night I came back to my body.

Broderick nods. "The one with the spell that freed Jack. Jack, who led us to you."

"And you freed me too." Now, I reach for his hand, tracing my thumb over the scar on his palm. I feel the stiff skin under the layer of fine powder he used to work magic.

The witch closes his eyes and rests his forehead against mine. "I wish I had found it sooner. That we'd found you before you spent years in the dark."

I cup his cheeks. "You're the reason I'm here." I press my lips against each of his lids. "I don't know if it was luck or fate, but you found exactly what you needed to. And now, I'm here." I kiss his cheekbones. "And I get the chance to live." I kiss the corners of his mouth. "I get the chance to love. To love *you*."

He sucks in a ragged breath, and then we're kissing frantically, full of need and passion.

And a little bit of fear.

But the useful kind that pricks at you to remind you that life is finite, so take advantage of the good things when they're in front of you.

I tear at Broderick's clothes, leaving scorched fingerprints in the fabric. But my fire doesn't hurt him, only makes the man groan and beg.

"I'm yours," he pants. "Tell me to do anything, and I'll do it."

"Lie back," I command. "I'm going to take you slow until I figure this out."

When I fantasized about having sex with Broderick, I never

imagined my knees would be pressing into dead leaves and I'd have an audience of stars above me.

But I wouldn't change a single detail.

Not how he restrains himself, like I told him. Not how heated his cock is when I slip him from his pants. Not how the muscles in his neck strain as I use the tip of him to stroke through my damp arousal.

And not the way he whimpers when I pause and say, "Do you see my purse anywhere? I think I dropped it. There's a pack of condoms."

The internet also taught me a lot about sex ed.

"We can look for it," Broderick offers in a strained voice. "But so you know, I have a contraceptive tattoo. On my hip. Still, I understand if you need more than that."

Well, that's something I *didn't* learn about online. Thank the gods for magic.

"I trust you." And I make sure to meet his eyes as I say so, loving the way his brows rise in wonder.

Broderick is tight at first. Or I am. Either way, it takes some time to work his length into me. But I put in the effort, and my well-behaved witch stays prone, his fingers tangled in his hair as he rattles off curses and prayers to the gods.

I've never felt more in control.

Then, I finger my clit until I'm grinding and squeezing and crying out his name.

And I've never felt more out of control.

"Amazing. So gods-damn amazing," Broderick groans, and I can feel him trying to see me in the darkness.

As pleasure pulses through my nerves, I allow a touch of my fire out.

Just enough to glow.

"Hold me," I command.

Instantly, he's upright, his arms wrapping tight around my torso, his lips dragging down my neck and along my collarbone. Broderick rocks his hips, thrusting up into me and prolonging my orgasm—or maybe starting a new one.

All I know is that when he shouts my name, movements erratic, I join him in the euphoria.

Even better than my freedom from fear.

16

OPHELIA

THE MORNING of Galen's Gauntlet, I find myself bending over a bush, throwing up.

I might be slightly nervous.

"This is normal!" Niko calls out encouragingly. "Lots of top competitors get nauseous right before a competition. Let it all out!"

I wasn't sure how I'd feel about having allies, especially when one is a well-known grump. But Jack and Niko have been awesome these past few weeks. We relocated my daily swimming lessons to the MacNamara dock since it was much larger than the library one and turned them into swim lesson/strategy sessions.

If Broderick was bothered by our sexy times getting postponed due to an audience, he kept his opinions to himself. Also, he spent most nights in the Airstream with me, making up for lost time.

In addition to coming up with plans for dealing with potential Gauntlet obstacles, I also used the time with Owen, Niko, and Jack to instill the knowledge that not all men are looking to hurt or imprison me.

My father and the sorcerer were outliers. Not the norm.

Though Niko did make it clear that our alliance lasted until the final task at the latest. There could only be one winner, and he intended for that to be him.

When I asked what his motivation was, the kappa explained to me that in addition to the prestige of the title and the cash prize, there were perks around town. Bonus prizes. And there was a particular complimentary service he had his eye on.

Back when I was fashioning my glass gifts, I'd stopped by the IT department at Ramla, where Jack worked, and asked him what his friend liked.

He'd simply said, "A wolf."

Not wanting to push, I had taken that and run with it. I hadn't understood it at the time, but when I was reviewing the prize list, I saw that there was a year of free haircuts offered by Veronica, who also happened to be the alpha of the werewolf pack that had moved into town last year.

Could it be that Niko has a *crush* on a certain werewolf?

I figure if we become close enough friends, one day, I'll find out.

When I asked Jack why he wanted to win, the werewolf shrugged and grumbled, "I don't."

Which I took to mean, the guy entered this competition with the sole intent of helping his best friend reach the finish line first.

After that, his grumpiness lost most of its intimidation factor.

But now, I'm plenty terrified as we make our way to the starting line.

What if I forget how to swim?

What if I'm too weak for this?

What if I'm better off hiding away?

Those self-deprecating thoughts batter at my brain, trying to overwhelm me with self-doubt and set off a panic attack.

"Here." Jack hands me a water bottle. "Rinse and spit."

At this point, I welcome the simple directions. Easy steps to follow. I slosh the water around in my mouth to get rid of the acidic taste of my sick.

"I'm going to hold you guys back," I confess. "You can leave me behind. I won't blame you."

Jack gives me a hard look, and Niko scoffs.

"No way. We're allies. We agreed that as long as we're in sight of one another, we help each other. All the way till the end. You won't get rid of us that easy." The kappa offers me a kind grin.

It takes me a moment to realize this warm, comforting feeling of connection must be friendship.

It's nice. Hopefully, I don't die in this magical competition before I get a chance to make more of them.

The three of us head toward the mouth of the inlet, where we were instructed to line up by noon. If you're late, then you've already lost. As we weave through a stand of trees, I pick out an almost-indistinguishable shimmer in the air.

"Wards," Niko explains when he notices the direction of my gaze. "Not a wall. We can walk through them. Ame said we should brace ourselves."

"For what?"

A moment later, I know.

Once we pass through the magical barrier, noise fills the air. A massive crowd stretches along the banks. Everyone cheers so loud that I expect the ground to start shaking. Somehow, above the cacophony, I hear my name.

A certain red-haired witch jogs up to me, a supportive smile on his face. Broderick scoops me into a hug, but the moment I realize his mouth is heading toward mine, I slap a hand over my lips, getting a kiss on my knuckles instead. His brows dip in the center.

"I'm sorry." He sets me down as his uncertain expression deepens. "I didn't mean—"

"I threw up!" I blurt from behind my fingers. "You can't kiss me until I thoroughly brush my teeth."

Broderick fully frowns now, though he doesn't retreat from me anymore. "You're sick?"

"Just nervous."

"You're going to do great," Niko announces as he sidles up to us. "Come on, teammate. Time to line up."

It's almost noon, and on a stretch of floating docks, a decent number of other competitors wait for the start of Galen's Gauntlet.

"He's right." Broderick speaks the words against my hair before pressing a kiss against my tight braid. "I'll be watching from the sidelines. Cheering for you the whole time even if you can't see me." He steps back, his hands braced on my shoulders. "You can do this, firebird."

The nerves don't disappear, but they become easier to ignore in the glow of Broderick's confidence.

"I can do this," I agree, then step out of his hold and head for the starting line.

Niko and Jack flank me, and we end up on our own floating platform.

The mythics around us look vaguely familiar. I see a lot of people I recognize from collecting recycling all over town. But I realize now how rarely I talk to anyone. Not even to offer my name. I still give in to the learned instinct to curl into myself.

But not anymore.

Today, there's nowhere to hide.

A siren soars overhead, the midday sun glinting off the bright white feathers that cover the wings stretching from her shoulder blades. The sight of her flying freely briefly stuns me.

Then, she calls out to the competitors, "Ready yourselves!"

I shake my head and refocus, following Niko's and Jack's lead as they line up at the edge of the dock. Just as doubt tries to overwhelm my mind, a horn blares from the shore.

There's no turning back.

The signal is still ringing off the trees when I jump—feet-first—into the water.

Other mythics stopped by our training sessions to help prepare Niko, Jack, and me for the competition. Our coaches included all the Shelly witches and the MacNamaras. Someone mentioned that obstacles could come at you immediately or there could be a calm before the storm.

When I come up for air, treading water, then pushing myself forward in an ungainly head-above-the-water freestyle with nothing stopping me, I assume we have a moment to get our bearings.

But then I hear the cursing. And when I glance around, I spy giant chunks of white that must have been hidden under a glamour a moment ago. And that's when I realize that the fire in my chest is steadily burning, not from excitement for the race, but to keep my body temperature regulated.

The water is freezing.

I pause and tread water, searching in front, then behind me for my teammates. I assumed they'd be far ahead of me and I'd have to try to catch up. But I spot Niko not far from the dock, his lips fading to blue, his jaw quaking. Jack has his friend by the arm, pulling him forward, but the wolf doesn't seem to be doing too well himself.

I can help them.

The realization is euphoric. Every moment they spent with me training for this, I thought of myself as a charity case. What help could I be to a powerful werewolf and a water mythic?

But neither of them has fire in their veins like I do.

In this, I am the powerful one.

I swim back to them as fast as I can, reaching the two mythics quicker because Jack is still managing some forward momentum.

"Give me your hands," I shout above the roar of the crowd.

Both men listen without question, slipping their frigid fingers into mine. With a gentle internal push, I guide the heat from my body into theirs—a skill I wasn't even aware I had—and watch with joy as their faces regain a healthy color.

"Thank the gods," Niko groans. " I knew Jack-olia was a good idea."

"Let's go."

The wolf doesn't have any use for hanging around to chat. And I find I don't either. My thoughts of weakness and unworthiness are gone. I'm ready to start competing.

The three of us arrow back into the competition, dodging other competitors going stiff from the cold. Any other day, I would stop out of concern, but Owen informed me that the Gauntlet wasn't meant to be deadly. If a competitor goes down past the point of recovery, they're removed from the course and taken care of by the on-call healing witch.

As we weave through miniature icebergs, the water slowly loses its frigid edge.

"Get ready!" Niko calls out. "Something new could pop up at any moment—ah!" The kappa's head disappears.

"Niko!" Jack dives forward, then lets out a curse as he's sucked into whatever grabbed his friend.

I consider trying to swim another way, but a current is drawing me forward, and I'm not a strong enough swimmer to get out of it. There's a tug on my body, a drop of my stomach, and then I'm falling over a waterfall I didn't realize was in front of me.

Oddly, the cascade of water and even my scream as I plummet into the pool below is silent. The sound of the world around me suddenly switches off in the middle of my yell. I resurface noiselessly, spluttering water until I can breathe again. A small corner of my brain is proud because only a little bit of the liquid went up my nose.

Then, I forget about my improved swimming ability when something knocks into my leg.

Something very large.

17

BRODERICK

EVERYONE around me is having a grand time, drinking and cheering. Meanwhile, I'm sweating through my clothes, watching as a gigantic metal fish circles the woman I love.

What if she has a panic attack?

I don't know if I can use my magic at long range, but I have a pound of red powder in my pockets, ready to assist me. But even if I can soothe from a distance, will the anti-cheating enchantments on the competition allow my magic to pass? If they do, Ophelia would certainly be disqualified. So, even though I spy fear on her face, I hold myself back.

We have a signal. If she needs me, she'll use it.

Until then, I have to trust her.

"Your mate is doing great!" Owen appears at my side, offering a beer, which I turn down.

I need to stay sober until this is all over.

"I am rooting for her. Well, her and the other couple of my employees in the race. I have a bet that someone from Clean Haven will win."

"You can bet on the Gauntlet?" Seems like that would up the likelihood of sabotage.

"Not officially. It's just a friendly wager with my brother Seamus. He thinks someone from Ramla will take the trophy. But I think he's just cocky from *his* win. I am so looking forward to him losing his title. I cannot stand another day of his champion strut. I would've rather had Moira win."

The selkie keeps chatting about his sibling squabbles. Meanwhile, I watch Ophelia drag herself onto an island with a lone tree in the middle.

The metal fish is one of many circling the small slip of land. Just as I am wondering if the creatures are aggressive, I watch a merman try to dive past one. He's too slow.

The thing swallows him whole.

"How is that allowed?" I choke.

Owen chuckles and sips from his beer. "I doubt he's actually hurt. Just wait."

After a count of three, the fish sprays an aggressive fountain of water from a blowhole. The stream carries the merman, who lets out a terrified yelp as he's flung into the crowd on the shore.

Out of bounds and out of the competition.

"Love to see a merman go flying!" Owen lets out a celebratory whistle.

"How are they supposed to get past them?" I ask, aghast at the idea of Ophelia getting chomped and rocketed through the air. Though, if she realized she was out of the game, the woman could always release her firebird form and glide to a gentle landing.

"My guess is they have to do something with those apples," the selkie says.

Then, he reaches into a fanny pack I just now realize he's wearing. Owen pulls out a fresh beer from the pouch and cracks it open. The guy came prepared.

"Apples?" I mutter to myself, squinting toward the island's

tree, and realize there are colorful fruits hanging from the branches.

"There's a wood witch in town. Root owns The Fernmore Pumpkin Patch, which includes an apple orchard. He has his own little competition around the autumn equinox. Bet that spell work is his doing."

Even after I've lived here for over half a year, there are still so many people I haven't met. So much about this place that I don't know.

But something I do know is that firebirds love apples. If anyone can figure this out, it's Ophelia.

She stands with Niko and Jack, the three of them staring up at the branches in deep concentration. Meanwhile, a guy I think I've seen behind the counter at the bank grabs an apple and bites into it.

Then, he collapses, rolls into the water, and gets the same abrupt exit that the merman did.

The group seems stalled.

That is, until Ophelia plucks an apple of her own. I hold my breath as she chucks the fruit toward one of the metal fish, her throw as good as her cricket bowling. The mechanical beast snaps it out of the air. Then, a second later, it floats, belly up.

A cheer goes up from the crowd, and I explode with pride.

Apples start flying, and fish start floating—but not for long.

The sedation only lasts for a few moments, and the audience watches a red-haired bear shifter get swallowed and catapulted toward the trees with a loudly roared, "I can fly!"

I about have a heart attack when Ophelia almost gets caught in a set of metal jaws, but Jack gives her a mighty tug forward across some invisible barrier the fish haven't passed. And I decide that Ame found herself a top-notch mate who I will never speak ill of to the end of my days.

"Come on," Owen calls over the excited shouts of other spectators. "Let's keep up."

The selkie grips my arm and pulls me along, all of us shifting our viewing spots to make sure we don't miss a single piece of the action.

Overhead, there's the ominous chorus of cackling, laughter, and steady beats, like wings in the air.

The sirens are here.

18

OPHELIA

"WATCH OVERHEAD!" Niko calls out.

The sound came back on once we passed the fish obstacle. It was eerie as I stood on that island, knowing danger lurked in the water on all sides, but not having the ability to communicate our next steps, even with Niko and Jack beside me.

Throwing the apple at the fish was a lucky guess. But Seamus, winner of last year's Gauntlet, said luck was an important factor toward him winning.

Hopefully, mine hasn't run out because we're still swimming and some gleefully determined-looking women with wings are arrowing toward us in the sky.

For a moment, I'm paralyzed by the sight. I thought one winged mythic was amazing, but here's a whole crowd, joy on their faces. No fear. No concern. No shame.

In this moment, I decide that two years from now, I don't want to compete in Galen's Gauntlet.

I want to be an obstacle in it.

"You're looking a little weighed down," Sonya, the siren co-owner of Coffee & Claws, shouts to the group of us who made it this far. "Let's take some weight off!" She fakes a throw toward Niko, who ducks under the water, but then she switches at the last minute to chuck a blue orb at Jack.

The wolf dodges, but isn't fast enough, and the ball catches him in the shoulder. The light ball soaks into his skin like water into a sponge.

"What the—" he starts, then snarls when his body slowly rises out of the water.

I've seen videos of astronauts in the space station weightlessly floating around, unable to move anywhere unless they push off something first.

That's exactly how Jack is now, hovering five feet over the surface of the water. Not flying, just hanging there.

"Fucking hells," he growls just as Niko resurfaces. "You two, go. Now!" His command leaves no room for argument, and with orbs smacking into competitors all around us, staying put isn't an option.

"Ophelia." Niko's voice is urgent as he hooks his fingers around my wrist. "Take a big breath. Hold it. When you need air, pinch my hand. Got it?"

I'm not sure what his plan is, but I trust the kappa. So, I nod, suck in all the oxygen I can handle, and let the mythic drag me underwater.

When Niko starts swimming, towing me forward, I realize that he easily could have left me behind. The guy is fast, even with my dead weight—although I try to kick my feet in a helpful manner. After probably too short of a time, my lungs burn—and not in the pleasantly heated way I normally enjoy. Reaching through the water, I pinch Niko's slippery skin. He immediately shoots us to the surface. We break into the air with dual gasps.

I glance around to see the field has thinned considerably.

Still, Seamus warned me that some obstacles might slow

competitors down, but not fully knock them out of the race. Mythics could catch up at any moment.

"Come on." Niko begins swimming again. "It looks like it gets shallow up ahead."

Thank the gods.

We paddle forward, and I spot a few competitors in waist-deep water, which encourages me to kick faster. My swimming lessons helped—hell, they saved me—but I long for solid ground under my feet. When my soles meet the muddy lake bottom, I feel like I can finally keep up with the kappa. Niko and I half walk, half paddle around a bend, and I do my best to ignore the audience crowding the shores. That's easier to do when the next obstacle appears.

Rocks.

Towering, view-obscuring rocks. And perched on each one is a woman with wide, feathered wings. As I take in the scene, I realize there are gaps between the boulders and that a siren is positioned near each one.

Georgiana stands above the pass Niko aims for.

I grit my teeth against calling out to him. My urge is to go to another. To avoid that mythic who holds a grudge, if her haughty glare is anything to go by.

But I won't let pettiness derail my ally.

"The maze isn't hard," Georgiana tells us when we get close enough to hear, and then her lips tilt in a smirk. "Simply heed my directions and warnings."

Warnings about what?

She opens her mouth, and a second later, I'm tilting forward into the water, suddenly dizzy and disoriented. A strong grip pulls me upright.

Niko.

"She sang to us," he explains, and my confusion clarifies.

Only sirens and their mates can remember their songs.

Everyone else immediately forgets and sometimes is left with a magical hangover.

Great. As if I wasn't worn out enough.

"Let's go." I don't spare the spiteful siren another glance as we pass through the boulders.

We come upon more giant rocks, and I swear I can hear more singing in the distance. I try not to listen, powering forward instead.

"What do you think the warning was about?" I ask, panting my question.

"If I had to guess, I'd say that." The kappa's voice is tight, and I stare in the direction he's pointing to see what looks like a massive fishing net.

A net that's moving.

19

BRODERICK

Galen's Gauntlet is always arranged so spectators have a decent view of the obstacles that competitors are working through. Which means Owen and I stand on a high bank, easily seeing into the maze, where Ophelia and Niko battle a sentient net. The thing scurries and lunges, moving like a spider, which makes it kind of terrifying.

But they aren't panicking.

"You can do it," Owen mutters, gaze intent on the face-off.

I expect him to be half drunk and bellowing, but the selkie seems focused.

How much money did he wager against Seamus?

Just when it appears like they have an opening, Ophelia loses her footing and disappears under the shallow water. Owen's hand fisting the back of my shirt is the only thing that keeps me from diving into the competition. A second later, she pops up, spluttering water and thoroughly tangled in the net.

The animated trap drags my firebird up a boulder.

"Go, Niko!" I hear her holler. "If I get free, I'll catch up."

But she has no knife or claws to rend the thick ropes. I expect a thick wash of orange to flood her aura. Ready myself to hear her panicked screams from the way she's bound. Captive, like her whole life before Folk Haven. My eyes lock on her hands, and I wait for her fingers to curl and press against her heart.

Calling for my aid.

Owen is going to lose an arm soon if he doesn't let me go.

She needs me. Niko is going to leave her.

Only the kappa doesn't. With the net distracted, he's free to power forward and possibly win the whole thing. A crown that only one mythic can claim anyway. Their alliance would have to end sometime, so why not now?

Instead, the kappa scrabbles up the rock after Ophelia, chasing the net as she struggles to claw herself free. He's almost to her when the net flops on the shoreline and falls loose.

"Stop!" Ophelia shrieks, and I'm sure her anxiety has finally arrived.

But then I realize her hand isn't clutched to her chest. Instead, they are both open in a staying gesture extended toward her ally.

"I'm free," she calls out. "And I'm disqualified." That's true. Like the fish did before with other competitors, the net dragged her out of bounds. "You still have a chance, Niko. Go!"

Finally, the kappa listens, giving her a nod of thanks before plunging back into the maze. But I don't pay him any further attention as I shove away from Owen, slide down the steep bank, and rush to Ophelia's side. My hands glide over her skin as I search for injuries. A few scratches and bruises, but that's all.

"How are you?" I pant the question, adrenaline pumping hard through my veins.

My magic searches her aura for sickly orange. For signs of fear.

There is none.

"I'm great!" she gasps and throws her arms around my neck, pulling me in until we topple onto the ground together. Her wet bathing suit soaks my clothes, but I couldn't give a shit because she's in my arms, laughing. "That was *amazing*! Did you see me?"

"Every second." I stare down into her golden eyes. "You're not upset about being disqualified?"

Ophelia laughs and shakes her head. "Not at all. I wasn't in it for a win."

"Then, why'd you sign up?"

Her hands cup my face, thumbs tracing my cheekbones.

"Because I wanted to live. To challenge myself. To be a little wild. A little dangerous." She sighs, and it's like a lifetime of tension leaves her in that one breath. "To show myself I can do anything I want."

"You can. You can conquer the world if you want." I lean down and press a gentle kiss to her lips, soothed by the steady warmth in her. "How do you feel?"

Fire sparks in her eyes.

"Free."

EPILOGUE

OPHELIA

Three Months Later

My professor is *hot*.

He stands at the head of the room, all of us students in a half circle, facing him as he lectures animatedly about the literary merit of first-person point of view. I think my panties are about to catch on fire.

But I keep that fact to myself.

No need to traumatize my fellow students or fluster the already-blushing professor.

After four weeks in his class, I'd have thought Professor Shelly would be better at ignoring my *I want to fuck you the second we get off this campus* eyes.

But the witch is hopeless, so I drop my horny gaze to my notebook and listen to him teach.

"Your assignment for the next class is to choose a prompt from the syllabus, write a five-hundred-word scene in third-person limited. Then, rewrite the same scene in first person. I want you to experiment with different writing styles so you can discover how you personally enjoy telling stories." He turns off the projector, which is a sign that we can start packing up. "Don't forget to swing by my office hours if you have questions. Have a good evening."

With that, we are officially dismissed. I take my time packing up my belongings, giving my classmates an opportunity to claim the professor's attention. A young woman with half her head shaved asks him about tense—our choice—and then he's free.

"That was a good lesson." I offer the compliment as I prop my hip on the table beside the podium and wait for Broderick to unhook his laptop and slip it into his bag. "I've already got ideas."

"Oh, really?" He tries to sound only mildly interested, playing the game we do here. Student and professor. Nothing more.

I enrolled at Ramla starting this fall, working toward a history degree.

Also, I'm auditing one creative writing course.

This way, I can learn about an interesting subject, but there's no true conflict of interest because Broderick isn't grading any of my work. Not officially anyway.

"Yeah. Only I'm wondering if there's a restriction on what I can write about." I keep my voice casual.

The witch adjusts the strap of his bag. "Only that it should fit with one of the prompts."

"I think this does, but"—I lean close, lowering my voice even though we're alone in the room—"the story might be slightly *erotic*."

He doesn't respond. Not other than clasping one of my hands in his and tugging me toward the exit.

"Wait," I gasp while grinning. "Where are you taking me, Professor Shelly?"

Broderick's spine goes rigid, and he turns blazing eyes on me. "Home. Where I can teach you a lesson about what it does to me when you call me *Professor Shelly*." My witch glances around quickly, eyes frantic, then drags me in for a hot, desperate kiss. He's breathing heavily when we part. "I love you so fucking much."

I cup his face. "I love you too." Then, I rub my nose against his. "Sorry for torturing you with sex eyes. You're too tempting."

He groans and drags me—laughing—from the room.

Days like this help me forget about the pain and fear from my past.

So does therapy. Jack got me in touch with a professional he talks to. A mythic. Ame had originally encouraged him to go to counseling. The wolf admitted that he was reluctant to talk to a stranger at first, but he's found it helpful.

And now, I do too.

The panic and anxiety attacks are less frequent, and I have tools for managing them when I can't avoid slipping into that bad space. Broderick's magic is always the final option, and when I'm struggling, I know his eyes are on my chest. Waiting for me to press a fist to my heart. Simply knowing that he has the power to ease the twisted pressure in my chest and head offers a sense of safety.

As we step into the twilight of the evening, a welcoming hoot sounds from overhead, and a large barn owl wings down from the branch where she's been waiting for us.

"Hello, Moonlight. Have a good sleep?" Broderick reaches up to offer his finger for a gentle, affectionate nip. The familiar trills another note before soaring away. She'll arrive at his window later tonight, tapping her beak on the glass of the kitchen window in a demand for admittance.

There's a perch for her in almost every room of the witch's house, though she spends most of her time in the woods.

Before I can break off and head for my truck, Broderick pulls me in for another kiss—chaste in case his students are around.

"I'll see you at my place?" he asks, as if there's somewhere else I'd rather be.

"I'll be right behind you."

But then his phone chimes, and when Broderick glances at the screen, he groans.

"What's up?"

"Mor wants me to close up the library for her." He turns his screen so I can see. "She has a monster emergency."

I grimace in sympathy. For his sister, not for him—Broderick will get laid tonight, just a bit later than he was hoping. A delay in his sex life is nothing compared to what Mor is going through.

She finally found a safe way to break the enchantment on the metal statue and free the being within.

Things have not gone well since.

Jack and I both caused our own slight disturbances in the town when we were freed of our curses. Even now, things with the wolves are still delicate, and Georgiana never offers me more than a clipped 'hello' when we run into each other around town. However, Jack and I have made efforts to find spaces for ourselves in the community and settle in. He's working as a sort of mediator between the two wolf packs, and I've met with some harpies and sirens—more open-minded ones than Georgiana—about establishing a safe space for flying in our mythic forms, probably aided by some helpful witches. Jack and I want to belong.

But this new arrival has a different, more destructive mindset.

Mor has her hands full.

The whole town does.

"Last I recall," I say in an overly casual voice, "the library has multiple bedrooms. At least two of which are unoccupied."

Broderick's face clears of disappointment. "You are a genius. Automatic A."

I laugh. "You're not grading me."

The witch leans in and presses a gentle kiss to my jaw before whispering in my ear, "You should still come by office hours. For extra attention."

"Are you about to tell me your bedroom is called *the office*?" I murmur back.

Broderick straightens with a chuckle, and I swear he's the handsomest being I have ever encountered.

"You know me so well, Ophelia Vatra."

I grin at his use of my surname. The one I gave myself, plucked from a memory of my mother. Was the name hers? Maybe not, but I like to think it was.

"I wonder though, would you still want to teach me a lesson if, one day, I called you Professor Vatra?"

In my time spent with other mythics in Folk Haven, I've learned it's common among many mythics for a male partner to take a female partner's surname when they officially mate. My comment was meant to tease, but as the words leave my mouth, I hear the weight they carry.

The future I'm hinting at.

Broderick cradles my cheeks in his hands, his hold gentle, as if I'm as fragile and precious as one of my glass creations. "Please," he says, "call me Broderick Vatra. Anytime. Anywhere. For as long as you want me."

And I'm sure that my happiness is pure fire spilling from my skin.

The End

~

Thank you so much for reading FLIRTING WITH A FIREBIRD. I hope you enjoyed Ophelia & Broderick's love story! Do you want to spend more time in the mythic-filled Folk Haven? Check out the following books for more magical small town romances.

SEDUCED BY A SELKIE
Folk Haven Book 1
Delta Novac hates Folk Haven, and as soon as she's done cleaning out her father's mess of a house, she's giving the town her taillights. But after she dives into the lake to save a drowning man that's not actually in danger, she finds herself with a sweet and sexy selkie shadow ready to do anything to get her to stay.

SUCKER FOR A SIREN
Folk Haven Book 2
Seamus MacNamara refuses to believe in the selkie mating myth: that his one true partner will rescue him from great danger. So, when the adorably beautiful barista he has a secret crush saves his life, Seamus ends up insulting her instead offering heartfelt thanks. Now he just wants a chance to redeem himself...and he's willing to go down on his knees to earn her forgiveness.

SWEARING AT A SEA MONSTER
Folk Haven Book 3
Moira MacNamara takes shit from no one, and that includes Levi Abadi, the enticing, infuriating monster who thinks he can dictate what she does with her own property. She makes a deal with him, sealed in blood. But now she can't help noticing how her veins thrum with heat every time he comes near...

SHELTER FOR A SHIFTER
Folk Haven Book 4

Ame Shelly found a cat, but this is no ordinary stray. She's almost certain her feline friend is a man stuck in an animal body. After years of searching, she's finally found the correct spell to release him from his fuzzy prison. Only, the man who appears in front of her demands two things: his witch mate and revenge.

If you enjoyed FLIRTING WITH A FIREBIRD, please consider rating and reviewing the book. Reviews help other readers discover my books, which helps me make a living and funds my ability to write more mythical romances for you!

WINNING OVER A WOOD WITCH

Blossom agrees to take part in an annual pumpkin-themed competition. She does *not* agree to play nice against a handsome, infuriating werewolf.

Blossom left the small, magical town of Folk Haven to prove to herself and her family that a wood witch could live out in the human world on her own. But she's drawn back to her childhood home during the autumn season, which puts her entirely too close to the werewolf who has taunted and teased her for years.

Manny has loved Blossom since they were teenagers, but he pushed her away. That was the worst mistake of his life. Now the witch is back in town competing against him in the Pumpkin Wars. This could be his chance to win not only the crown, but also her heart...

CONTENT WARNINGS

This book contains scenes with jumps off of dangerous heights, biting, bondage, and discussions of parental death.

1

BLOSSOM

Weddings are a time for joy, celebration, and resisting the urge to throw an elbow into the gut of the man standing too close to me.

Ignore him. If he knows how much he's unsettling me, that'll only make him happier.

To distract myself from the looming presence at my back, I stay focused on my sister and her beautiful mate-to-be as they exchange vows. Heather is a lacy masterpiece in a formfitting dress that flows into an elegant train and pools around her feet. The ivory fabric is a similar tone to her creamy skin. Light-brown hair—the same shade as mine—falls halfway down her back, the gentle waves stirring in the early fall breeze. Forget wood witch. She looks like a nature goddess with the flowers weaved into her strands. Helps that we're all standing under two towering oaks for this handfasting.

"Jenny," my sister says with a watery hitch to her voice, "I was never sure fated mates existed. But then I met you."

Standing behind Heather, I can't see my sister's expression.

But if it's anything like Jenny's, her face wears wonder and love and a touch of tears.

Everyone is getting misty-eyed. Jenny's parents sit next to my father in the front row, and the three pass tissues to each other. The small gathering of family and close friends fills a handful of benches in this forest beside Lake Galen, and I hear sighs and sniffles from the group.

My heart swells along with them—and then my errant brain wonders if *he's* crying.

Don't look. If you look, he'll know you're thinking about him. Best to never acknowledge his existence.

"Have you rings to exchange?" Selena, leader of the ceremony and head of the Folk Haven witch coven, asks the two women.

Heather slips her manicured hand into a pocket—because of course she would insist her wedding dress be equally breathtaking and practical—and pulls out a rose-gold band. The metal looks warm as it settles against Jenny's bronze skin. In return, the human presents my witchy sister with a silver band that cradles an emerald, the shade of the stone darker than the sage green Heather requested my dress be. I smooth my hands over the velvety fabric of my skirt before fiddling with my own ring.

The delicate piece of jewelry I wear isn't from a mating or human marriage, but instead was a gift from my father the day I left for college. The circlet is simple, without any stones, but beautiful with its intertwining tree and root design.

To remember where home is, his note said.

I had known my family wasn't overjoyed about me going to school hours away. But back then, I needed space. Papa and Heather had gotten into the habit of babying me and never seemed to grow out of it. I wanted to prove to myself I could survive on my own.

And I did.

Now, I've come back to Folk Haven. Sort of.

A year ago, I accepted a position as a faculty member at Ramla University, which sits a half hour south of my hometown. But I decided not to live in Folk Haven. Instead, I rent an apartment in Athens, Georgia. A slightly longer commute, but it's the space I need to maintain my independence. To show that despite being the coddled younger daughter, I'm not a child anymore.

No matter what some people might think.

Don't look at him.

I do my best to focus on the ceremony. The happiest moment of my sister's life. The joining of her with the amazing woman she loves. Our family growing by one as I gain a sister-in-law who is perfect for Heather.

Just as the coven leader drapes a light-green ribbon—the color matching my outfit and the floral arrangements—around the couple's wrists, I feel a brush against my back.

A slight tug.

And that's when I recall this beautiful dress Heather picked out for me, an outfit I loved the moment I slipped it on, is held up by two bows. One around my neck and one around my lower back.

And the latter is currently being tugged on.

He wouldn't.

Logically, I know the man behind me loves my sister like his own. They've been best friends since she found him sulking in Papa's apple orchard a week after moving to our magical town. She asked him to stand up here as the only other member of her bridal party. He wouldn't do anything to ruin her special day.

But another part of my brain panics.

If that bow comes undone, I'll look ridiculous. He won't be able to resist himself.

Trying not to draw attention to myself, I hold Heather's

bouquet with one hand and reach behind me with the other, seeking out the bow on my lower back. My touch brushes warm, rough fingers.

I grab them in a death grip and dig my manicured nails into the sensitive skin of his palm, wishing I'd gotten stiletto acrylics so I could do some real damage. Still, there's the softest grunt behind me, and he lets go of my dress.

But I don't trust him, so I keep his roaming fingers in mine as Selena calls for the blessing of The Dark One—the witch goddess we all pray to.

Luckily, Jenny comes from an open-minded family. She and her human parents accepted the knowledge that witches were real with excited curiosity rather than fear and disdain.

"Under her dark eyes," the coven leader intones, "I declare you two mated."

Heather whoops before lunging forward to wrap her non-ribbon-tied arm around Jenny's neck to drag the blushing woman in for a heated kiss.

In the joy of the moment, I briefly forget the nuisance at my back and cheer with the rest of the crowd. Heather and Jenny break apart and hold their bound hands up for all to see as the clapping and celebrating continue. On the other side of the forest clearing waits a cluster of tables full of food, a live band, and a dance floor. Time for the fun to begin.

Heather's cheeks might rupture from how wide she's grinning when her eyes meet mine.

I love you, I mouth, once again overwhelmed with happiness that she's found her life partner.

She blows me a kiss. Then, her gaze flits up and over my shoulder, and she sends another kiss through the air to the man at my back.

The one whose wandering hand I'm still clutching.

I drop it fast and whirl on him, allowing my fury forward now that the quiet part of the ceremony is over.

Much to my annoyance, I have to lift my chin to meet a set of slate-gray eyes. A stare that always seems hungry.

The eyes belong to Manuel Ramirez. Werewolf, Heather's best friend, and my nemesis.

"I'm about to rip your twig and berries off and feed them to you," I snarl, low enough so only he hears.

Manny tilts his head, smiling slow, the leisurely action pairing entirely too well with his crisp white shirt, dark dress pants, and ivy-patterned suspenders. His brown hair is neatly combed back from his tan face, showing off a strong jaw and dangerous cheekbones. He is all Southern gentleman in appearance and all Southern devil at heart.

And even after years of his subtle tormenting, my body still tingles, just standing near him. If only annoyance could eradicate attraction.

"You had a bee. On your back. Landed on that pretty little bow. I was protecting you, Blossom."

The way he says my name, practically purring the word, should not be allowed. He says *Blossom* like the flowery moniker is an endearment rather than what's printed on my birth certificate.

Product of having a wood witch father. Root Fernmore loves plants as names.

Couldn't have given me something slightly more mainstream though, could he?

"I didn't feel a bee," I snap. "What I felt was a handsy werewolf trying to untie my dress in the middle of my sister's mating." With a jerk, I wave toward the crowd that's rising from their seats to meander over to the party area.

Manny's brow dips. "I'm not about to strip you in front of an audience." A smirk pulls at his mouth. "I prefer some privacy for that." Then, he leans down, mouth next to my ear, warm breath teasing the short brown curls I've neatly arranged. "Maybe you should try to be less tempting to dangerous things. How's a bee meant to ignore a flower that smells so good?"

Heat flushes through my body.

What is this? What is happening?

It's almost like Manny is flirting with me. But that is impossible because we hate each other.

We have for years.

This must be some new kind of mind game. I refuse to fall for it.

I turn until my mouth is inches from his. "Maybe I want to tempt dangerous things." I watch his nostrils flare. "It's the best way to lay a trap."

Then, I twist my hand in a practiced gesture, tugging on my magic—the strands of power that constantly thrum just under my skin—and I wait a second in relish.

Only to watch as Manny whips his hand up in time to catch the shiny red apple hurtling through the air toward his dense head. He straightens and palms the fruit projectile I commanded a tree to chuck at him with a little mystical urging.

The wolf grins. "My reflexes have improved since high school, *Bud*." He emphasizes the annoying nickname he granted me years ago with a large, taunting bite of the crimson flesh.

I long for our younger days where he never saw the apples coming and I got to watch them nail him, the impact resulting in an explosion of juicy mush.

"Have they?"

I ram my fist into his gut, then whirl on my heel, sauntering away with the lovely sound of him wheezing blending perfectly with the opening strains of the wedding band.

I should've known Manny would expect the apple attack. It was my go-to revenge when we were teenagers anytime he would taunt me. I'll have to think of new methods to knock that smirk off his face. Because I can count on one thing: I'll never escape Manny Ramirez.

Not as long as he and Heather are best friends.

And the only thing the wolf loves as much as my sister is making me furious.

2

———————

MANNY

GETTING a fist to the gut shouldn't leave me hard, but that's what Blossom Fernmore does to me. To be fair, I deserved it.

There was no bee.

What there was, was a witch who smelled like warm apples and cloves, draped in soft fabric, with two tempting bows inches from my fingers.

I wasn't *actually* going to untie them.

I just wanted to feel the knots. Make sure they were sturdy.

Then store the sensation of my grip on them for later tonight when I'm in my bed and I take myself in my hand with fantasies where the sassy-mouthed wood witch lets me unravel her in all ways.

Keep it in your pants.

During my best friend's beautiful wedding reception, I should be focused on celebrating the happy occasion and not on how much I want to fuck her sister.

Although Heather would probably find my pining and

failed attempts at flirting hilarious. She knows about my infatuation with Blossom. Two years ago, after Heather told me her sister moved in with a new boyfriend—some human asshole named Teddy—I got roaring drunk. My friend hauled my wasted ass home from Local Brew—the town's werewolf-owned bar—and on the car ride, I confessed my yearslong obsession with her baby sister.

The next morning, once I was sober, Heather told me she wouldn't mind if Blossom and I ended up together. Only she doubted it would happen since I'd spent a good portion of my life making the little wood witch hate me.

Not the best pep talk despite the fact that Heather was only speaking the truth.

During our teenage years, I had done exactly as she said. Tried my hardest to make Blossom think I was a prick so she'd keep her distance. It was a form of self-preservation.

At least, that was what I had convinced myself of at the time.

When I have my arousal under control, I join the rest of the wedding party. The gathering is small but lively. Everyone invited to this ceremony knows about magic and the mythical creatures who live in Folk Haven. When Jenny moved to our small town for an engineering position at the Folk Haven Dam three years ago, she wasn't aware mythics existed. But then things got serious with Heather, and the witch decided to share the truth. Luckily, everything went smoothly.

My eyes catch on a flash of green velvet, and I wonder what words I could say to Blossom to untangle the mess I've made of our relationship over the years.

I need more time around her. She's always leaving before I can get my brain to work right.

"Manny!" There's a hand on my wrist, and I turn to find the smiling face of my best friend.

"Heather!" I shout back, then scoop her up in a twirling hug, which only works because she's no longer tied to Jenny. "You did it! You tricked someone into mating you!"

She laughs, and when I put her down, she punches me in the shoulder, but it's only a playful tap compared to her sister's sledgehammer.

I feel a spark of pride at how well Blossom walloped me. I'm the one who taught her how to swing a good right hook in the first place. She only agreed to learn when I offered to be the one she practiced on.

"Dance with me."

The bride tugs me onto the temporary wood platform next to the band, and I lead her in a dramatic waltz to a lively country song. Heather hasn't stopped grinning since the ribbon was wrapped around her wrist, and the sight is as satisfying as a chilled glass of sweet tea on a hot day.

"You're happy?" I ask, my tone taking on a rare note of seriousness.

She nods hard, her green eyes sparkling. "So much that I think I might explode."

"Let me know when that's gonna happen. I'll lay out tarps."

Heather chuckles and pulls me closer, just as I spy a mischievous light in her gaze. "I want you to feel this way," she says.

I smirk. "Sorry, not into the polyamorous thing. You and Jenny are on your own."

She keeps on wearing her *I've got a secret* smile. "Oh, no, Manny. Jenny and I wouldn't make you feel like this. I know that. But I know who would."

Suddenly, I find it hard to swallow.

She can't mean ...

"Things are in motion," the wood witch sings, and I watch as the tiny buds weaved into her hair begin to flower, her joyful magic spilling into them. "You just need to go with it." Heather pulls back to hit me with an intense stare, eagerness and concern warring in her eyes. "This might be your one shot. Don't mess it up."

"My shot at what?" I rasp. "What are you talking about?"

But Heather doesn't answer me, only takes the lead and whirls us to the edge of the dance floor, her concentration coming to rest over my shoulder. "Papa! I'm mated!"

As Heather's arms slip from my shoulders, I turn to meet the steady gaze of Root Fernmore. He's a short white man with ruddy cheeks, thinning brown hair, and an easy smile.

After my parents died in a hunting accident—two werewolves mistaken for real wolves, lurking near livestock—I had to move from New Mexico to this small Georgia town and live with my uncle. My father's brother was not a caregiver and had no idea what to do with an angry, heartbroken ten-year-old boy. When Heather found me wandering alone, she dragged me home with her and told her father I needed some apple pie. Root took one look at me, then slipped his apron on and started baking. That first bite was the first time I felt something other than devastation since I'd learned about my parents' deaths.

Heather forced me back into the world of the living.

Root comforted and supported me as I grew.

Blossom …

Blossom tormented me with her mere existence.

Now, she stands next to her father, looking like a fantasy in her green gown. The little witch also looks ready to sneak off, but Heather is too quick, looping her arm through Blossom's to keep her in place.

"I'm mated! Blossom, are you aware that I'm *mated*?" Heather holds up her hand, showing off the rock she now sports.

"New rule," Blossom deadpans. "Every time you say *mated*, you have to take a shot."

I snort, and the younger witch throws me a glare.

"Fine." Heather lets her hand fall, but her grin stays firmly in place. "I won't say the M-word anymore. I don't want to be hungover on the first day of my honeymoon. Not the best way to start off my mating."

"Mating. You said it. That counts." Blossom scoops up a glass of champagne. "Don't have a shot on me, so you've got to chug this."

And Heather—wild witch that she is—does as her sister demanded, letting out a burp when the bubbly is gone.

"You are the embodiment of grace," Root says, smiling at his two daughters. "We're going to miss you. You've never left for this long."

Heather and Jenny are departing soon to spend a whole month in Europe, country-hopping and sightseeing.

I agree with Root. I'm going to miss my best friend.

The bride's expression softens, but then I spot the spark of mischief again. "I'll miss you too. But we'll send pictures every day. And I expect a play-by-play of how Blossom does as Pumpkin Princess."

The witch in green stills at her sister's words, and my heart stutters.

Blossom is going to be the Pumpkin Princess this year? She's competing in the Pumpkin Wars?

The silly-sounding event was invented years ago by Root. The wood witch owns the most popular pumpkin patch in Folk Haven, and when Heather and I became friends, he decided to ring in the season by setting up a series of games for us to play against each other. Apparently, it was an attempt to burn off some of our endless kid energy.

He called it the Pumpkin Wars with Heather as Pumpkin Princess and me as Pumpkin Prince. Whoever won was the Pumpkin Queen or Pumpkin King for the year.

What started as a silly activity has grown into a full-blown, widely attended event in the Folk Haven mythical creature community. Mainly witches and wolves show up—the former rooting for Heather, the latter cheering for me. I didn't consider how Heather's honeymoon would have her gone for this year's event. Root always holds the Pumpkin Wars the last weekend in September to mark the opening of his pumpkin patch for customers.

Blossom has never competed.

As far as I know, she's never asked to. Root always gave his younger daughter special duties for the competition, but it was only ever just Heather and me battling it out.

"What?" Blossom croaks the question.

"You didn't tell her, Papa?" Heather asks, blinking her long-lashed eyes innocently.

Root wears his normal, pleasant, relaxed expression that gives nothing away. "Not yet."

"I can't." The youngest Fernmore shakes her head so hard that some of the flowers in her hair fall out. "I-I don't live here. And everyone is expecting *you*."

Heather scoffs. "It's only one weekend. And they don't care who the princess is. Everyone is expecting a fun time. A good show. Witch versus wolf." Heather clutches her sister's wrist and lets her gaze go soft and pleading. "Come on. You have to do it. The Pumpkin Wars is one of Papa's best business days. You want the patch to do well, don't you?"

I press my knuckles against my lips to hide a smirk. Heather will do anything to win, and that means playing on her sister's hidden heartstrings.

Blossom throws a wide-eyed glance her father's way, but the wood witch merely offers a gentle smile.

"Could really use your help this year, Blossom. If it's not too much trouble. Don't want your sister feeling bad when she and Jenny are away."

Oh gods, the guilt trip is piling on from both sides, and I love it.

Because I'll take anything that requires Blossom to interact with me.

My friend's words from the dance floor replay in my head. *"Things are in motion. You just need to go with it. This might be your one shot."*

Is this what Heather meant?

The witch bride meets my eyes and gives the subtlest of nods.

I scoop up the gauntlet but take a different tactic. "Guys, don't pressure her." I keep my voice smooth, as if I don't care about the outcome of this conversation. "If Blossom doesn't want to embarrass herself in front of half the town by losing to me, then that's understandable. We can figure something else out."

The scowl she throws my way could peel bark off a tree.

"I'm in," she snaps.

Success.

The younger witch mutters something about getting food and slips away from our group, and soon after, Heather sprints off to her mate's side. For the rest of the evening, I enjoy the festivities, keeping my distance from Blossom so I don't accidentally ruin my turn of good luck.

But she's always in my eyeline.

When I spy the little wood witch kissing her sister on the cheek, then grabbing her purse, I make my move.

A candlelit path leads through the trees, guiding partygoers back to the field, where a shuttle is running periodically to take tipsy guests back to town. Blossom is deep into the forest when I catch up to her.

"Aren't you going to say good-bye?"

At the sound of my voice, she whirls around, frowning deep at the sight of me. I'd rather have her lovely smile and some heated eyes, but I'll take this over cold indifference, which is what Blossom tries to affect around me most times.

"It's been twelve years," she spits. "When are you going to let this go?"

Absolutely fucking never.

"Hmm. Sounds like someone wants to go back on their word. I mean, if that's how you choose to live your life, Bud."

I swear she growls, and the noise does things to my gut.

Still, Blossom doesn't move to fulfill the bargain she made with me back when we were teenagers. The bet she was so cocky about.

An important thing to know about the Fernmore sisters is that they are both extremely competitive. Heather had been on a three-year Pumpkin Wars winning streak. A Pumpkin Queen unwilling to give up her reign. And Blossom loved poking me about it. Trying to get a rise out of the wolf, not knowing that simply being near her and that delectable scent of hers put me on constant edge. Young Blossom made a remark about how excited she was to watch me lose for the fourth year in a row, and I couldn't help myself.

I dared her to place a bet.

She scoffed with all the cocky confidence of a fifteen-year-old who thought her older sister was the coolest person on the planet and unable to fail at anything.

"Fine," Blossom said, her smirk taking on an evil twist that made me want to drag her against my body and tongue her lips. "If Heather wins, you have to lend me your car whenever I want."

"You're fifteen," I pointed out. "I'm not breaking the law for you." False. I would have broken tons of laws for her if it meant Blossom kept paying attention to me.

The sassy little witch rolled her eyes. "Obviously, I mean when I get my license."

I loved my Jeep.

But I loved Blossom Fernmore more.

Also, I had no intention of losing.

"Sure," I said with a shrug, enjoying her glaring response to the unconcerned note in my voice. "If Heather wins, you can borrow my Jeep whenever you want *after* you get your license. But ..." I dragged out the statement, partly to watch her mossy-green eyes narrow, but also to give myself time to think of the perfect prize to request.

One that straddled the line. That would give me a taste of her, but wasn't too much to have her running. One that was disguised as torture when, really, it was a desperate plea for her to want me back.

Inspiration struck, and I pasted on a mocking grin. "If I win, every time we part ways, you have to kiss my cheek and say, 'Good-bye, darling. I'll miss you.' "

The way the wood witch gaped at me was glorious. Before she could outright refuse, I offered another insolent shrug.

"Stakes too high for you?" I asked. "I'll have to let Heather know how little faith you have in her."

"It's a deal," sweet little Blossom snarled.

That was the first year I gave the games my one hundred percent. And when the pumpkin crown sat on my head, my eyes sought out Blossom, who stood on the sidelines, scowling. Because I was an eighteen-year-old asshole, I made sure to tap my cheek as a reminder.

And true to her word, for twelve years, Blossom has given me the good-bye I asked for.

Though never with the sweet intent the words alone might convey. She tends to wrap her fingers around my throat in a subtle threat as her soft lips barely graze my cheek.

"Good-bye, darling." She likes to hiss the words. "I'll miss you."

Sometimes, she'll lick my cheek after the kiss. Or give me a wet willy. Or pinch my side. Or yank my hair.

Every little attack coaxes my wolf to the surface in a way I doubt she intends.

And I always make sure to keep track of when she's visiting town. I've sprinted across Folk Haven to make it to her dad's place in time to claim her good-bye. It's a rush to drive up and see Blossom stepping off the porch, keys in hand, ready to leave, and a scowl on her face when she spots my approach, knowing what she has to do.

And despite the thrumming anticipation of her mock affection, I always have the urge to point out the obvious.

You wouldn't have to do this if you just stayed.

"I want to make a bet." Blossom's tart voice brings me back to the present moment and her current scowl, perfectly reflecting all the ones she's given me in the past.

"So confident you'll win?" I saunter closer, looming over her, even as I bend at the waist to put my cheek in range of her lips.

A subtle reminder she can't leave just yet.

"You've never competed against *me* before." Her finger jabs my chest. "And if I win, this is over. No more good-bye ritual."

Never feel her lips on me again? My wolf wants to howl in denial.

But I've been competing in the Pumpkin Wars for years. There's no way Blossom will beat me.

Which means this is an opportunity to get another boon from her. To draw her closer.

Closer. That's what I want. Not these random visits.

"Fine. And if I win, you have to move back to Folk Haven."

Blossom's mouth pops open, putting her pretty pink tongue on display. By The Clawed One, I want to suck on that tongue.

She clicks her mouth shut, as if hearing my thoughts. "Ridiculous. You hate me! Why would you want me around more?"

Frustration shoves all of the teasing out of my brain. "Why do you think I hate you?"

She sputters, waving her hands, as if the evidence were floating in the air around us, "Because you do. You always have!"

I grunt, dipping my chin to my chest to hide the sudden anger in my eyes. I'm not pissed at Blossom. I'm furious with myself. Of course she sees me as the enemy. That's how I acted when we were younger. The only way my adolescent brain knew how to keep distance between us.

But I'm grown now, and I'm done repeating the mistakes of my past.

I'm done driving Blossom away. I need to repair the damage I've done so I can woo her. And the only way I can do that is if she stays put in Folk Haven for longer than a few hours.

"That's the deal." I meet her bewildered stare. "Take it or leave it."

She studies me, her expression shut down so I have no idea what thoughts flick behind those glittering eyes.

"Fine," she snaps. "I'll take it."

Blossom steps forward, into my space, and I tilt my head and brace for the teasing torture that is her parting peck.

But then a set of cool, strong hands cup my cheeks and turn me to face her. I only have a moment to suck in a breath before her mouth smashes against mine.

The witch tastes like apples and spices, and I groan in hunger, wanting to devour her. But just as my arms reach to gather her close, there's a sharp sting against my lip and an unexpected force shoving me away from delicious perfection. I stumble back a step, one hand going to my mouth, one hand reaching for her.

But Blossom is already out of my reach, a triumphant grin on her red-stained lips.

Blood transfers from my mouth to my fingertips.

She bit me.

"Good-bye, darling. I'll miss you." She sings the words, a taunt beneath them.

Then, she's gone, disappearing into the woods.

And I know there's no way I'm ever letting her leave me again.

3

BLOSSOM

"Welcome to the twentieth annual Pumpkin Wars! Where two combatants battle for the coveted pumpkin crown. Witch versus wolf. Who will win?" Root Fernmore, normally a quiet man, always finds the voice of a circus ringmaster on these weekends.

In response to my papa's intro, the crowd gathered in his pumpkin patch roars their predictions. There are shouts of, "Witch!" and, "Wolf!" and, "Where's the pumpkin pie?"

That last one came from Owen MacNamara. The selkie grins as he holds a mug of spiked cider, steam rising into the slight chill of the sunny autumn day. From his silly comment, one might guess he has no stake in these games. But the seal shifter owns Clean Haven, the local recycling company Manny works for.

Which means he's on the side of the enemy.

I gaze out over the collection of attendees, a number that has shot up over the years.

The first time my dad arranged this, I think it was to distract

Heather from her melancholy. It was right around this time of year that our mother had left. I was barely two when she disappeared from our lives, so I don't remember her. But Heather was five and had formed a connection with the woman who decided a magical small-town life and motherhood weren't for her. Cornelia Fulmer didn't completely disappear on us. She's head of a law firm in Boston, and she responds to texts and calls if we make them.

I don't. Papa is the only parent I've ever needed. The man is creative and loving. Hence the pumpkin-themed tournament he set up for my sister and her best friend.

An event that has become an annual tradition in Folk Haven. Attendance is only open to mythics and mythic mates due to the magic sometimes utilized, and the crowd largely consists of witches and werewolves. When the coven and the pack caught wind of the playful battle years ago, spectators started to show up and cheer for Heather and Manny.

Over the years, I kept score, cheered for my sister, ate delicious fall treats, and tried not to let on how much I longed to join the games.

This year, I get my childhood wish.

But I'm not sure I want it anymore. Especially when competing means being within close proximity to a certain werewolf all weekend.

"Seems we have support for both sides!" My dad grins wide at the crowd. "And I'm glad to announce we have a special treat this year. Because Heather is away on her honeymoon, my equally talented youngest daughter, Blossom, has offered to take her sister's place and battle the veteran contender and last year's victor, Manny Ramirez. I present to you your Pumpkin Princess and Pumpkin Prince!"

Goddess save me from theatrical fathers. I silently send the comment to The Dark One as I step forward.

As corny as all this is, I've decided I'm going to embrace the festivities as fully as Heather does every year. In that vein, I'm dressed in neon-orange leggings and matching sneakers, paired with a pumpkin-patterned sports bra. Luckily, there's padding so no one can see how the cool air is making my nipples into icy points.

I spread my arms and accept the wild cheers from the gathered witches. Meanwhile, Manny is dressed in all black, and he grins toward the howling pack members here to support him.

Cocky asshole. I can't wait to rub a win in his face.

"The first test is one of the mind," Papa calls out when the crowd settles. "Bring forth the mega gourd!"

Behind my father, I spy a figure moving through the pumpkin patch. The creature looks massive and ungainly, but as they near, I realize it's only a man carrying a pumpkin.

A very large pumpkin.

"Here you go." My dad passes me and Manny each a small whiteboard and marker. "Whoever guesses the closest to the pumpkin's weight, without going over, wins the first round," he explains loud enough for the gathering to hear.

Suddenly, there's a roar of noise from the crowd as everyone starts shouting out numbers. None of it is helpful, seeing as how their guesses vary so widely, and I don't know if the witches are calling out to help me or to hinder Manny.

So, I let the clamoring fade to white noise and study the gigantic vegetable.

This isn't a new challenge. Dad has twenty or so he cycles through, using a different combo for each year. Some are brain-teasers, some are physical, some are both. There also tends to be an artist challenge and maybe a food thing. But we can all count on the fact that every challenge will be fall-themed. The autumn equinox might have been last week, but this is how my family truly welcomes in the new season.

I see now that the pumpkin carrier is Heath, a local bear shifter and co-owner of Coffee & Claws. The bear is a baker and has a contract with Papa for local produce. I wonder if that signed agreement includes a special clause, stating, *Must carry very large pumpkin for seasonal festivals.*

Admittedly, there aren't many others in town who could haul that thing around on their own. Dad must have worked some spells on that gourd to get it to grow to the gigantic size.

He puts more and more planning into these games each year.

And that—even more than the urge to defeat Manny—is why I agreed to be Pumpkin Princess.

As much as I'm proud of how I've done out in the world on my own, more and more, I realize the extent to which I miss my sister and my father. Being apart for weeks at a time has given me time to remember all the things I love about them both. The way Heather laughs with her whole heart and hugs me like she'll never let go. The way Papa always makes time for me and smiles as if I bring him nothing but joy.

When I was younger, their love felt stifling. Like a too-tight life jacket when I wanted to swim unencumbered.

But now that I'm free to float on my own, I long to enfold myself in their caring orbit again.

And if being here means I get to defeat an annoying, *too handsome for his own good* werewolf, then that's just a sweet bonus.

"Write down your guesses. Reveal your answers in ten seconds."

Papa begins a dramatic countdown, and the crowd joins him. Meanwhile, I concentrate on the height and width of the pumpkin while also taking in the strain of Heath's biceps.

Confident with my answer, I write out my guess.

510.

Manny is the type to write 501, in hopes that I'd choose a whole number. But he knows that *I* know he would do that, so I bet he expects me to write 502 or 505.

I figure 510 is safe.

"Time's up! Show us your boards!"

I hold mine aloft and glance over to see the werewolf's guess.

403.

I snort. Knew it. Only I'm sure he's wildly underestimated.

Then, Heath sets the pumpkin down on a scale, and half the crowd groans when the number pops up on the digital display.

"Five hundred six pounds!" Papa roars, throwing me an apologetic smile.

It's all I can do not to snap my whiteboard in half. When I see the triumphant grin on Manny's face, I can't help twisting my hand in the well-used gesture to tug on my magic.

And as if sensing my intent, the wolf's hand flies up in time to catch the apple hurtling toward his head.

The arrogant asshole sinks his teeth into the crimson flesh as he saunters my way.

And I recall how I dug my own teeth into his lip only a week ago. Manny's blood should have tasted metallic, but instead, it was full-bodied, like an expensive, dry red wine. I licked the droplets with relish and wanted more.

Then, I reminded myself that I was a witch, not a blood-thirsty beast, and admitting I liked anything about this wolf would only lead to disaster and mockery.

"If it had been closest guess, I would've had it," I snarl at him.

"But it wasn't." Manny holds the half-eaten apple out to me, as if I might want a bite. As if I might be tempted to put my mouth where his just was.

I *am* tempted, but he doesn't need to know that.

"The next challenge starts in a half hour in the east field," my dad calls out. Then, he throws Manny and me an eager grin before trotting off.

"Hear that?" I cross my arms over my chest and glare up at the aggravatingly attractive werewolf. "You have a whole thirty minutes to pretend like you're smarter than me."

Manny slips closer without seeming to move his feet. "Hmm," he rumbles deep in his throat. "Then, what?"

"Then," I hiss, pressing up on my toes to shove my face into his, "I will destroy you."

Instead of being cowed by my very frightening threat, Manny keeps on smirking. The expression only fades when his stare drops to my mouth, then lower to my heaving chest.

Wait, why is my chest heaving?

"You get so worked up," he mutters, his slate eyes finding mine again. "It's adorable."

"Adorable?" I grit my teeth when he goes to take another bite of the apple.

I can't handle seeing his perfect white teeth dig into that crisp skin again. Can't watch the sweet juice coat his lips. Can't listen to the pleased hum he makes after every taste.

I snatch the fruit out of his grasp and wing it into the pumpkin patch, watching the Red Delicious soar an impressive distance.

Maybe apple chucking will be one of the challenges. Looks like I'd dominate.

"I wasn't done with that," Manny says, his expression disgruntled.

"Good." Now, I'm the one smirking, enjoying seeing the grown man pout about his lost snack.

No need to dwell on my level of maturity. I will be an adult come Monday, when I have to go back to work as a college professor.

"That was quite a throw. Love this spirit of competition." The delighted comment comes from Owen as he strolls up to us with a collection of other people.

Everyone wears relaxed smiles, and most hold steaming mugs of cider. For them, this is a fun outing.

But they don't have a werewolf to conquer and a bet to win.

"Blossom is all about intimidation." Manny gives his boss a one-armed hug hello. Then, the wolf turns to me and points people out. "You know Griffith, right? He bartends at Local Brew. Then, this is Jack, newest member of the pack, and Ame Shelly, one of the witches who opened the library on the lake. Jack, Ame, this is Blossom Fernmore."

I'm thrown off-balance by Manny introducing me in his easy way. I was in verbal sparring mode, not *meet the new towns-folk* mode.

"Hello." I give them a jerky wave. "Welcome to The Patch."

Technically, it's called The Fernmore Pumpkin Patch, but everyone just calls this field of orange gourds The Patch. Papa loves the fact that his place has a nickname.

Manny slips up beside me and drapes an arm over my shoulders. As if this is the most normal thing in the world. As if I didn't recently try to assault him with fruit and make him bleed after kissing him.

"Nice to meet you." Ame returns my wave with a small smile of her own. "That was a good guess."

I try not to grimace, knowing she's just being nice.

"Yeah, but not the winning one, huh? Like to think I hire the best brains in town." Owen taps his knuckles on Manny's shoulder and puffs up his chest.

I'm tempted to poke the selkie right in his stomach to deflate him, but I tend to keep my physical assaults aimed at Manny.

Speaking of, I pinch his side in an attempt to extricate myself from his hold.

But the infuriating wolf only winces, then tugs me closer. And damn him, he smells good. The same way he tasted. Like a rich red wine that gets me drunk too fast.

"Just in case it wasn't clear"—Griffith, the bartending were-wolf, offers me an apologetic smile—"Owen and I are Team Wolf."

And that's when I notice their custom orange T-shirts that read, *All hail the Pumpkin Prince!*

Now that I acknowledge the design, I realize a decent portion of the crowd has them on.

"And I would like to make it clear," Manny says, "I specifically requested you *not* make shirts this year."

Owen shrugs, grin unrepentant. "I had to. If I ordered more than fifty, they gave me a discount."

"That's terrible logic."

Ignoring his Pumpkin Prince, the selkie turns his attention on Ame and Jack, the witch and the werewolf couple.

"What about you, newbies?" he asks. "Who are you rooting for?"

Jack fixes his dark eyes on the redhead whose hand he holds. "Who are we rooting for?"

Ame offers him a sweet smile. "Well, I'm a witch. So, go, Blossom!"

He nods, as if that decides everything. "Go, Blossom."

"Now, wait a minute, Jack," Griffith chimes in. "You're a wolf. You've gotta root for Manny." He points to the man at my side, who's currently running his thumb gently along my collarbone.

Wait, what is he doing? When did this start? Why is he touching me like this? Why am I letting him?

Why does it feel so good?

My nipples pebble again, but this time, it's not from the cold.

Jack's hard stare flicks between Griffith, Manny, me, then back to his mate.

"Go, Blossom," he repeats.

The show of loyalty—to his mate, not to me—has me smiling.

Then, the wolf, who's still manhandling me, opens his annoying mouth.

"Eh, can't blame you." Manny laughs. "If I didn't like seeing her in a temper so much, I'd be rooting for Blossom too." The hot fingers of his free hand pinch my chin, holding my face in place as he presses a loud kiss to my forehead.

A rush of emotion blots out all rational thought, and in self-preservation, my hands dance through conjuring motions before I consider the consequences.

Manny slips away fast, catching and dodging three separate apples I rocketed his way. Unfortunately, one misses its target and instead knocks Owen's cider out of his hand, sending the spiced beverage spraying through the air. Jack turns his body in time to shield Ame, blocking any of the splatter from hitting his witch.

"Damn. I was enjoying that." The seal shifter scoops his empty mug off the ground, voice mournful.

I'm not in the apologizing mood. "Well, that'll teach you to root for the wrong competitor." Nose in the air, I stalk away from the group toward the next challenge, where I plan to ignore the unwanted reactions my body has toward Manny Ramirez as I dominate the rest of this competition.

"Go, Blossom!" Ame cheers at my back.

4

BLOSSOM

Cornstalks stretch tall above us, their towering heads swaying in a light breeze. The corn is a wall with a single opening.

"Corn maze," I mutter before shooting a glare toward the grinning werewolf.

Of course he's happy. Speed is going to be a huge component in this next challenge. Sure, I go jogging a few times a week. But that hasn't prepared me to race a werewolf.

Maybe if I'd known I was going to be the Pumpkin Princess a year in advance, I could've joined a gym and practiced my sprinting.

But, no, I got a week to prepare myself, and now, I'm looking at the second L of the day.

Don't think like that. Mazes take speed but also brainpower. And Manny has always been shit at directions.

One time, he grudgingly agreed to drive me to my friend's house on the other side of Folk Haven, and he made the wrong turn at least five times. Practically doubled the travel time. I never thought I'd get to leave that car.

"Thank you, everyone, for joining us once again." My father claims the crowd's attention. "I hope you enjoy the spread! Make sure to fill your plates and settle in because we're about to say good-bye to our combatants. Who knows when we'll see them again?" Papa shares a grin between Manny and me from his temporary hay-bale podium. "This corn maze is full of twists and turns that could fool even the best puzzle master."

My father faces me with a delighted expression. The man loves a good game. Whenever I come home for a visit, he always has a new board game for us to try out. Usually, it is Papa, Heather, and me playing. But they often invite Manny to join, and I have to sit across from the wolf and tolerate his teasing taunts, cocky moves, and intense stares.

Now, the board game is life-sized, and Papa is giddy.

"Hmm. Alone in a maze with Blossom Fernmore. What could happen?" Manny smirks my way.

"Most likely, I'll beat you so bad that you'll be too ashamed to come out," I sling back, voice full of pure confidence that I don't feel. "Better get cozy in there. It's gonna be your new home."

The wolf's rumbling laugh disappears under the boom of my father's voice.

"Now, here's the tricky part, pumpkin competitors. You're not simply finding your way out. You have a goal." Papa taps his nose, eyes twinkling, and I think he could have done well as a TV game show host. "Inside the maze, deep in the twisting alleys of corn, are two scarecrows. They sit equal distance from this entry point." He waves at the break in the stalks in front of us. "To win, you must find a scarecrow and bring it with you on your exit journey. The winner is the first to return here with your scarecrow companion. However long that takes."

"Take your time!" Owen calls out from his spot by the cider keg. "We've got plenty to drink while you're away."

A cheer goes up from the crowd as they raise their glasses in a toast.

"I'm sure Manny would give you time to kick a keg. But I'm planning on getting back before the next round is poured," I shout back, grinning at the cackles from my witchy supporters.

Manny scoffs. "Think you can outrun me, Bud?"

At first, I was sure I couldn't. The man is part wolf after all.

But now, my magic thrums to life as my gaze glides over the field of corn before me.

This isn't some paved road in the middle of the city. I'll be running over dirt and roots and the living earth that sings to the power under my skin.

"We'll see." I crouch down to untie my shoes. The soles of my sneakers suddenly feel too thick and clunky on my feet. I need my skin against soil. My wood witch magic wants to touch the growing things of the world.

"Contenders," Papa bellows, "please approach the starting line."

There's a white line spray-painted on the grass ten feet from the entrance to the maze. Manny and I step up to the marker. I can feel the wolf's eyes on me, but I refuse to look his way.

"On your mark ... get set ... GO!" The shout is accompanied by the blare of a horn.

We dive forward. Manny reaches the entrance a step before me and immediately veers right. I choose the left route, wanting distance from him. Besides, there are two scarecrows to find. No reason for us to stay close.

With the sun starting to dip low in the sky, I have a good sense of direction, heading northeast toward what I believe is the middle of the maze. Sometimes, I have to make a series of quick turns, and sometimes, there're long, straightaway stretches. I prefer the latter because I can let my muscles loose and fly.

My hands dance in the air, calling out magical greetings to the corn. It's as though the very earth is moving my legs for me, powering me forward at a speed I've never reached before.

This—a wild running—might be what I've missed most about Folk Haven.

Living among the human population means adhering to certain social standards. Like *don't run barefoot in the woods*. I've had to train myself not to loathe jogging down a neatly paved path. One where everything is curated on either side, as if nature was always meant to be organized.

But when I run like this, there is no structure. Only exhilaration.

As much as the sensation threatens to intoxicate me, I maintain my focus on the branching paths, always on the lookout until—there! From the corner of my eye, I spot a flash of red. I turn my eager feet toward the break in the stalks where I spied the color, leaping into the small clearing to find a hay-filled scarecrow, dressed in a red flannel shirt.

"Got you!" I lunge forward and yank the straw-filled man off its wooden post before turning back the way I came.

There's no sign of Manny. Which could mean that he's still wandering aimlessly in this tangle of corn-strewn walkways.

Or maybe he found the other scarecrow and is already on his way back to the entrance.

Unwilling to let him claim victory, I gesture with my free fingers, seeking out the teasing magic within my soul, drawing on more of nature's power to give my feet gas. Sprinting, I choose paths that lead me southwest, my eyes on the sun and the gaps in the corn ahead of me.

Then, I hear it.

The steady *thump, thump, thump* of pounding feet.

I round a corner and almost collide with a sweaty Manny.

The wolf is breathing hard, pieces of corn sticking to his glistening skin, long brown hair tangled around his chin.

And in his right hand, he clutches a floppy scarecrow of his own.

"Hey, Bud." When his eyes drop to my inanimate companion, a grin takes over his mouth. "Well, look at that. You're keeping up."

"Get out of my way." I dodge around his hulking form and push my legs to go faster.

But just like at the wedding, I sense his presence looming behind me. Only the wolf doesn't overtake me, but instead keeps pace. After multiple turns and him not making any move to pass me, I can't put up with my annoying shadow any longer.

I whirl on him with my most seething glare. "What are you doing?"

Manny attempts an innocent expression. "Nothing."

"You're following me."

"We're headed to the same place," he points out.

"Well, get there on your own!"

The wolf tilts his head, wearing the most infuriating smirk. "Why would I do that?"

And as much as his answer enrages me, his strategy also makes sense. There's no point for him to break off from me, not when he can beat me in an all-out sprint. If we part ways, I might happen upon the exit before he does. But if Manny stays by my side, he can overtake me the moment we find the break in the corn.

The wolf wants me to solve this maze for him.

"You're such an asshole," I hiss.

"Am I?" He leans toward me with something in his eyes that I can't interpret. "Maybe I'm just doing everything I can to get you to stay."

The bet. Of course that's on his mind.

"Why? So you can torture me on a daily basis?"

Manny lets out a huff that sounds exasperated. "I can think of a lot of things I want to do with you, Blossom Fernmore. But torture is not one of them."

I narrow my eyes at the wolf the same moment he reaches out to catch a lock of my hair that's come free from my ponytail to tease my cheek. Gently, he tucks the strand behind my ear.

"What are you doing?"

Is that my voice? Why do I sound so breathless?

Must be from all the running.

He gives me a rueful smile. "I'm trying to figure out how to convince you to want me the way that I want you."

I choke on my next breath, shocked by his confession.

Manny Ramirez wants me?

No. This can't be real. He's up to something.

That's when I see his other hand out of the corner of my eye. Reaching for me.

No, wait. He must be reaching for my scarecrow. No doubt he's planning on chucking it over the closest wall of corn so I have to scramble to find it while he sprints off to victory.

And he thinks I won't notice because of this half-assed seduction attempt?

Well, two can play at that game.

And I don't do anything half-assed.

"Manny." I groan his name, trying to sound needy, and I swear there's a spark of fire in his eyes. Triumph at fooling me most likely.

Then, I lunge forward, wrapping an arm around his neck and pressing my mouth to his, as if all I want in the world is to devour his intoxicatingly delicious tongue.

I don't, of course.

This is all a ploy.

A ploy I'll put into effect in just ... a moment.

The wolf, who's been teasing and tormenting me since I was a teenager, grunts in surprise.

Then, he kisses me back. Hard and heady. The sensation so intense that my calculating brain is almost overwhelmed.

But not quite.

After taking a longer-than-planned moment to sup on his savory, warm mouth, I force my focus to get through the haze his solid body and hot kisses have cast over my brain.

Behind Manny's neck, where the wolf can't see, I twist my hands in the pattern of coaxing. Magic is an interesting thing. Part instinct, part trained direction. Some witches use words and substances to manipulate the powers of the world. Fernmore witches use our hands, speaking to the growing things through intricate finger movements.

The tingle of my magic surges, and my palms glow green, drawing the nearby roots to me. I feel them respond in the ground, rising through layers of soil to do my bidding.

"Gods, Blossom," Manny groans against my mouth. "I want you."

The moment he breaks contact enough to speak the words, I fully regain a handle on myself.

Well, *mostly* regain a handle. My pulse is still hammering in an erratic rhythm.

I shove away from the tricky wolf, skipping back a few extra steps to make sure I'm out of his reach.

"You almost had me. But I'm not falling for it," I taunt. "Have fun detangling yourself. I'll see you at the finish line."

I stick around just long enough to watch as Manny's wide eyes drop to his lower half.

While he was distracted by my awesome kissing skills, I had roots carefully but firmly entomb his legs from his thighs down.

"What the fuck?"

He barks out another few curses, but I have trouble hearing them over my laughter as I sprint away.

5

———————

MANNY

That gods-damn sneaky witch.

I stare at Blossom across the fire, where she chats animatedly with Ame Shelly, pretending she doesn't feel my eyes on her.

It's been a few hours since the last challenge, but I'm still not over her trickery in the maze. She kissed the hell out of me, got me hard as a rock, then ran off to claim her victory while leaving me tied up.

I knew she could get competitive, but the duplicity is downright sexy.

Fuck, I want you so bad, Blossom Fernmore.

But the question is, how do I convince her my interest is real? What do I need to do to prove I'm not trying to pull one over on her?

Heather thought Blossom taking her place in this competition would give me a good chance to woo her sister. Before she left on her honeymoon, she sat me down and spelled it out. Blossom's passion rose to the surface when she was chasing a win. And Heather claimed, by some sisterly bond, she could tell that part of the reason I was so good at pissing Blossom off was because I mattered to her.

But it's my job to turn that mattering into something good.

Something monumental.

Twice now, Blossom has kissed me on the lips. Both times with the aim of dealing me a blow.

And maybe I have an improperly flipped circuit in my brain because every time she ends a kiss with a menacing act, I only want her more.

"Attention, everyone." Root steps up onto an overturned log, gaining the crowd's notice.

There are at least ten fires spread out around this large forest clearing as we all congregate under the night sky, a half-moon shining down on our celebration.

"It's time for our third and final challenge of the day. A task that will require finesse and an understanding of your fellow mythic."

From the corner of my eye, I spy Blossom leaning forward, gaze rapt on her father, as if she thinks she can win simply by hearing him first.

"And like it or not, your fates will be decided by a single judge this next round. A special guest you both will try to impress. Everyone, please welcome our illustrious Mayor Nightson."

The crowd claps and whoops in approval as Belinda Nightson steps forward. Choosing a casual look for this gathering, our town mayor has her waist-length braids swinging loose and wears jeans and flannel, much like the scarecrows left for us in the maze. But even in her dressed-down attire, she still has an air of authority. The woman sits with a straight spine, a wide grin, and power rolling off her ebony skin. I've heard, in her griffin form, she's as large as a grizzly bear.

But when Belinda speaks, her voice is kind and welcoming.

"Thank you so much for having me. I'm honored to take part in this Folk Haven tradition."

"And we're lucky to have you here." Root turns his attention back to his daughter and me. "You two will have ten minutes to fashion the best, most delicious s'more you can create."

He waves toward a table, where I spy the normal s'mores ingredients stacked. Graham crackers, chocolate, and marshmallows.

But there's also so much more. There're at least five different types of chocolate, a jar of peanut butter, multiple jellies, different candy bars, a container of caramel, a collection of fruits, and a variety of spices, like cinnamon, nutmeg, and cayenne pepper. There's even a package of bacon.

Mmm, a bacon s'more? Sounds perfect to me.

"You'll want to be inventive. Or maybe you want to go classic." Root wears a teasing smirk. "But what you *need* to do is make the perfect s'more for Mayor Nightson, who will sit with her back turned, unaware of who is making what. And, Mayor, I expect you to judge based on your preference rather than mass appeal."

She offers a solemn nod. "Understood. I swear to be the pickiest of eaters."

"Love to hear it!" The wood witch returns his attention to us. "Once again, you both have ten minutes to create the perfect campfire treat and present it to me. I will then deliver the finished products to Mayor Nightson."

Interesting.

I glance over in time to see Blossom's brow crinkle in concentration, her expression thoughtful, her eyes locked on the mayor, as if the griffin is a puzzle that simply needs to be solved.

"Your time starts now!"

Immediately, the gathered wolves and witches start calling out suggestions, but I ignore them as I lurch to my feet, eyes scanning the table of ingredients. If I'm going to win or lose this, it'll be on my own ideas. I know I'd like to try a chocolate-coated bacon s'more, but would the mayor? I grab the package of meat and a collection of other ingredients, deciding to experiment. Ten minutes should give me just enough time for at least one practice round.

As I arrange food items with one hand and hold a skewer over the fire with a marshmallow, my eyes keep trying to watch Blossom instead of my food. The witch seems to be eating more than she's cooking. But her face still holds that focused expression that tells me a lot is going on in her mind.

If only I could read her thoughts. But I don't care about insight into her s'more plan.

I want to know if she thinks about *me*. If there's a single positive pondering about the werewolf who's secretly loved her for years.

"Three minutes!" Root calls out just as I'm hit with inspiration.

I don't know if it'll appeal to the mayor, but the combo can't be denied once I have my mind set. I hurry to re-create my mental image. And just as my marshmallow turns the perfect level of gooey crispiness, Blossom snaps her fingers and lets out a whoop of triumph.

Then, she sprints into the trees.

I pause, shocked by her abrupt departure.

"One minute!" Root calls out, the man also appearing confused, his stare on the shadowy trees where his daughter disappeared.

But she returns a moment later, a wide grin on her face. The witch runs back to the fire in time to scoop up her marshmallows before they scorch.

Needing to finish off my presentation, I can't watch Blossom's final arrangement.

As Root counts down from ten, I situate my top graham cracker and hurry up to him, offering the plate with my dessert.

Blossom is a step behind me, and I catch a flash of melting chocolate and golden-brown marshmallow before her father whisks the plates to the waiting mayor.

"One!" Root shouts, and the assembly hollers their excitement.

"What was that about?" I whisper to her as she saunters back to her seat.

Blossom's smile is pure cockiness, the expression tightening my groin.

"You'll see."

Root clears his throat, gaining the attention of the murmuring crowd. "If you would be so kind, Mayor Nightson, please describe the flavors for us all once you've taken a bite."

"Of course."

There's a crunch of teeth breaking through graham cracker, and the whole crowd seems to hold their breath in anticipation.

"Oh, yum," Belinda says after a moment. "This is delicious. There's cinnamon, apple, and caramel in addition to the classic milk chocolate and marshmallow. A great fall s'more." She takes another bite and swallows with a happy hum. "I could eat more than one of these."

I sit up straighter in my seat, chest swelling with pride. I tried the bacon, and it was delicious. But then Blossom's spiced apple scent teased my nose, and I couldn't think of anything other than tasting her.

I made the s'more version of my wood witch.

"That's going to be hard to beat," the griffin claims. "But let's see about this next one."

Another crunch and chewing moment.

Then, Mayor Nightson laughs.

Witches and wolves exchange glances, and Blossom worries her lower lip between her teeth. I want to drag her into my arms, press a comforting kiss to that lip, and tell her it's okay if she doesn't win every challenge—

"I love it!" Belinda exclaims, cutting off my thought. "Dark chocolate and mint. My favorite combo. Is this a fresh mint leaf in here? Goddess, that's divine. Sorry, competitor one, I have to go with option number two."

Well, fuck me.

I guess we know why the witch ran off. She went to find some fresh herbs that must have been growing nearby.

Blossom jumps up from her seat, fist-pumping both her arms in the air with a whoop before turning her taunting grin my way.

"Two to one, sucker." She leans toward me as she rubs the score in, eyes alight with her win.

Gods, she's beautiful.

"How'd you know?" I try to keep my voice unaffected as I fight the urge to lunge forward and steal a kiss from those sassy lips.

"Peppermint patty latte. I was behind the mayor one time at Coffee & Claws when she ordered." The witch taps her temple as she names Folk Haven's local coffee shop. "It's a steel trap in here. Don't forget a thing."

Don't I know it? As I watch Blossom saunter away, off to chat with Belinda about her creation and accepting congratulations from fellow witches, I wonder if not forgetting means never forgiving as well.

Two to one.

I stare at the ground between my feet, watching shadows from the dancing bonfire flames flicker across the flattened grass. Time passes as I try not to panic. Try not to think about losing and Blossom leaving again.

This time, without the requirement of saying good-bye to me.

As if conjured by my thoughts, there's a gentle press of lips against my cheek and the scent of spiced apples in my nose. The witch snuck up on me, and I turn my head so fast that my mouth brushes hers before she can fully retreat.

Blossom gasps in a breath, her pupils dilating when they meet mine, and we pause there, staring at each other until she whispers ...

"Good-bye, darling. I'll miss you."

Then, she's gone.

And I'm left wondering why those words didn't sound like a threat.

They sounded like an invitation.

6

BLOSSOM

It's well past midnight, but I can't sleep. The woods call to me.

I slip out from under the covers in my childhood bedroom, grab a blanket off the foot of the bed, and wrap it around my shoulders as I tiptoe downstairs to keep from waking Papa. Just because I can't get any sleep doesn't mean he should suffer and be drowsy tomorrow.

I need to rest, I remind myself. *How else am I going to beat Manny?*

The memory of his face from the corn maze comes back to me, and I allow myself a grin as I shuffle through the dark kitchen. The werewolf never should have doubted my devious nature.

The night air is cool against my bare skin, smelling of freshly fallen leaves and carrying the sounds of bats chirping, bugs humming, and the occasional hoot of an owl. Papa has cushy chairs set up on the screened-in porch, but I don't settle in one. The restless energy that has kept me awake draws me through the screen door and across the yard, toward the tree line.

Halfway there, I spy a shadowy form leaning against the thick trunk of a towering oak.

"Manny," I greet him, knowing immediately who the nighttime visitor is. "You're being a major creep. Do you lurk like this all the time?"

He lets out a deep, rumbling chuckle that makes me aware I'm not wearing a bra under my T-shirt. I pull my blanket tighter around my shoulders.

"What can I say? I'm a creature of the night." The last word rides a low growl.

"Is that supposed to scare me?"

"No." The shadows hide his eyes, but I still feel his gaze on me. "I know I can't scare you. Not that I'd ever want to."

I scoff, hiking the blanket higher to disguise the way my body shivers in response to him. "Why are you here? Missing your running buddy?"

The wolf tilts his head, as if confused.

I roll my eyes. "You and Heather might have thought you were being stealthy, but I always knew when she sneaked out to meet you in the woods. I used to think you were hooking up." I fight a smile at his grimace. "But after she came out, I realized you all must have just been enjoying the night together. Going for a run."

And damn if I wasn't wildly jealous of them. From my window, I'd watch Heather shimmy down her trellis, dressed in black and wearing her sneakers. When she reached the ground, my sister would sprint across the yard to the edge of the forest, where a wolf awaited her.

I wanted to follow them. The need to be free in the forest was a painful song in my body.

And I wanted to have a handsome werewolf waiting for me.

I wanted Manny.

But I didn't get to have him or to sprint through the woods with my sister at my side. Back then, Heather babied me and would have sent me back to the house like a misbehaving child. And Manny was always a surly beast to me.

No one invited me on secret nightly excursions.

So, I stayed in my room and tried to stifle my envy.

"We didn't go running," he says, surprising me. "Not together anyway. Heather is more of a climber. She'd scale some tall tree to study the stars, and I'd chase some unlucky rodent."

They never ran together? Apparently, my imagination got away from me. That seems to happen a lot around Manny Ramirez.

"If you want to go for a run," he says, "let's go for a run."

My body sways toward the trees, ready to take him up on his offer. My mind holds me back.

"Why? So you can prove you would've beaten me in the maze today if I hadn't tied you up?"

Manny leans forward, and I realize I drifted into his personal space at some point. His lips hover close to my ear. "Tie me up whenever you want to."

All the saliva in my mouth dries up, and I have to clear my throat. The taunting wolf straightens just enough for me to meet his eyes. To see the heated glint in them.

"What do you mean?" I rasp when, really, I want to say, *Why are you doing this to me?*

Did Heather finally spill the beans on me? After she came out and introduced Papa and me to her first girlfriend, I realized she wasn't in love with Manny. That they weren't destined to be together. After that, I guess I got lax about covering up my attraction to him. She caught me staring at the werewolf one day when he was shirtless and helping Papa haul pumpkins out of The Patch for a large order.

Heather can be relentless when she wants, and my sister

badgered me until I admitted that I'd always thought Manny was handsome. Too handsome for his own good. And that I knew he didn't see me the same way, so I refused to let him know how I felt.

Did she break our sister pact and tell her best friend that I'd had a crush on him the entire time I claimed to loathe everything about him?

I do loathe Manny. Hating the fact that, even while he teases me and growls at me, I want to strip him down, cover him in melted caramel, and lick his chest.

At least, in high school, I could claim adolescent hormones were the issue.

What's my excuse now? Misfiring horny spell that makes me want the closest asshole?

Whatever the reason, my body still responds to Manny in inappropriate ways. My skin heating in anticipation of his touch. My brain convincing itself that kissing him is the perfect kind of revenge.

Manny reaches out to tug on a lock of my hair before I can swat his hand away. "It means that I want you to truss me up, peel my clothes off with your teeth, and have your witchy way with me." His devilish grin slowly curls across his lips as I choke on my breath. "But only if you catch me first."

He's gone. Turning so fast that he seems to vanish into thin air. But deep in the shadows of the forest, I hear a pained grunt.

He's changing. The wolf is coming out.

He wants me to chase him when he's in his wolf form? So I'm guaranteed to lose?

Maybe that's why he made those suggestive remarks. Because he knows they would never come to fruition.

I grit my teeth, annoyance sparking through my veins that Manny might know about my crush and be using it against me. Suddenly, I want to catch him more than anything in the world.

I want to toss his body to the ground and strip him like he said. I want to bind him to the forest floor with thick roots.

Then, I want to leave him there. I want to walk away as he pleads for my forgiveness.

Pajamas aren't the best for a middle-of-the-night sprint. Neither are bare feet.

At least for someone who isn't a wood witch.

I bend one knee, then the other. Rubbing my bare soles before twisting my fingers in coaxing gestures. My power unfurls under my skin, a light-green glow emanating from my pores, and I feel my body respond to the spell. My feet touch the ground, and the connection is instant. This is more than my spur-of-the-moment conjuring in the corn maze. My magic is full of intention.

I am one with the earth.

It cannot cut me. Cannot bruise or harm me. Nature is a gentle cradle under my soles.

I don't know if this will make me any faster, but it'll keep a stray thorn in my heel from slowing me down.

"Ready or not, here I come," I mutter, dropping my blanket and taking off into the dark woods at a sprint.

My plan was to listen for the soft, thumping footfalls of a loping wolf, but the moment I start running, the race fades from my mind as I'm overwhelmed by the joy of finally letting myself go wild.

Letting myself run free.

Where I live, there are paths and trails in local parks I can jog on. And I do. But never with true abandon. Never with laughter bubbling from my throat and my arms stretched wide to brush my fingers against the foliage.

I wonder if this is what wood nymphs feel like when they dance through the woods. Those mythics commune with nature in a way I could only hope to achieve. I've seen them fully disappear inside trees as easily as stepping into the waters of Lake Galen.

That's a feat I haven't managed, but with my hand gestures and a force within my spirit, I can coax the natural world to move and respond to me.

We are friends of a sort, and now, I flow among them.

I'm supposed to chase the wolf, I remind myself.

But I don't know where to start, and I'm having too much fun, driving myself forward.

I whoop and keep going.

In the next moment, I feel a presence at my back. Imposing, but not threatening.

Just like at the wedding.

Manny is here.

"I'm not chasing you, wolf," I cry out, my legs pumping, my lungs sucking in the cool night air that smells like damp earth.

I swear I hear a huff, and then there's the slightest brush at my heels. With a squeak, I step higher, glancing back to find a massive black wolf loping behind me, his head ducked low. He gives a playful snap toward my feet.

"Are you herding me?" I intend for my voice to sound scathing. Instead, I giggle the question.

He offers me a fang-filled grin.

For some reason, I find his playful response hilarious, and I leave a string of chuckles in my wake as I fly forward. Like in the maze, I allow the power of the plants around me to infuse my limbs with extra energy.

The boost makes me faster, but not fast enough to outrun a werewolf. Manny sticks close, sometimes skipping in for another snap, as if he likes the way I hop and laugh.

Then, he slows and lets out a sharp bark of warning. Pointing my gaze forward, I realize there's a cliff fast approaching.

I more than see it. I *feel* it. The abrupt ending to the trees.

But I also sense where the forest restarts, far below.

The oaks and pines and yellow woods wait at the base of the cliff for me. Beckoning me toward them. Cheering me on.

I don't slow down.

Manny barks again, then snarls when I don't heed his warning. The ground shakes with his pounding paws. But he hesitated for too long. Too late to catch up.

"See you at the bottom!" I shout as the branches in front of me part to reveal the wide expanse of the Chattahoochee National Forest, lit by the half-moon.

My feet push me into a running swan dive, and I scream in pure delight as I free-fall through the air.

An animal's roar follows my plummet.

But I'm too busy calling to the woods below to concern myself with Manny.

Leaf-covered branches stretch toward me like my father's arms used to when I jumped from my bunk bed into his waiting hold. And just like then, I'm caught in an abrupt yet cushioned embrace.

"Thank you!" I call to the trees, my green-glowing hands stretched out in thanks.

They shiver their limbs in response, slowly depositing me on the ground. I sit there for a moment, grinning wide and panting. But as my heart rate begins to slow, I realize I'm not done.

I want to keep going.

"Blossom!" My name is bellowed through the trees.

Wow, he made it down fast. And he changed forms.

"Are you running naked through the woods, Manny?" I yell the question while rocking up to my feet.

"Thank the fucking gods."

I think I hear him groan, but I don't wait to check, setting off at a fast jog.

Will he turn back to his wolf so he can catch me?

There's the sound of crashing branches and crunching brush behind me.

Does he even need to change to run as fast as I do?

"Blossom! Get your ass back here!"

I almost pause. Almost. More because of his tone than his words.

He sounds pissed.

The last time I remember Manny getting truly angry was when Alvin Carter spray-painted a gay slur on my sister's locker. The guy was lucky he was a merman. A human wouldn't have healed from two broken legs so quickly.

Maybe I shouldn't have cannonballed off a cliff without warning Manny first. I guess that could scare a guy if he wasn't properly prepared.

Oh well. It's done now.

I pick up the pace, heading toward a familiar group of trees that isn't too far off. They call to me like old friends.

Two steps into the orchard, I'm lifted off my feet.

"Hey!" I yelp, my fingers scrabbling against the strong set of arms wrapped around my waist.

Next I know, my back is on the ground, and there's a glaring werewolf on top of me, pinning my body in place.

And the answer is, yes, Manny was running through the woods naked in his human form.

"What the hell were you thinking?" he growls.

"That you're heavier than a boulder." I jab a finger into his bare side, but he doesn't flinch.

Truthfully, the man isn't crushing me. But he's also an immovable force.

"I'm talking about that stunt you just pulled. You could've died."

I roll my eyes. "I knew the trees would catch me."

"*I* didn't know," he snarls.

And instead of my anger rising in response to his, I spy the fear in Manny's eyes, and the sight allows me to soften. Reaching up, I push the wild strands of his hair off his sweaty forehead.

"Poor little wolf. Did I scare you?" I tease gently, waiting for him to respond in kind. To bring us back to what we've always been. Two enemies who've established a fragile truce because we love the same people.

Instead, Manny's big body sinks closer to mine, his shoulders curving, as if to shield me. "I was fucking terrified." His face presses against my neck, lips on my skin as he speaks. "I think I could live with you leaving me. But I wouldn't survive *losing* you, Blossom Fernmore."

Once again, I'm left shocked by his words, blurting out the only question I can manage. "What does that mean?"

Manny presses a hot, open-mouthed kiss to my racing pulse before answering in a calm voice, "I want you."

This makes no sense. None at all. He's talking complete nonsense. Maybe he dived off that cliff after me and whacked his head on the landing.

Whatever the cause, I'm not about to put up with his teasing.

Or these neck kisses that threaten to unravel me.

"Manuel Ramirez." I'm proud of the stern tone I manage despite how breathless I suddenly am.

"Don't call me that," he rumbles, his lips brushing over my ear, hot exhale making me shiver. "Only my uncle uses my full name. I hate it."

"Fine," I snap, using annoyance to cover the effect he's having on my body. "Manny. I'll call you Manny."

"No." His voice is rough yet gentle. "Call me your wolf."

"My wolf?" I try to keep my voice hard, but it quivers. "You've never wanted to be mine."

Suddenly, Manny braces himself on his elbows, raised far enough to meet my eyes, his sharp gaze boring into mine.

"I've always wanted to be yours. Too much."

I shake my head. This is a game. It has to be.

But I find myself repeating my earlier question, this time with a tinge of desperation. "What does that mean?"

"It's not complicated, my infuriating little wood witch." He cups my face with one hand, tracing the curve of my cheek with his thumb. "I want you. I want inside you. And I want you to want me."

My body flushes with heat, every inch of me straining toward the wolf and his tempting words.

Words I've never admitted I've always wanted to hear.

7

MANNY

With fear still coursing through my veins after Blossom's plummet off a cliff, I can't find it in me to evade the truth a moment longer.

I listen to the ragged cadence of her breath, her chest pressing into mine with each inhale. As much as I want to claim her mouth and kiss the hell out of her—make her want me—that'll only drive the witch away.

And I don't want to force Blossom.

I want her to choose me.

With a shift of my muscles, I flip us over, rolling onto my back so Blossom is straddling me.

Giving her every inch of the high ground.

Not that I mind how the core of her is only inches from my half-hard cock.

"As you come to terms with the fact that I want you," I say, attempting a teasing tone, "I'd like it noted that I've confessed this in the middle of an apple orchard. I hope you take this as a sign of submission. The amount of ammo available puts me at a great disadvantage."

Blossom gazes down at me. "You're joking."

"I'm not." Carefully, I lay my hands on her thighs. Kneading the thick muscles with my fingers and trying not to think about how they'd flex if she rode me.

Blossom sits up straight, crossing her arms over her chest. But she doesn't climb off me, and I take that as a promising sign. As the beautiful, infuriating witch studies me, I pluck a few stray leaves off her cotton sleep shorts.

"So, this is a new thing?" she asks with narrow eyes. "You wanting me? You saw me clutching that scarecrow tight and were like, *Damn, I wish I were the straw-filled doll*?"

I snort and grin up at the sassy witch and fall for her a little more.

"No. I mean, don't get me wrong; I'm definitely jealous of every inanimate object you've ever held tight against your boobs like that." As I speak, I let one hand creep up to her rib cage and risk my thumb by brushing it over the lower curve of her breast. "But wanting you isn't new."

Her brow furrows in the most adorable scowl. "Explain."

"Happy to." Especially with her like his, astride me, as if I were her own personal mount, not protesting my sneaky, roving hands. "When you turned thirteen, you hit puberty. And you started to smell good. *Really* good."

Like *warm apple pie* and *teenage fantasies* good.

"Are you serious?" Blossom gapes.

I nod. "I realized it was the mating scent. That you and I had … potential."

My parents had explained how mates work for werewolves. How when someone smells amazing, that means The Clawed One is identifying them as a potential partner. Unlike some mythics, werewolves can scent more than one possible mate, which means a potential partner doesn't mean they're the only option.

But it's hard not to at least pay them attention.

"When I hit puberty ..." Her eyes widen, and even in the low glow of the half-moon, I spy a blush darkening her cheeks. "Oh my fucking goddess! Are you telling me you smelled my first *period*?"

Blossom's embarrassment has me wanting to strip her bare and do all manner of depraved things with her until she's burning alive with blushes.

But I settle for a shrug. "I smelled all your periods. It's a natural part of having a uterus. Nothing to be ashamed of."

The little wood witch presses her palms to her cheeks, as if that could cool the inferno radiating off them.

"I need you to shut your mouth," she groans. "Teenage Blossom is dead. Literally. I just felt the ghost of her leave my body, murdered by mortification."

"You're cute when you get dramatic." I drag my hands up and down her sides, enjoying this simple act of touching her.

And Blossom doesn't bother to stop me. Or to magically chuck an apple at my head.

This feels like progress.

"And am I the only potential mate you've met over the years?" she asks after a few beats of silent contemplation.

Not sure how she'll respond, I slowly shake my head. "There've been two more. Both times, I tried dating them. They were both nice. But ..." When an explanation doesn't immediately come to mind, I trail off as I reach for an answer that won't send her running.

"But what?"

I slip my hand up her chest, pressing flat against her pounding heart. "They weren't you."

Blossom scowls, but instead of pushing me away, she flattens her palm over mine, holding me in place. "I don't get it.

You've always been a dick to me. If you liked me, why didn't you *do* something about it?"

"I wanted to," I admit. "But you were thirteen. I was sixteen. You were my best friend's little sister. And you might not have realized this, but your dad was always more of a parent to me than my uncle was. I knew if I pursued you and messed it up—which I think we both know I would have because teenage Manny was a mess—I would've lost Heather and Root, along with you. So, immature kid I was, I decided to act like an asshole to keep you away from me."

Blossom glowers at me. "You did that spectacularly."

I can feel my rueful grin. "By the time you were old enough to date, you hated me. I'd screwed myself over."

She slaps my chest. "You told all the guys I dated in school that I was high maintenance and whiny!"

I grab her palm and bring it to my mouth for a kiss. "I was a jealous asshole." Needing a taste of her, I drag my tongue over the lines on her hand, like a horny palm reader.

Blossom gasps and squirms, which has her ass brushing my cock. A groan rumbles from my chest, and the witch freezes. Not that it helps when I can see how her nipples pebble against the thin cotton of her T-shirt.

"Can you forgive me?" I rasp, tense with restrained lust and fear of her answer.

She stares down at me, face unreadable.

As I wait for the final dictate, I catalog every piece of Blossom I can—from her round, flushed cheeks to the flare of her hips.

If she turns me down, what will that mean for the future? More avoidance? Will we be able to go back to our competitive banter?

I'd rather argue with Blossom for the next five decades than have her leave the room whenever I walk in.

Don't cut me off. Please. Don't shut down—

"I'm on birth control."

Now, it's my turn to gape. Blossom is still glaring at me, so I'm pretty sure I misheard her.

"What?"

"I got the contraception tattoo. The spell. You know about it, right?" She tugs down the waistband of her shorts, and I see the small symbol.

"Okay ..." I draw out the word, worried about coming to the wrong conclusion.

She huffs out a sigh, shoves my hand off her chest, and tugs her shirt over her head, baring her glorious boobs to the starry night and my starving eyes.

"So, we doing this or what?"

My mind is set in slow mode as I try to keep up. "And by *this*, you mean ..."

"Come on, Manny. You're naked, and you just told me I smell like your mate. You going to ravish me or what?"

My fingers grab hold of the remaining fabric on her body, moving out of sync with my mouth. "You don't want to talk?" I ask, my voice a deep rumble in my chest.

Blossom holds up her hands as if they were a scale. "Talk, orgasms. Talk, orgasms." She raises them up and down, as if considering both options, then lifts her right hand high. "Look at that. Orgasms it is."

"I mean, if that's what the scale says." With a fierce grin, I tear her shorts in half and then sit up fast to capture her mouth in an intoxicating kiss.

Blossom moans, wrapping her arms around my neck as she kisses me back and rocks her now-bare pussy against my quickly hardening cock.

This is everything I've hoped for and feared. A pivotal moment where she's giving me a chance.

Don't fuck this up.

Fisting my hand in her silky hair, I grasp the strands in an unforgiving grip as I drag my mouth from hers. Blossom whimpers, her lips looking bee stung from my aggressive kisses. What I wouldn't give to see them wrapped around my cock.

Not tonight. This is all for her. To show her exactly why she should forgive me. Give me a chance.

"You hold still, Bud," I growl at her.

Her wrist twists, and an apple pings off my shoulder, the magical assault more surprising than painful.

"Don't call me your buddy when you're trying to seduce me," she hisses, looking like she might bite me if I wasn't holding her head in place.

A slow smile steals over my lips. "Is that what you think that nickname means? Buddy?"

Blossom's lips pucker, and I let out a dark laugh.

"Oh, Blossom. You tasty little wood witch. I mean bud, as in flower." My cheeks ache with a grin as I watch her skin color. "That's right. A flower bud. Small, sure, but full of life and potential and beauty. Hiding all its secrets from the world until it's ready to burst forward in the most glorious bloom. Just waiting to blossom."

She bites her lip now, her eyes closed, as if she can't handle what I'm saying. But I plan to make it impossible for her to ignore my adoration.

"And how about this little bud?" My free hand slips past her intimate curls, pushing apart silky folds that remind me of petals until I discover that perfect bundle of nerves. "You want me to tell you how much I love this bud, don't you? How, most nights, I imagine you stroking this spot while I fuck my fist."

Blossom's body tightens, thighs gripping my hips. Chest rising and falling in a rapid rhythm with her pants. I can feel the puffs of her hot breath against the cool sweat on my skin. Each one brings the scent of her arousal, mixed with spiced apples, and I swear I'd never need another meal in my life if I could always breathe her in.

The delicate skin between her legs grows slick the more I stroke her. She wraps a clawing hand around my wrist, but not to pull me away. Instead, Blossom holds me in place as her hips rock. Each movement presses her ass against my cock, and I can't hold back my needy grunts.

"You close? You gonna be a good little witch and come for me?"

"Oh goddess." Blossom stares at me through half-lidded eyes, and the flames in her cheeks scald me with erotic heat.

"Say my name when you come," I demand. "Say it."

Her throat bobs with a swallow, and she whimpers. But I don't go easy on her, keeping my grip tight in her hair. I refuse to let her hide from me in this moment. The animal in me wants to speed up my ministrations, but I keep steady.

I'm relentless.

I'm rewarded.

"Manny!" she groans as her body shudders and tenses, curling inward as the sweetest inarticulate sounds spill from her throat.

Releasing her hair, I tuck Blossom against my chest, holding her head under my chin.

But I keep my fingers on her clit, pressing down to encourage the orgasm to linger, enjoying the way her body grasps at empty air.

A wordless request to be filled.

"You want my cock inside next time," I murmur against her hair, "don't you?"

Blossom's nails dig into my shoulders, but she doesn't say anything. Only drags in deep breaths.

And she nods.

"That's my good little wood witch. I've got what you want." My fingers shake with anticipation before I dig them into her hips. Then, I lift the woman I love and carefully ease her pliant body onto my shaft.

Blossom's gasp mingles with my pleased growl.

Right. This is exactly right.

Her tight grasp threatens to undo me, but I grit my teeth and push the orgasm back. Just for a moment. Just long enough to revel in this reality I was never certain would occur. Blossom Fernmore softening for me. Wanting me.

The wood witch presses her body closer to mine, rocking her hips.

"You slowed down," she complains. "Don't slow down."

I let out a satisfied chuckle. "You want fast?"

With a quick shift, I have Blossom on her back, and I drive into her, every thrust deep, demanding, and unrelenting.

"You're going to feel me tomorrow, Pumpkin Princess," I growl with a toothy grin. "I know you're still going to try to win. Try to beat me. But with every move you make, you're going to remember that I had you pinned."

Blossom smirks up at me, even as lust drags a dark flush over her cheeks. "Big talk for a wolf who hasn't even reached the finish line."

Then, she wraps her legs around my waist, arms around my shoulders, and crashes her mouth into mine. Her heated kiss ends with a sharp sting on my lip and blood on her mouth.

The animalistic move does it. With a low groan, I spill everything I am into the witch, her triumphant laughter almost as beautiful as the way she moans my name.

8

BLOSSOM

THIS IS IT. If I win this round, I win the whole thing.

True, there's still one more event after this, but it'll just be the final entertainment at that point.

After our world-altering sex in the woods last night, Manny and I didn't talk much. The orgasm made me sleepy, and after pulling on the clothes that survived the wolf's mauling, I got to my feet and swayed. The werewolf immediately scooped me into his arms and started to jog toward my childhood home. I would have protested if I hadn't nodded off, only waking up when he set me down on the porch, wrapped me in my discarded blanket, and nudged me toward the backdoor.

I slept well. Then, I woke up to a werewolf knocking on my front door with a mocha from Coffee & Claws. Turned out, I'd slept till noon, and I might have missed this next challenge if my competition hadn't wanted to caffeinate me.

I glance over to where Manny walks at my side, expecting to see a look of concentration on his face, an indication of his competitive nature rising to the surface. Over the years, I've

437

watched Heather and him get down and dirty on some of these bouts.

But he doesn't look determined.

He's just looking at me.

"What?" I wipe a hand over my mouth in case my breakfast bagel left behind crumbs.

Instead of answering, Manny sidles closer, scoops up my hand, and kisses the center of my palm. "Good luck," he says.

I snatch my hand back. "Is this a distraction technique?"

His brows dip, and then an evil smirk curves his lips. He hooks me around the waist, and the sneaky wolf presses my back against the closest tree.

"No, Blossom. *This* is a distraction technique."

Then, his mouth captures mine in a heady kiss that tastes like red wine and man. I moan and let my lips part so I can lick his tongue, wondering what terrible god gifted this wolf with such a tantalizing flavor.

Then, the terrible beast breaks the kiss, but uses his hips to keep me pinned to the tree and clasps my hands above my head, making manacles of his fingers.

"I'm not going to let you win," he says. "Not even if you say I can fuck you right here and now in exchange for me going easy on you."

I glare at him. "I'd never offer that!" I struggle to free myself, but Manny keeps me locked in place, nostrils flaring, chest heaving and pressing into mine. "I'm going to win because I'm awesome. And then *maybe* I'll let you fuck me again. But only if I have time between my Pumpkin Queen duties."

Manny firms his mouth in a line, trying to stifle a smile and failing. So, instead, he leans in and gently nips my lip.

But when he next speaks, his voice has lost its playful edge. "If you win, will you still stay?"

Will I stay?

The question is too heavy for our snarky banter.

Will I finally come back to this town that calls to me?

Will I come back ... to be with him?

But that's not what Manny asked.

What if I say yes, move back to Folk Haven, and this sultry side of him vanishes?

I couldn't stand to see him every day, only to get dismissed. Discarded.

With my life now, I'm the one who does the leaving. But that would be impossible if I set down roots in this soil that feels like part of my soul.

Can I trust the side of this wolf he's shown me since the mating ceremony? Do I believe the words Manny spoke to me last night?

It's hard to concentrate with his hard body between my thighs and the taste of him lingering in my mouth.

And the urge to battle him, to push back and never give an inch that isn't earned, rises in me.

"That wasn't the bet," I say.

Manny flinches, and his grip on my wrists loosens. When he backs away, allowing my feet to regain the ground, I spy a wounded expression on his face that has guilt spearing through my gut.

But he quickly clears the vulnerability away, replacing it with a smirk. "You're right. If I want Blossom Fernmore to stay in Folk Haven, I'll just have to win you."

Then, he stalks off toward our destination, giving me his back.

"That's not the bet either!" I call after him as I jog to catch up, feeling off-balance and defensive. "You don't win me." When I reach his side, I spy the tight set of his mouth.

"If you don't shut up, I'm going to kiss you again," he growls.

"I can talk if I—"

Manny hauls me into his chest and melds his mouth to mine. Without thought, I wrap my legs around his waist and my arms around his neck and kiss him back with equal fervor. When he breaks away, the wolf is panting, and I can see the animal in his eyes.

Then, the phone in my pocket starts buzzing, bringing my mind back to the present moment. Manny lets me slide down his body, and I pull out my cell to see my dad calling.

I answer it. "Hey, Papa."

"Is Manny with you? Are you almost here? We've got an eager crowd today!"

Through the phone speaker, I can hear voices chattering away.

"We're close. Be there in a minute."

When I hang up, Manny slips his hand into mine and tugs me forward, his eyes focused straight ahead.

Guess the guy is done talking. And kissing.

And I refuse to focus on how much I'd like to revisit that second one.

Soon enough, we're breaking through the forest edge to arrive on the shores of Lake Galen. The water glistens in the sunlight, and a short ways away, a group has assembled. But the spectators aren't only on the land. Out in the waves, a few pontoon boats float, anchored in the shallow water of the cove.

"There're our champions!" my father calls out, waving us toward the gathering.

I see now that there're multiple firepits set up, and I expect people will get them lit in a few hours once the sun has set.

Hopefully, this challenge doesn't last as long as all that. I'm competitive, but after last night, my stamina is questionable.

The werewolf beside me is probably doing just fine.

I tug my hand from his, not wanting to deal with questions and gossip. I swear I hear a soft, displeased growl from Manny, but I ignore him and hurry forward.

"Now that the Pumpkin Princess and Pumpkin Prince have arrived, we can commence the next round of the competition!"

Papa, nimble for his age, balances on the top of a barrel as he holds the attention of the crowd.

There's a tap in the side of the container, and once more, I see most everyone clutching a cup of cider. Papa brews a batch specifically for this weekend. A onetime-only tasting event.

"What do you have for the lucky pumpkin royalty today?" Selena calls out to my father, an easy grin creasing the witch's cheeks.

She sits beside a white woman with soft brown hair and an air of dangerous power around her. Violetta Radeva, the sea witch who now lives on a lake. The two magical women hold hands where they recline on a set of camping chairs.

"So glad you asked. Blossom, Manny, please join me."

My dad waves to the shoreline by his barrel, and we come to a stop beneath him. When we both face the crowd on land, searching for a clue to our next challenge, he laughs and points out to the water.

"Hope you two are ready for a dip!"

With growing dread, I rotate and watch as Heath steps up to the side of one of the farther pontoon boats and upends a basket over the water. A cascade of apples topples into the gentle waves.

My father's voice booms overhead. "Next challenge ... bobbing for apples!"

9

MANNY

Ten minutes. As many apples as we can gather.

The catch—as if we need another one—is that we have to use our mouths to bring them to shore.

Ultimate bobbing for apples.

Blossom has a furious frown on her gorgeous face as we line up where the water meets the red clay shore.

She knows I have the advantage.

And without her promise to stay even if I lose, I have no plans to go easy on her.

"Get ready!" Root calls out.

Blossom kicks off her sneakers and peels off her socks, left only in a matching set of green leggings and a sports bra.

Fuck, I want to drag her into the woods and peel the athletic gear off her and fuck her on the forest floor like last night, only in broad daylight this time.

Not now, I reprimand myself. *Win this. Get her to stay.*

"Get set!"

The wood witch crouches in a sprinting position. I leisurely

442

strip off my shirt, enjoying the way her eyes flick to my bare chest, then to the water, then back to my chest.

That's not all I'm releasing, my beautiful Blossom.

"Go!"

I drop my shorts, unabashed that I'm bare-assed in front of a good fifty mythics.

Blossom stumbles in the middle of her lunge toward the water before whirling on me with a heated glare. "Don't you dare!"

But I only grin, the expression turning into a grimace as I coax out my wolf.

"Foul! That's a foul!" the angry witch shouts.

"Sorry, Blossom," I hear her dad say, the man not sounding contrite in the least. "You used magic in the maze. That means fair is fair."

Damn right.

"Fucking wolves," she snarls.

Then, there's a splash, and I know she's off, her lithe body arrowing toward the closest apple. My eyes can't track her though, my sight blurring as I shift. I need another few breaths to push through the pain of the change.

Some of my kind can transform as fast as a blink with little more than a twinge.

Lucky bastards.

Still, even though the switch to my lupine form lost me half a minute, once I'm in my canine state, I charge into the water. The liquid parts easily as I paddle fast for the bobbing orbs, my strong strokes pushing me forward at a pace my human body wouldn't have managed.

Blossom has already reached her first apple. She's an adept swimmer, having spent most of her summers in this lake. The problem is, the chill water drags at her muscles while I now have a thick coat to protect me.

And there's also the issue of grabbing an apple with that sassy mouth of hers.

My lengthened jaw makes it easy to snatch a bobbing piece of fruit from where it floats. I kick my legs in a quick turn and shoot back to the shore. After dropping off my first treasure, I don't bother shaking the water out of my fur before plunging back in. As I plow through the waves, I spy Blossom's powerful freestyle, her teeth clamped on an apple of her own.

She's not giving up without a fight.

We continue on, back and forth, cheering from the shore following our progress. When the horn goes off, signaling the end of our ten minutes, Blossom and I return to land.

She collapses on the red rocky beach, her chest heaving with pants, soaking wet sports bra clinging to her chest and revealing the outline of a rigid set of nipples.

I want to warm the peaks with my mouth, and if we didn't have an audience—one that includes her father—I'd do exactly that. Instead, I focus on the competition.

Her pile has three apples.

Mine has seven.

Root steps forward, grinning broadly at the gathering.

"The winner of the apple bobbing challenge is the Pumpkin Prince! Which means we enter the last round with a tie!" He claps his hands together. "The final competition will begin at sunset."

10

BLOSSOM

A TIE. Damn it. I thought I could clinch my win, but now, we're back on equal ground.

As the sun dips behind the horizon, anticipation of the final challenge grows to a palpable hum in the tipsy collection of witches and werewolves.

Ever since my loss at apple bobbing earlier, I've avoided Manny, not sure how to feel about the conclusion of this festival. These two days were supposed to be a lighthearted seasonal celebration. But with the bet, there's so much more weighing on this outcome.

What happens if I win?

What happens if I lose?

One thing for sure is, I know *I* want to be the one making the big decisions in my life.

I should never had made that bet with Manny. Never have given him the possible power to demand I stay in Folk Haven. The wager never would have happened if I'd admitted an extremely obvious fact to myself.

I like having to kiss Manny good-bye every time I see him.

If only I'd acknowledged that, sometimes, when I visit town, I drag my feet while leaving to give him an extra moment or two to arrive. Because my lips crave the familiar warmth of his cheek, paired with the rich wine scent of his skin.

And my heart longs for a moment when I matter to him more than anyone else.

I could have kissed him good-bye for years and not minded. Not really. All the animosity I imbued those partings with had been born from frustration. From anger and upset that he never saw me as anything other than his friend's little sister to tease.

"I've always wanted to be yours."

That's what he said. Is it the truth?

Anxiously, I fiddle with the ring on my middle finger and watch my father chatting with the mayor so I don't stare at the wolf who hovers near my side. Close enough that I can feel the heat of his body.

"Will you still stay?"

I want to decide that on my own. For myself. But now, because I've played the *I loathe Manny* role with such dedication, I'm stuck on the verge of being forced to move back to Folk Haven based on my pride alone.

Would that be so bad? To live in this place again?

"Gather round, everybody!" Papa hollers, and voices hush as we all surround two stumps of wood with sheets draped over them.

With a dramatic flourish, Root Fernmore tugs away the white cloth, revealing ...

Pumpkins.

Two of them. One for me and one for Manny.

"The final task is a carve off!" The glee is apparent in his voice. Nothing gets people more excited about visiting The Patch than the idea of pumpkin carving. "You'll have to fashion an image that pleases our illustrious judge, Mayor Nightson." My father waves the woman forward as he sets out a range of tools beside each gourd. "If you would be so kind, Mayor, please tell our contestants what image you would like them to carve into their pumpkins."

Belinda shares a smile between Manny and me, then addresses the spectators. "As I'm sure everyone here knows, one of my greatest loves is this town." Her focus returns to us. "What I would like for you both to carve today is what you most love about Folk Haven. I think that would be the perfect way to ring in this fall season." She claps her hands together, the sound a punctuation on the challenge.

Goddess, it's like the griffin can divine the turmoil in my heart. It's obvious which way she would vote on stay versus leave.

"That's a fantastic theme!" Papa slaps his thigh and grins wide. "Can't wait to see what the pumpkin royalty come up with. You both have an hour, starting ... now!"

The crowd cheers and calls out suggestions for the first few moments as Manny and I snatch up our gourds, but everyone soon refocuses on the booze and food. Folk Haven's places and events they offer rattle in my head.

Lake Galen ... Main Street ... The Halloween Ball ... the Gauntlet ... Ramla University ... Coffee & Claws ... Local Brew ... Marlin's Marina ... the Public Mythic Library ...

The list goes on.

And yet none of them ring true for me. They're all wonderful things about this small town. But they're not what I love most. They aren't what had me staring at my soon-to-end lease agreement and wondering if I should let the claim on my townhouse lapse. They aren't what set my pulse thrumming and my breath quickening every time I drive past the *Welcome to Folk Haven* town sign.

Hugging the pumpkin to my chest, I close my eyes and let my mind soften around the simple question ...

What draws me home?

The answers come slowly, but they live in vibrant color once I let them free from my heart.

The forest.

Papa's cottage.

My family.

Him.

With a deep sigh, I allow a silhouetted image to form in my mind. It's simple yet detailed. If I start now, I should be able to fashion what I want in an hour.

When I set my pumpkin on the ground in front of me and snatch up my knife, I spare a glance Manny's way.

He's staring at me.

My heart beats hard, my cheeks heat, and old defenses slip into place.

"No cheating," I hiss to cover the way his unwavering attention affects every cell in my body.

The wolf grins, undaunted by my feigned animosity, then drops his eyes to his own vegetable canvas.

We both set to work.

If this had been the first task assigned to us, laid out for me yesterday morning, when I still set Manny in the Enemy category in my brain, I would've hacked away at this pumpkin frantically, desperate to create an image that far surpassed any the wolf could contemplate.

But now, I ease into the task. After I scoop out the innards, the pumpkin ends up cradled in my lap as I slip my sharp tool into the soft rind. My fingers grow sticky, the nail beds staining orange. But slowly, the picture in my head translates.

"One more minute!" My father's booming voice tugs me out of an almost-meditative state.

When I jerk my head up, I realize the crowd has finished their eating, and they're all watching us with held breath.

I set my pumpkin in the grass and wipe off specks of pulp before reaching for the short, thick candle left for me. With the strike of a match, the teasing scent of smoke fills the air. I light the wick, then carefully set the candle inside my creation.

"Time's up!" Papa claps his hands, and when I meet his gaze, I share his grin.

I've missed this. Being immersed in his fun. The past few years, I haven't even attended the Pumpkin Wars as a spectator. Now, I'm part of the silly tradition, and I find that I love it.

Even with the bet looming over my head.

"Pumpkin Princess, if you would be so kind as to show your creation to Mayor Nightson."

I stand and set my pumpkin on the wood stump where it first rested, turning the gourd so the crowd can take in all the details, though some might need to come closer to get the full effect.

"I call it *Home*," I say, keeping it simple, not looking to sell my creation to the judge. Either she gets it and she likes it or she doesn't. But I'm proud of what I made.

My pumpkin shows a small rendition of my father's house and trees towering above it. The windows flicker with the warmth of the candlelight, revealing silhouettes of people, and though they're indistinct, to me, I see my father and sister. A half-moon hovers above my carved forest, which resembles the pines and oaks that surround my childhood home.

Tucked in between the tree trunks—so small, almost impossible to see—is a set of eyes.

Wolfish eyes, though I might be the only one who knows that.

"Beautiful, Blossom," Mayor Nightson offers, tracing a finger over my image, and I can hear the sincerity in her voice.

Witches call out compliments, and I drop my eyes and fiddle with my ring, feeling exposed yet pleased.

"Pumpkin Prince," Papa prompts, "if you could show us yours."

Manny nods.

"I call it *Home*," he says, and I roll my eyes at his taunt.

Then, the wolf turns his creation to face the crowd.

His pumpkin is covered in flowers.

BLOSSOM

As my papa places the crown on my head, I can't help the silly grin that overtakes my face or the way my eyes seek out the Pumpkin Prince.

Manny is off to the side, clapping like everyone else. The wolf even has on a smile.

But his gaze catches mine, and I spy the regret in them.

We both know what this win means.

He lost the wager. I don't have to move to Folk Haven.

And I never have to kiss him good-bye again.

Last night could be a onetime deal. I could shrug it off as a hate fuck and move on. Forget the way he touched me. Stroked me. Lay beneath me with my name on his lips and awe in his eyes.

It was one night. One night can't rewrite years of animosity.

Still, after accepting congratulations from what seems like hundreds of witches, I gravitate toward a shadowy space between two trees, where he waits.

"You wear it well." Manny tilts his head toward mine, and I

reach up to finger the delicate metal construction.

"Told you I'd win."

"That you did." He stares at me. Into me.

I shiver under the weight of his attention. "Victory would have been sweeter if you'd tried harder on that last one. What even was that design?"

The smirk he gives me has a secretive edge. "You'll figure it out."

I squint my eyes at him, but then shrug. If the wolf wants to be elusive, then that's his prerogative.

Manny reaches forward and hooks a single finger in the belt loop of my jeans. He uses his hold to tug me closer, into the shadows with him until we can hear the gathering, but not see anyone. Effectively alone, he cages me against the trunk of an oak tree, leaves crunching under the thick soles of his boot.

"What's your plan, Pumpkin Queen?"

"My plan?"

He leans in to drag his nose up the column of my neck. "Now that you have the crown, will you conquer Folk Haven? Make this town yours?"

Having him this close, his heat surrounding me, makes my body tight and my voice hoarse. The tree at my back hums with life and encourages me closer to the man.

But my mouth sticks to old habits. "That wasn't the bet."

His fingers tighten, digging into my hips, almost hard enough to bruise, but not quite. "That's true." From the way he growls the words, I know Manny wants to add something. After sweeping his tongue over my pounding pulse, he snarls, "Fuck the bet."

For a moment, I consider giving in. Doing as he suggested.

But again, I speak from a place of self-preservation. "One night doesn't change everything."

Lies. Last night changed a lot of things.

But I'm terrified the changes were huge for me and only

passing for Manny.

The wolf pushes forward, crowding me, pinning me in place with his hips. "It changes enough."

All I give him is a shrug, trying to keep the intense way I want him to myself.

Manny's eyes glare into mine. "You belong here."

"With you?"

"Yes."

I've wanted that since I was thirteen. Since I started smelling good, apparently. I've ached for this man who always acted like I was a bother. He claims I've had the scent of a mate all along, but despite that, he's only ever teased me.

And there are the other people who smelled like mates to him that couldn't hold his interest.

Why should I trust that his longing reflects mine? Why should I tear down my defenses just because we had good sex?

Really good sex.

But the physical isn't all there is. I need more. I need to trust him.

I need to know that my returning to Folk Haven, that letting myself fall for Manny Ramirez, won't end in devastation.

But of course, instead of saying that, I go defensive, the way I always do around him.

I scoff. "Excuse me if you changing your mind yesterday isn't enough for me to upend my life."

Manny grasps the sides of my face, fingers delving into my hair, but he doesn't dislodge my crown. "I told you I've wanted you since I was sixteen."

"You *lusted* after me since then. I smelled good. But I don't let my pussy make my life decisions."

"If that's the case, then maybe you should stop humping my thigh."

Am I? Shit.

But he's the one that shoved it between my legs, pressing up against my greedy clit. I glare up at him.

Manny sucks in a deep breath and lets it out slow.

Then, he rests his lips against my forehead in a gentle kiss. "I'll be in the orchard again tonight. Come find me. Even if it's to say good-bye. Even though you don't have to."

The wolf steps away, releasing me. His face is in the shadows, so I can't read his expression.

"The crown was always meant for you," he says.

Then, he's gone, disappearing into the woods, leaving me behind, achy and confused.

No part of me wants to rejoin the festivities, so I turn my feet toward my father's house instead, mind reeling with longing and doubt as I stomp through the dark forest.

Once I'm alone in my childhood bedroom, I stare at myself in the mirror. Ridiculous neon-green outfit. Hair dried in random waves after the dip in the lake. Skin still flushed from being so close to the man I want.

I can feel him, between my legs, just like he claimed I would. The frigid water numbed the sensation for a stretch, but now, the subtle soreness is back, and my body misses his.

My eyes flit up to the top of my head.

The silly crown that I was so proud of weighs heavy on my forehead now. I snatch it off, and for a brief, petulant moment, I consider chucking it to the other side of my bedroom.

But I get over that urge fast. Manny made this crown. I remember Heather mentioning once that he fashioned it one of the years he won and she was determined to win it from him the next round. She did, flaunting her victory in front of the grumbling wolf.

From afar, I thought the headpiece looked beautiful. Twisted vines and amber beads twined into the thing.

But I never asked to see it up close, afraid that my jealousy of being left out of the competition would be obvious if I reverently cradled the circlet.

It's mine now. Won fairly.

"The crown was always meant for you."

What did Manny mean by that?

Instead of discarding the precious headpiece, I sink to the ground and hold it in my hands, letting my fingers trace over the metal. I follow the carefully crafted roots and spindly leaves hammered from metal into a perfect plant shape.

A familiar shape.

My ring glistens in the low light, the exact same shade as the crown. Side by side, it almost appears as if my ring was plucked from the larger piece.

As if they were a set.

It can't be. Papa gave me this ring.

But ... did he?

I found the gift box on my bedside table the morning I was leaving for college.

To remember where home is, the card read.

The note wasn't signed. I always assumed it was from my father.

But what if it was left by someone else?

What if this piece of jewelry I've treasured all my life, the reminder of home, came from the hands of a werewolf?

What if that werewolf has wanted nothing more than for me to come back?

He was telling the truth.

All this time, I've meant something to him.

Not just my body. This is not a means of seduction. If it were, Manny would have used it to his advantage. But this ring was a silent gift of love he never needed me to know about, only to have.

The pumpkin carving comes to my mind then, and the meaning behind the image is so obvious that I have to laugh.

The wolf covered it in blossoms and called it *Home*.

12

MANNY

"The thing you most love about Folk Haven is *me*. I'm *home*."

Blossom's snappish voice pulls a smile from my previously frowning mouth, and I lift my head, watching from my seat beneath an apple tree as the wood witch appears from the forest, striding toward me with the pumpkin crown still sitting snug on her head.

If Blossom competes next year, I don't know that I could put in my all. I never want to see that adornment on a head other than hers. She looks beautiful in my creation.

"Figured out the secret message of my pumpkin, huh?"

She scowls and crosses her arms over her chest. "Could you be any more obvious?"

"I don't know. Let me try." I lean forward and hold my hands out, palms splayed in surrender. "Blossom Fernmore, I'm gone for you. Please know that as much as I love teasing you, this is the truth. Please believe me when I say, you're all that I want, and your happiness means everything to me."

She's silent for an agonizing stretch, then extends her hand.

On it, I see the ring. The one I made.

I wondered if she would ever realize who the gift was from. I half expected her to know the moment she opened the box.

And then to chuck it at my head.

But I overheard Heather ask about the ring once, her eyes on me. My best friend knew I'd grown interested in metal-working and that I'd convinced a local dragon artist, Dimitri Novac, to let me apprentice under him. He taught me until he passed away a couple of years ago. I still miss that grumpy old mythic.

Now that I work for Owen at his recycling company, I have access to plenty of scrap metal for my hobby.

The crown was the first piece I fashioned that Dimitri approved of.

The ring was the second.

But Blossom told Heather that their dad had gotten it for her as a gift. That was when I realized the story she'd made up for herself.

One that Heather didn't believe, but was a good enough friend to keep her mouth shut about.

Now that I think about it, that must have been Heather's first hint that I was in love with her sister.

"I can't believe you never told me. You're a sneaky wolf," Blossom chides with affection in her voice, and I preen under the hints of her caring for me.

But will she stay?

Can I do anything to keep her here?

The problem is, I don't want to force Blossom into the decision. No more bets or tricks. I want her to choose Folk Haven on her own.

I want her to choose me.

"Let me know if you want a complete set," I tell her. "Necklace. Bracelet."

The wood witch saunters up to where I sit in the grass, back braced against the trunk of an apple tree. I told her to meet me here because even if she didn't show, I'd still have the scent of her around me. Still be able to stare at the flattened patch of grass where I held her last night.

Blossom sinks down, settling in my lap as her legs straddle my waist. "Nipple piercings?"

I rear back in surprise, shoulders hitting the tree trunk. My wolfish libido roars to the forefront, taking the joke entirely too seriously.

"Yes." I growl out the word, hands encircling her waist. "But I need to see the flesh I'm working with."

Blossom snorts. Then, her face turns thoughtful as she speaks. "Jenny owns a house on the lake in the human section."

Confused by the change in topic, I offer a confused nod. "She does."

Blossom wraps her arms around my neck and fiddles with the hair at the base of my skull. "Heather was saying they were going to move into Jenny's place permanently. Not go back and forth anymore. Heather's going to sell her house."

I remember my friend mentioning this too.

"She asked if I wanted to buy it."

My lungs clench, and I have trouble inhaling. "When?"

"Before the mating."

Before everything that happened between us. Did she tell her no and is now rethinking the refusal?

"I told her I'd think about it," Blossom says.

"You did?"

The wood witch scratches her nails against my scalp in a gentle caress.

Even though she's straddling my lap, Blossom isn't close enough. I tighten my grip on her waist, dragging her flush against my chest, and bury my nose in her hair.

Apples, spice, and warm woman.

Much better.

"I think I've always wanted to come back here," Blossom murmurs. "Once I realized I didn't have to. That I could survive out in the world on my own. Without Papa and Heather hovering over me and treating me like the baby of the family, the town stopped feeling so suffocating."

Every syllable out of her mouth gives me hope. I don't need Blossom to move to Folk Haven for me. All I need is for her to give me a chance while she's here. I'll utilize this proximity to badger her into loving me. Craft jewelry for every part of her body. Race with her through every forest. Give her orgasms in every orchard.

"Made any decisions?" My voice is rough on the words as I keep my begging at bay. To distract myself, I focus on the soft press of her against my chest and the way her intoxicating apple-pie scent fills my nose and my lungs.

Blossom hums and fiddles with the collar of my shirt. "I have. But I'm worried about something."

My stomach dips low. "What's got you upset?"

She sighs, heavy and long. "That you'll be completely insufferable when you find out I'm going to tell Heather yes. And that part of the reason is because I'm in love with you."

She's right. I will never let her forget this.

Cradling her cheek, I guide Blossom's face so her eyes meet mine. So she sees the incandescent happiness spilling out of every pore of my being.

"Bud—"

"I said, *part* of the reason!" She tries to scowl and pounds a not-at-all hard fist against my chest. "There are other things I miss about Folk Haven. It's not just you."

I roll us into the grass, pinning her sweet little body against the ground.

"But I'm the biggest reason." I pair the proclamation with a gentle, suggestive thrust of my hips.

My wood witch groans and digs her fingers into my hair,

pulling until almost the point of pain. "See? This is exactly what I was worried about. You're going to be impossible to be around."

"Only when I open my mouth," I argue. "There are plenty of ways to keep that part of me busy."

Blossom's cheeks go red, even as she smirks. "True."

More snarky, teasing comments come to my mind, but I don't let them out. There will be time in the future to get into verbal sparring matches with my witch.

Because she's staying.

I hold her gaze, remaining quiet for long enough that understanding flashes in her eyes. She knows the next words from my mouth won't be a joke.

"I love you, Blossom Fernmore."

Her gaze softens.

"Please, let me be yours. I want to carry the heavy furniture into your new house, and feed you s'mores, and fashion you hundreds of pieces of jewelry, and run through the woods with you. Let me love you, whenever you're ready. Let me in. Let me make up for every wrong I've done to you."

"Manny"—Blossom releases the grip she has on my hair to trace her thumbs over my eyebrows and down to the curves of my cheeks—"let me put apples in a pie for you rather than chucking them at your head. Let me kiss your cheek, not because I'm saying good-bye, but because I want to have the taste of you on my lips. Let me be your home. Let me love you."

The sneaky witch just plunged her sharp-nailed hand past my rib cage and gripped my heart.

But the hold, though it threatens to devastate me, is also a gentle cradle I can't live without.

"Okay," I rasp. "No arguments here."

Blossom's eyes sparkle. "None from me either. Look at that. I guess we *can* get along."

As our mouths meet in a kiss, a happy growl rumbles deep

in my chest. And when Blossom rolls me onto my back, I revel in the way she dominates me.

Suddenly, all her delicious warmth is gone, except for a tight grip around my wrists and ankles. I turn my head and realize vines have wrapped around my limbs.

"Bet you can't catch me, wolf." Blossom crouches at my side only long enough to smack a quick kiss on my cheek. Then, she takes off running, disappearing between the dark trees with light laughter and the sparkle of green magic reflecting off the pumpkin crown.

I grin, tugging at my restraints. And when I finally break free, I release a night-shattering howl.

Warning my wood witch that in every race with her as the prize, I intend to win.

The End

～

Thank you so much for reading the collection of Folk Haven Tales. I hope you enjoyed every magical love story! Do you want to spend more time in the mythic-filled Folk Haven? Keep reading for a peek at more mystical small town romances.

STAY IN FOLK HAVEN

You don't have to leave Folk Haven just yet! Keep reading for a sneak peek of *Seduced by a Selkie*, book one in the Folk Haven series...

SEDUCED BY A SELKIE

DELTA

When my father died, he left me a lake house, and I hate him for it. As if losing him suddenly wasn't bad enough, now, I'm back in this middle-of-nowhere town in northern Georgia, forced to set his estate to rights.

Estate. Ha. That word makes his house sound impressive. Maybe from the outside. But step in the door, and everything turns into a death trap.

When I got the call from Folk Haven's police chief about my father's passing a few months back, I half-expected the cause of death to be something more gruesome than a heart attack. Not that I wanted my father to suffer. They told me his death was quick, and even if someone had been nearby, there would have been an infinitesimal chance he could have survived.

With Dimitri Novac's hermit lifestyle, that chance had turned into zero.

Which leaves me here, sitting alone on the end of his dock in the early morning, listening to the hollow lap of the water against wood, contemplating Lake Galen and mortality.

Maybe my morbid thoughts manifest a response because,

suddenly, I'm sure I'm staring straight at a lifeless body floating facedown in the water.

"Oh hell," I mutter, scrambling to my feet, unsteady on the floating dock.

The higher vantage point shows me the same image. Just past the mouth of the inlet, maybe a hundred feet away, a person is rocking in the waves like the leavings of a shipwreck.

Adrenaline and panic make my decision for me. I rip off my long-sleeved shirt and unzip my jeans, pushing the denim off my legs without the hindrance of shoes because I walked down here, barefoot. Pulling on my muscle memory from a long-ago summer swim team, I dive into the water and plow toward the prone figure, using a strong freestyle. The distance first appeared closer than it is, and as I continue to pump my arms, I try to remember how long a human can go without oxygen and still survive.

Is it long enough for me to reach them, drag them to shore, and start performing CPR?

Doesn't matter. I have to try.

When I lift my head, shaking water from my eyes, I spot the lifeless form only a few strokes away. With a powerful kick of my feet, I cross the final distance. Despite my hope, the logical part of my brain informs me I am about to grab hold of a dead body.

Which is why I scream when the head pops up at my touch.

The man—because I see now that it is a man—jerks back at my holler, raising his hands above the water, as if surrendering.

"It's okay. I won't hurt you," he assures me in a rumble of a voice.

"You're not dead!" I shout, as if him being alive were an inconvenience.

His eyebrows creep up. "Would you prefer I was?"

"No." I suck in a deep breath, winded from my sprinting swim. "I ..." Words slip away from me as I glance behind him.

At this new angle in the water, I spy a pontoon boat floating outside the mouth of the inlet.

Unnecessary adrenaline keeps my heart pounding hard and makes it difficult to organize all this new information.

"Hey." The deep voice recaptures my attention, and I meet the set of soft brown eyes in an otherwise blockish white face. "Hi." He greets me again, his smile easing the harder angles of his jaw. "You were swimming up to a dead body?"

"I wasn't *sure* you were dead," I correct.

That only has him smiling wider. "You're here to save me?"

As understanding of the new situation dawns, I struggle to keep afloat—literally and figuratively. My body tries to remind me it's been a few years since I trod water for any length of time.

"Do you need saving?" My breathlessness comes from a combination of the swimming and his focused gaze.

At some point, we must have drifted closer, pushed around by the subtle lake waves.

The swimmer's hand rises from the water, catching a strand of my hair on the ascent. The black threads spill like ink about my pale shoulders, my skin turning a ghostly shade from the chill of the lake. He stares at where the lock wraps around his finger in a tentacle-like grasp.

"People rarely admit to needing help." His gaze laughs as his grin goes lopsided. "Please, continue saving me. Likely as not, I need it."

If I had time, I'd put in the needed mental energy to identify the subtext of his words. But a movement over his shoulder distracts me.

The good news: I don't need to come up with a response to his oddly philosophical statement.

The bad news: our conversation pauses because I'm transfixed by the sight of a head breaching the lake surface behind my not-dead acquaintance.

The appearance is only the beginning. One to my left. One on the right. All around me, more heads appear, all equipped with goggles and breathing pieces, identifying this crew as a gathering of scuba divers. Seems I've shown up in the middle of a scuba lesson. Soon, we're floating in a crowd of heads.

And every single one is facing me.

That's when I remember my outfit. Without my shirt and pants, I'm left with the most basic coverings. A matching bra and underwear set I got on sale at a department store. Both scraps of fabric are blue and covered in pictures of cartoon bananas.

No doubt, that's why they were on sale.

This group got an unobstructed view of my bargain boy shorts as they surfaced.

I hate this fucking lake.

I keep my curses to myself. "Well, looks like you've got this under control."

The man lets my hair return to the water as I paddle backward. Once I'm clear of the group, I turn on my stomach and swim back to my father's dock, possibly moving faster than when I thought someone's life was at risk.

Embarrassment is powerful fuel.

When I reach the dock, I grab the metal ladder and place my feet on the slick, algae-covered steps sinking below the surface.

"Please don't let them be watching me," I mutter as I pull myself out of the lake, soaked underwear clinging to my backside and rigid nipples. *Note to self: swimming in April is cold, even in Georgia.*

When I'm standing tall—because I refuse to cower and hunch over in my half-naked state—a quick glance behind me shows my audience is still watching the show.

"Fucking peachy," I mutter.

Thoroughly done with this miserable morning, I offer the

lot of them a salute, gather up my armful of clothes, and march toward the shore, reminding myself with each step that I will probably never see any of those people again, especially when I leave Folk Haven and Lake Galen for good.

So, what does it matter if they all have a permanent memory of soggy bananas decorating my ass?

This story continues in SEDUCED BY A SELKIE...

ALSO BY LAUREN CONNOLLY

Find a list of all of Lauren's books on her website:

Laurenconnollyromance.com/book-list

ABOUT THE AUTHOR

Lauren Connolly is an award-wining author of contemporary and paranormal romance stories. She has lived among mountains, next to lakes, and in imaginary worlds. Lauren can never seem to stay in one place for too long, but trust that wherever she's residing there is a dog who thinks he's a troll, twin cats hiding in the couch, and bookshelves bursting with the stories written by the authors she loves.